Angela Huth has written three collections of short stories and ten novels, including *Nowhere Girl*, *Virginia Fly is Drowning*, *South of the Lights*, *Invitation to the Married Life*, *Land Girls*, *Wives of the Fishermen*, *Easy Silence* and *Of Love and Slaughter*. She also writes plays for radio, television and stage, and is a well-known freelance journalist, critic and broadcaster.

She is married to a don, lives in Oxford and has two daughters.

Also by Angela Huth

FICTION

Nowhere Girl
Virginia Fly is Drowning
Sun Child
South of the Lights
Monday Lunch in Fairyland and other stories
Wanting
Such Visitors and other stories
Invitation to the Married Life
Another Kind of Cinderella and other stories
Land Girls
Wives of the Fishermen
Easy Silence
Of Love and Slaughter

NON-FICTION

The English Woman's Wardrobe

FOR CHILDREN

Eugenie in Cloud Cuckoo Land
Island of the Children (ed.)
Casting a Spell (ed.)

PLAYS

The Understanding
The Trouble with Old Lovers

Collected Stories

Angela Huth

An *Abacus* Book

First published in Great Britain in 2003 by Little, Brown
This edition published by Abacus in 2004

Copyright © Angela Huth 2003

'Loaf', 'Consequences', 'Thinnest Ice', 'Monday Lunch in Fairyland',
'Mind of Her Own', 'Loving Gourmets', 'The Fall', 'Azaleas for Sale'
and 'The Outing' first published in *Monday Lunch in Fairyland*
by William Collins Sons and Co. Ltd. in 1978.

'The Fuschia Auberge', 'Mother of the Bride', 'Donkey Business', 'Sudden
Dancer', 'The Bull', 'The Weighing Up', 'Irish Coffee' and 'Not for Publication'
first published in *Such Visitors* by
William Heinemann Ltd. in 1989.

'Dressing Up', 'Laughter in the Willows', 'To Rearrange a Room', 'The Wife
Trap', 'Squirrels', 'Mistral', 'Men Friends' and 'Another Kind of Cinderella' first
published in *Another Kind of Cinderella* by
Little, Brown in 1996.

The moral right of the author has been asserted.

A CIP catalogue record for this book is available from the British Library

ISBN 0 349 11575 3

Typeset in Fournier by M Rules
Printed and bound in Great Britain by Clays Ltd, St Ives plc

Abacus
An imprint of
Time Warner Books UK
Brettenham House
Lancaster Place
London WC2E 7EN

www.TimeWarnerBooks.co.uk

For Candida and Eugenie
with my love

Contents

Loaf   1
Consequences   15
Thinnest Ice   28
Monday Lunch in Fairyland   46
Mind of Her Own   58
Loving Gourmets   76
The Fall   87
Azaleas for Sale   100
The Outing   108
The Fuschia Auberge   123
Mother of the Bride   130
Donkey Business   139
Sudden Dancer   148
The Bull   165
The Weighing Up   174

Irish Coffee	184
Not for Publication	204
Dressing Up	221
Laughter in the Willows	231
To Rearrange a Room	258
The Wife Trap	264
Squirrels	284
Angels Bending Near the Earth	302
Mistral	309
The Wife and a Half	324
Another Kind of Cinderella	332
Men Friends	351

Loaf

Afternoons like this, Loaf hated. Afternoons like this he'd like to be up in the hills with his stick, bashing at the brambles or lying in the shade chewing a bit of gum. A man shouldn't have to work in this heat. Especially as there wasn't even any sun: just grey, dull, sultry heat so you could almost touch the stickiness in the air, and there was nowhere you could get away from it, no shady places.

Loaf sat on a bale of straw in the barn. His big legs in their khaki dungarees were slung apart to support a saddle. He polished its dark leather with an almost defiant feebleness, his big head hanging to one side, small strange eyes staring at the shining reflections that emerged, as he rubbed, from the dull surface. At his feet a couple of brown hens scratched at clumps of clover. Their silly clucking annoyed Loaf, a little, as it always did. Though once when his mother had taken him into the town for the day, a dreadful day with a tie round his neck and carrying paper bags of women's shopping, he'd said on the train coming back, 'I missed those bloody hens.' Now he said, 'Mind out, you pretty buggers,' and gave them a kick with one of his big, slow feet.

He didn't hit them but they squawked in their daft fashion and raised their wings, as if any such pathetic gesture could help lift their plump bodies out of Loaf's way. He looked up to see Gracie standing up at the barn door, lolling as usual, still in her school uniform.

'You hurt them and Pa'll go out of his mind,' she said.

'Ah,' said Loaf. Gracie with her airs and graces – he'd teach her one day.

'Tea's on,' Gracie added. 'But I should finish that saddle if I was you.'

' 'Tis finished.' Loaf put the saddle on the ground and stood up, newly conscious, as he was many times a day, of his own massive height. He looked far down at Gracie. She was small for fourteen, but had lovely breasts beneath her schoolgirl shirt, anyone could see that, and spindly legs under her short skirt. She gave him a funny look, challenging, like she often did, and pouted her pretty mouth.

'Come on, then,' she said, 'you got to have a bath tonight.'

Loaf followed her to the house, remembering. It was tonight he'd promised to go with her – well, been forced to promise by his parents. The thought of it made him roll his shoulders, and feel the huge wet patches under the arms of his shirt. He'd give anything, anything not to have to go. But there was no getting out of it now. For a week, since the suggestion had been made, he'd been racking his brain for some idea that would release him from the ordeal. But nothing had come to him and all the thinking had made him slow and clumsy. Pa had been sharp with him several times, and threatened to send him to work on a neighbouring farm.

At tea Gracie was all excitement but still managed to get

through a large amount. Loaf pushed his own plate of eggs and sausages away. He felt sick enough already.

'Eat up,' said his mother. 'I've no patience with poor eaters wasting good food.' She was skinny as wire herself, never ate a thing.

'Be glad when tonight's over and Loaf's back to his normal brilliant self,' said Pa. 'Done a good job on the saddle, have you?'

'Done a good job, Pa.'

'Hung it up?' There was a long silence.

'Well, I was going to,' said Loaf.

'It's on the floor,' said Gracie. 'Quite safe,' she added. Another silence.

'There's no call for tell-tales,' snapped her mother, taking away Loaf's plate of unfinished food. Gracie pouted.

'I only said because I knew Pa'd do his nut if it stayed there all night, and Loaf might forget, all the excitement.'

'You'll hang it up right after tea, Loaf,' said Pa.

'He's got to have his bath,' said his wife.

'He'll have his bath after he's hung up that saddle or he'll not be going to the dance.'

New hope leapt within Loaf. Gracie wailed.

'Shut up that noise,' snapped her mother. 'Loaf'll hang the saddle up *then* have his bath.' In the end, Mother always had the final word. She ran her hand through her son's short hair.

'And get that hay out of your head and put on some of Pa's grease.'

Loaf knew better than to protest. When his family wanted to do something they had their ways and means. They had quick tongues and a flow of words that always beat him. In his head, he could argue against them: in his head he was just as brilliant as they were, full of convincing arguments on his own behalf which, had he been able to articulate them, would no doubt have won them over. But getting over his own point of view was the trouble: translating thoughts to words was not a talent he possessed. All his life the easy spinning of words had eluded him, leaving him stranded, unable even to shout for help. And other people, even his family, in all their busy going back and forth, had little time for his predicament.

He had a bath and dressed himself in his only suit of baggy grey flannel. With it he put on a white nylon shirt and a plain blue tie, and greased down all but the most impossible spokes of his hair. Then he hung about in the kitchen, feeling more enormous than usual, waiting for Gracie.

When at last she arrived he understood why she'd been so long. She'd done something to herself, all right. She looked terrific, pirouetting about, aware in every fibre of her body of her own attraction.

'Like it?' She looked down at the bouncy pink skirt jumping about her legs as she moved, the neck of the jersey scooped out so that her breasts bulged above it. Her hair moved and shone: she had thickened her long eyelashes with black mascara and greased her pouty lips. Only her legs seemed frail and childlike: almost sad, their spindliness, Loaf thought. Weren't the ugly clumpy shoes too heavy for them?

'Oh yes,' he said, dully, because he was still thinking of her poor legs having to bear the weight of those shoes.

'Smashing,' said Pa, smiling. Gracie could always make Pa smile.

'And do hold your head *up*, Loaf,' said Gracie.

'Yes, chin up, Loaf,' said Pa. 'You've a sister to be proud of tonight.'

Loaf raised his head. His hair touched the beams of the ceiling. He tried to smile at Gracie, but she was frowning at him now.

'Couldn't you have worn anything more – you know?' she asked.

Loaf felt his heart quicken. He didn't much like Gracie, most of the time, but he didn't like to disappoint her, either. He didn't understand. Mother had gone to great pains to choose his clothes for the evening: she'd been pressing and brushing all afternoon.

'All this and I'm wearing the wrong things?' he said.

'Of course not,' said his mother, quickly. 'You're lovely and smart, Loaf, take it from me.'

'But all the others'll be in jeans and T-shirts,' said Gracie.

'Then Loaf will be much better turned out,' replied her mother. 'Now, you'd better be getting along.'

Pa drove them in his old car. Loaf sat in the back, brushing the seat with his hand before he got in. He didn't speak, but loosened his tie a little. Gracie chattered excitedly to Pa. When they arrived at the village hall, and got out, Loaf remembered about his head and held it up for a while.

Inside the hall an explosion of sound unleashed the sweat glands in his body. The wetness he had been dreading arrived with startling suddenness: with each new blast from the band the dampness spread, from arms to feet, to face to spine; it even trickled down his legs. Unnerved, Loaf put his big hands to his ears, then caught someone looking at him, so smeared his gesture into one of casualness, as if he was merely rubbing them.

He looked round for Gracie. She was already gone. He couldn't see her.

'Excuse me, you're blocking the door.' Someone had pushed him. There seemed to be so much room. It puzzled him he could be in the way. He moved.

As he walked away to a row of empty chairs by a wall he felt his head jerk in time to the music: he couldn't control it. When he sat down, he gave in and let it loll to one side. Sideways, he looked about him. The hall had been decorated for the occasion. A solitary string of coloured lights was strung across the ceiling. Paper roses were pinned to the glittery curtains drawn across the high-up windows, and posters of pop stars were stuck here and there on the shabby green walls. Loaf thought it looked very nice.

He turned his head to the band on the stage. It consisted of four very small, thin young men with long hair and scarlet hearts painted on their cheeks. They wore identical pink satin shirts, and winced and swayed as they clutched at their instruments, as if the wood and strings were hurting them. One of them was singing. Loaf couldn't catch the words. The voice was a shrieking groan that struggled to surmount the music. But the frenzy of their massive sound was successfully transmitted to the dancers. Forty or fifty young things, all in bright clothes and no ties, were springing about with a wild rhythm, their eyes rolled up to the coloured lights, every part of their bodies rippling with the music. Loaf watched their fast, skilful feet for a long time, then shuffled one of his own, so gently no one would notice, under the chair.

He caught sight of Gracie. She was the prettiest and best dancer in the room, definitely. People were looking in her direction. The man opposite her, to whom she seemed to be directing her sinuous movements, was the only one who had his eyes shut. He looked a decent enough sort of guy, Loaf thought, but with his eyes screwed up like that and his head thrown back, he, too, might have been in pain. Then Loaf noticed a message on the man's T-shirt. *F**k me*, it said. Loaf felt the hot dampness beneath his heavy clothes again. He stood up, head jerking. He'd have to rescue Gracie somehow, or he'd never hear the end of it from Pa.

He walked round the edge of the room, careful not to get in anyone's way, to a point where he thought Gracie, if she looked, would see him. For a moment she glanced in his direction.

'Gracie,' he said. But perhaps she didn't notice him, because she didn't stop dancing. Obviously she couldn't hear him. Loaf lifted one of his hands, looked at it, then waved it at her. She still didn't see. She was laughing at the man with the shut eyes, and stamping her skinny legs so that her skirt flew high. There was nothing left for Loaf to do, other than go over and drag her off the floor, and he'd never do that, not for anything. Maybe she'd be all right so long as he kept watching her. So long as he didn't let her out of his sight. If anyone tried to lay a finger on Gracie he'd bash them

over the head, in the stomach, everywhere, till they were unconscious.

He bought himself a Coke and a cheese sandwich from a long
table covered with drinks and food. He took them back to another
empty chair, further from the band, and settled himself to watch
Gracie. As the music ripped painfully through his head, and the
dancers confused his eyes, he thought how nice it would be to be
able to go home and say to Mother and Pa in the morning how
much he'd enjoyed it all. How much he'd liked the music and the
dancing. How nice it would be, too, he thought, if they really
were Mother and Pa, if he was their real son like Gracie was their
real daughter. He didn't have such thoughts very often, just sometimes when things went badly, when Pa shouted at him and he
forgot to do something he'd meant to do for Mother. Then, for a
few days, he'd find himself looking about more carefully: looking
out for a very tall old man who just might be his real father, and a
woman with very whitish hair, like his own, who could be his
mother.

Gracie was coming towards him, her body still wriggling with
the music, followed by the man whose eyes were half open now.

'Stop staring, can't you?' she shouted. 'Your eyes always on me,
gives me the creeps.'

Loaf blinked. He wanted to say he was unaware he'd been staring and he was sorry if he'd annoyed her. But the man put his
hand on her shoulder and pushed her away. They went towards
the food table. Loaf stood up, watching them. He felt himself
shaking. He saw Gracie point to the gin. The man poured her a
glass and added orange. Gracie wasn't allowed gin. If Pa knew
Gracie was drinking gin there'd be a row all right. He moved
towards the table and almost at once got in the way of some
dancer.

'Mind out, Loaf the oaf,' shouted the swaying girl, and laughed
at the hirsute man dancing opposite her.

Loaf dodged out of her way, looking at her. Familiar face.

Chemist shop – that was it, the girl in the chemist shop who'd made a rude joke when his mother had sent him to buy a laxative. Remembering, he blushed.

He sat down again, nearest chair he could find, gripping on to his empty Coke bottle with both hands. With a jerk of his head he saw Gracie and her man leave the hall, carrying their drinks. He swallowed, searching for moisture in his mouth, and looked at his watch.

He looked at his watch again two hours later when Gracie returned, alone. By now the evening was almost over. The satin shirts were packing up their instruments. The new quietness of the place had left Loaf feeling weak, and still he sweated. Gracie came up to him, perky as anything.

'We off, then?' Gracie was flushed, pleased with herself.

'Oh yes, if you want.' He didn't want to be any further nuisance to her. He wanted her to have her own way now, to make up for his staring.

'Come on, then. Derek's gone. He offered me a lift on his bike, but I said no, Pa'd do his nut.' Swing, swing, swing she went, towards the door in front of Loaf.

Outside it was still warm and airless, a faded summer night with a cloudy moon. Bikes revved up, white arms shuddering on handlebars, shiny girls on the back seats squealing to each other.

'Wish I could have gone with Derek,' Gracie said.

'Sorry,' said Loaf.

They walked down the quiet road between tall black hedges. Soon as they were out of sight of the hall Gracie took Loaf's arm. He couldn't remember her ever having touched him before.

'Quite gives me the spooks, the dark,' she said. 'Doesn't it you?'

'No,' said Loaf.

'The spooks . . .' She drew out the word, then gave a shriek. 'Ooh my God, there's a shadow moved, Loaf.' Her hand tightened on his arm.

'It's nothing, really.' Loaf was pleased to be able to reassure her. He looked down at her. He smelt gin. She seemed a little unsteady on his arm.

'You been drinking?'

'We had a couple. Gin and orange, my favourite drink. The gin brings out the taste of the orange, Derek says. He's right, mind.' She giggled. 'Did you notice Derek? I think he's smashing. Very gentle.' She was quiet for a while. 'He kissed me, you know. He wanted to go on, but I said no. I said you mustn't do that, Derek, or we'll go too far.' Loaf felt her small body stiffen.

'God, I wanted to go too far,' she said.

'Did you?' said Loaf.

They were walking very slowly now. The farm buildings were in sight. They walked the rest of the way in silence. There was a quiet stir of animals in the farmyard, the sudden darting flight of a bat, a smell of warm manure, and tobacco plants that grew by the barn. An owl hooted.

'Jesus, that scared me,' said Gracie. She stopped, forcing Loaf to do the same. 'You're brave,' she said. 'So brave you'd dare come with me into the barn for a fag.'

'A fag?'

'Derek slipped me one. You wouldn't tell Mother and Pa, would you? But Christ, I'm dying for it. I daren't smoke it in my room. Pa'd smell it out and do his nut.'

'We wouldn't want to set the barn on fire,' said Loaf, slowly.

'We wouldn't do that, silly.' Gracie broke away impatiently from Loaf and started towards the barn. 'We'll take great care.'

Loaf followed her, half flattered, half afraid.

The barn rustled, full of dark shadows and warm musty smells of clover hay. They sat on a bale of straw. Gracie lit her cigarette and puffed smoke at the doorway, a dim square of sky in which the moon floated halfway up.

'Wouldn't like to spend a night in here alone,' she said. 'I'd be dead scared.' She passed Loaf her cigarette. 'Have a drag.' Loaf shook his head. 'Go on, be a devil.' Loaf shook his head again.

Gracie sighed. 'I don't know what you *do* like,' she said. 'I some-times wonder what goes on in your head, what turns you on.' She shifted herself a little. One of her legs touched his. He didn't move, frightened of annoying her. 'What really gets you?' she asked.

'I like going up the hills with my stick,' said Loaf. 'I like beat-ing the bushes so's the butterflies come out.'

Gracie gave a small laugh. 'Big deal,' she said, eventually.

'Probably sounds silly,' said Loaf, 'but you did ask.'

Gracie leaned back, supporting herself on the bale behind them. She took another long draw at her cigarette, carefully watched the smoke filter up into the darkness. 'And mind the ash, for Pete's sake,' Loaf added. His limbs felt suddenly tight.

'I'm not a fool, Loaf.' Gracie sounded languid, slow. Not at all her normal pert self. 'D'you like sex?' she asked.

'Sex?' Just saying the word sent a quiver down Loaf's back.

'What d'you think of it?'

Loaf hesitated. 'I'm not sure.'

'Go on.' Grace laughed again, kindly. 'Have you ever had it?'

'Had sex?' The quiver again.

'You're being awfully dumb. You can tell me. Go on.'

'Well, I suppose, not exactly *with* anyone.'

Gracie sat up, interested. 'That way it must be awfully boring.' She nudged him. 'Aren't you dying for it with someone?'

Loaf looked at her.

'I am,' she said.

In the deep brown light her pinkness was mottled with shad-ows. She was warm and smelt of gin. Her lips shiny, her hair tangled prettily. Loaf was unable to move. Ever since she had been a small child Gracie had been able to exercise a carotic effect upon him, though never so strong as now.

'Yes,' he said, after a while.

Gracie shifted again. Her leg was touching his on purpose now.

'D'you think I'm sexy, Loaf? Derek does. He said he knew what he'd like to do to me all right.'

A strange havoc raged in Loaf's loins.

'If you've finished your cigarette, I think we'd better go in.' He felt his voice to be unsteady.

'Here. Your responsibility.' Gracie handed him the stub. He flicked it out of the door, glad to have something positive to do. Hand very weak.

'You ever seen a girl undressed?' Gracie was lying back again now, legs a little apart. Loaf studied her small sharp child's knees. He clasped his hands together to protect himself from touching them.

'No,' he said. He paused. 'Did you hear me? I said I thought we should go in.' He felt her hand on the back of his neck.

'Wait a tic, Loafy. I'll show you.'

Loaf tried to get up. Instead he turned to her.

She had pulled her jersey out of the skirt. It was gathered up under the chin, leaving her breasts triumphantly bare: firm, pale, two perfect round shadows at their centre, quite still, while the barn shadows trembled around them. Loaf looked, and looked.

'Go on, touch them. Do you good.'

'I'm your brother, silly. Gracie . . . come on.'

Gracie put a hand on his arm. 'Brother, phooey. Only in name.' Child's voice once more, sulky, wheedling. 'See if I can't turn you on. Promise I won't tell.'

'Pa'd do—' Loaf was up from the bale, free from her, head high in the darkness, running, breaking through the green square of sky, feeling the familiar catch of the back door under his fingers . . . The stairs, then, two at a time – the noise, never mind the noise . . .

He threw himself on the bed. His heart battered at his ribs, his trousers strained round the crotch, his whole body was clammy. He closed his eyes: darkness replaced by a million scarlet chips, spinning, spinning. *You'll pay for this, Gracie, with your airs and graces* . . . The words a banner in his head. He groaned out loud.

Loaf lay quite still for some time. He had no energy to get up, undress, put on the light, get into bed. Only a different kind of energy within him, disturbing, wakeful, prowling his blood, weakening him.

His door opened gently. He reached up and switched on his bedside light. He knew it was Gracie. *You'll pay for this, Gracie . . .* The interval without her had given him time to muster a little of his reasoning.

She stood there, defiant, beautiful, in a blue dressing-gown. Make-up still on, but stick legs bare now. Bare feet, too. She closed the door behind her.

'Sorry,' she said. Loaf swung his legs on to the floor.

'You must go back to bed, Gracie,' he said. The words were difficult. 'You must. You must, Gracie . . .' Looking away from her, he knew his head had lolled to one side.

'I know I must.' She giggled. 'It's just – I didn't want to go with you so mad at me. And I was feeling so – you know. I couldn't help it. I should've gone home with Derek.'

'Go, now,' said Loaf.

'Yeah, all right.' She opened her dressing-gown. 'Just thought you'd like a look at all of it before I do.'

Loaf jerked up his head. The scarlet chips, blasting his eyes again, crowded the slice of her body that the dressing-gown exposed. They gathered, crazed, round her breasts and stomach, darkening as his eyes lowered. Then she ran towards him.

'I'm not revolting, am I?' she screamed. 'Why won't you touch me?' She threw herself upon him so that for a moment he felt her soft warm flesh against his face, his hands. He pushed her from him, lifting her up as he did so. She weighed no more than a large box of apples. When her feet reached the floor again he supported her crumpled body, watching her sway. Then he hit her, heavily, on the side of her face.

'You little . . .' No word came. He watched her fall. She screamed. The noise was a profound exacerbation in his soul, causing his skin to contract, to go cold. He looked at her, lying on the rug, face down, dressing-gown covering the bony little back.

Breasts too heavy for those bones perhaps . . . She began to cry. Perhaps that's why she was crying. A child's noise. Loaf had forgotten she was a child. Forgotten why he hit her.

He looked up to see the door had opened. Mother and Pa stood there, Pa first, in old woolly night things. Faces askew.

'What happened?' Pa was at once kneeling beside Gracie. Loaf whimpered. Tomorrow, they'd send him away. Maybe tonight.

'What happened, child?'

'I don't know. Loaf . . .' Gracie was sobbing badly. Mother looked down at her, severe, drawn beige mouth.

'Best carry her to her room, Pa,' she said.

Pa picked the child up, averting his eyes as he wrapped the dressing-gown over her nakedness. He carried her out of the room.

Loaf hung his head, listening to her diminishing cries. He could feel his mother's eyes searching him, silent. He could see her hands kneading the clotted wool of her nightgown. She had brought a powdery, angry smell into the room.

'I didn't . . .' he said. 'I'll go in the morning. Pack my bags.'

'Look at me, Loaf.' Loaf raised his head. Mother's eyes, always small, were shrunk with tears that gave them an extra skin, but the tears stayed poised where they were, no signs of overflowing. He'd never seen her like that before.

'She'll have to be the one to go,' Mother was saying. 'We've had this trouble before, Loaf, so many times. Didn't you understand? Had you no idea?'

'I'll go,' Loaf persisted. 'I'll be the one. Gracie's your real daughter.' The words all rushed.

'I said: don't you understand, Loaf? Others . . . many others in the village. Complaints at school. Why do you think I asked you to go with her to the dance, to take special care of her? She's fourteen.'

Loaf found his mother's quiet words beating themselves into a pattern in his head. A shape he was beginning to understand, though not believe.

'What's the matter with her?' he asked.

Mother hesitated. Chose her words carefully. 'She's very precocious. But we thought at least with you, her brother—'

'But I'm not really her brother, am I?' New confusion: the chips gathering again in his eyes. 'I'm not, really . . . you know I'm not.'

He remembered quite clearly Gracie saying that in the barn, lying back, lying back. He'd always known.

Mother turned, eyes dried out and larger, neck pulled high.

'It's how we think of you, Loaf,' she said, and left the room.

They sent Gracie to a special school, far away, and Loaf continued his work on the farm. But since the dance an increasing listlessness came over him. He found it hard to concentrate on the simplest job. Pa snapped at him, doubly confusing him, and Mother seemed to notice him less than was her custom. From time to time he begged them to let Gracie come back. It was his fault, he said, and he didn't like to see her punished. But they wouldn't listen, said they didn't want to talk about her. She was ill, was all they would say: better get her cured while she was young.

Loaf spent more time than he used to in the hills. There, he was alone with his picture of Gracie lying back in the barn, the most beautiful thing he'd ever seen. She'd done something to him that night, Gracie had: just to think of her he trembled.

He trembled and bashed at the bushes with his stick. Restless, up in the hills, he'd bash till the butterflies flew out, pretty butterflies not half as pretty as Gracie, Gracie who'd done something to him that night damn her lovely mouth and breasts and eyes. Restless, bashing butterflies, he knew he'd not resist her when she returned. Mother and Pa'd do their nuts, send him away, next time. Still, he knew what he had to do. Restless, bashing butterflies . . . He'd wait.

Consequences

Professor Gerald Bravington met Leonora Thorne on the 8.15 from Pewsey to Paddington. He noted with pleasure that by some chance, for a Tuesday, the train was not crowded. The professor chose the compartment she alone occupied. He sat by the window, opposite her, back to the engine: his favourite seat, when he could get it. He observed that Miss Thorne, as he later discovered was her name, wore a red coat and was filling in *The Times* crossword with considerable speed.

It was a fine morning, but condensation on the window obscured the view. The professor wiped his hand across it, making a wide ribbon through which he peered at the familiar landscape. After a while Miss Thorne, who had been clicking her pencil against her teeth, said: '"Our sincerest something with some pain is fraught." Do you know what?'

The professor drew his eyes from the fields to her face. She had good teeth, white and even.

'Laughter,' he said.

'Thank you. That's it. I can never do the quotes.'

'They're all *I* can ever manage,' the professor answered, who was not a crossword puzzle man.

There were papers in his case that he should attend to: he had planned to read once more through his notes on Carlyle, in the hopes that he would not have to refer to them on the platform.

'If it wasn't so heavy I'd bring the *Oxford Dictionary of Quotations* with me,' said Miss Thorne. 'If it wasn't for the quotes I'd get it done most days by Hungerford. My father, before he retired, always managed to do it between Newbury and Reading.'

She folded the paper and put it on the seat beside her. Her eyes were restless, grey. They turned down at the corners, matching the slant of her mouth. The professor put a hand on his briefcase, making to open it.

'Haven't I seen you somewhere recently?' she asked, frowning. 'On television or something?'

'Could have done,' said the professor. 'I show my face from time to time.' He disliked being recognised, and thought attempts at conversation too bold, so early in the morning. Women's Liberation had killed the art of the subtle approach.

'Thought so. Do you live down here?'

The professor considered not answering her question. It was no business of hers where he lived, and probably of no interest. Yes, he did live down here, in a seedy rented cottage on the banks of the Kennet and Avon canal. Damp all year round: no heating, unreliable light. Three thousand books and a broken sofa. A willow warbler outside the kitchen window, milk in bottles left to clot, used tea bags cluttering up the sink. It had all got on top of him, somehow, since Mrs Jenkins had given up her weekly bicycle ride across the fields to help him out. Yes, he lived there, if you could call it living: reading, writing, eating out of tins, swallowing pills to induce a few hours of fretful sleep.

'I do,' he said eventually, eyes back out of the window. He heard her cross her legs, the rasp of her tights.

'Sorry to have interrupted your concentration, but I knew you'd know your Shelley.'

Was that sarcasm in her voice? Or merely the impatience of a woman used to men reacting to her swiftly? In any case, her guess might easily have been wrong. She was taking a silly line.

'Ah,' he said. 'I'm little acquainted with Shelley, as a matter of fact. Not very fond of him. I learned "The Skylark", at school. It was drummed into us along with "Ode to the West Wind".'

But Miss Thorne's head was bent over a book now. Huffy. She shrugged, but said no more. The professor had offended her, he supposed. In the old days, when he was more concerned about doing right by women, he was always offending them. He possessed no talents to charm them; that had always been his problem. He had felt uncommonly – quite disturbingly – inclined towards one or two of them in the past (the names Patricia and Teresa came briefly to mind), but the partial independence he had always insisted upon had not satisfied them. They required more than he had been prepared to give – his entire being, his every private reflection, a whole mass of promises concerning love and fidelity in the future. So far he had never felt all that was worth bargaining for, and so, some twenty years ago, the professor had abandoned the search for an ideal woman with whom to share his life. He decided that no such thing existed. Those who thought they had found perfection fooled themselves, as the years would show.

Out of the running, the professor was a happier man. Disillusion no longer disturbed him. The occasional woman who attempted to glut her own loneliness, desirousness, whatever, upon him, he could treat with impressive indifference: Madam, he would say, don't waste your time. I have no sympathy, no compassion. Go elsewhere. And at the ice in his voice they would give up, knowing he meant what he said. Now, the only women he depended upon were those he paid to ease the domestic side of his life. He missed Mrs Jenkins because without her the rubble of the cottage had become almost unbearable. When he could summon the energy he would have to try to lure some other woman from the village, by means of extravagant wages, to replace her. The professor sighed at the thought.

The train pulled into Paddington. He saw that the uncovered ends of the platforms were wet, and wondered at what moment of the journey the skies had changed without his noticing. Foreboding gripped him. He hated London rain.

'Taxi,' he said out loud, standing up.

'Taxi,' said Miss Thorne. 'I never take the tube, I'm afraid. I can't bear it.' She spoke vehemently, as if the tube was someone who had offended her in the past.

They walked together up the platform, stood side by side in the queue. A silent wait for ten minutes. It was always like this on rainy days. For practical reasons the professor asked Miss Thorne where she was going: to share a cab would at least halve the wait for one of them. Ludgate Circus was her destination.

'Well, how extraordinary,' remarked the professor, 'for I myself am bound for the City. Therefore it would seem sensible to share . . .' Miss Thorne nodded without interest.

In truth, the professor was going to Baker Street, the opposite direction. But there was plenty of time. If he had made his way directly to the lecture hall he would have had to spend a dull hour in the canteen. Half an hour in a traffic jam with this strange red lady seemed preferable. None the less the professor felt himself blush at his own lie. A man much concerned with the truth, to hear himself lie with such easy spontaneity was disturbing. He turned away to concentrate hard on an advertisement for hair oil that blared across the murky walls of the station. Goethe was right: 'Man thinks he directs his life, leads himself: but his innermost being is irresistibly drawn in the direction of his destiny.' Destiny had decreed that he and Miss Thorne should share a taxi. Therefore the lie was forgivable – indeed, imperative.

At last it was their turn. They sat side by side on the leather seat, encompassed in the stuffy air that smelt of old cigars. The professor's briefcase lay between them. Miss Thorne's gloved fingers played scales on her navy leather bag. She wore shoes of matching blue decorated with gold chains. Good ankles.

'Wish I could remember where it was I saw you,' she said, turning to look at him. 'Some programme about education, could it have been?' Her eyes held such enquiry that the professor felt afraid.

'Ah,' he said. 'I'm asked from time to time for my opinion upon diverse subjects, and find myself accepting with little relish.' What he had meant to say was that he did a bit of television in order to pay the bills. But the red lady's musky scent, which the professor had not noticed in the train, had stifled the cigar fumes and rampaged through his senses in a curious fashion. He noticed that the buildings of London, this morning, seemed to be made of coarse grain, shifting as if in a wind. Through the rain-pearled windows familiar streets were quite distorted so that it was difficult to be sure, on this well-known route, precisely where they were. And it was necessary to hear more of the lady's voice.

'You do have a funny pompous way of talking, if you don't mind my saying so,' she said. 'Wonderfully old-fashioned.' She smiled kindly. Extremely kindly, white teeth a-dance among scarlet lips.

'Really? I wasn't aware . . .'

'I shall look out for you,' she said, 'on television.'

As far as the professor could tell, they were passing the Savoy. It was then he asked her name, and was told Leonora Thorne.

'Beautiful name, Leonora,' he said, wondering if that, too, sounded pompous.

'Probably helped me more than anything to become an executive secretary,' she said.

'Is that what you are?'

'That's it.'

'Very impressive.'

'Quite dull. But well paid. In a year's time I shall stop commuting and stay at home.'

'What will you do at home?'

'Help my father with his orchards. We sell apples and plums.'

'Ah.' The professor could not imagine her, red-coated, up a tree, basket over her arm. 'Crossword in the lunch hour, then?'

'I suppose so, or I'll become a complete cabbage, won't I?'

A cabbage among the apples. The professor smiled as the taxi pulled up at the door of a stern building. Miss Thorne opened her bag, fumbled for her purse. The professor touched her gloved hand: he would not hear of it, he said. It was on his way. Miss Thorne looked at him in relief. She got out of the taxi, tossed her hair in the rain. The professor leaned out, shook her hand. She thanked him. He said perhaps they would run into each other again one day on the train. Perhaps, she said, and ran to the door. Rain splashed her shining blue shoes. Her red back disappeared quickly, impervious. As the taxi moved away the professor noticed the name on a small brass plate: Benson & Benson Ltd., Engineers. To whom in Benson & Benson was it the happy destiny to have acquired Miss Leonora Thorne, dreaming of her orchards, as executive secretary? Silly thought: but the professor would have given much to swap places with that person this morning.

As the taxi made its slow way towards Baker Street Professor Bravington found himself thinking about the exceptional whiteness of her teeth. Over a cup of tea in the canteen, guest of several students, he found the chains of her shoes glinting in his mind. On the platform itself he managed to banish Leonora while he concentrated upon Carlyle, and was rewarded by keen applause. But on the train returning to Pewsey – empty compartment very bare without her – she returned to him: the lilt of her voice, the funny way she boasted about her ability to do the crossword. The professor, repeating his earlier gesture, wiped a clear space in the steamed-up window, and watched the rain slant across fleeting trees. He thought about her father's orchards: apples and plums, she had said.

Professor Bravington was set upon a course from which he knew there could be no diversions. Exactly when the climax of that course would come he did not know, or care to know. It was a subject on which he would not question himself. He was content merely to let himself drift from day to day, without anticipation, until the right moment became recognisable.

When he arrived back that raining day from London, a feeling of unusual melancholy hung over him. His bicycle dripped in the station car park, its seat quite sodden. The rain battered into his eyes as he rode, and walking across the field to his cottage the mud seeped into his shoes. He was used to such things. They did not bother him. His mind was normally on bookish matters, too involved to be disturbed by the heaviest rain. But today, detachment from physical discomfort was suddenly not possible. There was no ignoring the wet, the chill, the bleakness of the evening ahead.

And the cottage itself, he noticed, was particularly desolate. The thatch was black with water. A thick curtain of raindrops fell from the eaves. Inside, the sickly smell of damp. Water dripped from a yellow patch in the kitchen ceiling and overflowed from a saucer the professor had laid on the floor in the morning. The sink was full of dirty plates, gaudy smears of dried egg yolk and baked beans – horrible colours in the gloom. The professor, still in his gloves, lit the kettle. Its instant hissing made a companionable noise, but the tin of tea bags was empty. With some distaste he plucked a damp tea bag from the pile under the plates in the sink, and put it in a mug. Through the window he could see that the solitary white duck, which of late had frequented this stretch of the canal, was huddled in the reeds on the bank. Head under its wing, it lay quite motionless.

The professor put logs on to the ash in the grate and lit a fire. The small flames had no power to slay the feeling of damp – they barely warmed his feet. He kept his coat on and lay back in the broken armchair, mug of revoltingly weak tea to warm his hands. Later, he ate some dry cream crackers and drank several glasses of whisky.

He watched himself steering his way down the narrow course he had set, eyes strictly ahead, not glancing in any direction for indications of help. There is no likelihood of rescue if signs of desiring rescue are not given, and the professor was not one for troubling others with his trivial depressions. The apparent futility of his life, he believed, was something that concerned him alone. He had always believed in the protection of one's friends from oneself. And besides, these days, due to his own apathy, his friends were scarce. They saw him from time to time on television and wrote letters of congratulation on his dazzling articulation and good sense. 'Saw you in excellent form as ever,' one of them had written only last week. 'Country life must suit you.' The professor was grateful, but only required that these few remaining friends should keep their distance. He never invited them to the cottage, and refused invitations so constantly to their London dinner parties that they had long ago given up asking him.

Professor Bravington played with a small pile of biscuit crumbs on his thigh, dividing and subdividing them into patterns. It seemed to him that what had happened today had caused the faintest – indeed an almost imperceptible – hesitation in his journey. Leonora Thorne, her wonderful conventionality shining brightly in train and taxi, had stood like a stranger on the bank and waved a wave of recognition. The gesture was a little unnerving. The professor desired no recognition on his solitary way. And yet . . . the smugness of her tailored coat, her dreary bag, her matching shoes – they symbolised a gentle pleasure he had ceased to imagine many years ago would exist for him. Perhaps to pause with her for a while, a mild autumn picking fruit in her father's orchards, would cause no harm. Not an affair, of course. At the thought of the absurd process of shedding clothes only to cling to another body in the dear privacy of his single bed, the professor blew all the crumbs from his thigh on to the floor. Not an affair in that sense: just a rewarding union of minds. (Maybe she would be interested in Carlyle.) The temporary cheer of companionship – a drink in the pub, scrambled eggs in here by the fire. (He could clean the place up, somehow.) Walks down the towpath. She might like the smell of wild chives in spring, if their association lasted that long.

The professor would not let her come too close, of course. All she would see of him would be the public man, the humorous intellectual who smiled on television. He would not warn her of his destiny: that would be unfair. All he would ask was her response: smiles and laughter for a while, before he pursued his way.

For a drunken fantasy, as the professor realised the whole thing was as he stumbled to bed much later that night, the idea had taken a curious hold. It had not faded next morning, as soberly he regarded more rain. And a week later it was still vivid, providing him with a new energy. He preoccupied himself with trying to clean the place though was soon diverted from this hopeless task by renewing acquaintance with old books. Each day he walked far along the towpath, watching swallows swoop to dip their breasts in their own shadows on the water's surface. He would walk until he was cold and wet and tired, and then have a lukewarm bath in his damp and peeling bathroom, which scarcely warmed him but afforded an illogical pleasure.

One afternoon, some three weeks after he had met Leonora Thorne, the professor, inspired by a silvery rainless day, decided to be practical. He would buy provisions at the post office, then make his way to the call box.

For once, he enjoyed the shopping: bought the entire stock of Ambrosia creamed rice, four dozen boxes of matches, firelighters, tinned pilchards, raspberry jam, sliced bread, sausages, margarine, Pears soap, and a packet of toffees, which he liked to suck on his walks along the towpath. He felt there were other things he should have remembered, but for the time being they escaped his memory. He tied the box of provisions on to the rack behind his bicycle seat, and pushed the heavy machine the few yards to the call box.

Inside, he gasped for air: vile smells of wet cement floor and stale cigarette smoke. He leaned against one glass-paned wall, heart beating jumpily like it used to in the early days of appearances on television. Directory Enquiries gave him the number of Benson & Benson. He made a small pile of ten-pence pieces, in case the call should be a long one.

'Benson & Benson, good afternoon.'

The chink of his coin.

'Miss Leonora Thorne, please.'

'Miss Thorne?'

Terrible silence, bringing back to the professor his first teenage date acquired through a telephone call to some nubile girl in Windsor. He remembered the trapped isolation of a call box, only possible to escape from by the cowardly act of putting down the receiver. He remembered the alarm of silence. The fear brought about by his own determination to hang on.

'Mr Wheeler's office. Can I help you?'

'Leonora?' Surely it wasn't her voice.

'I'm sorry, Miss Thorne is in South Africa for a month on business. Can I take a message?'

'No. No, thank you. No message.'

The professor put down the telephone. Silly not to have rung before. But a month was not so very long, he thought. Why, it was almost a month since he had seen her. Thirty days. Give him another chance to clear up the cottage.

But stacking the tins of rice and pilchards into the kitchen cupboard – mice droppings on every shelf – it seemed longer. Tea! That was it. He had meant to get more tea. The professor swore out loud. Tea-less, thirty days was hopelessly long.

Then he began to laugh at himself, at the absurdity of the whole plan, at the weeks he'd waited brooding upon it when it was in fact irrelevant to his central strategy. He cursed the disease of hope, for the restlessness it caused, the silly flutterings of the heart. Damn Miss Leonora Thorne and her thoughtless waving: she had lost her chance. He would not recognise the signals. Like all the others, having offered some fragment of hope, she had failed. He was no longer interested, he no longer cared. There was tinned rice enough till spring. Tomorrow he would clean the shelves – for himself, not for the benefit of Miss Thorne. Tonight he would read Carlyle, and eat pilchards straight from the tin.

Much later it rained again. The professor tried to block his ears against its battering on the window, but the sound penetrated the sparse feathers of his pillow. Miss Leonora Thorne, as he sailed once more down his course, still waved from the bank, smugly, in her tailored scarlet, with the mocking smile of one whose existence is to remind. Damn her: she would fade. Trespassers upon solitude were easily cast out. They had no power to distress, and what most concerned the professor at present was the itching of his eyes.

For several days he had been afflicted by irritation of the eyelids. Each time he blinked they seemed to scrape his eyeballs with filaments of glass. As a result, the eyeballs were raw and tearful. He bathed them night and morning, but felt no improvement. Now, in the dark, heart pounding from half a bottle of whisky, and head bleary from sleeping pills, they fiercely hurt. The lids scratched the balls in a way that made sleep impossible. Reluctantly, the professor got up and went down to the kitchen.

There, the fire was dead and water dripped from the ceiling again. Black rain slashed against the windows and the wind keened with horrible self-pity. In his half-drunk state the professor felt a sense of shock: he was used to such depressing things, but not in the middle of the night. He poured himself the rest of the bottle of whisky and, not counting them, swallowed a clump of sleeping pills. Then he went to the sink and chose two damp tea bags from the pile on the draining board. He had heard they contained anti-septic and could soothe sore eyes.

He carried them upstairs and returned to bed. After turning out the light he lay down and arranged the tea bags on his closed eye-lids. Almost immediately, he thought, he could feel some improvement. In celebration he drank the rest of the whisky – an awkward feat in his recumbent position: some of it ran down his chin and wet the neck of his pyjamas. Perhaps this is the right time, he thought: then, confused by the pills and alcohol, he remembered it was not so. Another thirty days. If Leonora Thorne had not faded in another thirty days . . . he might give her one last chance.

His eyes ceased to hurt and the wind faded. The sound of the rain dulled against the windows, no longer to be avoided, quite soothing in the dark.

They found him ten days later, decomposing in his narrow bed, tea bags dry but still in place upon his eyes. No one in the village could imagine his motive for suicide: he was a quiet man, the pro-fessor, they said – kept himself to himself, but always so charming to talk to. He seemed happy enough, full of smiles in the pub on the rare occasions they saw him – just as he was on television. Pity.

Leonora Thorne's trip to South Africa was cut short by three weeks due to an economic crisis in the firm in London. On the train, her first day back to work, irritated by the change in plans, she completed the *Times* crossword with particular speed. All but the quotation. Further irritated, she turned to the obituaries, which she always enjoyed. There she saw a picture of Professor Gerald

Bravington, described as an eminent man of letters. She had not thought of him since the day he had given her a lift in the taxi. Now, she remembered, he had helped her with the Shelley quotation on a rainy morning such as this. He had struck her – in as far as she had thought of him at all – as being an eccentric old thing, nervous – not at all as he appeared on television – and pompous at the same time. Inquisitive, too. He had asked her questions about her life, she recalled, with an eagerness which had exceeded the bounds of mere politeness. Perhaps she should have been more friendly in return, but she was fed up with men pestering her, seeking her out for comfort and all the rest of it, but never offering permanence. Still, it was always a pity when someone of such ability died before his time.

Leonora Thorne turned back to the crossword. For some reason the news of the professor's death inspired in her a determination not to be defeated by today's quotation, at least. She read it again.

The whirligig of time brings in his—

The line was quite unknown to her, she had never been good on Shakespeare. But, with uncanny speed, the word was suddenly there, dazzling her mind.

Revenges, she wrote, and smiled to herself, knowing it was right.

Had there been time, she might have paused to reflect upon the strange coming of her inspiration. But the train was already drawing into Paddington. Leonora Thorne stood up, smoothed her scarlet coat with her navy glove, as was her daily habit, and thought of the fortune she was obliged to spend on taxis, these days, due to so much rain.

Thinnest Ice

Laura's cheek was cold.

Apart from that, it was a perfectly normal evening, a Tuesday. Philip stuffed his glass full of ice before filling it with gin and tonic, a trick he had learned in America. He liked to show, through gestures rather than words, that he had been about a little in his time, although he had given up the travelling side of his business when he married. In spite of Laura begging him not to – she knew how much he had enjoyed his jet-set life – he had been insistent. Of course they could trust each other, but he had seen enough of what could happen to the most trusting married couples when one or the other of the partners was much absent. But his peripatetic bachelor days had left their mark. He still wore Indian cotton shirts and suits from Hong Kong, smoked Russian cigarettes and drank bourbon on the rocks.

Laura sat opposite him on the sofa, her evening face ready with

concern. In two years, he had never come home to find her anything but full of love, welcome and interest. She had learned,
from her meticulous mother, that a man is entitled to be selfish at
the end of a day. He needs to come home to a wife who casts
aside – at any rate to begin with – the petty cares of her own day,
and is all sympathy for his. On this score she never let him down.
She was always there, ice in the bucket, dinner prepared, curtains
drawn in winter, cushions on the garden chairs in summer. Philip
had come to rely on these things, and would no longer trade for
them a business trip to any part of the world.

He had, in fact, only the vaguest idea of how Laura spent her
day. He imagined she shopped, and took care of domestic things
in the morning; lunched with a friend, went to an exhibition in the
afternoon – he was quite proud of her interest in the arts. One day
a week, he knew for certain, she devoted to a group of disabled
people in Kensington. But she rarely spoke of her activities at the
Day Centre, perhaps for fear of boring him. Sometimes she mentioned taking a job – what job, exactly, was never discussed, and
none of the plans had ever materialised. She seemed content
enough with her quiet life. Soon they would have children and the
peace and privacy would be changed. It was her right to enjoy the
peace while it lasted. Philip approved.

In the dappled light of their sitting-room he studied her face.
Such innocence, he thought. Such innocence, and a fist of pain
screwed round in his chest. He had telephoned her at five, to
check what time they were expected for dinner, and there had
been no reply. There was never no reply at five o'clock. Laura was
always there at that time, in her apron in the kitchen eating ginger
biscuits (he liked it very much when he caught her on the telephone with her mouth full, barely able to speak), sifting through
her cookery books choosing something for their dinner. He had
rung at quarter past and half past. Still no answer, and he had left
for home. There, of course – and the underground had never
been so slow – she was waiting for him by the fire, holding up her

peculiarly cold cheek for him to kiss. He had managed not to ask where she had been. Now, he studied the familiar patterns of the room, aware that he was seeking something as he looked at the framed prints on the silky walls, plump cushions, fringes that hemmed the sofas and felt tablecloths – the autumn colours of the square conventional place, their sitting-room, that he loved so much. For a moment he found that each piece of furniture, each ornament, was backlit by a strong light, making it strange. He struggled with the illusion, fighting it off like the end of a nightmare, pressing his fingers against his icy glass, and the room returned to normal. First signs of flu, he thought. Several people had it at the office. Or, as Laura had often said recently, he had been working too hard.

'So what've you been up to this afternoon?'

Laura looked surprised. She shrugged.

'Nothing much. The cleaners. Boring things.' There was a lilt in her voice, an unusual brightness. She paused. 'You don't have to change,' she said, 'but I shall. We're meant to be there at eight-thirty.'

'What are you going to wear?'

The gin had melted the odd pain in his heart, replacing it with warmth. Laura's smile, with its power to reassure, had become part of his existence. The spell of black fantasy, the signs of encroaching flu, were over.

'You'll see. Surprise.'

She surprised him in a flurry of smoky velvet that he had not seen before; jet beads at her neck, amber gloss on her cheeks. Philip frequently suggested she should buy new clothes, but, with a nice sense of economy when it came to other people's money, Laura rarely took advantage of his encouragement. When she did, Philip was always pleased. She had taste, the girl. Wonderful taste. In the narrowness of their hall he congratulated her.

'Christ,' he said, 'all those husbands will be after you.'

'Nonsense,' Laura laughed, spiralling about, making the velvet flutter with shadows. 'You carry on just like a newly married man.'

They drove through fog to Hampstead. At dinner Philip was aware of every movement his wife made at the other end of the table. Bored by conversation with the high-pitched women on either side of him, he fell to musing, as he often did, on his luck in having found Laura. He quite understood why other men envied him. She was not only beautiful, as now, in the candlelight, but she was spirited. Exuberance blew off her like gold dust, touching other people, so that in her presence they found themselves reflecting her brightness. Her head was bowed. She was listening carefully to the man on her left, who taught Russian at Oxford. Philip heard the word Chekhov several times, and saw Laura smile. Ah! She was intent on educating herself. Having been unenthusiastic about coming to this business dinner party, she was now revelling in the don's company. *Revelling. Smiling. Smiling almost constantly.*

With a sharp movement Philip pushed back his plate. The duck stuffed with brandied plums quite suddenly sickened him. The old pain stabbed at him again. He closed his fists on the polished table.

Philip was a man of instincts: this he often claimed. Several years back, big game hunting in Kenya with experienced guides, he had suddenly sensed the dangerous proximity of an elephant. His companions had scoffed at him; they had seen it charge, enraged, in the opposite direction. It would never have returned so soon, they said. But such was Philip's conviction that they were persuaded to return to the Range Rover. No sooner had they done so than they saw the elephant a few yards from them, half hidden behind trees. It bellowed, prepared to charge; they escaped. Another time, alone in a bar in London airport waiting for a plane to Switzerland, Philip heard with uncanny clarity a voice telling him to switch flights. Without asking himself any questions at the time, he did so. A few hours later, he heard that his original flight had crashed in the Alps.

And now his instinct was at work again, gripping him in its horrible conviction. Laura, after only two years, was being unfaithful to him. What's more, she was being pretty blatant about it. The previously innocent, once embarked upon deceit, are often the most skilful. Here she was, not six feet from him, putting up an immaculate show. No one would ever guess she and the arrogant don had spent afternoons, days, months, for all he knew, in some form of contact. Not just talking about bloody Russian writers all the time, either. Christ, what a fool he was not to have seen it all before. Philip's mind jerked back to other occasions when they had met the don, Crispin – ridiculous name – with mutual friends in Oxford. Now he came to think of it, Laura had always made a point of paying him special attention, asking him questions and listening to his interminable answers with her big eyes. She said, he remembered, Crispin was shy – shy! But that when you got to know him, he was wonderfully entertaining.

Philip refused the cheese, the soufflé, the coffee. The heat of the room tightened about him; the candle flames, magnified by their own halos, pained his eyes. Only a lifetime's training in the art of politeness enabled him to contribute to a conversation about duck-shooting with the woman on his left.

After dinner, regathered in a beige drawing-room, Philip saw a look pass between Crispin and Laura as they chose their places: Crispin sat by his wife on the sofa, Laura talked to her host. Unspoken calculation. A tedious hour passed until the goodbyes, when Laura and Crispin merely nodded to each other. Admirable restraint. Philip took Laura's stiff velvet arm. Then they were in the car again, pushing through the solid fog.

'Well, that wasn't so bad, after all, was it? I was lucky getting Crispin. You know what he was telling me? He was telling me that the problem at Oxford these days –'

Philip wiped the windscreen with the back of his hand. Laura watched his face.

'Are you all right, darling? You didn't eat a thing.'

'I'm all right. Get that rag and keep wiping.'

They concentrated on their journey.

The next morning the feeling of unease had died. On his way to work Philip convinced himself he was being ridiculous. It had all been in his imagination, due to overwork perhaps. He spent a contented two hours reading through a long report, able to give it his full attention. At eleven Laura rang. This was unusual. She did not like to bother Philip at the office. There was some minor problem about servicing the car. The conversation was brief. Laura ended:

'See you at the usual time this evening, then.'

'Of course.'

It was only when he had put down the receiver that Philip realised what Laura had done. By ringing him now, she was making fairly sure that he would not ring at five: there would be no need. Thus he would not discover her absence. She would have no need to lie.

Philip's afternoon passed in a turmoil of disbelief. How could she? Laura? What had he done to deserve . . . ? Where had he gone wrong? At five, hand shaking, he rang her. No answer.

Laura's cheek was cold again. And again, apart from that, it was a perfectly normal evening. They watched a documentary on television and ate devilled chicken's legs in the kitchen. Philip opened a bottle of her favourite Sancerre.

'Why such extravagance?' she asked.

'I don't know.' He wondered if she noticed the quaver in his voice. He wondered why, when one human being can see a beast that haunts him, revolting as some creation of the devil, another person can remain unconscious of the vile, almost tangible presence.

'I don't know,' he said again. 'I was thinking. Laura: I was thinking – if ever all this . . . If ever you decided all this wasn't what you wanted after all, you'd tell me, wouldn't you? I mean, you wouldn't put up with it, bravely, just for my sake, without telling me, would you?'

Laura looked at him in amazement.

'What a funny idea,' she said. 'What on earth's on your mind? You look quite pale.'

With a tremendous effort of will Philip forced himself to laugh.

'I expect I sound quite mad. It's just that – I don't know. Such innocence as yours, such continuing innocence, makes one quite suspicious sometimes.'

'Oh, you silly idiot!' Laura laughed and blushed. 'You should find yourself something *really* to worry about.'

She was so convincing that for a moment, in the warmth of their kitchen, Philip felt the chill of shame. In bed he made love to her with unusual violence: she responded with surprised pleasure. If she was tired from her don lover all afternoon, then she did not show it. If there were recollections of his touch in the recesses of her mind, they stood little chance of survival while Philip thrust himself, full of his own agony and love, upon her. In his frenzy he bruised her, hurt her, and she cried to him to stop. She slept quickly, as she always did, her body curved into his.

Philip lay on his back listening to her breathing, and watched the picture show of his wife's infidelity glitter on the ceiling. She and the brute don lay on an anonymous bed, location impossible to define. Where did they go? How often and for how long? What did he do to her? The academic hands, luminous in the darkness, stroked Laura's thighs, Laura's cheeks, Laura's . . . Sickened by the vision, Philip took a sleeping pill, shut his eyes, tried to shut his mind. But sleep would not come. Both drained and alert, he watched the fogged dawn infuse itself into the room. When Laura eventually opened her eyes Philip buried his face in her hair, clinging to her, murmuring he had had a nightmare.

He drank only a cup of black coffee for breakfast, and left for the office feeling icy cold, flesh taut against his bones. He crossed the road and stopped to look back at the leaf-green façade of their house – a small, narrow house in a quiet street behind Notting Hill Gate. They had found it soon after they married. In summer, Laura filled its window-boxes with pansies and geraniums; now, they were planted with small evergreens bright with orange berries. It was a nice, conventional house, with a welcoming look about its windows. One of them, the kitchen, was lighted. Philip could see Laura moving about, a grey silhouette, gathering up the breakfast things. He wondered how long it would be before the telephone rang and she and Crispin arranged today's meeting. As he wondered Laura bounced towards the telephone on the dresser. Philip saw her nod. He saw her smile. He felt his breath come very fast – for a moment he opened his mouth and gasped the air, letting out a small moan – then struggled for control. Laura put down the telephone and left the room. A light went on upstairs, in the bedroom. As Philip's eyes travelled towards it he noticed a web of cracks over the green paintwork of the façade. The paintwork is cracking, he thought to himself: it's time we had it done. I must tell Laura to organise repainting. He turned away, began to walk towards the Underground. How strange, he thought, that green paint should last so little time. Must be pollution. Pollution destroys everything.

When he rang Laura from the office at five she answered the telephone. Relief confused him. He could think of nothing to say.

'It was just – I noticed cracks all over the front of the house this morning. The paint. It's worn so badly. We must get it done. Could you ring the builders before—'

'Cracks? What are you talking about?'

'Cracks, darling. All over the front of the house. Honestly.'

'But there isn't a crack to be seen.'

Philip could sense her puzzlement.

'Well, never mind. Maybe, in the fog – I must have imagined it.'

'You must have.'

'Be back in an hour.'

So today she and Crispin must have done it at lunch-time. Crispin must have had to get an early train back to Oxford. The weekend. Of course, the weekend. How would they communicate between tonight and Monday? Philip decided to make sure he would answer every telephone call. He could not bring himself to ask questions, but if he caught her out she would have to explain.

And there was nothing else for it. He would catch her out. Exhausted by the thought, he set off for home.

Philip unlocked the front door very quietly, a sense of horror at his own action. He could hear Laura talking on the telephone in the kitchen. Unusually low voice. A laugh. Noiselessly, Philip pulled the door shut behind him, crept a few paces further into the hall. Then he stood, quite rigid, and listened.

'That's funny,' he heard her say. 'That's terribly funny. I want to hear more when I see you.' Oh, they had their jokes, she and Crispin. Riotous jokes he knew nothing about, killingly funny jokes to make them squirm and giggle between kisses.

'So you'll be here tomorrow, then,' she was saying, 'about three. We might see if there's something good on locally.'

Tomorrow? Michael, her younger brother, was coming to visit them tomorrow. A great heat exploded in Philip's head. He swung round, opened the front door, banged it shut, pulled off his coat, ran up the stairs as the telephone clicked. Laura must not see him in this state.

He shut himself in the bathroom. Its familiar pinkness was unstable, as if he had cocooned himself in a shaking blancmange. Breathe deeply, Philip, he said to himself, leaning against the basin, and take a look at yourself.

He saw in the pink glass mirror the face of a man who had been spying on his wife: a man haunted by suspicion, convinced by instinct. Wild hair, huge eyes, fear.

'You're loathsome, you're despicable,' he said. 'How far will you go?'

Later, some measure of equilibrium restored, he poured himself an extra-large gin and tonic and paced the small sitting-room. Laura sat in one corner of the sofa doing her tapestry, half-smiling, innocent as usual.

'You're restless,' she said.

'I am, rather.'

'Anything the matter?'

'No. Not sleeping very well, I suppose.'

Sated by her own life, Laura had no notion how troubled were his nights. He had often thought of waking her, asking her for the truth which would put an end to his own suffering.

'Come to think of it, you seem to be rather thin.' Laura's eyes travelled all over him. 'Perhaps you're getting something.'

'Perhaps.' Philip sat down at last, crossed his legs, spun one ankle. 'I often wonder,' he said, 'how you fill your days. Sometimes at the office, you know, I try to imagine what you're doing, and I've really no idea.'

Laura glanced at him. Quickly smiled.

'I think I'd better keep you in the dark. If I told you the truth you'd not only be bored, you'd be ashamed of me for not thinking up better ways to pass the hours. But I've decided quite seriously that after Christmas I'll get a job – in fact I've more or less found one. That art gallery in Notting Hill Gate – you know – they apparently want someone part-time. That would suit me very well. Be a good idea, don't you think?'

'I should think it would.' Philip plucked at his Hong Kong trousers. Of course a part-time job would suit her well. Regular hours would mean terrible complications, maybe even the necessity of deceit. *Oh Laura! So quiet, so tranquil, in the lamplight, how is it that you love someone else, that you count the hours till you see him, that you let him into the most private parts of you . . . ?*

'Oh, Laura!' he cried out loud.

'Philip!' She ran to him, put a cool hand on his forehead. 'What is it? You're looking most . . . peculiar.'

'Don't touch me, please.' He removed her hand.

'What is it?'

'Leave me. I'm all right. I just . . . I'll ring Dr Bruce in the morning. Get some tranquillisers.' He rose and went to the tray of drinks. 'Worry about all this . . . redundancy. It's affecting us all.'

'Of course.' Laura's face expressed perfect concern. 'But you don't normally let office worries get on top of you like this. Perhaps you need a break. Perhaps after Christmas we should go away for a week.'

'Perhaps. But you wouldn't want to go away for a week, would you?'

'Of course I would!' Her indignation was genuine enough. 'What do you mean?'

'All right, then. I'll get tickets for one of those cheap tours to Venice.' *You lying little hypocrite, I'll take you at your word.*

'What a lovely idea!' *What's more, you bloody little actress, not for one moment will I let you out of my sight – no chance of your slipping off to the Poste Restante . . .*

Philip half filled his glass with gin.

As far as he could tell Laura and Crispin had no form of communication over the weekend, but the private canker within Philip spread. Tranquillisers did nothing to abate the torment of his suspicions. He could neither eat nor sleep. And yet, some basic habit of maintaining appearances kept him going, while within him a devil voice lashed constant abuse at Laura. Outwardly he was friendly, gentle: they continued to lead their quiet lives with little reference to Philip's disintegrating appearance. He could sense Laura's concern but, knowing he abhorred fuss, she refrained from questioning him, merely said all would be well in January.

Two weeks went by. During this time Philip rang Laura every day at five, and she was never at home. On his return each evening she flourished her cold shining cheeks, the sparkle in her eyes betraying her rewarding afternoon. Still Philip endured her condition in silence, though some evenings the physical pain in his chest was so bad he would shut himself in his study for half an hour, and bend double in the armchair to alleviate the ache.

Then, one morning after a particularly bad night, he came down early to make Laura breakfast. Having inwardly riled against her most of the night, he thought this was the least he could do for her, to make private amends. On his way to the kitchen he picked up the post from the mat, shuffled through the letters.

There was one with an Oxford postmark. Stiff white envelope, intelligent writing in black ink. Philip stared at it till the words blurred before his eyes, and a vile sweat pricked over his back.

He made two cups of coffee and took them upstairs on a tray with the letters. Laura was waking, stretching, smiling, pleased at the treat of breakfast in bed. For the first time for many mornings a pallid sun slanted into the room, cheering the timid blues of curtains and walls. Philip, conscious that the sweat that now covered his body smelt strongly, sat on the edge of the bed and watched his wife closely.

She was very clever. When it came to opening the thick white envelope she made no comment, simply slit it with a knife. She pulled out a white card, read it quickly, and passed it to Philip.

'Crispin and Moira want us to go to some lunch party on Sunday.' Voice quite level.

Philip held the card between finger and thumb as if it were edged with blades. This, of course, was all part of a well-constructed plan. Crispin and Laura apparently saw no treachery in organising social meetings as well as clandestine ones.

'Don't let's go to that,' he said.

'Why ever not? It should be rather fun.'

'Well, I'm not going. I don't like Moira and I like Crispin even less. Pretentious man, to say the least. And most of all I don't like donnish Oxford parties.'

'Oh, Philip.' Laura's mouth, rather thin, was not made for pouting. It curved downwards. 'That's silly of you. You can't generalise like that. You can't simply say you don't like *all* Oxford parties. Moira's and Crispin's might be quite different.'

Philip stood up.

'It might, but I'm not going. You can do what you like.' His dressing-gown fell apart. Glancing down, he saw the gleam of sweat on his stomach, realised the ridiculous sight he must be to Laura. She smiled up at him.

'No need to sound so fierce. I don't really mind—'

'And don't lie to me, Laura!' The roar of Philip's voice shook the room. 'Go to the party without me if you want to – I don't care a damn how many parties you go to, but don't lie to me!' The sudden fear and miscomprehension in her eyes goaded him. 'Go on, go! D'you hear me? All the way to Oxford for another little lesson in Chekhov. God Almighty!' He flung off his dressing-gown: the sour smell of his own sweat almost stifled him. He ran one hand down his stomach, wet flesh upon wet flesh: with the other he pulled back the bedclothes, watched the lilac slip of Laura's body cower into itself like a night flower at dawn. She screamed.

Philip was upon her. He was aware, from the way she turned her head from his mouth, that his breath was evil, and that his jowl scratched her cheeks, inflaming them with ugly red. He was aware of tintacks in his flesh, of the dryness of Laura, of terrible moaning noises from them both.

When it was over he left her exposed and crying on the bed. He dressed quickly and went from the house without saying goodbye.

In Holland Park the sun was gentle among bare trees. Philip sat on a bench, head in hands. I am ill, he thought. I have a virus that turns reason to unreason, makes me savage my wife, abuse her, suspect her. Dear God, he thought, I am a man debased by a feeling I should be able to overcome. I understand it to be irrational. Understanding that, perhaps it will go from me. He looked slowly about as if searching the air for a cure. The bare branches were cruel against his eyes, flaws in the winter sky. His whole body

ached with the kind of pain caused by flesh that is too thin to protect raw bone from the elements. He stood. He began to walk
back down the path, heavily as a man breast-high in water who
pushes against a strong current.

At the office, dully, no greeting to his secretary, he shut the
door. Telephoned Laura.

'I'm sorry.'

'Oh . . . that's all right.' Pause. 'I mean, it's the first real row
we've ever had, isn't it? It had to happen some time. Though I'm
not sure what it was all about.'

'Nor am I.'

'Are you all right?'

'Yes.'

'Well . . . thank you for ringing.'

'And thank you for being so . . . I don't know what came over
me.'

'No need to go on.'

Philip called for black coffee and a glass of brandy. The relief
of his wife's forgiveness gave him strength to start the fight. He
would rid himself of the disease through an act of supreme will.
He was, after all, a strong man. First thing to do was to resist
ringing Laura at five. He achieved this. But when, on reaching
home, he kissed her cold bright happy cheek, the physical pain
restruck with a force that overwhelmed all his good intentions. He
realised, as he lay awake that night, mind seething with vile possibilities, that it was going to be a long battle.

A week later, swallowing tranquillisers with his coffee in the
office – they merely misted the superficial pain, did nothing to
banish the fundamental ache and racing mind – he decided to tell
Laura what had happened. This would mean risking possible disaster. There was also a small chance it might save and cure. A
chance worth taking. Tonight. The positive decision fanned a
small flame of strength. Philip picked up a long report, began to

read. The uneasy looks of his colleagues, of late, had not gone unobserved; their concern for him was plain. He would now concentrate on putting their minds at rest. Then his private telephone rang. Laura.

'Sorry to bother you – but do you think you could *possibly* take the afternoon off?' She sounded breathless, excited.

'Well, yes, I dare say. But why?'

'It's quite important.'

'What is it?'

'I don't want to tell you now. Just come home in time for lunch. Please.'

'All right. How very mysterious.' He tried to sound lighthearted.

He put the report back in a drawer knowing that further work that morning would be impossible, and decided to walk home. It would take an hour and so exhaust him, in his weakened state, that, by the time she broke the bad news, he would have achieved a protective sense of stupor. He strolled along the City pavements, St James's Park, Hyde Park, afraid. When finally he reached the front door he felt faint and dizzy, as he had felt on occasions in church as a child.

For the first time Laura did not try to conceal her anxiety. He looked dreadful, she said, and insisted he should see the doctor again tomorrow. Philip, with little energy left to argue, let the warmth of the house seep into his cold flesh. Gratefully he drank a glass of red wine and managed to eat half a plate of soup.

'Now,' said Laura, 'I'd like you to come with me in the car.' She was authoritative, bossy, pretty. The warmth of her reached through Philip's fatigue. In the car, he wanted to touch her. But he remained quietly with hands in his lap, asking no questions. He assumed they were going to some mysterious rendezvous to meet Crispin and decide upon their future.

Laura drove to Queensway and parked in front of the skating rink.

'Here,' she said. 'We're here.' She paid their entrance money – Philip's reactions were too slow to reach for his wallet – and led the way downstairs. There was a heavy chill about the place that made Philip visibly shudder. It vaguely occurred to him that this was a strange place to meet with an Oxford don: too cold. Perhaps they would sit in the cafeteria behind the glass screen. It would be warmer there, round a small Formica table with a cup of tea.

'You wait here,' Laura was saying. 'I'll be back.'

Philip sat on a chair behind the barrier at the edge of the rink, no longer much in possession of his senses. Before him several dozen skaters, mostly women and children, skittered about the ice. A few of them were fast and competent, masters of their movements, spinning and zooming in tight-lipped silence, the keen wind of their own speed their only awareness. Others clutched, squeaked, fell, and rose again without the benefits of grace or balance. Nightmare people. None of them was Crispin.

A gong boomed. Philip jerked, afraid: felt a skein of sweat over his back. Clutching at his neck with a cold hand, he looked about for Laura. Where was she? And what was he doing here?

The skaters crowded to the exits in the barriers. Only the good ones remained on the ice. Music, suddenly: an organ blurred by bad acoustics playing a tune from a fifties musical. The skaters, in pairs now, began to dance.

Not far from Philip a familiar girl stepped on to the ice. Laura, it was. She wore a short pleated skirt, red tights and new-looking boots. She waved at him, smiled. Behind her came a thin figure all in black, except for a small badge on his breast. He had the impassive look of a skating instructor, his sharp face frozen into inanimation that comes from years of skimming over blank ice. He put an arm round Laura's waist.

The music changed to a slow waltz. Laura and her partner moved, cautiously. They were straight-backed, fluid. Gradually, they gathered speed, dipped and swerved in unison. They reached a corner: turning backwards, Laura quavered a little. The androgynous black arm tightened round her waist, supportive. Laura's face was pinched with concentration. She did not look towards Philip.

Philip's eyes never left the scarlet and black pair. They blurred and fuzzed, became dots, then fur, then for a moment hardened into sharp focus. All the while, beneath his raw skin, he felt the blood seep from his veins, taking with it the old pain in his breastbone, and leaving an overwhelming feebleness. He lifted one arm on to the edge of the barrier, lowered his head on to the coldness of his sleeve. Beneath his feet the black rubber flooring, holed like crochet, gleamed with the water of melted ice. The dreadful organ thumped out a Beatles tune. Philip put his free hand to his face to prod the numbness. He felt a hot mess of tears on his cheeks.

A hand ruffled his hair. He looked up. Laura was pink and laughing, leaning over the barrier. Her partner backed away, with little swerving movements, knees dipped.

'How about that? Are you all right?'

'Amazing. Cold.'

'Bet you never thought I could do anything like that?'

'No.'

'So you'll never again be able to say what do you *do* all day, will you?' Gently accusing. 'I was *determined* . . . I was determined to surprise you before Christmas.'

'You have.' Philip felt his icy lips draw back over his teeth into something which he hoped would resemble a smile.

'I didn't want to tell you. Though I nearly did because I began to think you thought . . .' She laughed. 'I'll just go round a couple more times, then we'll go home. You look frozen.'

She swirled away, too daring. Her partner darted forward, stretched out an arm, but she fell. Philip stood up, one hand on the barrier. Against the horrible slur of music, he heard himself laughing. Laura, scrambling up, regaining her poise, laughed with him.

Philip remained standing, hands in pockets, shoulders hunched, his breath regular globules ballooning over the rink. All those secret afternoons, he thought, and his instincts, a little late for once, flashed benevolently towards Crispin. Dear God, he thought, that such an innocent conspiracy should cause such thunder in a reasonable man: may she forgive me, should she ever guess.

But Laura came off the ice with no sign of ever guessing. Philip met her at the barrier, briefly aware of his own width compared to the svelte shape of her skating partner. He took her arm, kissed her cold cheek, and told her she was an amazing creature: yes, he could hardly believe it. Pleased, she strode off, unusually tall on her skates, to fetch her coat.

Philip enjoying waiting for her. Still weak from shock, he felt the strength seep gradually back along his blood, and refrained from smiling only for fear of looking foolish. His damned instincts had nearly destroyed him, but recovery was here. When Laura came back he would drive her home: he felt more able to drive, now. She would enjoy recounting the difficulties of carrying out her plot, words tumbling almost into incoherence, as they did when she was excited. When they reached their green and uncracked house, they would resume their normal lives.

Philip would listen quietly. Knowing the wisdom of occasional silence in marriage, he would admit only one thing: that in all truth he had not guessed she was learning to skate.

Monday Lunch in Fairyland

She met him at a party somewhere. Noticed the decayed state of his leather jacket before his face. Neither heard the other's name in the mumbling that goes for an English introduction. But they danced. When the music came to an end he said he was K. Beauford. The K stood for Kestrel. He liked it, but everyone else thought it so pretentious that he had long ago given up using it. Except his mother. And her name? Anna. O-oh, he said, giving the word two syllables. She thought, from his smile, it would have been nice to talk to him. But the music smashed into the room again, and he disappeared.

'Saw you having quite a dance with K. Beauford,' said Mark, driving home. They both sat upright in their lumpy marital car. 'Met him once, years ago, fishing. He kept us supplied with the best white wine I've ever drunk. Called something like Annaberg. Never met it since. Cooled it in rock pools. Bloody marvellous.'

He smiled. Fishing memoirs always made him smile. Smiling made his moustache hunch up to brush the keel of his nose. Sometimes this would tickle, and he would push it down with a thick finger.

'O-oh,' said Anna.

Breakfast in their London kitchen. Perhaps three weeks later. Feeling, as always, of an indoor storm. Flurry of cornflakes. Thunder of fists on the table. Rain of splattered milk on chairs and floor. Years ago, as lovers, Mark and Anna had calm breakfasts. Years ago they would speak, and gaze, and pour coffee absent-mindedly. Now, a child clutched a postcard in a sticky hand. Anna snatched it. For her. Picture of Buckingham Palace, Strange writing. *Nineteen days to track you down, am no detective. Love K. Beauford*. Oh, yes. Leather jacket. Pale as milk at the elbows. Fishing with Mark. Mark quite hidden behind *The Times*. Anna propped the postcard between two mugs on the dresser. If he hadn't been so deeply into Bernard Levin she might have said something about it.

'Get your *coats* on,' she shouted to the children.

Next card three days later. Buckingham Palace from the air, this time. *Would you consider lunch as my reward? Love K. Beauford*. Hooting outside of the school-run car. Lost satchels. Running noses. Smudgy kisses. Mark's baggy morning eyes dull with the promise of a hard day. All gone, suddenly. Alone with the silence of 8.45 a.m. This mess to be cleared before she could begin her own day. No immediate impetus, though. She sat. Dabbed at toast crumbs on the table, letting them prick her finger. Would she consider lunch? Yes, she would consider mere lunch. So innocent an event could not affect the order of her life. She had no wish for anything, ever, to affect the quiet order of her life. Its domestic tides, its familiar routines. Books for intellectual stimulus, flowers for pleasure. Small clinging arms for love, Mark's good-humoured laugh for companionship. Yearly holidays for adventure,

Christmas for excitement. Smug, perhaps, but orderly. Compared with so many, after fifteen years, happy. Untempted by the shoddy delights of extramarital associations. Those who had vaguely supposed had been severely snubbed. But lunch, just lunch. The smallest of treats. Preceded, if necessary, by a lecture on the lack of future. And of course not a secret. I'm having lunch with K. Beauford, she would say to Mark. If she remembered.

The quiet of the house, daytime, rose up: bulbous, engulfing, warm. Only to be shattered at four. That clatter of footsteps just as silence could be borne no longer, its peace grown chill. Squealing bell. Rush for television and instant tea. The noise. The telephone.

'I must have caught you at a bad time.'

'Rather. Only by five minutes Who is it?'

'K. Beauford.'

'Oh, yes.'

'How about Monday? That lunch.'

'Yes. Why not?'

'La Cuisine, at one.'

'Sorry, I can hardly hear. La Cuisine?'

'At one.'

'Lovely.'

'Bye.'

She had let the toast burn, felt no concern at the lack of peanut butter. 'You're so bloody *spoilt*, you lot. It's Marmite or nothing.' Unfamiliar puzzlement in their eyes. The whole weekend ahead – the smallest one in tears. Oh God, make up for it with an extra-long story . . .

. . . Increase of the size of the Round Pond that Saturday. Mark's kite entangled maddeningly in the trees. Hours till it was brought down. All absurd, such impatience. Just for lunch. Mark's hands efficient on her body after his favourite braised celery and *coq au vin* for Sunday dinner. Things she hadn't cooked him, come to think of it, for a long time.

*

Monday, noon, she thought she looked quite old. Brushed her hair to cover a lot of her face. Wore clothes she hoped might seem like ordinary Monday clothes. Paid for the taxi out of the housekeeping money, disloyalty shaking her hand.

K. Beauford sat in a distant corner of the restaurant. Its kitchen air. Strings of onions and garlic hanging from the ceiling, like unfinished chandeliers. He stood. Same leather jacket. Deep lines round his smile.

'Hello, hello.'

'Hello.' Anna sat.

'I thought I'd always send you pictures of Buckingham Palace.'

'I wondered at their significance.'

'No significance. I recommend the watercress mousse.'

'I don't know what I'm doing here, really. I'm not used to lunch. I never go out to lunch You're almost a blind date, aren't you? At my age.'

'Oh, do stop twittering,' he said.

Very pale green, the mousse. White wine that tasted of grapes. Trout. Fennel salad. He said he lived far away, by the sea. Hardly ever came to London. Had a wife, mostly absent, to whom he would always remain a husband. So no need for the lecture. Relief. Such relief Anna's hands sent her hair scattering backwards, revealing all her face.

'At last I can see you,' he said. 'Scrutinise.'

Confused, she told him something of her orderly life. Very brightly. Made it sound desirable. Which it was. The children would be having mince at school now. Mince on Monday, so fish fingers for tea. Never imagining their mother . . . Mark at the Savoy with a chairman. Making an important decision. Never imagining his wife . . .

In the end she had not told him. Would later. Tonight. K. Beauford was pressing her to pear flan. She was not resisting, liking his laugh. A furry quality. He was telling of his evenings. Alone with his dog. Not a reader, but a maker of complicated model cars for his sons. No, he felt no need to see people. So long as lunch appeared at one, and dinner at eight. Orderly, too, you see. That was the way to keep going. Invent one's own discipline to prevent floundering. Protect oneself from intrusion. Plant trees. Visit people's lives. Resist indulging in explicitness. Catch the train you first intended to catch. Which was in half an hour.

No word of ever meeting again.

Orderly life quite intact.

Goodbye, goodbye.

Nothing to fear. The children wanting tea. Full of relentless instinct. Mama, why are you wearing *that* dress? She knew quite well his part of the coast. Yes, darling, now I'll help you with your Geography. And after Geography, listen to news of Mark's lunch. Glad you've come to that decision at last, darling . . . No time to reflect. Seas very savage in winter down there. Dinner at eight alone with the dog. Postcard writer. Visitor.

Eleven days without a signal. Then third picture of Buckingham Palace by the second post. This one from an engraving, 1914. *Have discovered the Whitlaws nearby are mutual friends. Possibility of plans? Love K. Beauford.*

Possibility of what plans? The telephone, startling.

'Hello, hello. Are you coming to the Whitlaws?'

'What? I've only just got your card. I don't know what you mean.' Outside, movement of the one bare tree. In summer its shadows blurred the geometric shadow of the wrought-iron gate. Any minute now the car would be drawing up, bearing children.

'When are you coming?'

'When?'

'Couldn't you make next weekend?'

'Mark will be in Brussels . . .'

'Someone can look after the children. Surely.'

The children. There they were. Scrambling out of the car. One school beret falling into the gutter. Anna waved, smiling, through the window.

'What? Next weekend? I must go, I'm afraid. The bell.'

'I'll be expecting you.'

Apologies for keeping them waiting at the door. Exclamations at a cut knee. The *arrogance* of the man! The ridiculous nature of the summons. Of course, it was out of the question. Quite impossible. Where would the children go? She buttered their crumpets, full of love.

Mark, with the enthusiasm of the innocent, thought her idea a very good one. Nice to see the Whitlaws again and he loathed it down there. The children so pleased about going to their aunt. Plans falling into place with horrifying ease. For what?

On the long train journey she wondered. Just another lunch, perhaps. A long way to go for just another lunch. But no use speculating. In effort to remain calm, heart strangely beating.

The Whitlaws made no mention of K. Beauford for twenty-four hours. They were pleased to see her, pressed on her more food and wine than she cared for. The children rang her. She rang the children. Snow on the moors, forsythia in the court-yard. Mark rang from Brussels. Marvellous sun there, he said. But progress slow. Not back till Tuesday. Why had she come all this way to be without her children? Then it was announced: K. Beauford was coming to lunch on Sunday. Hadn't they met somewhere? He could give her a lift to the train.

Sunday was dour. Unbroken cloud. Anna pulled her belt into its tightest notch. She felt thin.

K. Beauford was punctual. Talkative. A bit wicked.

'Having discovered we all knew you, the next thing I hear is you're *down* here. It's an awfully long way to come for a weekend. Isn't it?'

'She'd come any distance to stay with us,' said the Whitlaws.

They left after tea. Late sun through a flurry of snow. Drove over the moors. In silence. Then K. Beauford said,

'There are all sorts of fairyland, you know.'

His car skidded through the thick gravel of his drive. In the snowy dusk, giant clusters of weeping copper beech trees. Indeterminate parklands.

He led her through outer and inner halls. Dark pictures. A room whose crimson silk walls twitched with firelight. She sank on to a broken sofa. Its stuff scratched the back of her knees. He pulled the curtains against huge panes of black snowflakes. Muffling a church bell.

'We can have dinner and I'll put you on the sleeper,' he said.

They explored the cellars. Gloomy stone passages veining the foundations of the house. Hundreds of bottles of orderly wine, dust obscuring the labels. Strongrooms of polished silver chalices. Crates of yellowing books, first editions waiting to be sorted. Kitchen tall as a barn. Old-fashioned black range. Mixing bowl and pile of chopped onion on the huge wooden table only signs of culinary activity.

Dinner at eight. The gong as the hall clock struck. Two places at the far end of a long white-clothed table. A silvery butler who poured Mark's remembered wine: Annaberg.

'I don't know what I'm doing here,' Anna said.

'Three postcards then a visit. That seems to me the proper order of things.'

'Do you eat like this, every night, by yourself?'

'Of course.'

'The table laid like this? The candles?'

'How else?'

'It seems so odd, these days.'

'Have to keep things going. There's not much of it left.'

'Kestrel Beauford,' she said. As if trying out the name for the first time.

'Silly whim of my mother's, really.'

'K. Beauford. I don't know what I'm doing here.'

'You keep saying that. I suppose you ought to be at home with your husband and children.'

'Yes.'

'Well, I'm glad you're not.'

They drank port by the fire. Wine red against fire red against red of silk walls. All reds confused. Billy Paul singing.

Me and Mrs Jones
Have a thing going on . . .

One hour, she was thinking, till the train.

'Alternatively,' said K. Beauford, 'you could go back in the morning. Or the afternoon. Or tomorrow evening.'

'Quite impossible.'

But there she was making telephone calls. Very calmly. To Brussels. Quite right, you stay on, said Mark. To the aunt. Oh, very well, she said. No, it won't be much of a bother. The children are quite happy. Elaborate stories. Everyone believing her. Guilt dulled by wine. Wine making the stories of her life quite funny, so that K. Beauford was laughing in his endearing fashion. Hand stretched out towards her. But at rest on the crumpled sofa. As if frozen on its journey.

Very late he showed her to a cold room. Switched on the one-bar fire. Double bed with icy sheets.

'Only three postcards and here I am. What am I doing here?' she said.

'Do stop asking that question,' he said. 'You can go tomorrow on the five-thirty. I promise.'

'You promise?' she said.

'I absolutely promise, my love,' he said.

Five-thirty. On the train in the stuffy carriage. She quivered. Next to her, cartons of farm eggs, pots of Devonshire cream. He had given them to her. Saying: for the children's breakfast. She would explain they were from the Whitlaws. The train jerked, moved forward. Dark bare platform where moments ago K. Beauford had been kissing her goodbye. I shan't wait and wave, he said. And had not mentioned when, or if, they would meet again.

Oh my love that wet and shining winter beach the sandpipers pecking at the frills of sea you said they were sandpipers I didn't know and you said quietly now if we go quietly we won't disturb them and we came so close before they flew away a small bush of wings in the grey sky urged higher by their own cries of alarm and me with my arm through yours absurdly bulbous in a puffed anorak of dreadful tangerine so out of place I said on this empty shore shouting against the wind so you could hear and laugh and feeling you shorten your step to coincide with mine . . .

All well at home. All pleased with eggs and cream. Stories of the aunt. Stories of Brussels. Scarcely a thought for her weekend. Thank God. For it hung, indelible, a double image upon her daily life. Which had resumed its normality so fast. Only, within, the orderliness had flown.

Impatiently she waited. Afternoons were worst. Then, in the silent house, the churning mind that nothing could divert. Fear of going out for fear of missing the telephone. The pacing, the trying of all the old familiar chairs. Mind a visible thing in the mind's eye: a yellowing ivory ball as carved by the Chinese. Intertwined rats of minuscule teeth and savage eyes. Twisting, turning, never still, gnawing at the memories. You're very thin darling, Mark said. Never usually noticed such things. And you're restless at night. Can't sleep? What's the matter? Concerned eyes. Oh don't be so silly, she said, hating his hands. And in the morning shouting at the children.

Because you are far away by the sea in the private ocean of your park knowing that lunch is at one and dinner at eight and your dog will

sleep by your bedroom fire and you plan the planting of more melan-
choly trees and spray silver paint on to plastic motorbikes and maybe
sometimes think of me though you didn't say you would you said in
fairyland the figure is there all the time unconsciously conscious if
you like you said K. Beauford why don't you ring me?

Complications of infidelity unimaginable to those who have not
experienced them. He rang too late one evening: Mark's car drawing up outside. So she sounded terse, bright. Yes, tomorrow, three
o'clock. No, not here. Not possible. She would meet him somewhere. Put off the dentist and the meeting with the headmaster.
Mark asking for ice. Nothing, nothing of the days that had passed.
I'm coming, Mark, with ice: her voice almost a scream.

And terrible hours, fighting for calm. Till she met him in a
dark wine bar in the King's Road. His jacket black with rain. They
watched its streamers liquidise the windows. Stabbed out cigarettes in a plastic ashtray. Arms touching, and their thighs.

'When are you coming again?' he said.

'I can't really come again, can I?'

'I hope you can and you will,' he said.

'It would be so difficult, another time. The plans. The lies. I'm
not very good at the lies.'

'Divided worlds,' he said. 'We should all have our divided
worlds. They shouldn't conflict, or be hard to separate.'

She laughed.

'Do you find that easy?' she asked.

'Well, yes, I do.'

'You're lucky,' said Anna.

'I mean, visits to fairyland are nothing to do with anything
else. If you plan them right they can go on for ever and ever. Just
things to look forward to, and to look back on. With tremendous
excitement. And pleasure. Aren't they?'

'Oh, yes.' She had to agree. Couldn't explain.

'Well, it's up to you,' he said.

'I've seen it happen so often. When people start this kind of thing,' she said. Trying. 'It's the stuff of divorce.'

'It needn't be,' he said. So easily. 'It's only difficult if fundamental, impossible changes are visualised. Best only to think of the good, possible times. Within their limitations.'

'The strength of you,' she said.

He drove her home on the back of his motorbike. Nose in his wet hair. Arms round his shoulders. He kissed her without heed by the front gate. Said she smelt wonderful in the rain. Some kind of flowers. And he'd be in touch. Exhilarated by such parting news, tea with the children was a lovely time. Mama, you look so happy today, one of them said. But such wet hair.

Well you see that's because K. Beauford insisted I should ride on his rusty old motorbike in all this rain dodging the buses I thought death every time smelling the earthy smell of his hair shouting into it be careful for God's sake I'm the mother of three children and now my love my love not many days will pass before we'll speak again . . .

Next postcard of Buckingham Palace behind the Victoria Memorial. From somewhere in Wales. *Am writing this in a bus shelter. Two days later – sorry I forgot to post it. Will ring Tuesday morning, much love K Beauford. Much,* Anna noted. Before it had been just love. Much love, and by now the destructive forces of infidelity crowded in all about her. Her family all strangers. Resentful of them. Resentful of their needing her presence. Their demands so irritating. Their puzzled eyes sniping her guilt at her own unfriendliness. Nothing was but what was not. Lady Macbeth's undoing. The house itself was an insubstantial thing. Tiny flaws in the fabric of daily life. The clear picture, familiar for so long, shattered. A private mosaic. It couldn't go on. She couldn't survive it: Mark's appalling tolerance. The children's constant forgiveness. The sleepless nights. Where had all the orderliness gone? Quiet content? Precious habit of unexciting love? All she had thought she wanted. Could never return, now. Not in the same way.

In the silence of a dun-coloured afternoon Anna stood by the tall windows of her house, fingers hunched up like spiders on the cold glass of the panes. Blasted, her life. Inadvertently, she had let it happen. Linen cupboard disorganised. Deep-freeze empty. Husband and children squeezed by the rats of her mind to a far-away place. No longer of prime importance.

Rain. It began to rain on the leafless trees. Falling silent on the square of plantless London earth she liked to call her garden.

Oh, I'm not as strong as you K. Beauford at dividing worlds perhaps because I love you and that's where it's all gone wrong though you must never know but in the spring I'll visit you again and we'll send postcards of Buckingham Palace for years and years until we grow old and calm and the visits between our separated worlds can't unground us any more. But oh, my love, can that ever be?

Mind of Her Own

'Think the big one'll win, Jack?'

'Chancy.'

'Small one looks as if he could do with a square meal.'

'Wiry, though. Muscle through and through.' Jack Lee tapped his thigh through his office trousers. 'Here, budge up, will you? You're cramping my style.'

Alice had slumped a little towards her husband's end of the sofa. She remembered the old days. 'Here, snuggle up a bit, Al. Keeps the chill out,' he used to say then. But that was twenty-eight years ago. Then, she would give him her hand. He would squeeze it, a passionless pressure that would cause no look of alarm in the eyes of his parents, who chaperoned Jack and Alice for five years while they waited, in their uncertainty, to marry. Now, she shifted her position obediently so that there should be a few more inches between them.

Co-operation was pale yellow in Alice Lee's mind. A primrose yellow, to be precise, sometimes almost metallic: a colour that started in her head, flowed down through her body filling it with warmth and making her limbs waxy, deliquescent, so that her movements, to onlookers, would sometimes appear clumsy. Most days Alice experienced these yellow sensations in some measure. The fact that she was used to them in no way diminished their rewards. They represented an inexplicable happiness that was her only secret, her only area of absolute privacy.

Alice Lee was born a good woman. As her friends said, there was no trace of malice in her. When all around her bitched and snarled, she remained full of charity. As far as she could tell – as she often laughingly said – the Lord had forgotten to plant in her any form of neurosis. In appreciation of this blessing she was a willing listener and adviser to many friends and neighbours. And as a wife and mother, Alice was conscientious and sympathetic. She put her family's interests always before her own, and thus never had the time to doubt that this was the best thing for herself. But for all her virtues, Alice ran no risk of being saintly. Sometimes, evenings like this, when Jack sat in front of the television thinking out loud about his day in the insurance office (he didn't require any response), Alice would find her concentration wandering far away from her husband's problems. Staring at the wrestling match before her eyes, she would see instead the woods of her childhood where she and her brother Sam would gather birds' nests and blow the pale eggs. Next best, she would let herself become enveloped in what she called her Brontë cloud: magically, she would turn into Jane Eyre at that climactic moment when Mr Rochester sees her through his veils of blindness. Not that she ever wanted Jack to be blind, of course. Alice would rouse herself guiltily, glancing at her muttering husband, important things on his mind. He was a fine, healthy man, for all his years of desk work. But in some strange way he'd never given her the thrill – not even in their earliest days, picnicking

Sundays on Box Hill – that in her view Mr Rochester had given
Jane Eyre.

'Where are Denise and Robbie?' asked Jack. He felt easier now
that Alice had moved. He asked the same question most nights.
Always prepared to be surprised by the answer, he was always a
little disappointed to find it much the same.

'Denise is washing her hair. Robbie's in his room.'

Denise washed her hair six nights a week. Robbie's habit was to
go to his room as soon as supper was over to fiddle with his home-
made radio set. Robbie was a mathematician, training to be a
teacher. Denise, presently working as a receptionist in a travel
agency, hoped one day to own a beauty parlour. Saving towards
this end, she followed carefully the rules of dedicated parsimony,
and grumbled at the self-inflicted hardship it caused. In his heart,
Jack would have been delighted if his children had been a little
more gregarious. But they didn't seem to have many friends.
Certainly, none of them ever came to the house. However, he
was not one to be ungrateful for his mercies. What he *did* have,
and it was a pretty rare thing these days, looking round – was a
close-knit family unit. As a family, they liked each other. They
enjoyed doing things together. And nobody should underrate
that, thought Jack. With a small twist of his head he went on to
reckon, as one wrestler flicked the other satisfyingly to the ground,
that he and Alice had been married coming up to twenty-five
years now. What's more, never a cross word. Alice had always
had the good sense to agree with him, so there had never been any
cause for dispute.

Denise came in, towel over her head, shaking her wet frizz of
hair. Jack couldn't ever remember having seen a shine on Denise's
hair, not even when she was a youngster. It was something she
strove for, but, Jack imagined, considering its natural hazy tex-
ture, it was something she would never achieve. But he wasn't one
to discourage anybody, let alone his own flesh and blood. So night
after night, when Denise came in shaking herself like a dog after

rain, Jack made an effort to restrain the criticism that welled up within him. It wouldn't do to criticise Denise on so vulnerable a matter as her hair.

A drop of water flicked Alice on the mouth. Even so small a drop smelt of expensive conditioner – Denise's only extravagance. A frail, flower smell. Alice brushed it away with her hand. She looked at her daughter. Looking directly at a real person like that, Mr Rochester vanished. Denise had a largish nose and large hands, like Jack. Her eyes were on the small side – though the blessing was she wasn't short-sighted. (Quite a wonder, considering Alice's mother, from Chippenham, had been nearly blind.) They were shut, as she towelled away at her wrinkled hair – cropped eyelashes barely reaching her flushed cheeks. In books Alice read the heroine's eyelashes always cast shadows upon her cheeks. Denise's didn't. Still, not everyone could give birth to a beauty, and Alice recognised the fact that Denise had a pleasant expression. What she'd call an open face.

'Cup of tea, Denise?'

'Thanks, Mum.'

Jack would be wanting his hot milk in half an hour, and no doubt Robbie would be down soon, that funny distant look in his eyes that always appeared when he'd been listening in to police messages – and he'd want something or other. Alice could never guess what. For a mathematician, Robbie was curiously irregular about his nightcap habits. To be on the safe side, Alice kept a good supply of everything so that she could never be caught off-guard. Sometimes, usually midweek, he liked a bedtime sandwich, too. You could never tell with Robbie.

Alice went to the kitchen. Denise took her place on the sofa, shaking her head, eyes smarting. Bloody wrestling. She could never persuade Dad to turn over to BBC2. That was the channel she liked: plenty of programmes about dwarfs and illegits and the educationally sub-normal – the sort of thing that reduced her to the warmth of compassion, and sent her to bed smug at her own good fortune. But she could only watch those sort of programmes when Dad was working late and she was here with Mum alone. Mum was easy. She'd agree to anything, and spoil her at the same time. Biscuits, little sandwiches made with salmon fishpaste and cress cut from the plastic dish on the window-sill. Mum spent her whole life looking after them a treat. Sometimes Denise felt bad about it – but then it gave Mum such obvious pleasure. You only had to look at her to see that. She was quite radiant, sometimes, faced with a pile of washing that would have caused Denise herself tears of frustration. Well, some people were born housewives: that's all there was to it. They had no ambition to be anything else, no matter what Women's Lib might say. Denise wasn't like that. *She* had her ambition – her talent – and she wasn't going to give that up for any husband on earth. It would be plain stupid. In fact it would be foolish even to think about marriage at the moment. Besides, it would be hard to give up the comforts of home life before she had to.

Upstairs in his bedroom, Robbie, who had had a good evening listening in to trouble in a pub over Uxbridge way, felt the desire for a plate of ham and chips come upon him. The strength of the feeling wrung his mouth with a fresh supply of saliva, and he hurried downstairs to the kitchen. Mum had better be quick. He couldn't wait much longer. His stomach was a burning pit, empty, lusting for the food that had come to his mind in so tantalising a way.

Alice was making tea for Denise. Arranging a tray while a kettle boiled. She always did a tray, even for one cup of tea.

'Plate of ham and chips, Mum, please,' Robbie said. 'I'm starving.'

Alice looked surprised. 'But you've had your tea. A good meal.'

'Can't be helped. I'm famished.'

'Very well. Just a minute, till I've taken the others their drinks. Shall I put it on a tray for you?'

'I'll have it in here.'

Robbie liked to eat by himself. He liked his food after the others had finished, alone at the kitchen table, staring at the calendar of English cathedrals on the wall, his mind on other things. But what he couldn't abide was that the room should be empty. So his mother – wonderfully obligingly, really – stayed with him. The music of her washing-up was of such comfort that people would laugh if he told them how much it meant to him. Sometimes, Mum would say something. He would answer her, politely of course, but not with the warmth that encouraged further observations. He required silence with his meals as other men need wine. On holiday, that was the one thing that bugged him, communal meals on the boat.

'Days getting longer,' said Alice. She passed him a tube of mustard. Robbie liked English mustard with his ham, French with his beef.

'Yes,' said Robbie.

'Enough ham?'

'Thanks.'

'Shall I do you a slice of bread?'

'Thanks.'

'And a lager?'

Robbie nodded. When there was nothing more she could do for any member of her family, Alice felt flat. They were the moments she most dreaded. The yellow of co-operation thinned in her blood, leaving her physically lighter, feeling she might take off like an autumn leaf in a west wind. Tasks were her anchor.

Empty, she returned to the sitting-room. Her husband and daughter were eating slices of the jam sponge she had baked that afternoon. There was nothing she could do for them so, second-best actions though they were, she plumped up the cushions and drew the blinds. She hoped they might all sit round for a while, now, and talk. She liked the sound of their voices. The drone of the telly, on most nights till closing down, was never the same joy.

But tonight she was to be rewarded. The news over, Jack switched it off. Robbie came in.

'You've turned it off.' His forehead was sweaty. It often glowed, like that, at any unusual change. Change of events confused him.

'Yes,' said Jack.

'You've turned it off earlier, though.' Robbie lowered himself into an upright armchair with aged caution. Five minutes and he'd go back to the set. See how Patrol 2 was getting on up in Uxbridge.

'Yes, I have,' said Jack, 'for a very good reason. Days getting longer—'

'That's just what I was saying to Robbie,' interrupted Alice.

'Days getting longer, and it's time to discuss our annual holiday. Not, I imagine, that there's very much to discuss. Need I ask where it's to be?'

'Broads, of course,' said Robbie.

Fifteen years they'd been going to the Broads, same boat, and Robbie liked it. He liked it best when it rained, sitting out on the deck, mac over his head, watching his mother peel potatoes at a sink no bigger than a pudding bowl. He liked watching the rain falling into the green weed on the water. He liked a drink in the local pub, evenings, talking to the local policeman in policeman's language, telling him some of the better stories he'd heard on the transmitter. Of course, the policeman had never been to Uxbridge but, as he said, he could credit the stories: the kind of thing the Force had to deal with these days. Robbie liked him. He liked everything in Norfolk but the communal meals, and more and more Mum was giving him sandwiches which he could take off and eat on his own.

'Broads, natch, silly,' said Denise. The thing that got her most about the place was the early mornings. You could hear birds and that if you woke early. Her sleeping bag, on the narrow bunk, was cosy. She could read her beauty magazines by the small light over the porthole, waiting till Mum got up to fry eggs and bacon for breakfast. *That* was a smell, on a boat. Not the same thing, in a house kitchen. Then, on the boat, Mum would offer her snacks all day long and she couldn't refuse.

'The *Lugger*, as usual?' Jack knew as he asked the question that it was rhetorical. There were many advantages to the *Lugger*. For a start, as the years went by and it grew more dilapidated, its rent decreased. To be honest, the Lees were the only family left who were still attracted to the boat: the only hirers. And in return for giving it a good spring clean on arrival – Alice was a wonder, the way she managed to clean a year's dirt and damp in an afternoon – they hired it for peanuts. That, in these days of economic crisis, was something to be considered. Moreover, it was *fun,* the *Lugger*. A good time was had upon her by all, come rain come shine. Been the same for years. They knew their way around. They felt easy on board. They respected their captain – Jack: they took his word. If he said the engine was snarled up and there would be no cruise that day, they'd all potter off, quite happy, believing him. And the engine often *was* snarled up. Increasingly, over the years. But, in truth, it was no hardship to Jack to put it to rights again. In his heart, the task was a positive enjoyment. There was something about kneeling on the boards of the deck, feeling the muscles pulling in your back, greasy black fingers coaxing the tired parts . . . After eleven months in an office shuffling through clean white papers, Jack loved tinkering with an oily engine. So much so that, sometimes, he even prolonged the job, anticipating the cheer that would go up when he straightened his back and declared the fault mended. He knew the feel of the key in the ignition, familiar as his own front door. There weren't many greater pleasures than turning it, face against the wind and hearing, distinctly, the putter of the gallant little engine as the *Lugger*'s nose pushed once more through the reeds and into the open grey waters . . .

He'd write the usual letter. Tonight.

' 'Course, the *Lugger*,' said Robbie. 'You're very quiet, Mum.' He turned to her.

In the barren heath of Alice Lees's mind the yellow of co-operation failed to flower. She waited, stranded, helpless. But no warmth surged through her veins, as it usually did at this annual family conference. For years, she'd been just as delighted as the others at the thought of a summer holiday on the *Lugger*. Where was that most familiar of feelings, now? As she waited for it to infuse her limbs, in the silence of the front room, the eyes of the family upon her, Alice saw a kaleidoscope of all their years in Norfolk.

Potato peelings. She remembered them best. Miles and miles of brown-spotted peelings uncurling from several tons of potatoes and overflowing the minute, discoloured sink. 'Here, be a love and get rid of these for me, will you?' she would say to no one in particular. But no one ever cared to hear her occasional cries for help. So – quicker to do a thing yourself, really – she'd push the peelings into a slippery plastic bag, feeling them curl like cold brown ribbons round her wrists, and squeeze the bag into the bin full of empty tins and eggshells and apple cores and lumps of cotton wool smeary with Denise's eyeshadow. Oh! The smell in the galley – Jack insisted they called it the galley. Funny the others didn't notice it. Tea leaves and baked beans, fried fish and pulpy fruit squashed under the superficial fumes of disinfectant. To Alice the smell was an obscenity, a tangible, creeping thing that crawled over her skin, into her hair, lapped in her nostrils at night while she tried to sleep. Not that she ever slept much. That awful plash, plash, thud, thud, a watery rapping hand against the boat. Then the lurching rock and the scrape of weeds when another boat passed, leaving behind its sickening wake. 'Jack!' she'd cry, queasy, head rolling about on the hard pillow. But Jack would be snoring, hands lumpy on the blankets, the oil washed to skeleton branches of black in the creases of his skin. Denise, too, slept peacefully beneath her face-pack, and Robbie was curled dreamingly under his mac on the deck. The moon, Alice knew, would be looking at itself in the black water. She didn't like the idea of two moons. They made her flesh prick. Also, she didn't like the idea of moorhens and water rats scuttling through the reeds on their night errands bumping, as they sometimes did, against the boat. The horrors of the night about her, Alice longed for morning. Stirring a tired fork among the bacon, at least there was light of a kind in the galley. The shopping to think of, the sleeping bags to be aired. Robbie's socks to wash; Denise's hair to set before she dried it, netted, in the sun or wind. Sometimes, on board the *Lugger*, every muscle in Alice Lee's body would protest, while the yellow of co-operation racing in her blood would urge her to go on. And go on she did. It was only conditions on board, being so different from home, made her so tired. Silly, really. The change itself probably did her good, and adversities were part of the fun, weren't they? Fun! Evenings, she'd let them all go off to the Jolly for a drink, and when they'd gone she'd sit out on deck, on the small plastic chair, alone, scuffing at the midges. Dreading the night. Counting the hours to going home. But not wanting to dwell on her *silliness*: for that's what it was. A five-minute sit-down, a glance at the sunset clouds that dyed the water (she'd never been much of a one for sunsets herself, preferred grey skies that needed no comment) then back to the galley to peel more potatoes. They'd come back ravenous, wanting a big fry-up supper at once. Oh God! The bin would be full again, plate scrapings from lunch. Lumps of meat Jack hadn't been able to chew. They'd arrive to find her started on the frying, smiling.

'Well?' said Robbie.

'I'm not going,' said Alice.

'Not what, dear?' Jack, a careless listener, could rarely believe what he heard.

'Not this year.' As she saw her own words spin into an incredulous void, Alice felt the gradual induration of her body. She leaned back in her chair, but her spine remained stiff.

'Mum says she's not going. Hark at that. She wouldn't miss it for anything.' Denise, filing her nails, was full of sarcasm. Robbie rubbed at the sweat that had accumulated on his forehead.

'Not going?'

'Am I to believe my two ears are deceiving me?' asked Jack, looking his wife directly in the eye.

'No, Jack.'

'Then what's all this about? I want to get the letter off tonight.'

'You can do that. You can get the letter off, go on your holiday. It's just that I'm not coming too.'

A film of blackness, like a year's dust, had gathered over the room. Alice felt faint. She held on to the arms of her chair.

'Mum's gone mad,' said Robbie, 'haven't you, Mum?'

'She's having one of her turns,' said Denise.

'She hasn't had one of her turns for twenty years, since she was pregnant with you. Or was it Robbie?'

'Could someone get me a glass of water?' Alice asked quietly.

Jack went to the sideboard, momentarily alarmed. He poured a glass of brandy from a full bottle which he kept for victims of possible car crashes in their street.

'I said water, please.' Alice hated spirits.

'Go on. You need some of the hard stuff.'

Obediently, Alice drank. Jack watched her, uneasy at her paleness. Best to get her to bed as soon as possible, he thought. Then he could write the letter and post it in the morning. By then, she would have come to her senses. This turn was something to do with her time of life, more than likely.

When she had washed up the cups and plates and her own brandy glass, Alice went willingly to her room. In the morning she, too, knew she would feel better.

It was raining when she woke. Alice was immediately glad. She liked grey days better than bright ones. Her own internal yellow illumined the hours more satisfactorily when there was no real sun outside to compete with. Besides, there was more to do on rainy days. The lulling pleasure of sweeping and re-sweeping the kitchen floor, and the hall carpet where they all forgot to wipe their shoes. She sprang out of bed, looking forward to the day. Gently pulled back the curtains so as not to wake Jack for another ten minutes.

'I've written the letter,' he said. 'I trust you've come to your senses, so I'll be posting it this morning.'

Alice stood still by the window, a bunch of curtain hitched up in her hand, staring at the rain. She wriggled her toes in the warm burrows of her slippers.

'You can post the letter,' she said, 'but I've not changed my mind. I'm not going.'

Jack sighed. He threw back the bedclothes, sat up, slinging his legs on the floor, knees left wide to support his arms. His hands cradled his head.

'You're barmy,' he said. 'What's your objection?'

Alice was going to say the lavatory, the spilling bin, the potato peelings, the water rats – but it was none of those things, individually, or even together. What *was* her objection, she asked herself?

'Nothing in particular I could explain,' she said. Any more than she could explain how her body felt when it was drained of yellow. They'd think she was mad.

'You're barmy,' Jack said again. 'What you need is a tonic, too. A change. You don't look after yourself all that much.'

'Oh, I'm fine,' said Alice. 'I'll be getting the breakfast.'

And the strange thing was, getting the breakfast, she felt just as usual: the same subdued pleasure, a lovely saffron colour at this time of day, soon to flower later into the inevitable chrome. It was only when she let her mind alight on the holiday that the warmth of the colour in her veins ebbed from her. So she tried not to think. That wasn't easy, considering how the others kept on with their remarks. Then Jack gave her a strange look as he left.

'I'll be posting the letter,' he said.

For three evenings they tried to persuade her to change her

mind. She resisted, simply, strongly. Nothing they could say would alter what she felt: she didn't want to go. Then what did she want to do? Denise, near to tearful exasperation, demanded.

'Go to the Lakes, perhaps.'

Alice had a vague idea in her mind of looking up Wordsworth's birthplace. Daffodils up there – she loved the poem. Though of course it would be the wrong time of year. Still, she could imagine them, a host of golden—

'What, alone?' Denise's voice, so hard.

'Yes. Why not?'

'Huh.' Robbie, gleaming again, his forehead.

'Don't be daft.' Jack kept saying, Don't be daft. Don't be daft, he said; don't be barmy; don't be mad. 'And who would look after us?' he added, this evening.

'You'd manage very nicely.' They wouldn't in fact. They all knew that. Denise would never get things going in the galley: she could scarcely fry an egg. No one would air the sleeping bags and check the bread bin for damp. Without her, it would be a disaster, not a nice holiday at all. But what could Alice do? Her mind would not change. Set on its own course, first time for years, it was quite adamant. No yellow to the rescue. A terrible black of stubbornness. And yet the red, somewhere, a strong and crazy flag, of knowing she was right.

Within a week a letter came from Norfolk. Jack read it and passed it to Alice with a silent smile. It confirmed, unsurprisingly, that the *Lugger* was available to them again this year. Alice smiled back.

'Well, you'll have to take a lot of cleaning things to get it into shape,' she said. 'I'll collect them up for you. I expect Denise'll manage.'

'You're off your rocker, Mum,' said Denise.

Off your rocker. It was a phrase which had begun to haunt the household. They all said it. They said it straight out to her, over and over again, no attempt at hiding what they thought. Their questions *why*? flagged in the face of her taciturnity. She could not answer them. She remained silently knowing she was right, and as her silence increased so did their taunts that she was barmy, stubborn, selfish, foolish . . . The adjectives sprayed out, each painful new dart a further incentive to her resistance.

The day the letter came Jack left the house for work with a grim expression.

'You in all day?' he asked. He never asked such things: he knew she was in all day. The small mystery alerted Alice. When the front door bell rang, mid-morning, she was unsurprised. It was Dr Cairn, concern twisting his face.

He had been requested to do a difficult job by his old friend, Jack, and he did his best. He was gentle with Alice, quiet and patient. They drank tea in the kitchen, and he suggested she wasn't sleeping well. He could prescribe her something mild. Oh, but she was, said Alice. She was sleeping beautifully. Then she had something on her mind? Alice smiled. Only the usual domestic things, the horrifying price of . . . No, no. He didn't mean that. He wasn't making himself clear. Oh, but he was. Alice felt unusually bright this morning. In her brightness everything was particularly clear.

'What you're trying to say, like the rest of them, is because, for once, I've a mind of my own, I'm sticking to my decision, there's something *wrong* with my mind. A nervous disorder, perhaps? My time of life?' She was quite enjoying herself.

Dr Cairn crumbled a biscuit between his fingers. He had been convinced, by Jack's description on the telephone, that Alice was suffering from some kind of temporary aberration that a small bottle of tranquillisers would put right in no time. Now, facing her, he wasn't quite so sure. The problem seemed more complex. If there was a problem. Perhaps it was simply a matter of a spiritless woman – he had always thought her a wan old thing – showing a little temperament. But Jack had been so positive she was suffering. The way she had been going on – her silences. You could tell, he had said.

'Well, I don't know.' The doctor met Alice's eyes. 'But you can say anything you want to me, you know. Get it off your chest. Professional discretion.' He smiled a little. 'I wouldn't tell Jack.'

There was no clarifying response.

'I've nothing to tell you except that I don't want to go with them on the boat this year. No particular reason. I just don't want to go, that's all.'

From what he had heard of the Broads, Dr Cairn thought that mighty reasonable. It was Alice's calm and unshakeable determination not to change her mind that he found baffling. He left in some confusion, knowing he would have to think quickly. Jack wanted some kind of answer that afternoon. What should he recommend? All part of a GP's practice, mental disorders were not his forte. Best thing to do, obviously, was to pass Alice on.

Jack conveyed the message when he came home. Privately, in the kitchen. Gently. Worried eyes. Dr Cairn had said there was only one thing for it – and he was sorry, incidentally, that he had sent the doctor round without saying anything, like that, but he knew Alice would never have gone to the surgery. Dr Cairn advised she should see someone up at the hospital. Some kind of specialist in psychiatry.

Oh, the easiness of such a request! The yellow flowers leapt. Alice clapped her hands, startling her husband. Of course! Why not? She didn't mind going to see anyone at the hospital if it would please him. She'd do anything to please. Except go on the boat.

The interview with the specialist, a few days later, took place in a small cubicle of frosted glass. The gas fire, a red-blue honeycomb on the fragile wall, filled the silences with its roaring, and the sun, through the ribbed window, made a halo of thorns above the specialist's head. He took off his spectacles and looked at her.

'They think I'm mad,' said Alice quickly, giving him no time to make up his own mind, 'because I don't want to go on holiday with them this year. Well, we've been going for fifteen years. It seems to me quite reasonable to want a change, but they're convinced I'm mad. Have you ever heard anything so ridiculous?' He didn't answer, but allowed his mouth a slight widening. His coat was blazing white. It would be good to iron, Alice thought. The idea exhilarated her. She liked the feeling of being enclosed with a man who was at the top of his profession. The blue of confidence swelled about her. At least he would understand, would dismiss the concept as nonsense . . .

'It isn't quite as simple as that, I think,' he said, and wrote something on his piece of paper.

'Surely it is.' Alice had imagined her voice would come soaring out. Instead she heard with surprise its minor tone.

The specialist tipped his head back to look at the ceiling. He made his fingers into a spire, their tips just touching, so that if prayer was made of incense, and he was praying, it would float through the stubby mesh quite easily. Nearer to God with unclenched fists. Alice hadn't prayed for years, not since she had asked Him to send her a Mr Rochester, and He had failed.

'Tell me all about it,' said the specialist, 'from the beginning.'

Although there was nothing to tell, nothing at all, really, the yellow of co-operation was flowing fast within Alice, and she tried. She spoke for a long time, twenty minutes, perhaps, saying how nice it had always been on the *Lugger*, how they'd always had such a good time – not mentioning the bin, or the two moons or the smells. There was no need to go into all that. But she ended, boldly, by saying the Lakes had taken her fancy. Wordsworth, the daffodils fluttering and dancing. They had a few in their own garden and, in the March winds, that's just what they did. Fluttered and danced. Didn't he think? For the first time in her soliloquy, the specialist revealed a touch of impatience in the arc of his fingers. He demolished the structure, which had weathered the whole of Alice's explanation, to take up his pen. He thanked her, told her not to worry, and she left.

In the next few days, Alice noticed, the jibes at home died down a little. There seemed to be a conspiracy of reticence which for the most part was kept to, although when discussing the holiday Denise, the most incensed by Alice's betrayal, continued to use the word daft. Robbie took a more tactful line.

'Poor old Mum,' he said, many times, 'think what she'll be missing.' Pity, it seemed, was now strongly within them. Strong as resentment.

On the night Dr Cairn arrived Alice was feeling particularly happy. The whole family had enjoyed her apple crumble for supper, and there was a good long play on television with three commercial breaks in which to fetch everyone their special drinks. But with Dr Cairn's entrance, the play was switched off. Denise, at some private sign from her father, fetched a tray of small glasses, and the brandy. Everyone seemed to know what was going to happen. Alice waited.

Dr Cairn explained it had come to this: all Alice needed – according to the specialist, who had diagnosed in a moment what was wrong – was a short spell in a home. A very nice Home, all comforts, not too far away, no restriction on visits. There, they would look after her. Wouldn't fill her with pills – oh, no, nothing like that. Just, well, look after her in the way that she needed – in a way that her family or any unskilled person could never hope to accomplish – and after a while she'd be quite herself. How long, he couldn't exactly say. It would be partly up to her, depending on how she responded to the treatment. On how she co-operated.

Alice looked round her tidy sitting-room at the grave figures of her family. She felt a warmth of love for them, that they should care for her so. She felt guilty at their concern. And then their faces, very precise in their anxiety at Dr Cairn's words, wavered into marvellous oblivion behind the bands of surging yellow that rose before her eyes. The brilliance of the colour pounding in her veins made her very sure, very strong, with the pleasure of instant co-operation. Dr Cairn, had he known, would have been proud of her.

Jack was unsurprised at his wife's calm. He would not expect her to flap in a crisis. She wasn't like that. She had always been able to cope. They would miss her. But it wouldn't do to be selfish in a case like this. She would come back her old self: it was, after all, for her own sake she was going. They were doing the best thing for her. Denise sniffed a bit, rubbed at her eyes and shook her damp head.

Robbie studied the carpet, thinking he would go and see his mother twice a week. A firm resolution, that. It would be an effort, the long bus ride. But he would keep to it. She deserved that from him.

And so, with no murmur of reproof, Alice packed her things and made arrangements for the perpetual delivery of milk and bread, and stuck reminders on the kitchen wall about the laundry and how to work the spin-dryer. They all went with her to the Home, and saw her settled comfortably into her pastel room, with its linoleum floor and bright narrow bed. There was a nice garden outside, with a cedar tree and a bench made of knotted branches. The corridors made footsteps quiet, there was television in the lounge, only a few cries in the wakeful hours of the night. The staff were all so kind, always asking her if she would like tea, and the specialist who built prayers with his fingers came only once a week to ask her questions to which she had no answer.

They gave her a glass of pink stuff to drink every morning, saying how wonderful she was not to complain, how co-operative she was. She didn't worry much about life at home – Jack assured her, when he came on Saturday afternoons with a packet of chocolate wafers, that Denise had come out of herself surprisingly. She was being a good little housewife, doing very well. They all came quite often, as they said they would, interrupting her thoughts about Mr Rochester sometimes, but she didn't really mind. Then, in the summer, there was a break in their visits. Their holiday on the *Lugger*, of course. Alice quite understood, simply asked them to send her a postcard if they had time. A picture of the reeds at sunset arrived, with messages from all three of them. Having a lovely time, they said they were, but they wished she was there. Alice thought of their time, as she sat in her pastel room, and remembered the smells, the water, the potato peelings, the bin, and she saw the petals of the yellow flower in her mind were wilting, dying, falling all about her. She stretched out her hand to touch the petals, to feel again their warmth. But she knew, as she thought of them all in the boat, the yellow of co-operation would not come to her, and she was glad.

Loving Gourmets

We met again in Elizabeth Street, George and I. There he was, carrying a blue nylon shopping bag with immeasurable dignity. Flowering broccoli sprouted from its holes, brushing his legs as he walked, very upright, ignoring the purple heads that flirted with his twill knees. He stopped at once when he saw me, clicking his heels together: he'd never been able to shake off his military style.

'Why, good heavens, Diana,' he said.

'*George*,' I replied.

He had changed very little: same blunt face, a little baggier perhaps, startling green eyes. Red veins splintered his cheeks now (they were once solid red) and his paunch, safe as ever in its tweed waistcoat, had expanded by many pounds. I felt him looking me over, taking in equivalent changes, down to the waist. He once told me he never looked further, on an attractive woman, as this prevented him from being disillusioned by bad legs. I wondered if he noticed I had quite a show of bosom now (the menopause had brought that on) solid under my beige cashmere: I wondered if he recognised the same dull pearls with their magnificent ruby clasp that he'd played with sometimes between his finger and thumb.

'It must be twenty years,' he said. 'I live round the corner now.' It came back to me: I'd read in some gossip column he was married to his second – or was it his third? – wife. They had a penthouse in Eaton Square. The wife wouldn't speak to one of his hippy grandchildren, something like that. George had always had a penchant for difficult women. He swung the shopping bag a little.

'I enjoy doing the shopping – well, *you* know.' He smiled, darker teeth. 'Bloody Spanish servants always fiddle the bills.'

'After all this time,' I heard myself saying.

'Indeed, indeed: my dear Diana,' he was mumbling, and from the look on his face I realised he was having some difficulty in recollecting, too.

We met at a cocktail party in the days when it was considered normal rather than daftly grand to send printed invitations to such functions. Him: blue pinstripe suit, red carnation in his buttonhole. Me: insignificant black dress, wavy hair. An immovable waiter held a silver dish of particularly ostentatious canapés between us, and we talked about mock caviare. We had to shout against the noise. He seemed to have a nice, resonant, shouting voice.

A week later he asked me to lunch at the Savoy – the restaurant, by the window, being summer. There was champagne waiting by the table, real caviare – my first, poached salmon with *sauce verte*, and a salad of translucently thin cucumber. Finally, *fraises du bois* flown from somewhere with, of course (*of course*, I quickly agreed) kirsch instead of cream. I remember coming away feeling, for the first time in my life, excited about food. Except for the caviare I had eaten all the things before, and was even acquainted with the Traminer and the vintage Moët et Chandon. But George, with his enthusiasm and knowledge, had a way of making them a new experience. I think we only talked of food: funny stories about some woman in Beirut who had forced him to eat rose-petal jam.

The lunch must have been a success because he then asked me out to dinner at the Caprice – iced sorrel soup and roast baby kid: marvellous. But we deplored the general standard of restaurant food in England – this was, of course, a few years before the birth of even the first trattoria. It was then that George admitted, diffidently, that he was shortly off on his annual gourmet holiday round France. Would I like to come?

This, it seemed, was a compliment. In previous years he had always been alone. In me, apparently, he confessed, he had found a soul mate. I had little knowledge but instinctive appreciation. It would please him so if I would come.

I looked at George. The red of his cheeks was a little deeper after two bottles of wine: his smooth, army hair was greased immaculately back, the thick silk of his tie an unblemished blue. I felt a sudden stirring of anticipation. The wine had made the crimson room dance like tendrils in a wind. I imagined us eating like this – better – every night. Then making love in small auberges in the Dordogne, Normandy, Brittany, the South. I'd never contemplated any such escapade before – indeed, never before had I been offered the chance. I had been to bed (as it was referred to in those days) with only one gentleman to date, in conditions of utmost secrecy and discomfort. Today's permissive society was unborn: among my friends a week away alone with a man was rarely achieved and even more rarely acknowledged.

I accepted.

Along with his red Sunbeam Talbot, we boarded the ferry from Dover. In his holiday clothes George was perhaps somewhat less spectacular than in London, but very polished and neat in tweeds that merged into each other in a Scottish fashion. I noticed several middle-aged women turn their heads in admiration at the bar. After we'd drunk several pink gins we found two deck chairs on the deck. We sat enjoying the sun through the sea breeze, and looking in easy silence at the green-grey rocking waves. I thought perhaps he might hold my hand, not that he had ever done so before. In fact, he took a packet of pâté sandwiches and a bottle of hock from his briefcase. In my delight at his forethought (all around us people were eating packets of crisps) I made some extravagant remark about the receding cliffs of Dover. But George, concentrating on opening the wine, didn't seem to hear.

'It came to me in the night, about the sandwiches,' he said. 'I got up and made them then and there, in case there should be a rush in the morning.' I think it was at that moment I wondered how I should ever get through to George, apart from food. Maybe the nights would do it.

We landed at Calais, and with great modesty George fell into perfect French, only when necessary. No inessential observations to the porters to show how good he was. I was grateful for that. Leaning back in the comfortable seat of the Sunbeam Talbot I knew for certain that should we cross the border into any European country, George would be just as at home, just as fluent in the language. Oh! he was wonderfully in charge. I shivered at the pleasure. He noticed, and covered my hand, which had strayed close to the gears, with one of his – gloved. Just for a moment.

'*Maintenant, mon chou*,' he said.

We sped away into northern France, dusk falling, the silence between us agreeable. Some hours later we drew up at an auberge set back a little from the main road. The Auberge Bonne Femme, I seem to remember it was. A warm and cheerful place, a wood fire in the hall – the auberge of my fantasies. They seemed to know George there. The *patron* greeted him with many a jest, and kissed my hand, and called me *madame* with the seriousness of one who is always willing to partake of an English joke. We were shown to a room under the eaves, most of which was taken up by a vast double bed with brass ends. George began to unpack with great energy, almost filling the cupboard with his uncreased suits, leaving only two hangers for me. He seemed awfully happy. His walk, from cupboard to bed, bed to cupboard, was an anticipatory bounce. He hummed to himself, French tunes. Then suggested I should have a bath and change while he went downstairs to have a *verre* with the *patron*. We would dine at eight-thirty.

At eight twenty-five I made my entrance into the bar. I was wearing a modest little dress, sort of rhubarb colour which, I had noticed, glancing into the speckled mirror before coming down, enhanced the almost silly look of rapture on my face. The effect did not go unnoticed by George. He slid from his seat, welcoming.

'*Mon chou, mon ange,*' he said. 'You're beautiful. What will you have to drink?' He put an arm around my shoulder, his exuberance perhaps encouraged by the two or even three *verres* he had had with the *patron*.

We had the best table, by another fire. And a most exquisite dinner. Pâté first, the *spécialité de la maison*. Slices of dappled, skewbald stuff that lay glinting on clouds of lettuce. As we ate it, with great reverence and much sighing, George recalled so many pâtés in his past: those smooth, bland concoctions of whipped goose liver spotted with fragments of truffle; the rougher, country pâtés full of zest and brandy. He had had such experience of pâtés, George. I was amazed. He liked to amaze me, I could see. He ordered wine without looking at the list, and when it came he sniffed it with just the right amount of disdain before acknowledging it perfect.

We ate *rougets*, next: such *rougets*, simply grilled. And finally a cheese soufflé that was a buttercup puff of foam – a *poem* of a soufflé, as George said. By this time my head was cloudy bright from the beautiful wine. George's memories of past meals diminished a little with the petits fours, and he was quite silent by the time we went to bed.

The wine had made me careless. I undressed in a disorderly fashion, leaving my clothes in heaps on the ground. George was more meticulous. Under the camouflage of his dressing-gown he slipped into silk pyjamas. There was some confusion about which side of the bed each one of us should have.

'You wanted . . . ?'

'No, no. I don't mind. You go there.'

'Which side of a double bed do you normally sleep?'

I blushed, I know.

'I don't normally sleep in double beds.'

'Very well, if you really don't mind.' He chose the side with the bedside table and the small lamp that glowed brownly under its antique shade. In bed, he took a tortoiseshell comb from the pocket of his dressing-gown and resmoothed his already flattened hair with two quick, decisive movements. Then he lowered himself in the bed, and politely lifted the sheets for me to get in.

'Tomorrow,' he said, 'we shall go somewhere that has the best burgundy you've ever tasted.'

'That was a marvellous dinner,' I said. We lay a yard apart. My skin stretched too tightly over my surging veins.

'That was only a beginning,' he said softly. Lovingly, I thought. I let the words seep into my flesh. Then peered up at him.

'Do you always sleep in your dressing-gown?'

His eyes were shut, his hands folded on his well-filled stomach. The position reminded me of those stone saints who lie on their graves, worn out by their good life, now happy in their good death. He snored a little. I reached across to put out the light. Well, I thought: I'm glad. It wouldn't have done, tonight. Not with him being so tired. It might have been an anticlimax. It's much better that he should get a good night's sleep. For one so young, I was something of a cynic.

*

George slept very well. He hardly moved all night. In the morning he woke vigorously, ringing at once for *deux cafés complets*. I realised, then, how I had misjudged him. He was not, after all, a predictable man – a perfect dinner, a heady bottle of wine, make love. Such a conventional pattern of things, thank goodness, would not appeal to him. No: his method was more interestingly spontaneous. He would ask for love when he felt the desire come upon him, no matter what time of day. And judging by this, his eager early face, it could well be morning. I trembled.

How delighted he was by that first breakfast! The warm *croissants* flaked away in our fingers even as we touched them. The rich black coffee flared through my wakeful body filling it with longing. I felt my legs squirm under the bedclothes – careful not to touch George, just to let him know of the movement. Outside the open window a blackbird sang, the sky was cloudless. It was going to be a good day, but I didn't want to enter it just yet.

'George!'

He turned to me, specks of croissant on his mouth and dressing gown. Took my hand, shifted himself a bit.

'Now. We're going to leap out of bed and get to the market while it's still early. It's always best, early. There I shall choose for you the most perfect peaches and cheese for our lunch, which we shall eat under a poplar tree that Manet might have painted.' His eyes strolled far away to this *déjeuner sur l'herbe*. 'Does that suit you?'

An infinitesimal silence. Then new hope: a checked tablecloth, the car rug spread in the long grass – why else would he have brought the car rug? A few more hours, that's all.

'Oh, yes,' I said.

He was wonderful in the market. His fingers skimmed up and down fruits and vegetables, he muttered 'Bah!' sounds if he touched upon too ripe a flesh. Eventually he chose: two frail, dewy peaches and a wedge of Camembert that trembled on the brink of runniness. He bought butter and a knife and long flutes of fresh bread, and we roared off down empty roads between fields of smudgy lavender. He stopped at a place beside a small river for lunch: it seemed familiar to him. We spread the rug and sat in a cage of long grass, butterflies our only visitors. George took the corkscrew from his briefcase and uncorked a bottle of red wine, château something.

'This is the life,' he said.

In the sun, his brown shoes shone very brightly. There was something vulnerable about those shoes. I felt a surge of love for him: affection, regard, respect, desire. While he poured the wine I undid the top button of my shirt. After lunch, drowsy, we would sleep, perhaps. It would all happen, so drowsily, so drowsily. George's mind seemed to be following my own. He lay propped on one arm and lifted a gentle hand to my cheek, his eyes melting.

'There's a little place not far from here,' he said, 'that sells the most irresistible truffles. We'll go there directly after lunch, which will leave us plenty of time to get to the Bellevue by tonight.' And he broke the long, sweet-smelling loaf.

We accomplished it all, of course: stacked a dozen tins of truffles into the boot, and arrived at the Bellevue in time for dinner. There we had a room crowded with Louis XIV-type chairs, and extravagant satin curtains. There we drank a sharp little muscadet on the leafy terrace before dinner, and between the quenelles and the profiteroles he fiddled with the ruby clasp of my pearls.

'You haven't enough bosom to show off such pearls,' he said, 'but you're becoming a delicious little gourmet.' In the confusion in my head I sifted the compliment from the criticism and hugged it to myself, and quickly drank another glass of wine to ameliorate the sadness of my inadequate bosom.

Then, to my shame, in the dreadfully hard historical bed, I was the one to fall asleep first. Thoughtfully, George did not disturb me.

By the third day of our tour I learned that to join George in spirit, if not in body, was the only way. And so it was with greater, more desperate relish I came to appreciate the food. The days spun by, a galaxy of four-star interludes. I remember a hotel on a mountain top that overlooked half of France – the most delicate of boiled chickens under whose skin the *patron* himself had slipped fine slices of secret pâté. I remember the lightest of omelettes singing with fresh herbs (some of George's phrases rubbed off on me); I remember pale fish whose sea-taste glowed through the creamy sauce. And then the puddings – my particular weakness: the irresistible trolleys of cream cheeses spun with white of egg into airy blobs, and floating through primrose-coloured sauces. I remember sorbets, and exotic pastry things oozing with cream and *fraises du bois*, and whipped *marrons* hazy in chocolate sauce. Less clearly I remember swaying up many a staircase to a sagging French bedroom whose once grand wallpaper was now quite faded. There, in a dozen different beds, exhausted by our gourmet day, overblown with food and wine, George and I slept at once. At least – did we? I could never be quite sure. Wasn't there the odd night when our bodies churned together, essaying some feat of love quite beyond us? I only positively know that we would wake each morning with our appetites for food renewed.

Somewhere in the Loire country I became aware of feeling a comfortable fatness. It slowed my movements: it happily dissipated all desire except for further food. George, I noticed, was at one with me in this feeling. The warmth of compatibility was upon us, and the days went fast.

We spent our last night in Paris. Began with champagne and those incomparable crisps at the Ritz Bar. Went on to a place whose menu, even to our experienced eyes, was dazzling. We took our time, weighing up the pros and cons of each dish, and indulged in a bit of connoisseur talk.

'How about the *pâté maison*?'

'But it couldn't be as good as the *Bonne Femme*.'

'Nor it could. But dare we try the *agneau*, after Mère Bise?'

In bed that night – a soaring cathedral of a bed, four posts and a domed ceiling of silk pleats, George remembered it was almost over. Sleepily, he held my hand.

'I don't know what you expected of this little *vacance*,' he said. 'I hope it hasn't been a disappointment.'

'Oh George! How could you? What an idea. I've never eaten such food in my life.'

With some effort he focused his eyes upon me.

'I wondered, from time to time, if you *really* loved food. If it could ever become a way of life to you, like it has to me. I thought, tonight – your face – that perhaps I've accomplished one thing: I've made you a gourmet for life. Haven't I?'

'Ooh, you have.' A slight, desirous stirring somewhere. But his eyes were half closed.

'I'm so pleased about that. Diana?' His stumbling hand felt for the clasp of my pearls. 'I'm really so pleased about that.'

On deck next day, on the way back to Dover, I tried my best to thank him. Without my knowing, he had slipped out early that morning and filled his briefcase with charming things for our lunch. We huddled to eat it, once again, in deck chairs in the shadow of a lifeboat.

'Thank you, tremendously, George.'

'Glad you enjoyed it.'

'Oh, I did. *Tremendously*.' This time, the rocking of the boat made me feel a little uneasy. 'But I think I was probably a disappointment to you, in some way.'

'Whatever do you mean?' His army hair glittered in the bright sun, his flushed cheeks bulged with surprise.

'I don't know, really.'

'Utter nonsense. We came to France to eat, didn't we? That was the idea, wasn't it? Thought we had some damn good times, myself. I'll never forget those meals. I shall remember them for ever and ever.'

'So shall I,' I said. 'Definitely. For ever and ever.'

Back in London he kissed me goodbye on the forehead, and gave me a couple of tins of truffles

'Just to remind,' he said. And that was the last I saw of him till we met again in Elizabeth Street.

His face was beginning to clear.

'We had some good times in France, that, eh – wasn't it? That time. Lots of good grub.'

'Those *rougets*,' I said. 'Those puddings and pâtés.'

He paused. 'There's a new little French place somewhere near here. Not up to much, but the *escargots* aren't bad. I was wondering, would you like a spot of lunch?'

I looked at my watch.

'I can't really, George,' I said. 'Not today.' The shepherd's pie was already in the oven. I had to do the sprouts.

'Oh, well. It was just a thought.' He swung his bag of flowering broccoli so that it banged against his leg. He glanced at my mature bosom, gave an almost imperceptible sigh. 'Still, you might just come to Justin's with me and choose a decent bit of quiche. I can never decide between the spinach and the mushroom. What d'you think?'

In memory of our gourmet heydays I went with him. His pleasure among the shelves of delicious foods was as inspiring as ever. For a moment I caught my plump, middle-aged breath; remembered some distant thrill. Should I change my mind about the *escargots* after all? Would this not be my chance to find out the answer to that silly question, which had been puzzling me all these years? Would George remember?

But suddenly he was on his way, three boxes under his arm. How nice it was running into each other like that, after all this time, he was saying. We must . . . some time. But he turned as he spoke, so I was unable to hear what we must do some time. But knowing George – dear George! – I supposed it might be to experience once again the absolute happiness of a gourmet lunch.

The Fall

Mrs Grace Willoughby, seventy-three years old and reduced by circumstances to a diminished way of life, endured the present while she lived with the past.

She understood, philosophically, that there were good times and bad times, and when good times came to an end they were inevitably replaced by less good ones. That was the rhythm of things – it had to be accepted. Not unwillingly, therefore, she accepted it. Nourished by the better past, she concerned herself with making tolerable the present.

But it was a struggle. For all her efforts, she could never quite accustom herself to this high living. Her two-roomed flat was on the top floor of a tall block. Outside, when Mrs Willoughby dared look, were the summits of three other identical blocks; thin, soulless buildings with no form of life at their windows. Mrs Willoughby had looked *down* only once, on the occasion she had first been shown the flat by the estate agent and her married daughter, Rose. The small patch of green 'recreation ground', the ant people and toy cars had looked so terrifyingly far away that Mrs Willoughby had never repeated the experience. Rose, however, thought the view was 'lovely'. But then Rose was one of those people who, exhilarated by any journey up, only had to look down to find any view a delight. She was indiscriminate like that, Mrs Willoughby thought privately. The estate agent, too, expressed an enthusiasm not only for the view but for the sparse qualities of the two rooms. He advised her to snatch at her lucky chance. Between them, they convinced Mrs Willoughby. Reluctantly, she snatched.

The idea of moving to London, after Edgar had died and the chemist's shop was sold, was to be near Rose. What had not come into the calculations was that while Rose lived in north London, Mrs Willoughby's new flat was south, and miles of difficulties lay between them. To begin with they tried to keep some form of routine. Every other Sunday Mrs Willoughby would set off early, negotiate a complicated route of trains and undergrounds, and arrive at her daughter's in time for lunch. Once there, she never felt wholly welcome. It wasn't that Rose was unfriendly, just busy. She had her own worries: five children and a tight income. Her engineer husband, Jack, surly at the best of times, spent their every spare penny on flying lessons. He fancied himself as a swashbuckling pilot. Rose half approved the fantasy and meanwhile had to do without a washing machine. Mrs Willoughby, for some reason cynical about others' marriages despite the experience of her own happy one, once suggested to Rose that Jack might fly away for ever one day. Rose had just laughed.

The first winter in London put an end to Mrs Willoughby's visits to her daughter. A November fog gave her bronchitis, and when she recovered she no longer had the energy, or, to be truthful, the desire, to re-establish the old routine. Instead, on one occasion, Rose came in the Mini to south London. But it wasn't a success. There was no room in the flat for five children, nothing to do. Rose was in a dither about getting the car back to Jack in time to get to the airfield: she and her mother had little to talk about. No mutual interest helped them, not even the past. Rose had left home at fifteen. Her parents, puzzled and hurt by this, agreed at the time their caring for their daughter would never be quite the same again. And things hadn't changed.

Mrs Willoughby hadn't seen Rose and her grandchildren for three years now. They were simply coloured snapshots on the fireplace of shiny tiles above the electric fire. They sent each other cards, Christmas and birthdays, but ceased to have any real concept of the other's life. Rose would never have guessed that her mother, so energetic, independent and gay, now spent three-quarters of her time communicating with no one more rewarding than the budgerigar.

In her three years alone, Mrs Willoughby's struggle to accept her present life had become easier. In fact, it had almost come to the point where she had no energy, or even wish, to change it. She had long since ceased to hope for any companionship from her neighbours. They were a reticent, dour lot who went up and down in the draughty lift with secret and uninteresting faces. Mrs Willoughby once invited the harassed young mother who lived next door for coffee one morning. But the woman said she hadn't time, thank you, and no reverse visit was suggested. It seemed that the policy of the building was to keep yourself to yourself. After several rebuffs at the beginning, Mrs Willoughby fell in with this pattern.

All she had ever required in her life was to love someone in an atmosphere of peace. With Edgar, she had happily managed that for thirty-nine years. Now, she still had peace, but empty peace was a different matter. And as she could think of nothing to enliven the present – abhorring as she did any attempts to join old people's clubs – her days became a prolonged reverie of old times.

That was not to say she let things slide. A strict upbringing had had its impact for life: wash the dishes straight after the meal – no leaving them till later. Hair to be brushed fifty times night and morning, though all the brushing would not bring back its shine now – the shine that Edgar had so admired. Keep to a sensible diet – proteins, a little meat once a week, one slice of wholemeal bread and butter for tea. Lights out at nine-thirty after the news. These determined adherences to her own rule gave Mrs Willoughby an inexplicable satisfaction, and as a reward for keeping them she treated herself to a few minor luxuries: a box of milk chocolates once a fortnight, African violets the year round, an occasional expensive magazine.

She left her flat – each time dreading the precarious journey in the lift – only once a week, to do her shopping. She had no friends in the shops – after three years still none of the assistants seemed to recognise her, and the trips were not a pleasure. One summer she had gone to Kent for a holiday to stay with the doctor and his wife, old neighbouring friends. But she hadn't liked the experience, going up the stairs that for thirty years neither she nor Edgar had ever gone up, to their chilly spare room. Besides, she had been unable to resist taking a look at the chemist's shop. It was unrecognisable, brash with neon lights and selling shoddy clothes. After that, she decided holidays were of no use to her. She still wrote once a month to the doctor's wife, but stayed at home, reading, knitting, watching the news, and reflecting.

One October morning Mrs Willoughby's alarm clock failed her. It had been a wedding present from her mother-in-law and for over forty years had awakened her with its shrill old-fashioned voice at seven-thirty. The morning it died Mrs Willoughby slept till eight o'clock. When she did wake up she was surprised to find herself put out by the uncalled-for change in her custom. After all, there was nowhere she had to be at any time. It was her shopping morning, but there was still plenty of time to do the chores before setting out at eleven, which was the time she always left. Quite angrily, she rattled the clock. Its lack of response, for some reason, brought a ridiculous tear to her eyes. Silly to get so upset about a clock. She dressed quickly and went to boil the kettle.

In the kitchen Tina, the balding budgerigar, was chirping to herself in her usual monotonous fashion. Mrs Willoughby had hung her cage in the window to break the view of gaunt sky and neighbouring block of flats and she managed, when pressing her face to the wires of the cage, to distort her vision so that the cheerless sight beyond the cage became out of focus.

Now, as always, Mrs Willoughby talked to Tina at breakfast.

'Morning, my lovely one: my lovely one. Slept well, did you? I'll tell you something, my clock didn't go off this morning. That's why I'm late. That's why I've kept you waiting for your breakfast. I'll have to get it mended somewhere. I can't be sure where. Now just a moment and you shall have your clean water . . .'

Mrs Willoughby fed the bird and herself. Even without looking directly out of the window she couldn't help noticing it was a fine day. Blue sky, sun. Wind down there, though, she wouldn't be surprised. She made a mental note to wear a hat-pin.

She washed up and wiped down the small Formica-topped table. Then, passing Tina's cage, she let her fingers slip along the wire sides gently as a harpsichordist feeling for her strings.

'We're all right, Tina, you and me,' she said. 'There's no doubt about it, we're very fortunate, all things considering.'

On mornings like this, she remembered, Edgar would be very alert at breakfast. She had never known anyone like him for responding to weather. There only had to be a glimmer of sun for Edgar to be out in the garden, checking that its life-giving rays were injecting themselves into the palm tree. That palm tree, that poor old palm tree! Mrs Willoughby smiled at the thought of it, battling for life like no plant she had ever known. She and Edgar had spent their honeymoon on the island of Tresco in the Scillies. There, Edgar had become so entranced by the tropical gardens that he had tried to recreate them, on a smaller scale, of course, in their patch behind the shop in Kent. But the climate in Kent is less temperate than in Tresco, the soil less sympathetic to highly strung plants. Exotic blooms withered before their prime. Only the palm tree, fed on strange potions from the chemist's shop that Edgar concocted over the years, clung tenaciously to life. This morning Mrs Willoughby remembered that, in her last letter, the doctor's wife had told her she'd heard the old tree had finally died, and the people at the boutique planned to chop it up for Guy Fawkes' night. Once again she wiped away a tear, despising herself for having to make the gesture as she did so.

Mrs Willoughby went to her bedroom and opened the small cupboard beneath her dressing table. There, in neat army rows, stood twenty-nine small bottles of old-fashioned lavender water. The sight cheered her immediately. The store meant much to her. When Edgar had died and the shop and all its contents had been sold, Mrs Willoughby had forced herself to go back to check the place finally. She had opened each mahogany drawer, each cupboard, all unfamiliar now they were empty, and on the shelf beneath Edgar's mixing sink she found the bottles. Somehow they'd been overlooked. Without a second thought Mrs Willoughby had taken them for herself. She knew quite well Edgar wouldn't have minded.

In her widowhood Mrs Willoughby had preserved the lavender water carefully. She wanted it to last till she died. She sprinkled a few drops on her handkerchief every morning, and every morning the smell brought back to her the polished wood of the shop, the sun making a streak of lightning in the scarlet liquid that filled the huge pharmacist's bottle, the anticipation that never dulled as to who would be the first customer, the reassuring early cough (never a worry till the end) as Edgar mixed the contents of his old brown jars.

Today it was time for a new bottle. With some reluctance Mrs Willoughby unscrewed the cap.

It was, as she had predicted, windy outside. She bent herself in the direction of the all-purpose shop, where she bought herself a small selection of tasteless packaged things, thinking all the while that she'd give her soul for warm crusty bread like their next-door baker used to bake, a bit of fish still smelling of the sea, muddy eggs instead of these anaemic things. Outside the shop again, buffeted by the wind whose direction changed every moment, and made it more disconcerting, Mrs Willoughby wondered where to take her clock. Opposite, through tears the wind made in her eyes, she could see a jewellery shop. Maybe they could help. Rattling her shopping bag, suddenly concerned for the future of her clock, she stepped off the pavement.

Mrs Willoughby was aware of a sharp pain in her leg, a screech of brakes, a shout, and a small patter of glass on the road. Then blackness. When she came to, a crowd of faces bobbed like yo-yos up and down at her. She was unable to feel her leg, but through a strange rug that covered it seeped a widening stain of dark red blood. A folded mackintosh had been put under her head, but the pavement was hard beneath her spine.

She couldn't make out what they were saying at all. A confusion of voices, like a foreign language. She tried to ask them if they had seen her clock, but thought they wouldn't understand.

'Don't you worry about anything, dear,' a kind voice said, then, in a language she understood, and she heard the wail of a siren. At that moment the black spots cleared before her eyes and she gave herself up to the marvellous attentions of the ambulancemen.

In a life of consistent good health, Mrs Willoughby's only suffering had always been from an incurable fear of anticipated illness and accidents. It was therefore with some surprise she found herself almost enjoying the trip in the ambulance, and still she felt no pain. They'd bandaged her leg and wrapped her up in a scarlet blanket to match the blood, and there was a nice fresh smell of disinfectant.

'What happened?' she asked. Her voice sounded shaky, she thought, but the ambulanceman didn't seem to notice.

'Seems you had a fall, dear, and a car just missed you.'

'Oh. Anyone else hurt?'

'Not a bit of it, not a bit of it. Now you just keep still.'

'It doesn't hurt,' said Mrs Willoughby.

'You just wait,' grinned the man, cheerfully, but his warning didn't frighten her.

In the hospital they were swift and kind. She was wheeled to a cubicle, a doctor looked at her leg, a nurse cleaned it and dressed it and said they'd like to keep her in for a couple of days. When Mrs Willoughby protested, they insisted: it wasn't the wound, they said, but the shock. Shock had to be looked after carefully.

'Especially at my age,' conceded Mrs Willoughby, and two pretty young nurses smiled at her, even though they were so busy. One of them asked her about her nearest relative: they'd like to get in touch. Mrs Willoughby gave them Rose's number but asked that she shouldn't be troubled. The nurse made no reply, no smile this time, and wheeled her to a ward.

Mrs Willoughby was given a pain-killing injection and something to make her sleep. When she woke up the two old ladies either side of her, neither of whom looked very ill, were drinking tea. Drowsily, Mrs Willoughby began to heave herself up into a sitting position: she was immediately helped by a nurse who plumped up her pillows and went off to fetch her something to eat. There was a dull pain in her leg now, but it wasn't too bad. Quite bearable.

Glancing round the ward, Mrs Willoughby wished she had her own pink nightdress and wool dressing-jacket instead of this stiff hospital thing: still, it didn't really matter. She was warm and comfortable and they were all so nice and concerned.

Suddenly, through the swing doors at the end of the ward, she saw a familiar figure. Rose came stomping towards her, in a scarlet coat (so much scarlet today), bag swinging from her shoulder, a look of slight concern on her face which had, Mrs Willoughby thought, grown heavier.

'Oh, mother, there you are. You gave us all an awful fright.'

Rose looked down at her mother. As soon as it was apparent that she was in no actual danger, or even in any great pain, Rose's thin mouth drooped.

'I managed to get here,' she said, sullenly.

'That was good of you, Rose,' said Mrs Willoughby.

'It was a devil of a job finding someone to baby-sit at that short notice,' Rose went on, 'and then the traffic.'

'You shouldn't have bothered,' said Mrs Willoughby. 'I'm all right.' They kissed.

'Glad to see you are,' said Rose. 'They sounded fairly adamant that I should come. I've brought you these.'

She put a paper bag on Mrs Willoughby's bedside table. It contained half a pound of small white grapes. Mrs Willoughby, who had never liked grapes, thanked her daughter with convincing appreciation. There was silence between them for a few moments. Then:

'Your clock's stopped,' said Rose.

Mrs Willoughby turned to her bedside table again. This time she noticed the clock. In an instant she realised that someone must have rescued it, taken care of it, and seen it delivered safely to her. The thought of such care on the part of a stranger caused a constriction in her throat.

'I was going to get it mended,' she managed to say eventually, 'when I had the fall.'

'Poor old Mum,' said Rose, looking at her watch.

She left five minutes later and Mrs Willoughby drank her tea. The old lady on her left turned to her.

'That was a smart young woman,' she said.

'My daughter,' said Mrs Willoughby, surprised at her own pride.

'Lucky to have a daughter like that. I've only got a sharpjack of a husband. What's more, when he comes, he only talks to other people. You'll see.'

Mrs Willoughby smiled.

There was boiled fish and rice pudding for supper, and very good it was too. Then the visiting hour: the old lady's husband arrived, very smart, as she had warned, in beautiful big-checked tweeds and a stiff collar. He made several cheering remarks to his wife but she, who had apparently looked forward to his arrival, now wouldn't answer. He offered her a chocolate but she pushed the box away. So he offered one to Mrs Willoughby instead, who accepted with delight. They fell into conversation. He was a Mr Potterville and used to be in market gardening. His wife had insisted on their moving to London when they retired, but he was not enjoying the life. He missed his greenhouses. Mrs Willoughby understood. Then suddenly, without meaning to, she found herself telling Mr Potterville all about the struggle she and Edgar had had to keep the palm tree alive.

That night Mrs Willoughby's leg ached a little harder but the pain was still quite tolerable. Her last thought, before going to sleep, was that she was enjoying herself. Who would ever have thought it? Here she was in hospital after a nasty fall, with a wounded leg and the effects of shock, no doubt, to come, quite positively enjoying herself. Even the thought of Tina, alone in the flat, could not spoil the strange feeling of contentment. It coursed warmly through her body and she smiled in the dark

Mrs Willoughby continued vigorously to enjoy herself in hospital for two days, then she was taken home by an ambulanceman who escorted her to the lift. By coincidence, a middle-aged neighbour, face vaguely familiar, was also going up.

'We heard you had a fall, Mrs Willoughby,' she said.

Mrs Willoughby who had never, as far as she could remember, imparted her name to anyone, seemed surprised by the news. She stuck out her bandaged leg, tapping it with her stick.

'Oh, nothing to worry about,' she said.

'You can't be too careful,' replied the woman. 'I'll give you a hand to your door. Mrs Winner's the name.'

Mrs Winner ended by staying for a two-hour tea. She was remarkably interested in Mrs Willoughby's fall, and when the detailed story of it came to an end told three stories in return. They were about friends of hers who had had even worse falls, all with disastrous consequences. It seemed that the hospital, who had thought of everything, had arranged for Mrs Winner to look after Tina and the African violets. She was a friendly if somewhat tiring woman, and Mrs Willoughby asked her to come again. She quickly accepted.

When she had gone Mrs Willoughby felt quite tired, but pleased to be home, even if it all looked a little strange since her absence, and since the visit of Mrs Winner.

Next morning there was, surprisingly, an unexpected ring on the doorbell: Eileen – the young housewife next door, previously so cold, now full of offers to do the shopping. Mrs Willoughby made a short list, hands trembling with gratitude and excitement as she did so. From that time on it could be said that her flat was almost a-bustle. The news of her accident seemed to have spread round the building and, from whatever motive, strange neighbours came with offers of help and advice. They drank her tea and talked for hours, so that each night Mrs Willoughby fell into an exhausted and grateful sleep. Rose rang three times – the unexpectedness of the calls gave her mother three separate frights, but it was nice to be able to say to the companion of the moment, 'That was my daughter, you know, just checking up.'

On several occasions Mr Potterville, on his way back from the hospital, dropped by. Once he brought a bottle of sherry; another time Mrs Willoughby made him sardines on toast and they listened to a radio play.

'I positively enjoyed myself, Mrs Willoughby,' Mr Potterville said one night, as he left. 'The visit has quite bucked me up.'

'And so did I, Mr Potterville. I haven't had such a good time for several years. Please come again soon.'

'I will, I will. Never doubt that.'

But Mr Potterville failed to keep his word. As Mrs Willoughby had no address for him, and felt reluctant to go back to the hospital to see his wife, lest she should take it wrong, there was nothing she could do. Still, with so much coming and going these days there was little time to think. Mr Potterville's few visits had been pleasant while they lasted, but there were still many others, even if they weren't handsome men with bottles of sherry. As Mrs Willoughby said one evening to Tina, testing her leg for a small skip, 'I'm happy as a lark.'

Two weeks passed in which neighbours dropped in three or four times a day. Then a district nurse came and took off the bandages. She declared Mrs Willoughby fit enough to go out now, provided she took care. She found herself strangely disappointed at the news. Eileen had got into the way of doing her shopping, bought just the right brand of soup without being told. With some reluctance she explained to Eileen she had to get back to normal now: there was no need to carry on with her kindness. Eileen appeared quite huffy, and in the following week only dropped by once for a few moments.

It took Mrs Willoughby a week or so to realise that visits from her new friends, as soon as her health was back, were dropping off. They still smiled at her slightly should she see them in the lift, but it seemed as if the sudden flare of their interest had been eaten up. They needed her no more: as a target of their transitory benevolence, or curiosity, she was a spent thing. Gradually, the small flat returned to its former quietness: only Tina chirruped on, without cease. 'Funny what a fall does for you,' Mrs Willoughby said to her one evening. 'They're all round you, to help, then they're gone. We're back on our own again, Tina, but very fortunate, all things considering. Very fortunate indeed.' And for the first time for several weeks she took down the photograph album of her wedding. This reversion to her old ways, her old reliance on the past, took a little getting used to, but it wasn't long before she accepted the inevitable pattern of things once more.

Though just occasionally she had to exert a little extra self-control, like the morning she went shopping and found it was a windy day, very much the same kind of weather as the day of the fall. She stood at the edge of the kerb, for an irresistible moment, where it had all happened. Holding on to her hat, she remembered. And a wicked thought suddenly came to her.

Wouldn't it be nice if . . . She wouldn't really be sorry if . . . Quickly, she cocked her chin in the air, ashamed of herself. Then, she raised her stick defiantly, stepped off the pavement, and crossed the street without misadventure.

Azaleas for Sale

The 'Azaleas for Sale' notice was nailed outside the fence, uneven letters painted in tar on a piece of board, and immediately you entered the gate you saw them: plantations of azaleas, frail bushes not more than a couple of feet high, and here and there the first spotted flower.

The house itself, a great slab of a house, grey stone, defied the daylight to make it sparkle. Its heavy portico was supported by plain thick pillars, and one of those shrubs that clings to stone grew thickly round the windows, its blackish leaves gloomy as funeral gloves. In the cold January day of Marina's visit, dull sky, it was a forbidding place: difficult to imagine that fifty years ago a butler flashed instantly in the door at the sound of wheels and, according to Colonel Adlington, gay young things tripped across the lawns to pluck azaleas for buttonholes and hair.

No one heard Marina arrive. She pushed open the huge front

door, stood shivering for a moment in the flagstone hall. She could feel the bite of salt in the dank air, though the coast was a mile away. High on the walls stuffed things in glass boxes began to register – fish and birds. There were footsteps, squeaks, the muffled thump of doors. Then the husky bray of Mrs Adlington's voice which had, as late as 1940, she claimed, thrilled audiences all over the country.

'Marina!'

'Isabella!' The names small bells in the semi-darkness.

'What a morning! Bloody dank, gets into you. You arrived? Marvellous, marvellous. Come on in and have a drink. Gerald can't wait to see you.'

They kissed. Isabella's breath, staled by years of gin, was superficially refreshed by the drink she carried in one hand. She swilled the liquid around.

'Hope you don't mind I didn't wait? Got to have something to keep out the cold. Should keep your coat on for a bit, if I were you. Gerald, you know, has been hopping up and down all morning waiting for you. Filthy old thing.' She pulled her cardigan more tightly round her large bosom which once, too, no doubt, had thrilled audiences. The cardigan was an aged, matt thing, dullest ever navy, which must have been pulled from years of slumber in a drawer earlier this morning, and was still clumsy with lack of use. 'You look marvellous, darling,' croaked Isabella, 'you really do. Gerald'll have a seizure.'

Marina followed her through tall dark passages past doors that smelt faintly of cloakrooms and kitchens. Isabella finally flung open the door of the drawing-room, with a theatrical sense of timing.

'We're in here in honour of you,' she said. 'Your first visit. It'll warm up soon, the fire. Gerald! She's here.'

Gerald stood at the window – huge panes, eighteen inches high – surveying all he could of his land through the mist that rolled in from the sea. He turned towards them, his nose bigger than Marina remembered, his cheeks one tone deeper than the old rose of the walls. If in reality he had been hopping up and down all morning in anticipation of Marina's arrival, the exercise had exhausted him: for now his very stance was tired. His tweed shoulders sagged. Lustreless eyes revealed nothing of the wicked desires that his wife warned were raging within him.

'Look at him waiting for you, Marina, you see! What did I tell you? Gerald, come along! Open the bottle. What are you dithering for?'

Gerald shuffled towards Marina, greeted her politely.

'Like to come and see the pantry?' he asked. 'We've turned one of the old kitchens into a pantry, makes it much nearer.'

'For heaven's sake, darling!' Isabella clutched at Marina's arm. 'For God's sake, *don't*! He'd pounce on you before you can say knife, wouldn't you, Gerald?'

Ignoring the question with a dignified tilt of his head, Gerald moved towards the door.

'I'll go alone, then,' he said.

Marina huddled on a stool by the fire. The flames crouched pathetically low over the three damp logs, overawed by the size of the chimney into which they were expected to rise. They gave no heat. Isabella thumped down on to a sofa, spreading her legs. She had fat knees and good ankles.

'We're keeping body and soul together,' she said, 'skin of our teeth. Economising like crazy, just the odd nip to keep ourselves going, and we see a lot of the grandchildren, which is nice.' Her voice was a bandaged rattle, the sound of an old steamboat grinding sluggish water. With it, once, she had lured an international film star to love her. And, for a time, to marry her. 'We're having oysters, as I promised on the telephone. Oyster pasties and a bit of lamb. Now, tell me your news.'

A long time later Gerald returned, a champagne-shaped bottle in his hand.

'Pushing out the boat,' said Isabella. 'I told you, darling, the old boy's nutty about you.'

'Don't worry, it's not the real thing. Just something sparkling.' Gerald opened the bottle with difficulty, poured two glasses. Isabella heaved herself up.

'Don't try to give *me* any of that rubbish, now. I'm off to have a decko at the pasties. For Lord's sake scream, darling, if the old sod gets too fresh.' On the way out of the room she filled her glass from the bottle of Gordon's Gin which stood beside a small vase of pale dried flowers on the mantelpiece.

Gerald chose an armchair as far as possible from Marina's seat by the fire. Due to his deafness, conversation had to be a series of barked shouts. Marina enquired about the progress of the azalea farm.

'Very good, really,' Gerald replied, 'considering admin. isn't all it might be, but we're seeing to that. It'll all fall into place, gradually. But we get a lot of orders, you know. We get orders from all over the place. People seem to like azaleas.' His slow eyes flitted among the damp patches that bruised the old pink walls. ''Course, when it all takes off, we'll be made. No more worries. Be able to get it all done up a bit.'

'I'd like to buy about a dozen bushes, if I could,' said Marina. 'They make such good presents.'

'Really? Want to buy a couple, do you?' Gerald sounded surprised. 'Ah, well. We could see about that after lunch, perhaps.'

'Didn't Isabella tell you that's what I'd come for? I wrote you several letters asking you to send them. In the end I thought it best to come myself and collect them.'

'Don't think she did,' said Gerald, 'but then we don't look at the post much these days. Think she just said you were coming all this way for lunch, wasn't that nice? She thinks the world of you, of course. Wish the bloody mist would clear, and I could show you the view.'

Isabella returned to announce that lunch was ready. She was unable to resist enquiring how their five minutes alone had passed.

'Kept his hands off you, sly old fox, has he? I only have to turn my back, you know. Any pretty face. You'd never think he'd had two heart attacks in the last eighteen months, would you?'

'Never,' said Marina, watching Gerald totter to the door, one arm weighed down with the half-empty bottle of sparkling white wine. They made their way through a series of high-ceilinged rooms: faded walls, curtains drained of colour, left only with the skeletal print of patterns: the odd dark portrait clenched in a gilded frame. There was no heating in any of the rooms, but each one was furnished with a single bottle of gin. To keep out the cold as you passed through, Marina supposed.

Lunch was in the kitchen. Here, any risk of disturbing ancient planning by modernisation had been avoided. No bright Formica noises – sounds redolent of the past: drip of tap into an enamel sink, splutter of kettle on top of ungainly black Aga. Smells of coal and sprouts and steam; tenebrous light through the one small window, designed in the days when it was not considered that staff required much light to work by.

Isabella had laid the lunch with care. Small silver knives and forks – the last of the Georgian stuff, she said – were arranged on the pitted wood of the table. Real linen napkins, unaired, so limp they dipped into the shape of the Crown Derby side plates. Fine-stemmed wine glasses, home-made mint relish in a crystal bowl.

'Got to keep things going,' said Isabella, and Gerald uncorked a bottle of dusty claret.

Lunch, it was evident, was the high spot of the Adlingtons' day. After their morning chores, checking the wood store, pottering among the azaleas, peeling potatoes, stretching up to dust some of the high fireplaces, it was there to reinvigorate them, to give them strength for the lesser delights of the afternoon (shuffling bills) and the long, cold evenings. Besides, the kitchen was warm: only warm room in the whole bloody house, for God's sake, said Isabella, and the two high-backed benches each side of the table made an agreeable feeling of enclosure. This was the vantage point of their fortress against worrying conditions. Here, armed with the knowledge that they could flog the remaining silver as a last resort, they allowed the warmth of possibilities to cocoon them for a while. In the First War, shoulders braced, Gerald had received the VC for bravery. He had been taught to face the enemy without flinching. In old age, a new kind of enemy, he did not find it hard to adapt. Same tactics, really. Take each blow as it comes, and plan to fight the next one. But don't let them shoot you out. Stick to your territory. Be cunning in your strategies. (Azaleas turned into a business.) Gerald would happily die starving in his house, but while he lived he would protect it from being sold for institutional purposes – and who, these days, would want it for anything else?

Fired by the mixture of gin, claret, and oyster pasties, the courage of the Adlingtons grew. It took diverse turns, but Marina recognised it in all its disguises, and admired. Isabella, in a vitriolic attack on paper napkins, showed the strength of her own determination. She banged a speckled hand on the table. The English upper classes would never allow *all* their standards to slip, no matter what happened to the pound, she said. We had all reduced our living standards, of course, but who cared about that? We had probably had it too good for too long. Besides, the war had trained us to regard hard times as a challenge. Well, they were a challenge. And we should face them. But paper napkins – no, never. Paper napkins would be like . . . the Blues giving up horses in favour of Japanese cars.

Gerald said she had gone too far, as usual. Isabella shook her head, agreeing. She poured her husband more wine with a merry lack of reverence for its age, making it swirl in the glass like her own gin. Gerald averted his eyes from the swaying liquid.

'I'm off to the South of France for a short break in March,' he said.

'By himself,' explained Isabella. 'I never want to go further than the village these days, you know. Had my travelling. Bloody

South of France every year when I was young. Grew out of it. Bloody mean Frogs.'

'You didn't see many of *them* in the Negresco,' said Gerald.

'Don't like to imagine what he gets up to down there by himself, anyway.' Isabella bent towards Marina. 'He comes back looking a wreck, I can tell you.' She turned to Gerald. 'Anyway, unless the azaleas take off whizz, bang, ducky, what about the fare?'

'Marina's come to *buy*,' explained Gerald. He smiled. Suddenly, the idea of selling her two plants seemed like his whole salvation. 'Didn't you know?'

Isabella's mouth fell open in surprise.

'Hadn't a clue. That's lovely, darling. Awfully generous idea. But of course we'll give you some, can't let you pay.'

Marina was firm.

'No, really,' she said, 'business is most especially business among friends.' She felt her strength to be ineffectual in the wash of their generosity.

'Well, we'll throw in some extras,' conceded Isabella.

'We might go down after lunch, what about that?' asked Gerald. 'Choose some good ones. Then I better ring the travel agent, confirm my ticket. March nearly upon us . . .'

'Sleep, for me,' said Isabella, cutting into a beautiful apple pie. 'We have very regular lives, you know. We like being old. Nothing much changes. My energy runs out a bit quicker, perhaps. But Gerald's the same as ever, the old dog . . .'

'God Almighty,' interrupted Gerald, looking deeply into his wine, nose quite blue now.

'Yes, I sleep. Only go to the village when I have to,' went on Isabella.

'You should come to Monte this year. Give you a break.' Gerald nodded at his wife with the optimism of one who knows his own suggestion will be rejected.

'Never! Me, risk an aeroplane just to see you hobbling after starlets, making a fool of yourself? Never. Besides, someone's got to stay at home and look after the flowers.'

Her voice had ground incredibly low. The claret was finished. Gerald blinked at his own drowsiness. Marina judged it time to go. They protested at her leaving, but could find no reason to urge her to stay.

'Just the plants,' said Marina. 'Could we put them in the car? So sorry for the trouble.'

Azaleas! The very thought of them caused the Adlingtons a sudden, mutual exhaustion. They struggled against it.

'Tell you what,' said Gerald. 'I've got to get on about the wretched tickets before three, but we could send them to you. Trust me to pick out the best ones.'

'Or better still, you could come *back*!' Isabella was clinging to Marina's arm in the hall. Echoes of their footsteps overlapped. 'Just write and give us a little warning and we'll have them ready, won't we, Gerald?'

'Of course, of course.'

'And it's been so *lovely* having you, darling. Someone young about. I'll see Gerald doesn't go too far next time, sexy beast.'

They were steering her across the gravel, through the cold, grey, salt air. They were waving goodbye, shouting at her to promise to come again. Azaleas . . . good excuse, what?

She drove away along the drive, past the acres of thriving plants, wonderfully protected from audacious buyers. They stretched into the distance, finally to be lost in mist now coming more thickly from the sea: mist which by tea-time would quite obscure the Adlingtons' afternoon, blot out their view entirely, so that the azaleas would only exist in their imagination again, a brave idea with which to defend themselves against alternatives too terrible to contemplate.

The Outing

Mrs Christopher Radcliffe, as the wife of an MP, was a practised speaker. Since she had married she had made dozens of
speeches, opened numerous shows, shops and fêtes. Nevertheless,
she still felt slight unease before a public occasion, however small,
and this nervous tension always seemed to mar her judgement
about precisely how long it would take to reach her destination.

On the Saturday afternoon of the local fête, which was held
every year in early summer, Mrs Radcliffe drove her car very
slowly along the narrow road that twisted over the moors. She was
a good ten minutes early. Just before entering the village she
stopped the car in a gateway to check her appearance. Navy straw
stetson at a nice angle; neat belted coat; navy gloves; sensible
shoes for tramping from stall to stall. Not too ostentatious for the
country. She should do, she thought.

Miss Warburton, head of the local branch of the Country

Women's Guild, was looking out for Mrs Radcliffe as she drove up to the village green.

'Oh, Mrs Radcliffe. How kind of you to come.'

'Hello.' Mrs Radcliffe brandishing her practised smile. 'How nice to see you again. All right if I park here?'

She was aware of a small flutter among the onlookers as she got out of the car.

'I hope we'll be lucky with the weather.' Miss Warburton was a little nervous. She led Mrs Radcliffe across the village green. The grass was a sour yellow: the colour grass goes before a storm. Huge oak trees surrounded the green, towering into the thunderous sky, their leaves an ominous colour, too. Behind the trees stood the small village houses: built of West Country grey stone, the deep-set windows in their gaunt façades afforded glimpses of snug rooms lit with flowers.

'It looks as if it might hold out,' said Mrs Radcliffe. 'Let's hope it does.'

They reached a trestle table that had been set with a cloth and a long, narrow vase of carnations stuck into a ruffle of fern. Mrs Radcliffe took her place behind the flowers and nodded at a few familiar faces. She looked about her: the stalls weren't up to much, at a glance, but she would make straight for the home-made cakes. It was easy genuinely to appreciate *them*. There wasn't a bad crowd, for a dull day. But they were a bit scattered. With no microphone, she'd have to raise her voice. She could be away, she calculated, in just under an hour.

'I am so pleased to be able to welcome today,' Miss Warburton was saying, 'Mrs Christopher Radcliffe – wife, of course, of our local MP.' A smattering of claps from the listeners. Mrs Radcliffe smiled in response and turned to take an interest in the introduction. She would keep on smiling, now, till the end of the welcome, which Miss Warburton was having some trouble in reading from a small piece of paper that fluttered nervously in her hand.

*

A couple of hours previously Miss Pears had been told it was time to get ready for the outing. This news, like almost any news that involved action on her part, put her mind into a considerable flurry. What should she take with her? Her lunch, for one thing. That was sure. She had it beside her on the bed, in a scrumpled up paper bag. Two hard-boiled eggs, a piece of cold fried bacon and a buttered roll. That would be nice, later on.

She glanced out of the high windows to the dull sky. Scarf, she thought. My pink or my blue? It might come on to rain, but then again it might not. But when in doubt wear a scarf, had always been her motto. Mrs Grace had only set her hair yesterday. It would be a pity to have it all come out in a sudden shower. Money – how much money should she take? They'd been told it would be a nice outing, to a garden party or a fête or something – she had forgotten exactly – up on the moors. There would be a chance to spend.

Miss Pears scrambled about her locker for her purse. It was a worn old leather purse appliquéd with a giraffe that was coming unstuck, but somehow there was never any glue handy. Janet, her only niece, had sent it to her, Christmas '68, before she'd married and become too busy to send more than a card. The purse contained exactly forty new pence – eight shillings to Miss Pears. She'd die before they got her round to decimals.

She tied her blue scarf round her head, pushing it well forward so that her fringe, should it rain, would at least be partially protected. There was no mirror, but the hefty knot she tied felt secure: it felt as if it gave her chin a good lift.

She set off down the dormitory. There was no one else there. She was the last, as usual, but then she'd never been quick on her feet. She laughed out loud a little to herself, anticipating the chiding she'd get from the others on the bus. 'Good old Apples,' they'd say, 'late as usual.'

'Buck up, Apples, we haven't got all night,' one or two of them did shout, as they climbed the steep bus steps. But by this time the laugh had died in her throat and she knew her face looked quite stern. Funny how she wanted to laugh with them, just as she'd done a few moments ago alone in the dormitory. But when it came to the time that they actually teased her the laugh always vanished, and some of them, the grumpier ones, said she was stuck up.

Miss Pears found an empty seat next to Mrs Grace. She sat down beside her. Mrs Grace was almost her friend. She didn't say much, Mrs Grace, but she'd made her mark by doing things. Little things, like setting your hair or giving you a cigarette or a chocolate, all for nothing in return. She had a temper, of course. Sometimes, she went wild. Semolina all over the place, for no apparent reason, more times than Miss Pears could remember. And then Mrs Grace would be taken away for a few days, and come back sleepy, and start doing things for you again. Miss Pears liked Mrs Grace. She would have shown her the Valentine card she got this year, had some sudden intuition not told her that it was Mrs Grace herself who had sent it.

Miss Pears looked down at her hands. They were indeed shaking, so that the bag made quite a noise.

'I'm all nerves, going out,' said Miss Pears, quietly, so that no one else should hear. She envied Mrs Grace her composure. Nothing seemed to shake *her* – outings, medical check-ups, anything. But then of course she'd lived in villages, she'd worked for the nobility, she'd probably experienced many a garden fête.

The first thing Miss Pears noticed when they arrived at the village green was the brass band. The musicians sat in a semicircle, legs apart, shaking spit from their instruments and flipping through their sheet music. In her excitement Miss Pears tightened her grip on her lunch bag and tore it at the corner.

Then, as she dithered down the steps, causing a lot of complaints from those behind her, the musicians struck up with 'Whenever you feel afraid'.

'Well I never,' said Miss Pears to Mrs Grace. But Mrs Grace was thinking about something else and only answered, 'Nasty sky.' Then she turned away and waddled off in the direction of the church. Miss Pears considered shouting after her that she was going the wrong way, and to mind the road: but then she thought it wasn't worth it.

She was left standing on her own, her mouth slightly open, looking up at the giant trees – terrible thing if one of them crashed down – and listening to the music. Then she noticed most of the people seemed to be herding towards something, past the band. She set off to follow them – something must be going on. Mrs Grace would miss it, but perhaps Mrs Grace had been to too many of these sort of things to mind.

Mrs Radcliffe wetted her lips as the applause died down at the end of Miss Warburton's speech, and reset her smile. After a suitable pause, she began:

'Ladies and gentlemen, I find it a great honour and pleasure to have been asked here today. As you know, I myself am a firm supporter and indeed a *member* of the Country Women's Guilds, and I honestly believe that the day we open membership to men, your first new member will be my husband.' (Small laugh. That line always went down well with women's institutions.) 'As you know, although he's a very busy man, he takes a great interest in all our activities, and he has asked me to tell you how very sorry he is not to be able to be here today. But you know what a politician's life is . . .'

Her eyes trailed round the listeners. A Miss Burrows, the district nurse, she recognised; the farmer, she forgot his name, from whom she used to buy free-range eggs; a few strange mothers and children. And then a small woman with sloping shoulders and wide hips, hands lolling at her sides, a detached expression on her square face. Mrs Radcliffe found her eyes paused when they came upon this woman. There was something odd about her. Mrs Radcliffe hesitated, then returned to her speech with a jolt she hoped no one would notice.

'Looking round –' (she gave another quick look round, this time determined not to stop at the woman with the odd face) – 'looking round there seems to be a most impressive display on the stalls, and I know how much trouble this means you must have all taken: what hard work behind the scenes it must have been.' Her voice was rising. People at the back of the crowd were beginning to fidget. Bloody stupid of Miss Warburton not to have arranged a microphone. It was difficult enough to hold their attention . . .

Her own attention was on her listeners again. This time she caught sight of a woman a little apart from the crowd – a woman standing alone looking up at the trees, solid legs planted wide, blue scarf round her pudding face, hands clutching at a small paper bag. – Of course.

It was then that Mrs Radcliffe remembered. Well, it would make a lovely afternoon for them, poor things. She renewed her smile and decided, with a spontaneity unusual to her, to cut her speech short. A quick word about all the good work the Country Women's Guilds do, and on with the opening.

'And so I ask you to give as generously as you can to this very good cause. And now, I won't keep you any longer from enjoying yourselves – and *spending*. And so it is, with great pleasure, I declare this fête open.'

Miss Pears heard the clapping – it sounded a little muted from where she stood – and gave a brief dab at her paper bag. She could see a small girl with a satin bow in her hair shuffling up to the lady in the big hat and smart red coat. The child curtsied and handed the lady a beautiful posy of carnations and fern in a twist of silver paper. The lady laughed, and held it up to her lapel. It was a pretty sight, thought Miss Pears. She wondered if her niece Janet's little girl would be about that age now.

The crowd round the table began to break up and make for the stalls. Miss Pears noticed several of her lot seemed hesitant, dithery, compared with the villagers. Well, she for one knew where she was going. The home-made cakes.

She walked towards a stall under one of the largest trees, the long thick grass tickling her ankles above her shoes. But when she managed to reach the stall, pushing her way through the nattering women, there were no cakes, but only second-hand clothes. Hands were holding them up: a very large bathing suit with boned breasts, and a tatty old scarf, no better than a duster, blew in the breeze. Nothing that Miss Pears wanted. A lot of old rubbish. She saw Mrs Grace nearby, sniffing at the stuff, not touching anything – so she knew that she was right about that. It *was* a lot of old rubbish.

She turned, and made her way to another stall. This time she found the right one, a long trestle table covered with tantalising cakes. It was difficult to take them all in at a glance, with people shoving and pushing and asking the price. But there was a particular one which caught Miss Pears' fancy: chocolate-iced and decorated with a swirl of pink sugar roses. It was hard to tell, just looking, whether the icing was soft or hard. If it was soft, she'd have it. She put out a finger to prod it, very gently – she wouldn't harm it in any way, of course, just test the icing, when a lady with a biting voice behind the table snapped: 'No touching please.'

Miss Pears' finger whipped back in fright. She'd meant no harm. Oh well, have to risk the icing. She took out her purse. The ticket on the chocolate cake said 35p. She tipped all her coins into the palm of her hand, still holding her paper bag, all very awkward. She began calculating in her head. Counting the odd coins was difficult because the paper bag was in the way, and yet if she didn't put her finger on them she forgot which number she'd got up to. Very muddling. She realised, though, if she bought the chocolate cake, and she could just manage it, there'd be precious little over for tea. Though of course that didn't matter so much, seeing as she'd still got her lunch.

Miss Pears was about to ask the snappy lady if she could have the chocolate cake when the people around the stall suddenly began to drift apart, as if to make way for someone. Miss Pears turned round. There before her, so close she was almost touching, was the lady in the big hat and the red coat, the posy of carnations pinned to her lapel now. The lady gave a huge smile, her lips all glossy red. She seemed not to be looking at Miss Pears, though, but at the snappy lady behind the counter.

'What lovely cakes!' From under the big hat her voice brayed, close-to. 'I must take some home for the children. They're real fiends for cakes.'

'There's a good selection, isn't there?' A middle-aged woman in silk polka dots edged up to the lady in the red coat. She had a kind face under a shiny straw hat that danced with cherries.

'Which ones will you have, Mrs Radcliffe?'

The snappy woman's voice was all sweetness now. Miss Pears' hands tightened on her paper bag and her coins and her empty purse. Several people craned forward to get a good view of Mrs Radcliffe's decision.

'Well, I don't know, do you? It's so difficult to decide.' She put a navy blue finger to her chin then suddenly pointed it very fast at several different cakes. 'That, that, that, that, and er, that, I think.' She took a £5 note from her bag and handed it over the counter. 'Why don't you keep the change as my contribution to the afternoon?'

'Well, that's really very kind of you, Mrs Radcliffe,' the snappy woman glowed.

'Thank you so much, Mrs Radcliffe. We'll get Mrs Radcliffe's cakes boxed up, won't we, Mrs Leigh, and get someone to put them in her car?' The nice lady with the cherry hat sounded efficient. 'Would you care to come and look at the garden produce, now, Mrs Radcliffe?'

The two ladies, red coat and polka dots, moved away. Miss Pears stood by the stall and watched Miss Leigh snatch up the five chosen cakes, including the chocolate one, and put them under the table. Without them, it was almost bare. A couple of dull sponges left, sprinkled with icing sugar, and a weedy-looking jam roll. Miss Pears began to put her coins back into her purse. Then she opened the paper bag to check on the bacon, shining pinkly through its piece of greaseproof paper. She might as well go and have her lunch.

*

Miss Warburton was privately disappointed by the bring-and-buy stall. There, not much imagination had been shown – tinned pears, dishcloths, a silver-painted horseshoe, a baby's dummy. Mrs Radcliffe had had quite a difficult time choosing anything. Eventually, she had settled for a bottle of tomato ketchup.

Miss Warburton was also disappointed in the weather, as she kept repeating to Mrs Radcliffe.

'Just our luck, after so many good Saturdays.'

'Well, at least it isn't raining.' Mrs Radcliffe made it quite clear, by her determined step, there was no point in her stopping at the second-hand stall. Miss Warburton took the hint, and didn't suggest it. Instead she guided her guest of honour towards the village hall, where she could be certain a good tea had been laid on.

The band struck up again, this time 'Getting to Know You'. They seemed to have a particular liking for the music of the fifties. Mrs Radcliffe sprang a little on the balls of her feet, in time to the music.

'My husband and I used to dance to this before we were married,' she said. Anything to get off the weather.

'Really? How very interesting.' Miss Warburton herself hadn't danced for fifty years.

The village hall was a bare, lofty place which smelt of newly scrubbed wood and warm scones. Mrs Radcliffe noticed that its high windows were edged with skimpy maroon curtains, and she wondered why it was that nine out of ten village halls she went to chose that particular colour for their curtains. She'd have to tell Christopher.

A couple of dozen tables were laid with white cloths and jam jars of cow-parsley and honeysuckle: someone had taken a lot of trouble. Extra chairs lined the walls of the hall, and on the stage a trestle table was stacked with thick white cups and home-made things. Miss Warburton introduced Mrs Radcliffe to the tea helpers, and pressed her to choose a lot to eat. But Mrs Radcliffe picked only one salmon fishpaste sandwich, besides her cup of tea. Miss Warburton laughed understandingly.

'We all have to think of our figures, don't we?' Then she waved her hands in a flurry as she saw Mrs Radcliffe beginning to open her bag. 'No, no, please! Tea on the house.' Mrs Radcliffe thought it wise to accept the offer with no fuss.

She and Miss Warburton wound their way through the tables, nodding at people, looking for a free seat. Mrs Radcliffe noticed that the woman who wouldn't budge out of her way at the cake stall sat at a table alone. But instead of eating the provided tea, she seemed to be having trouble cracking a hard-boiled egg on the table. Miss Warburton hurried past all the tables that were occupied by only one, drab woman, and finally asked Mrs Radcliffe if she would care to join the Bennet sisters at their table. They were the people responsible for the raffle. Miss Warburton knew they would be honoured if Mrs Radcliffe would be so kind as to call out the winning numbers. Mrs Radcliffe cheerfully agreed to do this. She calculated that could decently be her last duty. She could still be home by five-thirty. She began to nibble her sandwich.

Miss Pears had never come across such a tough-shelled egg. She banged it on the table, thwacked it on her knee, but it wouldn't break. In the end, with great patience, she laid it on her plate, waited till it stopped rolling about – till it was quite, quite still, then crashed her fist down upon it with all her force. This caused not just the shell to break, but also the white and even the hard-boiled yolk. Miss Pears began picking at the shattered bits, peeling away small chunks of white from small pieces of shell.

She noticed, meanwhile, that quite a lot of her bus-load sat at tables by themselves, while the villagers chose tables with their friends and sat together. The child who had given the lady the flowers passed nearby Miss Pears' table. She held out a small chip of egg to her and the child smiled. But then a fat woman snatched at the child's arm and hurried her away to the other end of the hall.

Still, she was happy with her lunch, on her own. She liked to eat alone. That's why she always saved her meals till past the proper meal times. No one seemed to mind. Perhaps they didn't notice.

All the others seemed quite happy, too, as far as she could tell. There was Lily, at the next table, squinting over her pile of sausage rolls. She'd always been greedy as a pig, Lily, and her table manners were nothing to write home about, either. When the lady in the red coat passed her table, Lily looked up, still chewing, mouth still open, with no respect at all. Then her eyes watered – she couldn't take bright colours, they always hurt – and the tears trickled down her face.

Mrs Grace, Miss Pears noticed, had chosen one of the chairs at the edge of the hall. But then she wasn't eating anything, just sipping a cup of tea. Miss Pears looked at her quite hard. There was something up with Mrs Grace, she could tell. She had that look in her eye. She'd been obliging for so many days, too: perhaps the time was up. Miss Pears looked round for the supervisor – not that she ever listened to anyone, stubborn old bitch, but it would be worth giving her a hint about Mrs Grace. However, the supervisor was nowhere in sight, so Miss Pears began on her bacon.

As soon as she had finished her lunch she made her way to the stage to choose her tea. On the way she passed Mrs Grace.

'Coming up for something to eat?' she asked. Mrs Grace didn't answer, or didn't seem to have heard. 'There's some lovely gingerbread,' Miss Pears went on, 'and scones. Shall I treat you to something?'

Still Mrs Grace didn't answer. Instead she got up, as if Miss Pears didn't exist, put her unfinished tea on her seat, and left the hall. She'd always been unpredictable. Muttering to herself that there were some people who looked a gift-horse in the mouth, Miss Pears climbed the stage. She decided to spend every penny she had on tea.

Half an hour later, feeling pleasantly full, she made her way back to the village green. She had no money left, so there was nothing else she could buy. She would sit on the grass beside the band and listen, until the supervisor told them to get back into the bus.

Outside, the sky was darker, the green of the trees and hedges more vivid. Miss Pears shuddered. Sometimes, millions of pellets of sky, black as soot, streamed through her eyes, her mouth, her nose, till she could hardly breathe, and her hands and feet went icy cold. She hadn't had an attack like that, mind, for several weeks now: not since they'd been giving her those new red pills. But she didn't like anything black: it always reminded her.

She walked carefully back to the band, heavy with tea. It swayed and gurgled in her stomach, a comforting sound.

But the musicians weren't there: probably gone for tea themselves. They'd left their instruments propped up against their chairs, their peaked caps on the seats, their sheet music making little snapping noises as the breeze pecked at the pages.

Mrs Grace sat on one of the seats, in the front row. Her feet, not quite touching the ground, swung backwards and forwards, hitting a trombone. She stared into space, sulky looking. Still, Miss Pears thought, might as well have a go at her.

'Understand the music?' she asked. No answer from Mrs Grace. 'I used to be able to play a few notes, years ago.' She paused again. Mrs Grace just didn't seem to be interested in anything today.

Oh well. She'd tried. Nobody could say she hadn't. Anyhow, here was the band coming back. Now Mrs Grace would have to budge.

A dozen large men in silver-buttoned uniforms tramped back to their places. The one who should have occupied Mrs Grace's seat had a bristly red beard.

'Had a nice sit-down, have you?' he asked. 'Afraid I've got to shift you now. Back to work.'

Mrs Grace took no notice of him. She stared unblinking at his stand of music. The man touched her shoulder.

'Come on, now, love. Up you get.' The conductor was tapping

his stick impatiently on his knee. Everyone was looking at Mrs Grace, now. The man with the red beard tried again.

'I said come on, dear. Very sorry and all that. Up – you get.' He tried to lever her gently up from the chair.

But with startling speed Mrs Grace leapt to her feet herself, spun round, picked up the slatted chair, brandished it for a moment above in the air, then brought it crashing down upon his head.

'Bugger off, you fucking creep,' she screamed. 'No one's going to bloody turn me off a fucking chair if I bloody want to be on it.'

Her voice ripped the heavy air. At once every member of the band stood. The conductor edged forward to protect his trombonist, whose face was spattered with blood from his head: it streamed down into his beard. The conductor tapped Mrs Grace on the shoulder with his stick.

'Now, now, madam, we don't want any trouble—'

'And as for you, you toady old bit of bullshit—'

She lashed out at the conductor with hands tightened into claws, and kicked at his shins.

Miss Pears was aware that all at once everyone at the fête seemed to be crowding round Mrs Grace and the musicians. All her lot had appeared from nowhere, very fast it must have been: usually they moved quite slowly. There was Lily, eyes full of water, screaming abuse at the whole band; Wendy the Egg running round and round in small circles, cackling with laughter, her head quite bald: her wig must have fallen off somewhere. Barbara the Giant was standing on a chair, almost as tall as the oak trees, fists clenched, ready to punch someone; Annie and Mavis, hand in hand as usual, stamping their gym shoes – when it came to revolt against authority, they were a loyal lot, the girls.

Quickly, Miss Pears decided she must do her bit. Mrs Grace after all was her friend – well, more or less her friend. She'd done her hair so nicely yesterday, not pulling once. She'd every right to her seat. She deserved support.

Miss Pears ran faster than she'd run for years across the green, the screams and weird laughs pounding in her ears. The home-made cake stall was empty now except for the one dreary sponge. With a heave Miss Pears tipped over the table. The single cake rolled away like a coin into the grass, brushing it with icing sugar. And there, exposed by the tipped-up table, lay Mrs Radcliffe's cakes in a box, waiting for arrangements to be made to get them to her car.

With an almighty cry Miss Pears jumped into the box, and felt them squashing beneath her feet. She stamped on them with all her force, bashing the chocolate and pink roses to an ugly pulp: coffee icing, white icing, strawberry fillings, crushed almonds oozed over her shoes and ankles, warm and soft. She began to laugh, her mouth widening over the whole of her face. The strong knot of her scarf snapped and the scarf fell off, but she didn't care. She kept on stamping, mincing the cakes to a multicoloured mud, and then the rain came. It fell into her mouth, turning black, and began to fill her eyes and nose and mouth till she cried out to breathe. She felt her feet turn to ice in the mess of cake, and her hands, icy too, rose like rags in the air, calling for help.

Miss Warburton and Mrs Radcliffe had just finished their tea when they heard the screams. With everybody else left in the hall, they hurried out to see what had happened. Mrs Radcliffe shoved her bottle of tomato ketchup into her pocket so that she could run. Miss Warburton held on to her hat.

As soon as she turned the corner and saw the fight, Mrs Radcliffe hissed out loud: 'You can *never* rely on those people. They should be properly supervised.' But Miss Warburton was far behind her, so her observations went unheard.

Mrs Radcliffe quickly made up her mind that there was nothing she could usefully do to help the situation. A fat policeman was blowing his whistle and grappling with a woman who appeared to be having hysterics by the bandstand. The district nurse was lead-ing away a bloody man with a red beard. A thickset woman in a navy uniform and her stocking seams all askew was running about shouting unheeded orders, and a monster woman, standing on a chair, fists thrust into the sky, screamed obscenities. And there was Miss Warburton, suddenly very fast on her feet, chasing a woman with a completely bald head, dabbing at her with her straw hat, as if she was trying to catch a butterfly.

I hope to God the local reporter has gone home, thought Mrs Radcliffe. This sort of publicity wouldn't help the next election. For Christopher's sake, in fact, it would probably be better to make a discreet exit and write a letter explaining to Miss Warburton – who was in no way fit to say goodbye to at the moment.

She threw away the bottle of ketchup, which was digging into her hip-bone, cursed the rain, and began to tiptoe as inconspicuously as possible round behind the trees. At one moment a man crossed her path – he looked like a bus driver – dragging a crying woman, the one who'd had the blue scarf, and whose feet were now covered in some kind of revolting mess. The woman's cries, and ugly twisted face, made Mrs Radcliffe feel sick: she had never been any good at coping with scenes, as she was the first to admit.

Unnoticed, she got into her car. Quickly she closed the window, which half shut out the hysterical yells of fear, hatred, abuse and despair. She switched on the wipers. The water on the windscreen blurred the writhing people among the upturned tables, and scattered brass instruments of the band. She shut her eyes for a moment as the bald-headed woman ran quite close by, still screaming – Miss Warburton still chasing her, her wet polka-dotted dress now clinging to her thick body.

Mrs Radcliffe switched on the engine, glanced at her watch, very calm. If she put her foot down, she reckoned, she could still be home by half past five.

The Fuschia Auberge

On the eighth day of the holiday, mid-afternoon in Angers, Anna McGull suffered a crisis no one noticed.

She stood apart from the rest of her family who, for the second time that day, were looking at the famous tapestries. Her husband Michael and her youngest son, Patrick, huddled together, seemed to find as much interest in the guidebook as in the tapestries themselves. Simon, the eldest son, stood some distance away, his earnest stare fixed upon the Apocalypse. When contemplating any work of art, Simon managed to exude an air of superiority, as if he alone were granted understanding. His father and brother, a little awed by this attitude, believed Simon had a vision they lacked: hence their endless perusal of guidebooks to make up in facts what they lacked in spiritual communication. Anna had no such feelings. Simon's loftiness drove her wild. She thought he looked quite goofy, peering through his thick spectacles, fingers

twitching at his sludge-coloured anorak. For years, she had struggled to fight the annoyance his physical presence caused her. It
had never been so bad as on this holiday.

Outside, it gently rained. A flat, plum-coloured light in the
galleries darkened the tapestries. Anna wondered if any of the
women who had put thousands of hours of work into these hang-
ings of gloomy beauty had ever rebelled. The younger ones,
surely, must have woken some mornings and thought to themselves they would go mad if they had to do another bloody stitch.

Anna's reflections were cut short by a Norwegian tourist. He
stepped in front of her, blocking her view and provoking the
crisis. His mackintosh skimmed calves latticed with veins: bare
toes splayed beyond the edges of his sandals, clenched in concentration. Anna thought: in the past week I've seen forty-three
Romanesque churches, fifteen museums, eleven châteaux, seven
picture galleries, the tapestries *twice* . . . and now a Norwegian is
thwarting my view. I can't bear it any more.

She left the gallery, hurried outside. It was raining harder, now.
Sheltering under a chestnut tree, she looked up into the great
dome of sharp green leaves and thanked God there was nothing in
the guidebook about *this*. The very thought of the guidebook
made her cry for a moment. Soon she would recover herself,
return to the gallery, wait.

But as she was dabbing her eyes an English couple walked by.
Plainly happy, the man took the woman's arm and guided her
towards a café. His innocent gesture caused Anna a second crisis,
this time of jealousy. Michael and the boys would never consider
stopping mid-afternoon for a drink. Three more churches before
dark, they would say.

Anna followed the couple into the café. She chose an empty
table by the window, ordered a croissant and coffee. (Lunch had
been a bag of apples eaten beside an ancient tomb.) Her aching
legs and feet recovered. The pleasure of sitting alone at a foreign
table uncluttered by guidebooks was almost tangible.

After a while she saw her husband and sons leave the gallery. They looked briefly about them, then set off towards the church. The English couple rose to leave.

'Where are you going?' Anna heard herself asking.

'Delange, ten miles north. We've been staying in an auberge there, but we've got to get back to Paris.'

The woman smiled, friendly. Then Anna heard herself requesting a lift.

They sped along a small road that followed a curling river. Silver birches shimmered high above white cows, and higher still white clouds feathered the sky. What am I doing? Anna thought, just once.

The auberge was the sort of place she had been hoping to find ever since landing in France. In her mind a fuchsia auberge (baskets of flowers hanging round the terrace) represented warmth, peace, an hour or two to herself. Michael and the boys, of course, were not interested in such things. Convenience for the sights was all they cared about. Station hotels. But she was alone now. She could do as she liked. Anna quickly decided the place was much too agreeable to leave within the hour. Besides, there was no transport. She booked in for the night.

Her room had blue-striped walls, curtains dizzy with flowers, a freckled mirror in a heavy frame. The window looked on to a narrow garden of apple trees and lupins. A grey cat, ears laid back, snaked across the grass and jumped up on to a wall. Small gusts of windy rain, splattering against the window, were the only cracks in the silence.

So this is freedom, Anna thought, and put out her hand to touch it: the silky bed cover, the cold brass of the bedstead. She climbed under the eiderdown and with no feelings of disloyalty reflected what a relief it was to be in a *silent* bed: no Michael beside her rumbling on about tomorrow's plans or today's churches. Then she fell asleep.

It was almost dark when she woke. Away from the family for

four hours . . . Guilt brushed her lightly. Much stronger was a kind of nefarious excitement, a feeling of adventure. The word caused her to smile to herself with a touch of scorn. If an afternoon's sleep in a French auberge was an adventure, how dull was the rest of her life?

Downstairs in the salon – open fire, smell of lavender – the guilt vanished altogether. Half a dozen couples – here for the fishing, she supposed – all seemed to be drinking champagne. The place reminded her of a small hotel in Galway where she and Michael had spent a last holiday alone before the children were born. They would sit on the bank of the river all day, Michael tweaking at his rod, she reading *War and Peace*. After a dinner of grilled fish they would play Scrabble by the fire, and have a glass of Irish whiskey before bed. That had been a good holiday, long ago.

Michael, these days, hated spending money on frivolous drinks. In private defiance, Anna ordered herself a glass of champagne. Careless of her light head, she chose a seat and drank fast. Then, rising cautiously, she went to the telephone and rang the hotel in Angers.

Michael and the boys were out.

'*Sortis pour le dîner,*' the receptionist said.

Anna was silenced for a moment. Loyalty and compassion had forced her to make this call. She had imagined them worried, searching.

'Were they looking for me?' she asked at once.

'*Absolument pas.*'

'Please say I'll be back tomorrow.'

Returning to the bar, annoyed by her burning cheeks, Anna found a full glass of champagne on her table. Puzzled, she caught the eye of a man she had noticed before. He sat alone.

'*Je vous en prie, Madame,*' he said quietly, and lowered his head into his newspaper before Anna, in her confusion, could thank him.

Her hand now trembled on the glass. The extraordinary gesture had blasted all thoughts of her family from her mind. She felt the warmth of vanity. Her profile, she remembered, had always been good. Perhaps the remnants of other attractions were still recognisable. After a while she allowed herself to glance at the sender of the champagne. Nice face, hair drooping endearingly over one eye.

Suddenly, the way things were going became marvellously clear to her. She thanked God for the double bed, though how would she manage without a dressing-gown? The man raised his eyes.

They looked at each other searingly, recognising their mutual intent. Anna got up, left the salon. She would go straight to her room, rip off her clothes and let the stranger begin.

Somehow she found herself guided by the friendly proprietor to the dining-room. A candle burned on her corner table, a vase of blue lupins made pearly shadows on the white cloth. She ordered dinner. Passion would have to be postponed for an hour or so. Soon the man would follow, make his next move.

As she sipped at the stranger's champagne, Anna found herself wondering at her cold-blooded lack of guilt as she contemplated imminent infidelity. After twenty-three years of absolute faithfulness, here she was suddenly confronted by the prospect of adultery, determined to break every rule she had ever lived by, to behave like a whore. She shivered, enthralled at the thought.

She was halfway through her wild duck when the man eventually entered the dining-room accompanied by a girl of about twelve – plainly his daughter. He gave Anna a brief smile full of purpose, then sat with his back to her and started a conversation with the child. Pity, considering the scarcity of time, Anna thought. But there was also something luxurious about *not* being able to have dinner with him.

By ten o'clock she was naked in bed, waiting. The sound of voices and the banging of cooking pots came from downstairs.

Two hours went by. Footsteps creaked outside her room. Doors shut. Silence.

Tense with anticipation, Anna found herself wondering if just one night with a stranger would do anything to jeopardise twenty-three solid years of marriage. Might the placing of one foot on the slippery slope mean a general descent? Would it whet a long-dormant appetite, underline her discontent? It was hard to judge in advance. The self is so surprising. Maybe, from now on, she would break out in all sorts of directions. Maybe she would start to acknowledge the looks that Jack, Michael's oldest friend, had been giving her for years. Maybe she would become impervious to the boys' lack of consideration and, with other things on her mind, be irritated by them no longer. Maybe she would spend some money on herself, for once: resuscitate her rusty smile . . . cut and redden her hair, go off to London on Michael's nights out at the Round Table, the Parish Council, the Rock Gardeners' Club, and the Regiment's endless reunions . . .

The silence continued. Anna lay awake all night. The man did not come. The cold she felt became the cold of foolishness and shame. Desolate, she dressed at dawn, stood for a long time at the window watching a hard sun rise over the lupins. Escape had been quite spoiled by her own stupidity, her own crushed vanity. Also, she must now query her own judgement. How could she have been so wrong about the man's intentions?

By eight, she was downstairs settling the bill. Through stinging eyes, she observed a mistake. She had been charged for two glasses of champagne.

'A gentleman paid for one,' she explained.

'Apologies,' said the proprietor at once. 'Of course: Monsieur Cadeau. He gave instructions. Whenever he's here he buys everyone in the place a glass of champagne. Good for – how do you say? Public relations.'

Anna felt the blood scour her face.

'Who is Monsieur Cadeau?' she asked.

The proprietor's smile indicated it was not the first time he had had to solve this puzzle.

'He works for a champagne firm,' he said.

A taxi took Anna back to Angers. At the hotel she found Michael and the boys at breakfast. They showed no surprise at her return.

'Had fun?' asked Michael. 'You might have left a proper message. Still, we didn't worry. We knew you wouldn't do anything silly.'

The boys, engrossed in guidebooks, asked no questions.

'Delange is the plan for today,' Michael went on. 'Looks like an interesting church.' He turned almost contrite eyes to his wife. 'I see it has a pretentious auberge, your sort of thing. Would you like—?'

'Oh no,' said Anna quickly. 'I went there. You wouldn't like it at all.'

From a long way off, she registered Michael's relief, and her sons' clumsy hands thrashing about among their guidebooks and maps, eager to be off.

'Buck up with your coffee, Mum,' said Simon.

Was there anything more bleak than return from a flight that had failed?

In the car, Michael said, 'Let's take the small road, follow the river.'

I could always try again, thought Anna.

'Did you look at the church?' asked Simon, zipping up his horrible anorak.

'No,' said Anna. 'I didn't go there to see the church.'

Turning her attention to the map, she found the road that led to Monsieur Cadeau of the champagne firm.

'On our way then,' said Michael.

But I don't suppose I will, thought Anna.

En famille once more, the McGulls then set off for the ninth day of their sightseeing tour of France.

Mother of the Bride

After much deliberation Mrs Hetherington decided against taking any tranquillisers. Better, she thought, to witness the whole thing with a clear mind than through an unreal calm induced by pills. If a tear should come to her eye – why, that was the prerogative of every bride's mother. Few people would see and those who did might understand.

When she had taken her decision Mrs Hetherington had not envisaged the strength of emotion that would affect her on the Big Day. So it was with some surprise, here and now in the church, the journey up the aisle having been accomplished with dignity on the arm of her brother John, that she felt frills of sweat at the back of her knees. And her hands, stuffed into navy gloves one size too small, trembled in disconcerting fashion.

She had chosen to wear navy with the thought that it was the most appropriate colour for her particular role at the wedding.

Nobody could accuse her of trying to steal the bride's thunder –
as did so many mothers, perhaps unconsciously – and yet, if they
observed her closely, Mrs Hetherington's friends would see that
her clothes conveyed the quiet chic she had always managed to
achieve. She had chosen them with care: silk dress, matching coat,
straw hat bearing the only small flourish of which she could be
accused – an old-fashioned rose on its moiré band. On a
November morning of early snow she had taken shelter in
Debenhams and come upon the whole outfit, piece by lucky piece:
even bag, shoes and gloves. In the small changing-room she had
examined her appearance with the sort of critical eye no bride's
mother can afford to be without. How would it all look five
months hence under a blue April sky? Mrs Hetherington would
have liked to have asked Alice's opinion – after all, it was by tradition supposed to be Alice's day – but her daughter was off on a
'holiday' raising funds for overseas famine relief. She was funny
like that, Alice. No interest in appearance – never had had. It had
been all Mrs Hetherington could do to persuade her daughter in
March – cutting it pretty tight – to concentrate on her own wedding dress. No: Alice had never so much as asked her mother
what *she* was going to wear, and in all the flurry of getting ready
it was unlikely she had noticed. Or cared.

Precisely what Alice did care for, Mrs Hetherington was sometimes at a loss to know. As a child she had been straightforward
enough – ordinary, really, except for her freckles. A fondness for
rabbits rather than ponies; some talent at the high jump, which
petered out at puberty; an inclination towards history, which
petered out after 'O' levels; and no traumas that Mrs Hetherington
could recall. Except perhaps for the time Alice had thrown scrambled egg at her father on the last morning of their holiday at
Brancaster, calling him a fuddy-duddy (and worse) for not allowing her to stay at the village disco later than midnight. But that had
been an exceptional time, and David had made his point clumsily,
Mrs Hetherington had to agree. She put the incident down to

teenage wilfulness and considered herself lucky she had such a comparatively easy offspring.

It was only when she thought about it later that it occurred to her that Alice's 'distance', as she called it, dated from that holiday. This 'distance' itself was so hard to define that Mrs Hetherington refrained from mentioning it even to David, lest he should consider her ridiculous. But to Mrs Hetherington, who could never be accused of insensitivity, the widening gap between their daughter and her parents seemed noticeably to develop. It wasn't that Alice changed in any outward way: she remained the polite, willing, quiet creature she had always been, dutiful to her parents and apparently content to come home most weekends. But of her weekday life in London Mrs Hetherington was aware she knew nothing beyond the facts: Alice had a research job in television – exactly what that meant Mrs Hetherington had always been a little unclear and never remembered, somehow, to ask. She shared a flat with an old schoolfriend in Shepherd's Bush: not a very salubrious part of London, but still. What she got up to in the evenings Mrs Hetherington had no idea, though several times when she had rung after nine at night Alice had been in, giving rise to the comfortable thought that at least her daughter spent many evenings at home watching television. Once, when Mrs Hetherington had conversationally mentioned a demonstration in Trafalgar Square that had been given much attention in the papers, Alice casually remarked that she had been there and it wasn't half as bad as the publicity made out. Well, thought Mrs Hetherington at the time, Alice must have been passing. She had never been a *political* girl, that was for sure. She could happily have bet her bottom dollar Alice would have no interest in the terrible carryings-on of the National Front, or those dreadful Militants.

As for men in her daughter's life – Mrs Hetherington's speculations flailed about in a total void. No evidence of any kind to go on. Some weekends Alice would stare into the distance, sandy eyelashes (from David) fluttering thoughtfully, and make a point of answering the telephone first. When the call was for her she would speak in a low, unrecognisable voice: hard to hear from the other side of the door where Mrs Hetherington would hover – not out of curiosity, of course, but from natural anxiety about what was going on. If Alice had any boyfriends she never brought them home. Mrs Hetherington could not understand why. She had always made it clear she was eager to entertain any of Alice's friends. 'Do bring whoever you like to stay, darling,' she would say every Sunday evening Alice was at home. But Alice would always reply she preferred her weekends alone.

Then, out of the blue, no warning, there had been the event of Alastair. Mrs Hetherington would never forget it. Glancing at the stained-glass windows above the altar, whose unkind colours recharged the tears in her eyes, she remembered the occasion once again. Alice had not acted in the most thoughtful way, it had to be admitted. Not a warning telephone call, even. Just, that Friday evening, arriving with him.

'Thought you wouldn't mind, Mum,' she said, 'if I brought Alastair Mead. We're going to get married.'

David, bless him, had taken it very well. Fetched the last bottle of Krug from the cellar and was talking easily to Mr Mead, about mortgages, within moments. (Mr Mead, it seemed, was something to do with mortgages 'for the bread and butter', Alice said. In his spare time, his real vocation, he raised money for famine relief.) Their conversation gave Mrs Hetherington time to study her future son-in-law: she saw a shortish, chunky figure, head slightly too big for his body, the loose smile of lips not quite in control, falling socks. She sipped rapidly at her drink to conceal her disappointment. In her heart of hearts she had always hoped her son-in-law would cut something of a dash: the brutal truth about Mr Mead was that he would not turn a head in the most plebeian crowd. Still, he had been to Charterhouse, as he let drop with his second glass of champagne, and perhaps his charm lay in his mind. He must be given a fair chance, Mrs Hetherington told herself, and in time Alice might wean him off tweed ties. Dreadful to be so prejudiced by appearances, but Mrs Hetherington had always been like that. It was unfair that a stranger's cast of nose or choice of shoe could breed in her such instant prejudice, but there it was. Suddenly Mrs Hetherington knew that she hated Alastair Mead, both for himself and for his proprietory talk about Alice. But she smiled bravely, and no one could have guessed her feelings.

Next morning the two of them appeared at breakfast blatantly haggard. Well, Mrs Hetherington and David had done a bit of passage-creeping in their time, but at least they had had the decency to disguise the effects of their naive kisses next morning. With a shudder Mrs Hetherington handed Alastair a kipper. He should have known better than to lay hands on Alice the first night under her parents' roof. Also, he had cut himself shaving and a thread of blood looped down his chin to join a clot of dried toothpaste in the corner of his mouth. All distasteful to her, poor man. In twenty-nine years David had never cut himself shaving: it wasn't necessary. As for Alice, she could have combed her hair, surely, and done something to conceal her satiated state. It wasn't that Mrs Hetherington disapproved of sex before marriage, naturally: everyone did it these days and Alice, she had no doubt, had relinquished her virginity some years ago. But up to now she had had the tact to protect her mother from evidence of her affairs. Would that she had not let matters slip just because she had an engagement ring – and a very minor pearl, at that – on her finger. Mrs Hetherington's thoughts were only interrupted by Alastair's irritating pecking at his kipper, and his boring remembrances of childhood kippers in Scotland, implying criticism of the Macfisheries' pedigree of the present fish. In all, Mrs Hetherington found the whole weekend a trial. She could not deny the probity of Alastair's character, but kept furiously to herself the disappointment at his lack of humour and style. Worst of all, he supported Alice in her desire for a quick register office wedding. But on that point Mrs Hetherington was adamant, unbudgeable. It was to be a white wedding with all the trimmings, for her sake if not for theirs.

The organ played Bach, swelling to greet Mrs Hetherington's present feeling of satisfaction as she reflected on her efforts in the past months. She had tried, and she had triumphed. There was genuine love in her heart, now, for her son-in-law. Even admiration. The way he worked such long hours in his mortgage business and then gave up his weekends to famine relief. His solid principles: only live in the way you can afford (they were to start off in a small rented house in Twickenham) and put work before pleasure. He had planned with touching care a honeymoon trip around Inverness. Mrs Hetherington wouldn't have cared for any such thing herself, of course: she and David had cruised to Panama. However, Alice seemed happy in general. And, in trying to see Alastair through her daughter's eyes, Mrs Hetherington had almost certainly succeeded in discovering his charm – if devotion counts as a charm. She found it hard to forgive his dandruff and his anorak, a particularly nasty blue – but they were unimportant externals, weren't they? It was his character that counted and, by God, by now, she loved that. She really did. The love had been flamed by others' approval: his prospects, his solidity, his charity. But no matter how it had been come by, it was there. The real love of Mrs Hetherington for her son-in-law Alastair Mead.

She glanced at the gold watch embedded in her wrist. Only a minute to go. Very moving, the music, whatever it was. Half an hour ago she had witnessed the poignant sight of Alice struggling into her white satin. She looked – cliché or not – *radiant*. Alastair was a very lucky man. Mrs Hetherington let her eyes fall upon his back view. He had had a haircut, it seemed. And he looked a little taller in his morning suit. Rather endearing, the way he kept nervously whispering to the best man. Of course – and this was a wicked and secret thought – in Mrs Hetherington's

experience of weddings, Etonians undoubtedly made the least
nervous bridegrooms. She'd noticed that over the years. (David,
in the Guards' Chapel, had been wonderfully untrembling, giving
her courage.) But given the less noble training of Charterhouse,
Alastair wasn't doing too badly so far. Straight shoulders, almost
as if he'd been in the army. Mrs Hetherington wished her brother,
who was still in the army, could contain his asthmatic wheezing,
irritating at such a solemn time. Still, the marguerite trees at the
altar had been an inspiration. (Hers.) Oh dear God, where were
they? A minute late and her left shoe was hurting.

She heard the hush that precedes a bride's entrance. With a
supreme effort of will Mrs Hetherington remained facing the
altar. Alastair, weaker, turned. His face was pale, the jowls loosened by trepidation. Dear Alastair. Would he were just a few
inches . . . But all right so long as Alice never wore stilettos. Had
David ordered enough champagne? And Alice's heart: was it
beating like her own? Funny how such disparate thoughts topple
over one another at such moments. What on earth could they be
doing? Darling Alice, such a loving daughter.

Glorious things of Thee are spoken . . .

Ah, they must be on their way at last. Oh my Alice . . . the way
she laughed in the bath so much at two; and how she cried that
time she fell off her bicycle into the shrubbery at four. And all
those things she had made at school: painted fir-cones and potato-
cut calendars. No better presents in the whole world, were there?
Impossible to think of her as a married woman. Oh dear, they
must be halfway up the aisle by now. Well at least Alice wouldn't
be in fearful anticipation of It, as Mrs Hetherington herself had
been. Rather a shame, really, that particular excitement already
over. But it was awful to be thinking of her own daughter in such
terms at all, wasn't it? And here she was at last, misty faced under
her veil. Pity about no posy of gardenias, as Mrs Hetherington
would have liked, but Alice had insisted on the austerity of a
prayer book. Anyway, she was beautiful. Well, almost. David's

handsome bones were a bit strong on a girl, perhaps: it had to be said Alice's face was not one of infinite delicacy. But today it was at its best, all for Alastair Mead.

'Let us pray,' said the vicar.

Navy patent bow dug less into her foot now she was on her knees. Thank God. Thank God for having given her a daughter like Alice. That time she had been so homesick at her finishing school in Paris – oh God forgive me for all my inadequacies as a mother. Darling Alice forgive me too and try to be happy. Try to keep those promises like Daddy and I have done. It may be awfully boring sometimes, but it's worth trying. And don't desert us. Why didn't I put my handkerchief up my sleeve instead of in my bag – it would make too much noise, opening it. Mustn't sniff . . . Come home whenever you want to and bring your friends. And I promise to be a good grandmother. Baby-sit at anytime. Oh you were such an adorable baby, and so good. Mrs Alastair Mead. Well, who on earth would want their daughter to marry a flashy duke? Who'd really want their daughter to be a sudden duchess?

They were in their seats, now, listening to the address. It was a little hard to hear, even here in the front row: something about the importance of putting someone else *first*, for the rest of your life. Very moving. Pity those further back wouldn't be able to hear the message. But then the servants of God were inclined to mumble too humbly. Putting Alastair Mead *first*: what a thought. Who on earth could want . . .? Mrs Hetherington glanced at her husband, firm beside her, slight smile. Dear David: his handsome rugged face, the calm of a good colonel in all crises. Though naturally this wasn't a crisis, was it? But a very happy day.

There was much kissing in-between signing the register. Alastair's cheek was damp with nervous sweat. He smelt of the worst kind of after-shave. Alice glowed at him, brown mascara clotting her eyelashes. No words: what could Mrs Hetherington say? Thank goodness this part of it was nearly over. Called upon to be efficient at the reception, her role would come more easily. It was all this hovering about, second lead to the star, that caused the strain. Stiffly she followed David back to their pew, eyes down, aware of the blur of wedding hats and curious faces. Mean thought: mostly *their* friends. The Meads' side was half empty . . .

Optimistic blast of the organ. Finale. Darling Alice. As she appeared on Alastair's arm Mrs Hetherington briefly shut her eyes to protect the scalding balls. On opening them she felt them lashed with tears in spite of all the self-control. Perhaps she should have taken a pill after all.

Alice smiling, now. Alastair smiling. Stupid flaccid smile of triumph at his catch. For after all, Alice *was* something of a catch. Sparkle of dandruff on his shoulder. Wedding socks no doubt wrinkled. God forgive her, but Mrs Hetherington couldn't love him any more. Her first instincts had been right. Nothing could alter the fact that he was a humourless dreary prig: there was not a single thing about him over which she could rejoice.

Still, sons-in-law are sent to try us, and she would battle on. She stepped into the aisle, let Alastair's dreadful father, pink-eyed, take her arm. She gave a wonderful smile to the congregation at large, acknowledging the happiness of the day. And with eyes never leaving the distant white cloud that was her beloved daughter, refusing to limp in spite of the agony of her shoe, she made the kind of irreproachable journey down the aisle which can only cause the wedding guests to observe: what a perfect mother of the bride.

Donkey Business

The first day of the season, the donkeys were always hesitant. Ears pricked high, remembering the way, they walked close to the pavement, re-accustoming themselves to the sound of the traffic. Their nervousness would be gone within the week. For the moment, Jo, at the back of the line with his ash stick, encouraged them.

'Along there, Pat! Lulu, Oliver, Fancy, Skip. As for *you*, young Hasty!'

He brought the stick lightly down on Hasty's grey haunches. She was a good-tempered beast, but slow. Nothing could hurry her, or excite her. A bit like Jo's mother, in many ways, and Jo, who was a patient man, was fond of them both.

The only one to whom Jo gave no commands was Storm. A small, brown donkey, Storm was a natural leader: an animal of exceptional intelligence. As Jo often said, Storm could *think*. His instincts were always right. There was that time a silly woman insisted her screaming infant should have a ride. She put him on Storm's saddle. The child sobbed. Storm refused to budge. He listened unmoving to the noise for a while, then lay down on the sand. The child was able to dismount, and ran away gratefully. Jo would never forget that occasion. It was one of the many times Storm had shown wisdom and kindness.

He led the way, now, down the concrete slope to the sands. There, hooves sinking into the soft stuff for the first time in six months, he gave a small bray of pleasure, and broke into a trot. The others followed, eagerly. Jo ran behind them, the wind keen about his ears. When they reached the hard sand, washed by an early tide, the donkeys' hooves made a gentle puttering sound that Jo often remembered, but could never quite recapture, during the long winter months that he spent in the stables polishing the tack.

At an invisible point on the sand, precisely the right place, Storm came to a halt, turned his body parallel to the sea, and looked towards the far-off cliffs that edged the bay. The other donkeys copied. Unused to the spurt of exercise, their breath came bulbous from their grey muzzles, and they sniffed the raw smells of salt and seaweed in the air. They were all pleased to be back, Jo reckoned. Like him, they felt this was the life, down here on the beach.

Jo tucked his stick under his arm, put his hands in his large duffel pockets. Legs slung apart, he looked about the wide familiar territory of beach, sea, cliff, sky. The tide was far out. It had left a stubble of white foam drying on the ribbed sand. There was a whitish, cloudless sky that made the tracery of shadows very pale between the shallow mouldings of the beach. The coast, Jo liked to think, was gathering together its brighter colours to splash out in the summer months. Meantime, everything was nice and Aprilish – easy on the eyes.

It was too early in the year for anything but the rare customer.

The crowds began mid-May, depending on the weather, but Jo didn't care. He liked it best when he had the beach to himself — just he and the donkeys. Then, he felt, privately, it was all theirs.

Jo had spent much of his thirty-two years on this beach with the donkeys. He knew no other life, desired no other life. His father had come from a long line of distinguished donkey breeders. He had died three years ago from a heart attack, while helping Lulu give birth to a stillborn foal. His mother, the daughter of a Punch and Judy man, had had hopes of being an actress. She settled, instead, for the chance to be Judy to her father's notorious Punch. From the dusky canvas box beneath the puppets' stage, she sent up a cacophony of Judy voices that soon became quite famous. Jo's father, as a young man in the audience, fell in love with the funny, raucous voices. He enticed the real Judy from the tent with the offer of free donkey rides, and married her at seventeen. They never left the northern resort where they met, and from his youngest days Jo remembered views of the bay from a donkey's back, two pricked ears spiking the huge blue sky.

Now that her husband was dead, Jo's mother over-worked herself in the small tobacconist's shop they had bought some years ago, to help pay the increasing bills for donkey food and bedding. For his part, Jo saw to the old stables that his father had built round the yard behind the shop. He spent every winter patching the roof, creosoting the weatherboarding, struggling to keep the rot at bay. But in his heart Jo knew that one day he would have to give up, and pull the buildings down. Their state of dilapidation was a great worry. But, away from them, on the beach, he could forget them.

He could forget everything, here, wind blowing a veil of sand on to his boots. It was hard to remember, even, what the skyline of the old town looked like before they built tall concrete hotels between the pretty Edwardian houses that used to have the front to themselves. Still, Jo was all for some change. So many people had come to the place last summer, attracted by the new holiday camp, the glassed-in swimming pool and the famous television comedian twice-nightly on the pier, that Jo's donkeys had made enough money to ease the winter months of no employment. Should be the same again this year. The long-range weather forecast had predicted a fair summer and, no matter what the state of their finances, parents could never resist donkey rides for the children.

Jo's reflections, practical rather than ambitious, were interrupted by a gentle bray from Storm. Most observant of donkeys, he had seen, before Jo, a figure in the distance. Jo screwed up his eyes. Seemed to be a woman: long skirts under a thick coat. Yes: definitely a woman. A small child walked at her side, holding her hand. Jo felt a fluttering of nervousness, as he always did with his first customer of the year. For she surely *was* a customer: she was approaching fast, now, eyes determinedly on the row of vacant donkeys.

Soon Jo saw her quite clearly: long hair billowing out to one side in the wind, bony face webbed with faint lines, surprisingly young grey eyes, pinkish cheeks but pale lips. A gypsy, most likely, Jo thought. It was too early for tourists, and local mothers never came down in the mornings.

She came right up to him, rather bold. The child clung to her dark skirts, burying its head in her side.

'How much?' she asked.

The question left Jo speechless. He had thought there would be several days in which to determine his rate for the year. He had intended to think about the matter at leisure, fixing on a fair price which, while keeping pace with inflation, would not be so high as to restrict his customers' enjoyment. But he was blowed if he knew, at this moment, what that price should be. Eventually, fearing that the lady might grow impatient, he said, 'Off-season rates, definitely.'

The lady nodded, smiling slightly, as if she didn't care at all what the off-season rates amounted to. She patted Storm – they always patted Storm first – running a long white hand through the shaggy winter growth of his coat to where, Jo knew, she could feel the warm and softer fur beneath. The hand, curving through Storm's mane and down his shoulder, put Jo in mind of a fish: it was a graceful thing, somehow: gentle and slithery all at once. Not at all like the normal clumsy pat.

'You look like a bit of an expert,' he said.

'Oh, I'm used to animals, all right,' she answered. 'Can we take this one?'

Jo nodded. He knew she was the kind who'd like to lead Storm herself – not that Storm needed any leading. She swung the child on to the saddle with one skilful movement. Jo could see now it was a boy: curly flaxen hair, happy slanting eyes, huge grin.

'Mind if we just go to the farthest breakwater and back?'

The lady spoke so quietly Jo could hardly hear her words in the wind. 'Course he didn't mind. Delighted, he said to himself, to find such early custom. My pleasure, madam, he said to himself, because it would not be in his nature to say any such thing out loud.

It was his pleasure to watch the lady walk away in step with Storm, one hand on the donkey's neck. She was definitely no gypsy. Not with that voice, that walk. He watched till they were a tiny shape on the horizon. Then they turned. Slowly, they grew bigger, clearer, till they were life-size. The lady's grey eyes, though sad, looked quite pleased.

'Thank you,' she said, 'we enjoyed that. I'm sorry we've been so long. Must have been a good half-hour.'

It had seemed like minutes to Jo, their journey, but he did not disagree. The lady brought out a pile of coins from her pocket. She handed Jo a pound. He stepped back, shocked.

'It's nowhere like a pound, especially off-season,' he said.

But she insisted. 'Go on. You've had a long winter, and I've got plenty of money – that's one thing I have got. Please take it.'

Having no idea how to argue with women, Jo took the money. He watched the lady lift her child from Storm's back. The boy's smile faded, on the ground, but he made no sound of protest.

'Goodbye, then,' said the lady, and, taking her child's hand, she turned away.

To Jo's surprise, she came again at the same time next day. The child made straight for Storm, and they went for the same long ride. While they were away, Jo determined to make some conversation on their return. His mother had taught him always to be polite to women and, out here, no one listening, it was easier to put away the shyness that gripped him, stealing his words, that came in crowded indoor places.

So when they returned, Jo put a hand on Skip's saddle to steady himself, and said, 'You come from round these parts, then?'

The lady seemed to hesitate, rubbing at the fur between Storm's ears.

'No,' she said at last. 'I just have to be here for a while. And you?' She smiled at him politely.

'Me? I'm here always. I live here the whole year round.'

The lady swung the child down from the saddle, perhaps no longer interested. Where to go from here? Jo knew she would be off in a moment, if he didn't think of something.

'My name's Jo,' he said.

'Mine's Ida.' She was feeling in a pocket for the money.

'I live with my mother above the old tobacconist's by the church. We sell mostly souvenirs, now, what with the price of cigarettes. Ices in the summer . . .' He trailed off, confused by his own rush of words. Then added, '. . . and postcards.'

In the silence that followed, Ida gave him the most beautiful smile Jo had ever witnessed from any human creature, making him oblivious to the boniness of her face, only aware of the pretty puckering of skin round mouth and eyes. Wonderfully unnerved, he kneaded Skip's mane with his free hand.

'What you ought to do,' she said at last, 'is to have postcards made *of the donkeys*. Each one separate. Then everyone who rides them would buy one. You'd make a fortune, I bet.'

The brilliance of her idea rendered Jo quite speechless. He

stood a full minute in silent wonder at his luck in meeting anyone so inspired.

'That's a grand idea,' he said at last. 'Thanks.'

Ida shrugged. 'Oh, I'm always full of ideas. Usually, people don't do anything about them.'

Then, before Jo could protest, she slipped a pound into his lunch bag on Hasty's saddle, and hurried off.

Ida and her child came back every day after that: Jo lost count of how many days they came. He began to look forward to seeing her every morning and dreaded the day she might not turn up. But she was always punctual, never put off by rain or a cold wind. Sometimes, Jo would leave the rest of the donkeys and accompany her and the child — her son, David, he learned — as far as the breakwater and back. They didn't talk much on these occasions: Jo had no wish to appear inquisitive, and Ida was not one to offer up much information of her own accord.

Then one day — it must have been late May — Ida asked him if she could bring David to see the donkeys in their stables. Jo agreed at once, but the idea of her visit put him in a state of some agitation. He had never mentioned Ida to his mother, not knowing quite what to say. Once, he had been about to confide to her that this was the best spring he could ever remember, no particular reason — then he had thought better of the idea, and kept his silence.

Ida and David came to the stables early one evening. Jo's mother was out, so there was no fear of her discovering the visitors. Away from the wide spaces of the beach, Ida seemed to Jo taller, and nervous. He himself was in much the same state. Having come home early to give the yard a special clean, he was aware he smelt strongly of manure. But Ida did not seem to notice. She went from stall to stall with the child, stroking each donkey's muzzle, murmuring things Jo could not hear. When they reached Storm, the child flung its arms about the animal's shoulders.

'He's grown very fond of them,' said Ida.

Jo thought there was sadness in her voice, as if her son's affection could somehow be destroyed.

'Still, there's a while yet. Thank you for letting us come.'

She fetched the child and hurried off, as if fearful of being late for someone or something. When she had gone, the yard seemed empty as it had never been before, and Jo longed for the safety of the next morning on the beach, and all the comfort of their more familiar meetings.

Just a week later, long after dark, Jo was in the stables cleaning bridles by the light of his father's old oil lamp. He could not hope to improve the shine on the soft, gleaming leather which he polished every day. But it was something to take up the restlessness of his hands: he felt very awake, a little uneasy.

He looked up, saw Ida standing in the door. He had heard no footsteps in the yard. She was by herself, wearing a long grey cloak. With no child at her side, she seemed strangely alone.

'Sorry to disturb you,' she said, 'but we suddenly have to go tomorrow. I wouldn't have been able to come down to the beach, so I've come to say goodbye.'

The reins in Jo's hands turned to ice. He put down the bridle.

'Come on in, won't you?' he heard himself saying.

'I can't stay more than a moment.'

All the same, she moved nearer Jo. The flat light from the lamp illuminated silvery marks of dry salt beneath her eyes, reminding Jo of the crusts of waves left on the beach by a strong tide. So close, Ida smelt like the interior of the warm flower shop on the front where he went on Mothers' Day. Standing there, she blotted out the stables' own smells of manure and hay. Jo wanted to put his hand on her arm, just touch her for a moment, more than anything he'd ever wanted in his life.

'One thing, can I ask you?' she was saying. 'It's David. He's grown so fond of the donkeys. Storm particularly. I wonder if you'd let me buy him? We'd be a good home. I'd pay you anything, anything.'

She sounded quietly desperate. Jo scratched his head. The desire to touch her had not diminished in all the confusion caused by her question.

'It wouldn't be a matter of money,' he said, to give himself time.

'I could send a trailer for him tomorrow morning.' She sounded oddly practical.

Jo stared at her. He thought of her small silent son David – his unhappiness without Storm. He thought of his own future without Storm. Well, he could always train one of the others to lead, he supposed. And somewhere in the jumble of conflicting feelings, Jo realised that if Ida owned Storm she would have a reminder, perhaps, of their days on the beach.

'That'd be all right, then,' he said at last. 'I'd like young David to have him.'

They made arrangements for transport. Jo refused any money. When he finally managed to persuade Ida that to give her the donkey would be his pleasure, she turned to go. Raising her fish-like hand to her mouth, she blew him a kiss in the semi-darkness. Then the fingers flew away in an arc, and disappeared beneath her cloak. Jo could think of nothing to say, and in silence watched her leave.

Some time later, when he had finished the bridle, he went to Storm's stable. The animal made a small welcoming noise. Jo remembered the night of his birth: a wicked night, thunder, lightning, rain through the roof, the lot. Now, running his hand down the black line of Storm's spine, came disquieting thoughts of the emptiness of tomorrow. But soon, because he had an orderly mind in which optimism swiftly followed upon melancholy, he began to imagine the summer ahead: the record crowds, the happy children, the sounds of sea and laughter – all the pleasures that Jo had learned come every year in the donkey business.

Sudden Dancer

'There's not much point, far as I can see,' said Joan Cake, 'keeping on going to these things. With someone who can't dance, that is.'

'You enjoy yourself,' said Henry.

'I'd enjoy myself more if I could dance with my husband.'

'You enjoy the outings.'

'It's not the same.'

'I couldn't get my feet to dance, no matter what.' Henry sighed.

He and Joan sat together on the late bus home, their bodies rolling slightly, used to the journey. They were splattered with rain. From the hem and neck of Joan's mackintosh sprouted frills of pink net. Her hair, piled up in meringue-like curls, was covered with a transparent plastic hat. Her mouth was down.

'I don't like to remind you,' she said with a small sniff, 'but when you've been champion at something, once, you don't like to have to retire before you're ready. You don't like to have retirement forced upon you.'

'You dance with plenty of others,' pointed out her husband. 'You're never wanting for partners.'

He took her arm, as the bus drew up at the stop. He liked to think the descent from the bus might deflect her train of thought.

'Not the same as having someone you can always rely on,' retorted Joan, stepping recklessly into a puddle and soaking the toes that pudged through the straps of her golden sandals. 'The last waltz, this evening. There was no one to do the last waltz with me, was there?'

'I knew that's what was getting you down.' Henry was sympathetic. 'Still, you had a lovely foxtrot, just before, you said.'

Home, glittering mackintoshes hung side by side in the narrow hall, Joan smoothed the skirt of her bulbous pink dress.

'Only three months till the Christmas Ball,' she said. 'That should be a big do, if it's anything like last year.'

'Certain to be,' agreed Henry, dread in his heart.

Joan straightened herself, punching the rhinestones on her bosom.

'If we never went to another dance, it wouldn't make a mite of a difference to you,' she shouted. 'I shall have to think about a new dress.' She knew the last suggestion, at least, would provoke her mild husband: he hated the very idea of anything new in the way of dresses.

'That one's very nice,' he said, sadly scanning the mass of pink. 'It's always been my favourite.'

'Huh! Not for a Christmas party.'

She paused, suddenly feeling all the despair of being wasted: all afternoon setting her hair, ironing her dress, doing her face, and for what? For a disappointing evening dancing with dull old men, and now this late-night confrontation with a husband who did not know the meaning of the word appreciation.

'I wish you could *try*,' she said.

Henry coughed. He longed to go to bed. After a dance, this was always a long ordeal, what with the ungluing of the false eyelashes, and the stuffing of tissue paper between each layer of the pink net. He tried to be patient.

'There are some things a person can't bring himself to do,' he said. 'But I do try in other ways, don't I? To make up?'

Joan laughed nastily.

'Lots of things you think I want. Bringing in the coal – I'd bring in the coal. Beating the doormat – I'd beat the doormat. Clearing out the bird – I'd . . . None of the things I really want. All I want is just the one thing. I'll put the kettle on.' She turned and stomped off down the passage to the kitchen.

Confused by the outburst, Henry followed Joan, watched from the door while she slammed mugs down on the table. The rhinestones on her bodice glittered at him like a swarm of angry red eyes, as she pirouetted to the fridge for milk and foxtrotted towards the sugar.

'One day, perhaps, you'll give some serious thought to what I'm saying.'

'Oh, I will,' said Henry, and the great mercy was that as his wife cha-cha'd towards the kettle, an idea came to him.

On the walls of the studio Fred Astaire danced with Ginger Rogers: huge, blown-up photographs, a little muzzy, for the cameras of those days were not quite up to the speed of their twirling. Henry stood in the middle of the bare floor marvelling at the sight of them. His hand closed more tightly on the small paper bag that held his lunch. He listened to the thirties music that oozed from a small grille high up in one of the walls. He half-closed his eyes, felt himself spinning as fluently as Fred Astaire . . . Wonderful. Joan, light in his arms, smiling up at him.

When Henry looked down, eyes fully open, he saw he had raised one leg, slightly, but had not moved an inch. Fearful that he should be caught in so foolish a position in the middle of the floor, he hastened to a chair at the side of the room and took out his sandwich. A moment later Madame Lucille entered. Madame Lucille was well into her sixties, but you could see at once she had been a famous dancer in her time. Her bouncy walk set the muscles of her calves twinkling up and down.

She made an impressive entrance for Henry alone, coming right up to him before she spoke. She had white-blonde hair and powdered wrinkles. Her multicoloured dress clung everywhere.

'Mr Cake?'

'That's right.'

'I'm sorry to have kept you waiting, Mr Cake.'

'No trouble.'

Madame Lucille's eyes jumped with great disdain to Henry's sandwich.

'Have you come here for your *lunch*, Mr Cake? Or to learn how to dance?'

'Oh, I'm so sorry. You see, it's my lunch hour. I thought a quick bite . . .'

'I'm afraid we cannot entertain eating and drinking in the studios, Mr Cake, though I'll close my eyes to it this once.'

'Thank you.'

He slid the sandwich into the pocket of his mackintosh, and laid the mackintosh on the chair.

'You'll have to make your appointments after work. On your way home. I'm open till seven.'

'I'm not sure I could work that in—'

'It's up to you. Now, shall we begin?'

Madame Lucille offered Mr Cake her hand, led him into the centre of the studio.

'What stage is it you're at, Mr Cake? As a dancer?'

'Oh, quite a beginner, I should say.'

'Then we shall start at the beginning.'

Henry felt a freezing sensation in his legs. The flesh of his hand that Madame Lucille clasped in her warm little fingers had turned entirely to bone. Anything to put off the moment when she would urge him to move . . .

'But my wife, she's a champion,' he said. 'She won cups all over the Midlands before we married.'

'My. Did she?'

'That's the trouble, really, with her being the champion. I didn't think it would be, but it turned out to be.'

'So you're here secretly – a few lessons – to surprise her?'

'How did you know?'

Madame Lucille smiled. 'Thirty years of secret plotting husbands, Mr Cake. I can tell the look in their eyes. I'm the heroine of many confidences. I've sent so many on their waltzing way, happy. Thirty years.'

'Oh.' Henry inwardly marvelled, already happier at the prospect that he might be added to her list of successes.

'Right. So, let's get down to it, shall we? We begin like this. By relaxing.' Her fingers loosened a little on his hand. 'What I'm going to do is to ask you to shut your eyes, to hold up your head, as if you were sniffing something nice, like spring in the air, and then let yourself feel the blood flowing right down through your body and into your feet.'

And just how does blood flow through bone, Henry wondered. He watched as Madame Lucille, close beside him, shut her eyes and sniffed. She seemed to be all puffed up, somehow, in a way that he could not imagine he would be able to imitate. She opened her eyes and looked at his feet. He felt his toes wince in the privacy of his shoes.

'So many beginners are frightened of their feet, Mr Cake. The first thing to learn is: they're nothing to be afraid of. You must learn to feel they're a part of you, *at one* with you. Not things you take off, like shoes.'

Madame Lucille had put into words something that Henry had suffered all the years of his marriage to Joan: fear of his feet. Now that the words had been said out loud he gave a small sigh of relief. The merest trace of courage quickened his stiff-boned body. He should have sought Madame Lucille's help years ago . . .

'Now, on with the dance,' she was saying. 'I think we'll start with the waltz.'

'My wife loves a waltz,' said Henry. 'The Blue Danube.'

'That's a fast waltz, Mr Cake. Lesson eight or nine, depending on progress. If you can be just a little bit patient . . .'

She took his hand again, and pointed her toe.

'Still raining?' asked Joan, when Henry arrived home.

'Pouring.'

'I haven't been out, what with my hair.'

She patted the rollers. Henry had never been quite able to accustom himself to the sight of his wife in rollers, but knowing they were necessary to the dazzling pyramid she concocted for nights out, it was a feeling he kept to himself.

'Anything untoward?'

Henry gave a small inward jump. Surely his face betrayed no trace of guilt?

'That's a funny word, for you.'

'I heard it on the radio. It appealed to me. You know I like to adopt new words. You know what I am for extending my vocabulary.'

Henry laughed.

'I love your sense of self-education,' he said.

'It's you who should have more sense of self-education. In some areas, I mean. The arts. Who cares about *gas*?' All their married life, Joan had scorned Henry's job with the Gas Board. 'There are some things any man who calls himself a man should know how to do.'

Henry sighed. 'Come on, Joan.'

'I've pressed your suit,' she said, lips pursed.

'What for?'

'Tonight.'

'What's happening tonight?'

'The do up at the Winter Gardens. Live band.'

'But I thought there was nothing else on this week?'

'Maybe it slipped my mind to tell you.' She paused. 'I could always go on my own, of course, if you didn't fancy coming.'

'Don't be daft,' Henry snorted. She had never made such an outrageous suggestion before in her life.

'I dare say I'd be all right. I wouldn't mind.'

'Well, I would. Letting my wife out alone at a glittering function.'

'My age, I don't suppose I'd be fighting off the rapists.' She watched her husband stiffen. 'It's all over by midnight.'

'There's no question of it.'

'It's quite inhibiting, sometimes, knowing you're there all the evening just watching.'

'But I don't watch with disapproval, do I? I'm happy to see you enjoying yourself. You know that.'

'You're always watching. I can feel your eyes right through my back.'

'I'm sorry. There's not much else I can do. Not much I have in common with dancing people . . . They all go there just to dance.' Something in his voice diverted Joan's attack.

'I'll take the entrance money out of the housekeeping if you like,' she said.

'Don't be ridiculous, love,' said Henry. 'I have the money.'

Some hours later Joan came downstairs in a foaming mass of lime tulle.

'You must be mad, thinking I'd let you out alone looking like that,' said Henry. Joan flipped his cheek with her lime glove.

'Sometimes, you know, I dream you're Henry Cake Astaire. Off we go, and when we get there you whirl me round all evening, keeping up the compliments in my ear!'

'Ah,' replied Henry, the bony feeling stiffening his limbs again. 'I've filled the log basket, laid the breakfast.'

In Joan's eyes he saw a sneer that pierced his heart.

'Come on, Fred,' she said.

To Henry, one dancehall was much like another. Each glittering function, as he had learned to call it, was identical in its crowd of elderly, overdressed dancers dizzying their way about the floor to the old tunes of a tired band. He failed to see the glamour that enchanted his wife. Her eyes, as usual on arrival, swept about the place with an anticipation out of all proportion to the occasion, so thought Henry, privately. He suggested a drink.

'I haven't come here to drink,' snapped Joan.

'No need to look so frantic,' returned Henry.

Two nights out running and he found his normal reserves of understanding severely tried.

'I'm not looking frantic! And I wish you'd sit *down* somewhere, Henry. Nowhere near the dance floor.'

Her eyes swerved from her husband to a middle-aged man with crinkly hair who was approaching.

'What did I tell you?' said Henry. 'Here's Romeo.'

'May I have the pleasure?' the man asked Joan, for all the world as if Henry did not exist.

'Why, Jock,' smiled Joan warmly, 'I do believe we meet again.'

Henry watched them glide away, merge with the dancers, sway easily together, their feet in perfect harmony. He watched the crinkle-haired man, Jock, look down on his wife's careful curls, and smile. He remembered Madame Lucille's words at the end of that first, difficult lesson. He was plainly not a born dancer, she said. But with a lot of practice, maybe . . .

Henry took her advice and changed to longer lessons after work. At first, his progress was definitely slow. But in the fifth week he felt for the first time some small sense of achievement, when Madame Lucille accorded him her first praise.

'There's really a breakthrough, this evening, Mr Cake,' she said. 'We're really getting somewhere, now, don't you feel?'

'If you say so.'

'How about one more turn?' She fluttered her lashes.

'No. Really. I must be getting back. My wife'll be wondering.'

'Of course. Well, there's Thursday to look forward to, isn't there? I thought we might try a quickstep, Thursday. I think we should try to race ahead a little if you're going to be ready for the Christmas Ball.'

The Christmas Ball. Just seven weeks to go, the evening Henry had planned for his surprise. He hurried home, noticing with alarm the time. It went so quickly, dancing.

He arrived almost an hour late, somewhat flustered. At first, it didn't seem as if Joan had noticed.

'Do you know what a sissoo is?' she asked.

'No. Why? Should I?' He wondered if it was a guilty man.

'It's a valuable Indian timber tree.'

'Is it really? That's most interesting.'

Joan dug a fierce needle into a froth of chiffon, a pink that hurt Henry's eyes.

'I learned that today. Some magazine. I like to pick things up.'

'That's good.' Henry sighed. He could see the way things were going.

'I like to try, you see. To extend my accomplishments. Which is more than can be said for some of us.' She paused, took a pin from her mouth, leaned across the table, crushing the silk. 'And why are we so late tonight, Henry Cake?'

Henry glanced at the clock on the wall to give himself time.

'I'm sorry,' he said. 'The traffic. Terrible jams.'

'Forty-five minutes to be precise. Am I to believe there have been traffic jams every Tuesday and Thursday for the last five weeks, Henry?'

'Very curious, I must say –'

'Very curious indeed. Very curious, too, that you're such a bad liar. If you'd been more clever you wouldn't have met her on such regular nights. You'd have jumbled them up –'

'Met who?'

'Whoever she is. I don't know.'

Joan dug her needle more fiercely into the material. Henry heard himself laughing.

'You mean, you think I'm meeting a woman, having an association, just because of a few traffic jams? Oh, Joan. Oh, love. Would I ever? Have I ever looked at another woman?'

'Not as far as I know.' Joan sniffed, almost convinced. 'But it's never too late. All I'm saying is, you've had your head in the clouds these last weeks. Your mind seems to have been elsewhere. That's all I'm saying.'

'You're daft,' said Henry, his heart racing.

'Maybe,' said Joan. 'But I'm not a fool. After all these years, I know when there's something up with you.'

The awkward encounter that evening alerted Henry's sense of urgency. Joan's suspicions, once aroused, would be hard to quell. It was imperative Henry should take extra care in the future, so that he would not be forced to spoil his surprise in self-defence.

For several lessons he made sure he left punctually, despite Madame Lucille's pleading with him to do a few more turns 'on the house', and arrived home in time. Joan made no further mention of his imaginary girlfriend. But then came the evening of the second breakthrough: Henry mastered the reverse turn in the fast waltz. In his excitement, he twirled Madame Lucille round the studio till she was quite out of breath.

'*Beautiful dancing*,' she declared, when eventually he stopped and they stood, with arms about one another still, panting. Henry glanced at the clock. Ten minutes late.

'Madame Lucille, I must *rush*.' He made to leave her, but she clung to him.

'No need to go on calling me *Madame* Lucille, is there, Mr Cake? After so many lessons? After all, all I want is that *your* wife should be happy with your dancing, isn't it – Henry?'

Quite violently, Henry wrenched her hands from his shoulders, and fled the studio. But he was out of luck. His slight lateness did not go unobserved.

'It's which one of us?' asked Joan, in greeting. 'That's what I want to know. Which one of us is it to be? Her, the trollop, or me? It's up to you. The choice is yours. Give one of us satisfaction, stop mucking about with us both. That's all I ask.'

'What's all this?' said Henry.

'Such innocence! The game's up now, that's what. You can't draw wool over my eyes any longer. I know when I've been made a fool of, and I know when the time's come to put a stop to it.'

'Let me explain—'

'You explained last time. The traffic. I almost believed you.'

'It wasn't the traffic this time. But I'm not having an association, I promise.' He looked at her face. 'I have to admit, there are reasons I've been late. But they're reasons that will benefit you in the end. Can you believe that? It's the truth, I promise.'

'Huh, I don't know what to believe, I'm sure.' The edge had gone from her anger. 'There's never been any of this secrecy business before. Double bluff, most likely. Still, if that's how you want it, that's fine with me. Because I've made my decision.' She paused, pursed her lips. Henry dared not ask her the question. 'Nothing lofty, mind,' she said at last. 'Just, things will be a little different. I'll go my way and you'll go yours. I shan't worry any more if you're kept late by traffic jams. You mustn't worry if I join my partner for a cigarette after we've had a dance.'

Henry sighed, nodded silently. With any luck, before all that sort of gallivanting came to anything, it would be the Christmas Ball, his chance, and dancing together happily ever after.

'How long till the Christmas Ball?' he asked.

Joan snorted. 'You can't butter me up like that! I know you're not interested. Three weeks. There's bound to be a lot of Charlestons, always a favourite at Christmas.'

Henry turned away, dejected. He had not reckoned on the Charlestons. Another hurdle . . . More overtime, more difficulties. But he would manage it somehow.

And he did. In three weeks he had mastered the art of the Charleston, much to Madame Lucille's surprise, and his own. His rendering was a little cautious, but foot-perfect. With confidence, Madame Lucille assured him, he would become more flamboyant, twirling his hands and giving little flicks of the head, just as she did.

On the afternoon of the ball, Henry had his last lesson. For the first time in his working life, he had taken an afternoon off. (It was easier to lie to the Gas Board, he discovered, than to his wife.) It was also the last lesson of his course, and he felt quite sad. He had enjoyed the lessons. Judging by Madame Lucille's farewell, the feeling had been mutual.

'Not much potential, Henry, when you started,' she said, 'but you've come on surprisingly. Your wife will never believe her eyes. I wish you luck tonight. You're one of my successes.'

'Well, thank you for everything, Madame Lucille.' His hands were trapped in her small warm fingers. The Charleston still played through the grille.

'There are some pupils, my dear Henry, that stand out in the mind . . . years and years. If ever you want a little course of revision, I'd be only too delighted, on the house . . .' She gave him a peck on the cheek, and they parted.

On his way home Henry had not known the thrill of such anticipation for many years. In fact, he felt quite dizzy, a little peculiar. His legs ached from all the Charlestoning, his heart was thumping. Not wanting Joan to observe anything unusual in his appearance, he decided to slip into the pub at the end of their street, and have a single medicinal brandy. He needed strength, courage, calm.

The pub was crowded, it took a long time to be served. Then Henry drank slowly so that the brandy's effects would be beneficial rather than inebriating. What with one thing and another he found that, to his dismay, it was past seven by the time he left. Still, they weren't due to catch the bus till seven-thirty. Henry hurried down the street, knowing Joan would be fretting, waiting for him to do up her hooks and eyes.

Home, he found the house empty. No sign of Joan. A note on the kitchen table.

I've gone on early, it said. *Please don't follow me, I want to go to this Ball alone. Seeing as how things have been this past few weeks, I'm sure you'll understand. P.S. All the same, don't worry.*

Henry crumpled on to a chair at the table, sunk his head to his hands.

It took him a few moments to make his decision. He changed quickly, ran for the bus, arrived at the dancehall soon after eight. It was already crowded, the ceiling strung with balloons, Christmas trees in the corner. All very pretty, the perfect setting to put his plan into action . . . But the beneficial effects of the brandy had worn off. His heart reverberated all through his body. His courage had quite gone.

Henry soon caught sight of Joan. She was waltzing with the crinkle-haired Jock, laughing. Henry decided to waylay her when the dance was over, and ask her for the next one. But when the music stopped, and she walked with Jock unknowingly towards her husband, something in her face made Henry abandon his plan. He hid behind a pillar, watching as they made their way to the bar.

Henry remained hidden, dodging from pillar to pillar, most of the evening. His eyes scarcely left his wife, dazzling as ever in some new dress of gold sequins. The strange thing was, although she was rarely off the floor, she did not seem to be entertaining her usual amount of partners. In fact, dance after dance, she stuck with Jock. It was no doubt he was a very good dancer, though Henry could see little charm in the red puffiness of his face and the greasy gleam of his crinkled hair. Still, it was the *dance*, not the *man*, that Joan went for, as she always said.

The first Charleston added to Henry's distress. His toes leapt in his shoes – what he would have given to show Joan how he could do it! – while he watched her and Jock, flushed and laughing and winking, as they kicked up their heels. When the music came to an end, Jock took a handkerchief from his pocket. Joan snatched it from him and with a sort of secret smile – or so it looked to Henry from his distant viewpoint – dabbed his sweating neck. Henry could bear no more. He left.

He sat in the silent empty kitchen brooding for many hours. It was almost three when Joan returned. She came bouncing in, humming, snapping on lights, and was none too pleased to see Henry.

'What on earth?' she said. 'There was no need to wait up for me.'

She took off her coat. Henry observed that the expanse of chest above the gold sequins had a bruised, flushed look. And there was something strange about her face – her mouth. It was pale as first thing in the morning. The carefully painted plum red had quite gone. He made no comment, rose from his chair stiffly.

'Lovely dress,' he said. 'Nice evening?'

'Very pleasant, thank you. Someone said they saw you. I said they must have been mistaken.'

'Quite. Got the last bus, did you?'

Joan looked at him. 'No. Missed it. Got a lift.'

'Oh, good. Wouldn't like to think of you so late, walking . . .'

'I was all right, don't worry. I can look after myself. Now I've broken the ice I can do it again. You won't need to come any more. All it needed was to break the ice.'

She pranced over to the stove, began to make tea. The gold sequins twinkled conspiratorially in the harsh electric light. Henry would have done anything on earth to have been able to have seen through their eyes, tonight: to know what she had been doing, just how her evening had passed. He gripped the back of a chair, spoke softly.

'Joanie, if I was to say . . . What if I was to say I could dance?'

Joan laughed. She did not bother to turn round.

'Huh! I'd say that was a good one. I'd say I'd believe *that* when I saw it. After all these years of stubbornness.'

'Well, I'm saying it,' went on Henry. 'I can dance.'

Joan turned to the table with two mugs of tea.

'It was quite easy, breaking the ice, when it came to it,' she said again, as if she had not heard him.

'Would you like me to prove it to you? That what I'm saying is true?'

Joan sat down. 'You do what you like, one way or the other.'

Henry left the room, went to the sitting-room, and put a record on their old gramophone. 'The Very Thought of You.' Back in the kitchen, the sound was very thin.

'There,' said Henry. 'Well, would you care to dance?'

'What's all this?' Joan wrinkled her nose. 'Be a bit silly, here in the kitchen, wouldn't it?'

'If my plans had worked out, and you hadn't wanted to be alone, we would have been dancing together at the Christmas Ball.'

'Likely story! So who's been teaching you to dance?'

'Come on. Give it a try.'

Joan stood, half reluctant, half intrigued. She stood with hands at her side, grasping bunches of sequins on her skirt.

'Not much room in here, is there? —'

'The heater's off in the front room.'

'— For you to show your paces.'

They were suddenly shy of each other.

'You could make allowances,' said Henry. He stepped towards her, nervous. Held her stiff arms. He waited for a bar or two, counting under his breath. Then they began to waltz, moving cautiously round the kitchen table.

'How'm I doing?' he asked after a while.

'Amazing.' Though Joan's feet responded naturally to the rhythm, her voice was flat. 'I would never have believed it.'

Henry laughed, tightening his grip on her golden waist.

'Thought I'd surprise you. I'll tell you all about it, one day. Those traffic jams.' More confident now, he twirled his wife more firmly. 'Dance with anyone special tonight, did you?'

'No. Well, the usuals.'

'Jock included?'

'One or two with him.'

'He's a lovely dancer, Jock. Brought you home, did he?'

'He lives this way,' said Joan.

'The very thought of you,' murmured the singer, making Joan shut her eyes with a small wince of pain that Henry did not see. Then the music changed to a quickstep. Henry was all delight.

'Hey! I can do this too, you know. I can do all sorts.'

But Joan was pulling away from him.

'Come on, Henry. That's enough. Tea's getting cold.'

'Just a minute more. I'm beginning to get the feel of it. Come on, Joanie, be a sport.' She ceased to struggle against him. They moved round the kitchen table once more. 'Tell me, honestly – am I any good as a dancer?'

'You're a lovely dancer.'

In his exuberance, Henry did not notice that Joan's voice was weary, and that her dancing, for all its accuracy, was uninspired, automatic. 'Turns out, though, it isn't just the dancing that counts. Not just the dancing,' she sighed.

Henry, his head pressed excitingly close to her myriad curls, could not be sure what she said.

'What's that?'

'I said you're a lovely dancer, Henry. A lovely dancer.'

'Just think . . . years ahead. What you've always wanted. Me to dance with. How about that?'

With unbounded happiness, Henry twirled even faster,

undaunted by the surprising heaviness of his wife in his arms. He tripped slightly in a reverse turn, but no matter. They both recovered together, Fred Astaire and Ginger Rogers, whirling through timeless space between kitchen table and stove.

'How about that, indeed,' answered Joan, seeing a grey dawn through the window.

Despite this sudden dancing, she was feeling the cold. She hoped to goodness Henry would soon be finished with his quick-stepping, and let her have her cup of tea.

The Bull

The bull had spent a restless night. Through the shallows of her sleep Rachel had heard him snarling and groaning, sometimes angry, sometimes sad. Now at dawn she peered through the curtain of the small window to look at him: he stood knee-high in mud, curly forehead stiffly silvered with frost, furious pink-lashed eyes staring at the cows on the far side of the field. Maddened by the way they ignored him, he roared again, a sound that ended in a high-pitched whine: a sound pathetically thin from so large an animal.

Rachel shivered and got back into bed. She wished Jack was there. But he was away on one of his conference trips, the Canary Isles this time. She had had a postcard saying wonderful sun for the time of year, and too much wine. He always sent her postcards but never said he missed her. Sometimes Rachel wondered how the evenings on such trips were spent. Jack often said they were very boring, endless talking shop at the bar with the boys, and Rachel liked to believe him. But occasionally the nastier part of her imagination activated itself, and she imagined her husband slapping his thigh in delight at strip shows, or flirting with a passing air hostess. She never, of course, spoke of her suspicions: they only came to her because her days were too empty. In their idyllic cottage, a mile from the nearest village, there was little for her to do: no defences with which to keep lurid thoughts from an empty mind. Every day she wished she had never agreed to leave London. But it was too late now. Nothing on earth would make Jack return.

The last time he had been home, ten days ago, Rachel had mentioned the bull's restlessness, wondering what it meant. Jack had laughed at her, seeing the unease in her face. He often scoffed at her for her lack of understanding of the countryside. When she could tell an elm from an ash, he said, he would take her fears seriously. As it was, the bull was like a frustrated old man – feeling sexy, but overweight and not up to it. No wonder he bellowed all night. Wouldn't anyone?

Rachel managed to laugh. Standing in the kitchen in his vast gumboots, Jack seemed very wise. When he was at home there was no worry that the bull, suddenly enraged, might trample over the flimsy fence that divided their garden from the field, and storm the cottage. When Jack was there, throwing huge logs with one hand into the fire, or tapping his pipe on the hearth, any such thoughts seemed absurd. When he had gone for a while, they came back to haunt her, and she made sure she never went into the garden wearing her red skirt.

Back in bed Rachel knew she would not be able to go to sleep again. She stretched a foot into Jack's cold part of the sheet, and wondered how she would pass the day. Squirrels in the roof scurried about: she tried to imagine the dark warmth of their nest, and felt grateful for their invisible companionship. At first, thinking they were rats, their noises had alarmed her. But now she was used to all the sounds of the cottage, the creaks when the central heating came on, the gurgle of pipes, the flutter of birds nesting in the eaves. Now, none of them alarmed her. Even on stormy nights alone, rain pelleting the windows, wind keening down the chimney, she was not afraid. She was only afraid of the bull.

Smiling at her own stupidity, Rachel got up and put on her dressing-gown. She went down to the kitchen and switched on the kettle. Outside, the morning was pale. A yellowy light, reflected in the waterlogged field, meant a weak sun was rising. The distant cows, lying down, were almost submerged by mist. The bull stood up at the fence, chest rubbing against it. The wire bent beneath his weight. Rachel could hear the animal's soft, patient lowing. Hand curiously unsteady, she cut herself a piece of bread and put it in the toaster.

Then she looked at the bull, eye to eye. It jerked its head back, increasing the large folds of reddish skin round its neck. Its dilated nostrils smoked streams of warm breath. The small mean eyes remained on her face.

'Bugger you, bull,' said Rachel out loud.

There was a loud roar. Rachel jumped back from the window. The bull moved away from the fence. Turning its back on the cottage it rumbled towards the cows, hunch-shouldered, long scrotum swinging undignified as a bag of laundry against its muddy hocks.

Rachel heard a click behind her. In her nervous state, she jumped again. It was the toast, blackened. Smoke filled the room. She opened the back door, felt a blast of cold air, watched the blue smoke seep on to the terrace. The bull had almost reached the cows by now. So far away, Rachel felt quite safe. The pomposity of his shape reassured her. If that bull had been a man, he would have been a chairman – a stumpy-legged, huge-bellied chairman, rolling down executive corridors chewing on a fat cigar. He would have been disliked, not trusted, but respected for his power. At office dances he would nudge secretaries with plump knee or elbow – even as now the bull nudged one of the cows which, in awe, heaved itself to its feet.

Rachel ate her breakfast at the kitchen table. She would begin the day, she decided, with a long bath. Then, in preparation for Jack's return at the weekend, she would defrost the fridge. The igloo appearance of the freezer, which somehow she never noticed, had annoyed him on many occasions. He said she took no care of possessions. Their attitude to possessions was very different. Their attitude to most things, in fact, was rarely similar. For the hundredth time, that winter morning, Rachel wondered why she had married Jack. Strange how you sometimes make major decisions without meaning to, she thought: strange how you bury your real will beneath a floss of superficial good reasons and act against your instinct. She had met Jack not long after her turbulent affair with the irresponsible David had ended. Exhausted by months of alternating hope and despair, she had in her weakened state settled for the promise of peace and security. They were assets she now regretted. It was danger, she had been forced to admit to herself, that she most relished. Without the possibility of danger her life lacked an element necessary to maintain her spirits. Often, these last, lonely months in the cottage, she found herself wishing for a fire, a burglary, a local drama – anything to menace the dull rhythm of her life.

Upstairs, after her bath, Rachel sat at her dressing-table carefully making up her eyes in the way that had always pleased David. Sometimes she imagined that one day he would arrive, unannounced, to rescue her. She would not want to be caught looking less than her best. And so most days she made an effort with her appearance, in weary expectation.

She was thinking of David – the funny way his left cheek crinkled when he smiled – when she heard a crash downstairs. Then an almighty roar. Her skin shrank icily, pressing tightly over a wild heart. Glancing out of the window she saw the useless wire fence was flattened on the grass. She remembered she had not shut the back door.

With the speed of terror she ran downstairs and into the kitchen. The bull stood by the sink, its huge form blocking the door to the terrace. Beside it on the floor lay the smashed crockery it must have knocked off the draining board. Steam rose from its back, clouding a shaft of pale sunlight. It took a step forward, mud squelching from its hooves on the tiled floor. Then it raised its head to meet Rachel's look, and gave a deep noisy sigh.

For a moment Rachel was hypnotised into silence. For a moment incredulity overcame her: perhaps this monster in her kitchen was but an hallucination sprung from a despairing mind. The whole room caved about her, the thick stone walls suddenly no protection. All the familiar objects – china, dried flowers, candlesticks, basket of eggs – cracked in their vulnerability. The bull growled. It was no illusion. Rachel screamed.

She fled, slamming the door behind her. But even as she ran to the telephone in the hall she knew it had not closed. With useless fingers she stumbled through the telephone book for the farmer's number. When the ringing was answered by an unknown voice she shouted an almost incoherent message. She could hear the bull whining and snorting in the kitchen. With great effort of will, as she slammed down the receiver, she forced herself to turn round. The bull had nudged open the kitchen door, was surveying her with malicious intent. It stamped a forefoot. Mud on the pale carpet. Rachel screamed again.

She ran to the sitting-room, snatched up the poker. While one part of her terrified mind told her to run up the back stairs and lock herself in the safety of the bathroom, another, more reckless part urged her to fight the bull, to protect her possessions. Suddenly, for the first time, they seemed important.

Waving the poker she now approached the animal, shouting obscene threats. Confused, it backed away from her, until it was wholly in the kitchen once more. Rachel was sparked with the adrenalin of courage: with no thought for the foolishness of the action, she struck the bull on the nose. It gave an agonised roar and lowered its swinging head. One of its horns hit the television on the dresser. The screen splintered, cracking the small reflections of the quiet day outside. Further angered, the bull moaned again, prepared to charge. But its muddy hooves skidded on the polished tiles. Its knees buckled. It fell.

Rachel took her chance. She dashed past it, hitting it again on the nose. She dived for cover under the kitchen table, peered through the legs of the chairs, shouting all the time.

The bull, infuriated by its own foolish position, managed with difficulty to get up. It then spun round with astonishing dexterity and lowered its head towards the chairs that were Rachel's only protection. Snorting, it banged one with its head, sent it crashing to the floor. Then, seeing that Rachel was out of easy reach, it turned its revenge on the television set. One butt, and it smashed to the ground. China eggs, a jug of leaves, fruit, followed, different-shaped noises piercing the bull's now constant roaring.

From her position under the table Rachel watched the bull's campaign of destruction. She saw in close-up its spongy hooves slide in the mess of egg yolk and mud. She saw the dark matted hair of its belly and knees as it slid about in monstrous fashion, slashing at everything with its head. But by now all fear had left Rachel. With only the small risk of the bull reaching her, its livid roaring and thrashing thrilled rather than terrified. At last an outside force was smashing up her life. Here was reason to go. The brief protective feeling towards her possessions had disappeared. For all she cared, the bull could destroy as much as it liked. When, all too soon, she heard voices, and saw two farm labourers enter the back door, armed with pitchforks, she felt the chill of anti-climax.

The men's appearance calmed the bull, or perhaps its rage was already spent. Willingly it allowed itself to be led by the ring in its nose on to the terrace, and back over the fallen fence into the field. The men were full of apologies and concern: the farmer was coming over at once, they said, to see about the damage. But the damage, for the moment, was of no concern to Rachel. Clearing up her shattered kitchen would nicely fill the days until Jack came home, then, with the weight of good reason on her side, she would make her announcement.

The men set about mending the fence. It would be replaced later in the day with a stronger one, they said. No need, Rachel replied: the bull's curiosity is sated. He wouldn't attack again. They chuckled knowingly, and said you can never trust a bull. It was pointless to argue. With a sense of real purpose – a strange and unfamiliar sensation – Rachel set about the long task of clearing up the mess.

When Jack came home two days later Rachel patiently listened to his week in the Canaries before telling the story of the bull.

Consumed by his own dreary tales of seven innocent evenings of drinking at the hotel bar, he failed to notice the television set was missing, as were many pieces of china and other objects long established in their place on the dresser and shelves. When Rachel told him what had happened, he was incredulous and concerned. His concern, however, was not so vital as to cause him to suggest a change of life. No: he merely guaranteed he would assess the strength of the new fence himself, and have some pretty sharp words with the farmer about damages. Rachel mustn't be frightened in future: it would never happen again, he could assure her.

In return Rachel assured Jack she would certainly feel no fear in the future, because she would be far away. She was leaving him. There was no point in Jack making promises for the future, or trying to persuade her to stay. It would be a waste of breath. Her mind was made up. Also, as it would be pointless to spend the weekend together, she would be grateful if he would run her to the station in the car. She would leave her own car behind and go by train to London. She had no idea where she was going. She would make up her mind on the train.

Seeing the seriousness of her intent, and knowing she would change her mind in a few days' time when the reactions of her nasty experience had spent themselves, Jack, with a small secret smile, obligingly took her to the station. He handed her the suitcase – rather a large one, admittedly, but then she had to play out her silly game to the full, of course – in a friendly manner, and kissed her on the cheek. As for his part, he congratulated himself on playing it impeccably. He said he would send extra money to their joint bank account, and Rachel should feel free to draw on it as she wished. Driving back to the empty cottage he felt full of understanding. Rachel had always thrived on a bit of drama: perhaps in future when this silly incident was over, he would try to provide a few more excitements in her life. What an effort, though: the price of not having married a peace-loving wife, as he had always intended, after all. Ah, well. He looked forward to a quiet evening by the fire.

Rachel arrived at Paddington just before midnight. She lugged her suitcase to the taxi rank. Before she had time to think – which she had resisted doing on the train – a taxi appeared. The driver asked where she wanted to go.

Rachel had not been in London for a long time. It was too late at night to arrive on the doorstep of friends she had not seen for many months. There was only one place she could be certain of being received with real pleasure, wasn't there? She gave David's address.

David had said so often he would always love her. They had not communicated for nearly a year, but that would not change things, surely. He was a man who kept his word. She did not doubt he would be alone: he was not the sort of character who would replace his women in a hurry. Rachel was certain he would be pleased to see her again, for all the ugliness of their parting.

No: it wouldn't be too late, she was sure. But as the taxi sped through the empty streets towards his house, Rachel felt the thrill of fear again, the snarl of danger in her bones. She was reminded of the bull – its rage spurring her own excitement and fear. She felt grateful to it for rousing her from an apathy which had gripped her for far too long. Had it not been for the bull's attack, she would never have been here, now, boldly returning to her old lover with no idea of what kind of future awaited her. As the taxi drew up at David's house – a light on in his bedroom – for one last moment Rachel imagined Jack, alone in the kitchen at home, smoking his pipe by the fire, listening to the roar of the bull outside. Smiling to herself at the thought, she rang David's bell and waited.

The Weighing Up

The last time I weighed myself, yesterday morning to be precise, the scales registered twelve stone and one ounce. That is not a record. I have been several pounds heavier. On rare occasions, these last five years, and quite by chance, I've also been a pound or so lighter.

You may be surprised by my saying this, and possibly not believe me, but I am not depressed by my weight. Passing shop windows, or the occasional glance in a mirror, confirm that all hope of ever retrieving my old, slight shape, has quite gone. And I don't mind.

The funny thing is, nor does Jeremy. We married twenty-three years ago when I was a mere slip of a thing – an old joke was that he referred to me as a *slipover* rather than a pushover. Food, then, did not concern me much. I cooked because I had to: meals for the children, dinner for Jeremy on the rare occasions he was home.

But I did make quite an effort, for years, with Sunday lunch. There were constant disputes about whether it should be chocolate pudding or Brown Betty (as a family, we all love apples) each week. I made whatever they finally decided upon, and enjoyed their appreciation.

It was after Sam and Kathy left for university and only Laura, our youngest, was left at home, that I became unstuck. The trouble was, used to making enough for five healthy appetites, I miscalculated when cooking for two. I always made too much, to be on the safe side. There were always things left over. Remembering the post-war economy of my own childhood, and not liking to see things go to waste, I found it hard to leave them in the fridge or larder to await reheating. It became impossible to throw them away. Finishing them off myself – cold rice pudding for elevenses, cold chicken curry for tea, time doesn't matter to an anarchistic eater – became my habit.

By the time Laura finally left, too, to go to Durham, I had noticed the conspicuous change in my figure. I should have taken some strong hold – gone on a diet, changed my eating habits, whatever. But no. One of the pleasures I came to look forward to was a proper three-course dinner alone in front of the television. Plus half a bottle of Jeremy's nice white wine. He always said, 'Help yourself from the cellar whenever you want to,' and I would take him at his word. Another pleasure was breakfast: all those fried glistening things I had cooked for years for the children and never eaten myself, I now found immensely enjoyable. They gave a good start to the morning. They would keep me going till the chocolate biscuits and coffee at eleven, later followed by home-made bread and soup for lunch.

The children, when they came home, teased me mildly about my middle-aged spread. They found it odd I had put on so much weight considering I seemed to be eating no more than usual. For, out of habit, or perhaps secret shame, in front of them I remained quite abstemious, piling their plates with second and third helpings but toying with just one small helping myself. I contemplated confessing to them my secret vice, but then couldn't face it. Besides, they didn't go on about it, accepted me lovingly as always. As for Jeremy – home less than ever despite retirement being only four years off – he made no comment at all.

Jeremy is in shipping. It has always been his job, ever since he came down from Balliol. I'm ashamed to say after twenty-three years of marriage I still don't know *precisely* what it is he does in shipping. Sales, I think. 'Do you have to sell a liner like a man who sells double glazing?' I once asked, but he was concentrating on something else, or perhaps considered it a question not worth answering, though he would never have been so rude as to say so.

For Jeremy is a very kind man. In matters of consideration, you could not fault him. That is not to say he is a man of declarations. His appreciation is expressed in other ways. Compliments have never sprung readily from his lips, and indeed I'm sometimes unsure he even observes things that might inspire other men to words of praise: Laura's new short hair, or one of my better souf-flés, for instance. And yet he plainly cares deeply for his family. When he *is* home – and his business takes him all over the world, sometimes for weeks on end, for most of the year – he gives us his full attention. He asks questions, goes for walks with Sam, talks about Renaissance poets to Kathy and the history of politics to Laura, and takes an interest in my herbaceous border and the state of my old-fashioned roses. 'Sorry I've got to go again,' he says, when his time is up. And I know he means it. He looks full of regret.

Away from us, he sends postcards, calls occasionally at inconvenient hours – though, heavens, the sound of his voice is never inconvenient – from Australia or wherever. I always get a decent warning of his homecoming. Mrs Manns, his secretary, gives a ring saying what time he is due at Heathrow, so there is no chance of my letting him down. A company chauffeur meets him at the airport these days, but I can be sure of having ready his favourite shrimp vol-au-vents, or risotto, or, best of all, baked red mullet. Plus, of course, a bottle of good wine in the fridge.

He always seems to be pleased to be home. Lately, he's taken to bringing me chocolates. He apologises they have come from the airport, time being very scarce – but they're invariably very expensive and elaborately beribboned. Particularly good, of course, when he returns from Brussels or Zurich. We have established a funny little routine after our first reunion dinner: I offer him one of the heavenly chocolates: he refuses. 'You have them all for yourself,' he says with his generous smile. And once he's gone away again – I don't open them till then – that's just what I do.

I'm sitting now by the study fire, the latest box – a fine assortment of soft centres – by my side. I've watched the nine o'clock news, and *Panorama*, and am quite content. I choose my third – fourth? fifth, perhaps? – and last for the evening: a walnut cluster. The hand that plucks it, I notice, is a plump, puffed-up thing compared with what it used to be. The nails are still a pretty shape, but my wedding ring sits deep beside two banks of flesh. I could never get it off, now: it will have to be buried with me. The ankles and feet, stretched out, match the hands in puffiness. No longer can I wear the pretty shoes that I used to love to find, and which caused people to pay many a compliment. The arms are large and heavy. Once delicate wrist and elbow bones now quite obliterated by fat, and the stomach is swollen to the same size as when I was six months pregnant. None of these things worries me dreadfully, but I do observe them. Thank God we are designed so as not to see our own faces – that was an almighty piece of tact on the Lord's part. For on the occasions I'm forced to study the face, I admit to a certain desolation. Simply because it doesn't look like the one I remember best. 'If you'd just lose a stone or two, Mum,' Laura said a week or so ago, 'you'd be exceptionally good-looking. I mean, you've got the features. It's just that they're becoming obscured.'

It's true. (Laura has always been the most loving and most

honest of the children. She's the one who minds most about this metamorphosis.) I did have fine eyes: but as the cheeks have swollen their size has diminished. And the once pointed chin is now indeterminate, mingling with underchins that ripple down to a doughy chest. My hair still shines from time to time, I think. But I'm not attractive any more. I'm fat, fat, fat.

Perhaps if Jeremy were to complain, I would make a serious effort to do something about it. This I reflect on sometimes: I am so much less busy now and have time for introspection. (A dangerous pastime, I always think. I don't indulge too often.) But as Jeremy does not complain, and remains as considerate to me and appreciative of home life as he is able in the brief times he is here, why make the effort? As it is, I am peaceful, lazier these days, and happy. And it's time to go to bed.

It's a windy night. Draughts slightly move the curtains. The weather forecast warned of tempestuous autumn days ahead. Well, if it rains tomorrow I shall stay at home with bean soup for lunch, and make a list of ingredients for the Christmas cake. Some people might be daunted by my solitary days of trivial pursuits. I like them. Besides, it's not a barren life. There is always Jeremy's next return to look forward to.

Yesterday he rang from Tokyo to say he doubted if he could get home by the weekend. He would ring again if plans changed. I stir, meaning to get up. The telephone on the table beside me rings. It can only mean that plans *have* changed.

'Hello?' says a woman. I do not know her voice. 'Is that Ada Mullins?'

'Avril,' I say.

'Sorry. I knew it was something beginning with A. Couldn't for the life of me remember what.' She gave a small laugh, but not a friendly one.

'Who are you?' I ask.

'I'm Richenda Gosforth.'

Silence.

'Richenda . . . ?'

I do not know a Richenda, I'm almost sure. Perhaps she's a friend of one of the children.

'Gosforth.' Silence for a moment or two. 'I'm – the mother of Jeremy's baby. Your husband Jeremy.'

'Yes, yes. I know Jeremy's my husband,' I say. My fingers fiddle with the velvet ribbon twisted into a multi-looped bow on the lid of the chocolate box. I feel very calm.

'Look, Av – Mrs Mullins,' says Richenda Gosforth. 'Jeremy wanted to keep all this from you. He'll probably be livid with me when he finds out I've rung you. But I think you should know the truth.'

'Really?' I say, but it isn't really a question as I'm not sure what she's talking about.

'Well, the truth is, Jeremy and I have been together for nearly two years now. I've been like a second wife to him in a way. I suppose you could say I've had all the glamour but none of the real advantages.'

'None of the real advantages?' I echo.

'Absolutely not. I mean, yes, I've had the trips abroad, the first-class flights, the champagne, the hanging about in hotel suites while he's in his conferences. But what I've never had with Jeremy is a *base*. That's been your privilege. You've got the base with Jeremy.'

'That's true,' I say. 'Jeremy and I have certainly had a solid base for a good many years now. Man and wife.'

'Exactly. And you hold the trump card, *being* his wife.'

'I am his wife, yes.' Another pause.

'You're being very nice,' continues Richenda Gosforth. 'I thought you'd be screaming mad at me. I had to have three whiskies before making this call. Anyhow, about the baby. I thought you should know about the baby. When I first told Jeremy, heavens, was he put out! Wanted to whizz me off to an abortionist straight away. He didn't want anything to *rock the boat*, as he put it.'

'That's always been a concern of his, not to rock the boat,' I reflect. We give a small, clashing laugh. When the laughter dies, Richenda Gosforth goes on with her story.

'But I said: no way, Jeremy. I'm not going to be pushed about for your convenience. My baby's not going to be murdered just to suit you. I'm going to have it.'

'Quite right,' I say, being anti-abortion myself, and to end another silence.

'Jason was born three weeks ago,' says Richenda, 'and when Jeremy saw I had no intention of changing my mind, I must say he was very decent about it all. He set me up in this flat near Richmond Park, and he's paying for a part-time nanny so I'll be able to go back to work. He was in Canada for the actual birth, but he comes to see us as often as he can. I'm expecting him for the weekend when, I've told him, we've finally got to thrash things out.'

'He'll be with *you*, this weekend?' I say. 'To thrash things out?'

'Exactly. Unless, that is, his plans change, and he can't make it.'

I feel the merest smile twitch the corners of my mouth. 'His plans do change,' I say.

'I'm sorry if all this is coming as an awful shock to you,' says Richenda. 'But I thought if I could tell Jeremy I'd spoken to you, although he might be angry, it would make things easier.'

'I hope so,' I said.

It might not make things *much* easier, I think, Jeremy not being a man who thrives on confrontation.

'The thing is *this*. In a word, Mrs Mullins, Jeremy is the love of my life. I want to marry him. I think, to be honest, he feels the same.'

She is silent again. I feel I should help her out.

'And I'm the stumbling block,' I say.

'Exactly. You're the stumbling block. Jeremy's told me a million times he can't leave you, break up the family. *Yet*, anyway. *Some time*, he says, perhaps. But he says he can't bring himself to leave you at the moment, whatever he feels for me and Jason, for reasons he can't explain. You're a taboo subject, actually. So I don't know anything about you. I don't know if you're old or young or middle-aged, fat or thin, whether you work or not, whether you're a good wife and mother. I don't know *anything* about you. Jeremy goes all blank if I ask any questions. He simply won't talk about you –' She breaks off with a sob in her voice. I wait for her to recover. 'Mrs Mullins, forgive me for saying this, but although he keeps his silence I get the impression that *there's not much going on between you and Jeremy*. Would you mind if he left you?'

I see my dimpled fingers twirl faster through the pretty loops of the velvet bow. Would I mind if he left me? It is a question I have never asked myself.

'It's a question I've never asked myself,' I tell Richenda Gosforth, 'and a question I trust I shall never have the need to ask myself.'

I glance down at my feet, slumped inwards upon themselves, conveying the weariness that seemed to be congealing my veins, making me hungry. I lift the lid from the chocolate box and rustle through the crisp, empty, pleated brown-paper cases that once held the delicious collection of soft centres.

'Oh,' says Richenda Gosforth, eventually. 'Really?'

She does not sound deflated. She's obviously a determined young woman (I presume young, anyway) out to get her own way.

'Well, I think you should think about it all, if you would. I mean, after all, nothing's ever going to be quite the same again, now, is it? Knowing Jeremy has a mistress and baby tucked away somewhere. As you can imagine, Mrs Mullins, I shall be insisting on no less for Jason than your children had – private education, holidays with Jeremy, all that sort of thing—'

'Quite,' I hear myself interrupting. I am still thinking calmly. The impertinence of the girl. The weariness turns into a heavy, physical thing that clouds my whole body.

'So you think it over and I'll ring you back,' she suggests in a bossy voice.

'Oh no, don't ring me back, if you don't mind,' I say, wanting this insane conversation to end, now. I put down the receiver.

The wind still shuffles the curtains. The silence is broken only by the small cracking sounds of the empty chocolate papers as my hand despairs through them in hope of a last one: but no, there are none left. But Jeremy, when he comes early next week, I must now suppose, will not let me down. Jeremy is a loving man. He will bring me new chocolates, lovingly chosen by himself. He is not the sort of man to hurt his wife and family. If there is a complicated side of his life, he will protect us from it. Perhaps he has always done this. Perhaps there have been other . . . complications over the years.

This whole daft matter is, in fact, scarcely worth thinking about, because nothing can ever affect us. The solid base Richenda Gosforth seemed so to envy cannot be disturbed by an outside force. When Jeremy comes, I shall welcome him. He will be pleased to be back, as always. I shall offer him the chocolates he has brought me. He will refuse. We will laugh, exchange news. Naturally, I shall not mention the silly business of Richenda Gosforth's telephone call. I would never dream of intruding in that way. Where there is trust, there is no place for intrusion. I would rather not have known about this squalid girl, of course, but Jeremy will deal with her. He is very competent at sorting out all manner of things. Never will he know, from me, that I know about his son. That is the least a wife can do, keep her silence, if she is to practise her real love for her husband.

I shall lash out on Monday evening: I shall lash out on turbot and a mousseline sauce, and he'll chide me a little for my extravagance, but really be pleased at the effort I've made. We will have one of our quiet and peaceful evenings together – happy, easy with each other as is our custom. As usual, he will be suffering from jet lag – funny how after flying so many thousands of miles it still affects him – and fall asleep instantly his head touches the pillow. Sometimes I watch his sleeping face for hours. Good, kind, searingly familiar. Oh Jeremy. I think I know you well. I *do* know you well.

Somehow it is nearly midnight. Long past my normal bedtime. In the circumstances, I think I shall treat myself to a mug of hot chocolate and a piece of toast and dripping, the stuff of midnight feasts as a child. Now, standing, in anticipation of such pleasure the weariness has fled. I am large and strong and Jeremy's wife. I am warm with trust.

After a while, I go to the kitchen, pour boiling milk into the mug of chocolate powder, and stir the creamy bubbles. I choose a pretty tray for the drink and toast and dripping, and make my way, quite sure of our unchanging love, to bed.

Irish Coffee

It was Magda McCorn's custom to holiday alone. There was not much choice in this matter, but even if there had been she would probably have preferred it that way. She was well acquainted with the many conveniences of the solitary holiday and in the bad moments (which she would scarcely admit to herself, let alone anyone else) remembered to appreciate them.

Last year Mrs McCorn had gone to Sweden. The year before, Norway. Now, she was sick of fish, and twilight afternoons. A yearning for her late husband's country of birth had assailed her one April afternoon, admiring the bilious sweep of King Alfreds in her Cheltenham garden, and within the week she was booked into a first-class hotel in Parknasilla, Co. Kerry.

Mrs McCorn did little at random, and it was only after thorough research that she chose Parknasilla. As her efficient eye swept through the brochures, the name came back to her with a sparkle of nostalgia. It was not her husband, Patrick (born in the shadow of Croagh Patrick, a charming Co. Mayo man), but Commander Chariot, eligible bachelor on a spring cruise to the Canaries some years back, who had recommended the place most warmly. They had been drinking sherry at the ship's bar: the scene was an indelible picture in Mrs McCorn's mind. Commander Chariot wore his panama, despite the overcast skies, while Mrs McCorn had undone the top button of her floral bolero, which would indicate, she felt, a nice distinction between normal reserve and long-term possibility. But if the subtleties of his companion's dress made any impression on the Commander, he did not show it. His bleak grey eyes hovered on the horizon which tilted a little perilously, for Mrs McCorn's sherry-flushed stomach, through the window behind the bar. He chatted on in his charming, impervious way, about Parknasilla (often visited in July) and other places he had enjoyed over the years. All the while calling her Mrs McCorn.

But then the Commander was not an easy man to get to know. The very first evening aboard, Mrs McCorn, well-trained antennae highly tuned for potential companions, sensed his reserve. Reserve, however, was a challenge rather than a deterrent to the good widow. On many occasions she had found herself quite exhausted from exercising her sympathy on shy fellow holiday-makers and often, as she wore them down, she had recognised the breakthrough, the light, the reward: sometimes it was the offer of a drink or a game of bridge. On other occasions there were confidences, and it was these Mrs McCorn liked best. For in persuading a stranger to 'unwind his soul', as she called it, she felt of some real use, and the satisfaction kindled within her in the bleaker months of the year between holidays.

She had worked very hard upon Commander Chariot, trying to put him at his ease, to draw him from his shell, with the delicate lift of a sympathetic eyebrow, or an almost indistinguishable pat on the arm by her softly padded hand. And indeed, by the last night, amid the coloured rain of paper streamers, she had persuaded him to call her Magda. But she knew he had only complied with her wishes out of politeness. The name had not burst from his lips in a rush of warmth and natural friendliness, and Mrs McCorn had felt disappointed. It was some consolation, of course, to know the other passengers were firmly convinced a shipboard romance had flared between herself and the handsome Commander, and she would not give them any indication that the truth was quite different. She returned to Cheltenham with the Commander's Suffolk address and the promise to 'drop in for a cup of tea if ever she was that way' (which, one day, she would most certainly arrange to be). The Commander made no such promises in return. In a brief farewell, he mentioned – in a voice that was almost callous, Mrs McCorn thought later, considering all the trouble she had taken – that Gloucestershire was not a part of the country he ever had occasion to visit. They did exchange Christmas cards, and Mrs McCorn rather boldly sent postcards from Norway and Sweden – by great strength of will managing to refrain from saying 'Wish you were here'. But her greetings from abroad remained unacknowledged and in terms of *development*, Mrs McCorn was bound to admit, the Commander was a failure.

But hope is often confused with inspiration, and on the journey to Ireland Mrs McCorn could not but help thinking that Fate may have planted the idea of Parknasilla in her head. On the aeroplane she bought herself a small bottle of brandy to quell the feeling of pleasant unease in her stomach: a glittery, excited feeling she had not experienced for many years. But the brandy's medicinal powers had no effect on a state which no medicine can cure, and by the time she set foot on Irish soil Mrs McCorn was as dithery as a girl, her heart a-flutter, her cheeks quite pink.

She walked into the lobby of the Great Southern Hotel mid-afternoon on a fine July day, accompanied by her family of matching suitcases. She moved with head held high, bosom thrust forward, knowing that should her entrance cause a rustle of interest, then those who looked her way would take her for someone. She had persuaded her cautious hairdresser to be a little more generous with the Honey Glow rinse than usual, and by great effort she had lost two pounds through cutting out her elevenses for the last month. She felt she exuded health at this, the beginning of her stay, which is more than can be said of most people, and it was with a symbolic flourish of well-being that she signed her name at the reception desk.

Then Magda McCorn, glowing in oatmeal dress with tailored jacket to match, and a butterfly brooch (made from a deceased Red Admiral) sparkling on the lapel, tripped up the wide hotel stairs behind the friendly Irish porter. She admired the high Victorian passages, with their thick and shining white paint, and the ruby carpets. Commander Chariot was a man of taste, of course: he would only recommend the best in hotels. Should he not appear, then at least she would still have benefited from his recommendation and would thank him in a single sentence on the left-hand side of this year's Christmas card.

In her fine room overlooking the bay, the porter relieved himself of all her suitcases and asked if there was anything Mrs McCorn would be requiring. Mrs McCorn paused, smiled, fumbled in her bag for a tip, to give herself time. The only thing in the world she wanted was to know whether Commander Chariot, regular visitor to the Great Southern, was expected. The porter would surely know. But Mrs McCorn was not a woman to indulge in questions that might bring forth a disappointing answer, and after a short, silent struggle, she decided to shake her head and give the man a pound. He could be useful in the future, should she change her mind.

When the porter had gone, Mrs McCorn surveyed what was to be her room for the next two weeks with great satisfaction. Then she went to the window and looked out at the grey waters of the bay. There were palm trees in the hotel garden, reminding her this was a temperate climate and, more distantly, wooded slopes that went down to the sea. I am going to be happy, here, she thought, and sighed at the idea of such a luxury.

Some hours later – having furnished the room with small touches that made it more her own (crochet mat on the bedside table, magazines, travelling clock) – Magda McCorn returned downstairs. It was time to perform her first important task of a holiday: establish her presence. This she did by arming herself with a small glass of sherry, then drifting round the lounges (three of them, with open fires), nodding and smiling with fleeting friendliness in the direction of anyone who caught her glance. The idea was to stamp a firm image in the minds of the other guests: they should instantly understand that here among them was a middle-aged widow of considerable attractions, alone, but in good spirits and certainly not a case for sympathy. While her smile was calculated to indicate enthusiasm, should anyone wish to offer her to join in their conversation or their games, her firm choice of a chair near the window, and apparent engrossment in a book, conveyed also that she was a woman quite happy with her own resources. Her establishing over, her search for the Commander thwarted, Mrs McCorn set about hiding her disappointment in the pages of a light romance.

In the magnificent dining-room of the Great Southern, Mrs McCorn had a single table by the window. There, she enjoyed a four-course dinner cooked by a French chef, and drank half a bottle of expensive claret. Nearby, at other tables, families with children, and several young married couples, chattered their way through the meal. Mrs McCorn did not envy them: it was her joy silently to watch the sun – which put her in mind of a crab-apple rather than a tangerine, but then, as Patrick used to say, she was an original thinker – sink into the silver clouds which, if she half shut her eyes, looked like further promontories stretching from the bay. Her measure of wine finished, Mrs McCorn's thoughts took a philosophical turn: the frequent lack of clarity between boundaries (sea and sky, happiness and melancholy) struck her with some hard-to-articulate significance that sent a shiver up her spine. In fact, it had been to Commander Chariot that she had tried to confide some of these private thoughts – as the sun then had been setting over Santa Cruz – but he had shown a lack of response that Mrs McCorn had quite understood. It wasn't everybody who was blessed with such insights, and after all they were of no practical use and the Commander was a wholly practical man.

After dinner, to continue the establishing process, Mrs McCorn made her way to the lounge where the life of the hotel seemed to have gathered. There, an elderly lady wrapped in a mohair shawl, the occasional sequin twinkling in its furry wastes, played the piano. The prime of her piano-playing years was evidently over and, accompanied by a dolorous young man on the double bass, their rendering of fifties tunes lacked spirit. It was as if the music was emerging from under a huge, invisible cushion, oppressed. But it was good enough for Mrs McCorn. In her time she had had quite a reputation on the dance floor, although partnering her husband Patrick there had been little opportunity to show off her prowess at the quickstep. It would have been disloyal to complain, and she never did: although for all the happyish years of their marriage, Magda McCorn secretly deplored the fact that her husband was such a lout on the dance floor. But her feeling for the dance, as she called it, never left her and here, suddenly as of old, she felt her toes privately wiggling in her patent pumps in time to the steady thump of 'Hey, there! You with the Stars in Your Eyes' which, she recalled with a stab of nostalgia, had been played every night on the cruise to the Canaries.

Mrs McCorn chose herself a tactful armchair. That is, it was within reach of a middle-aged Norwegian couple, should they choose to talk to her: yet far enough away to make ignoring her within the bounds of politeness if that was how they felt. She gave them a small signalling smile and was delighted, though not surprised, when immediately they drew their own chairs closer to hers and began to converse in beautiful English.

Due to her holiday in Norway, Mrs McCorn was able to tell them many interesting things about their country, and to captivate their interest for some time. Occasionally she allowed her eyes to glance at the dance floor, where she observed the deplorable sight of unmusical men shunting around their wives with not the slightest regard to the beat of the tune. The long-suffering expressions of the wives did not escape her, either. She felt for them, poor dears, and envied them, too. Varicose veins a-twinkle, at least they were on their feet.

Something of her feelings must have registered in Mrs McCorn's eyes, for the Norwegian gentleman was standing, offering her his arm, asking her to dance. Taken so unawares, Mrs McCorn hardly knew whether to accept or refuse. But she saw the friendly smile of the Norwegian wife urging her, urging her, and knowing everything would be above-board, with the clinical Norwegian eyes of the wife following their every move, Mrs McCorn said yes.

On the small floor, they lumbered round in imitation of a fox-trot. Mrs McCorn, confident that the delicate tracery on the back of her own calves was well hidden by her Dusky Sunbeam tights, gave a small shake of her hips to encourage her partner.

'You dance very well,' this spurred him to say, and Mrs McCorn began to enjoy herself. Should Commander Chariot come in now, he could not fail to observe the way in which people were drawn to her wherever she went, and surely he would be moved to admiration.

Mrs McCorn's two-week holiday passed happily enough. She befriended many of the other guests in the hotel, and every evening found herself in the desirable position of joining in games, drinks and conversations. Her new acquaintances included many foreigners, and Mrs McCorn was able to let the fact be known that she was a much-travelled woman herself, for all her quiet life in Cheltenham – with quite a flair for Continental cooking and with some talent for making herself understood in French.

The pounds of flesh that Mrs McCorn had so industriously lost before coming to Ireland were soon regained, and indeed increased, by her indulgence in the delicious food. But Mrs McCorn did not care.

Realising that Fate had slipped up and been unkind in its choice of dates, and there was little hope Commander Chariot would appear, she sought consolation in cooked breakfasts in bed (beautifully arranged trays, flat grey water unblinking in the bay outside her window), hearty lunches and enormous dinners. But as her plumpness did nothing to diminish her evident popularity, she saw no reason for cutting back until she returned home.

On the last day of her visit, Mrs McCorn – who for the most part had spent sedentary days – decided to join a trip to the Skellig Islands. She was all for a little adventure, and felt the breath of sea air would be of benefit to her complexion.

It dawned a disappointingly grey and misty day, a light drizzle swirling so weightless through the air you could not see it at all. Mrs McCorn contemplated abandoning the trip, but then felt that would be faint-hearted, and cheered herself with the thought that Irish weather was wonderfully changeable, and at any moment the sun might drive away the cloud.

And indeed, by the time she was seated snugly in her poplin mackintosh and silk scarf on the fishing boat, along with some dozen foreign students, the gloom had begun to lift and the sun threw a first pale rope of light along the horizon. Mrs McCorn did not much like the bucking motion of the boat as it lumbered over the waves, but she sucked on her boiled sweets and concentrated on the feeling of enjoying the proximity to young foreigners. Widening her horizons, she was, she felt. Perhaps before the day was over she would find the chance to make herself known to them, although for the moment she could detect no openings.

They were a dour lot: unwashed, unshaven, dirty clothes and unhealthy skin. But then Mrs McCorn, who was sensitive to the hardships of those less fortunate than herself, supposed they could not afford to live on anything but fish and chips on their camping holiday, and was not surprised. She could have wished they had appeared friendlier, more willing to talk: a little conversation would have been agreeable, but perhaps they kept their interest for monuments rather than people.

After an hour of bumping over the grey sea, Mrs McCorn and the other sightseers were rewarded by the sight of the first island. It loomed out of the misty sea like a single tooth. The fanciful thought came to Mrs McCorn that the whole Atlantic Ocean was a vast, grey tongue, hissing and snapping and drooling with white-spittle foam, armed with its one hideous giant tooth. And the sky was a grim upper lip. The vast and dreadful mouth, made from the elements, only waited for the right time to swallow the boat-load with a single flick of its lapping tongue . . . Mrs McCorn sucked harder on her raspberry drop and listened to the wail of forty thousand gannets, who fluttered round their island thickly as a snowstorm. Occasionally one of them would swoop quite close to the boat, dismissing the passengers with its beady red eye, then diving into the waves to snap at an invisible fish.

The second island, their destination, came into sight. It was another monster rock, sheer and black and menacing. Waves thundered round its base, thousands more gulls screamed their indignation at having to live in such a God-forsaken spot. It was here that seven hundred years ago a small band of monks chose to build a monastery on its summit. To climb hundreds of steps to see the remains of this monastery was the aim of the expedition.

The boat moored at a small concrete pier. Mrs McCorn looked about her in dismay. She had imagined it would be quite primitive, of course: a simple tea shop, perhaps, and a small cluster of cottages. But there was nothing. The petulant gulls were the only inhabitants, balancing on the edges of precarious rock nests, screaming all the while. Close to, the rock was no less intimidating. While the waves pounded upwards, other water streamed down the jagged sides, gleaming, oily. Mrs McCorn was afraid.

Gritting her teeth, remembering she was British, she followed the students up the dangerous little flight of steps. There, they abandoned her with peculiar speed, scampering up the steep path with an eagerness Mrs McCorn found herself unable to share. She followed them slowly, tucking the lunch box the hotel had given her under one arm, and telling herself she must persevere, however undesirable the climb may seem.

Although Mrs McCorn's progress was very slow – students from another boat passed her with uncaring speed – she soon became out of breath and listened to her own panting against the dimmer noise of waves thudding far below. She was forced to conclude that she should have to rest before the top, or she might risk a heart attack. And who, then . . . ? She chose a small, flat rock at the edge of the steps, sat down, and unbuttoned her mackintosh. The hotel had provided her with an unimaginative lunch, but she found comfort in the sliced-bread sandwiches, tomatoes, biscuits and cheese. Her breathing returned to its normal pace, and after a while she began to feel cool again.

When she had finished eating, Mrs McCorn looked about for somewhere to bury her empty lunch box. There were no litter bins, of course, and the sea was much too far away to throw the wretched thing over the edge. Mrs McCorn scrabbled about the springy green stuff that grew among the rocks, and eventually managed, by squishing it quite small, to hide the box. Plunging her hands into the greenery gave her a nasty turn: its cold sliminess was surprising. But she completed the job to her satisfaction, and turned for another look at the bewildering expanse of grey Atlantic before continuing on her way.

The sky was whitish-grey, mists swirled blotchily about the sheer sides of rock. In the distance, the sea kept up its perpetual snarl, and the gulls their angry screeching. Mrs McCorn had never felt so alone. To lift her spirits, she thought of the ordinary things of her life: her small, neat garden, her well-hoovered carpets, her Silver Jubilee tin of biscuits, always full, in the kitchen, her cat Tibby, the absolute regularity of the Parish Newsletter – things which sometimes she found lacking in excitement, but which now she appreciated with all her heart. Then, for the first time that day, she thought of Commander Chariot.

As she did so, Mrs McCorn stood up. No point in dwelling on the unlikely, she thought, and at that moment a small chink of sun appeared in the sky, making the wet rocks glint. An omen, thought Mrs McCorn, and at once forced herself to abandon the idea as silly. But, trudging slowly up the rough steps once more, she could not cast aside the Commander. He filled her being in an unaccountable way: she longed for his presence. With him this day on the island would be an agreeable adventure, instead of the frightening experience it was in reality. Alive in her mind, the Commander then spoke to Mrs McCorn in a voice so real he might have been at her side.

'Ruddy masochists, those monks must have been,' he said ('ruddy' was his favourite adjective), and Mrs McCorn smiled.

Somehow, she got to the top. It was no great reward. A cluster of stone-built cells, gently rounded structures, putting Mrs McCorn in mind of house-martins' nests. Very uncomfortable, they must have been, with their slit windows and damp floors, the mists and rain flurrying about outside, and nothing to comfort in the sight of the grim Atlantic sea. Mrs McCorn ventured into one of the cells: it smelt wet and spooky. When her eyes had grown accustomed to the dark, she noticed three of the students sitting on the floor in a corner. They passed an evil-smelling cigarette between them, and gave her an unfriendly look. Mrs McCorn hurried out.

She was quite cold by now, and thought with longing of the hotel bath and her warm candlewick dressing-gown. Only a few more hours . . . And it would, of course, be a good story to tell friends at home, not that she'd ever be up to describing the strange sense of horror that the island of rock had given her.

Before returning to the path to descend, Mrs McCorn leaned over one of the ruined stone walls and looked down, down at the spumy sea battering for ever the base of the rock, and she listened to the endless evil screeching of the gulls. It was then it came to her why the silly old monks had chosen such a place to live: they had wanted to confront the devil head-on and this was the perfect spot. There was no grain of comfort, of soft or easy living on the rock land or the monster sea. The gannets were devils incarnate, the brief flashes of sun a simple mockery. On this island was the rough face of God – quite unlike the God Mrs McCorn was acquainted with in the church at Cheltenham with its carpeted aisle and central heating. On this island, you'd have to be tougher than she, Mrs McCorn, to go on believing.

Physically weakened by such thoughts, and by the day's exposure to relentless elements, Mrs McCorn put the last of the boiled sweets in her mouth and began her slow descent. She found her knees were shaking and she was sweating quite hard into her poplin mackintosh. But for all the loneliness, she was glad there was no one here to witness the way in which the island had unnerved her – that is, except for Commander Chariot. He would have scoffed at any talk of devils and talked knowledgeably of the breeding habits of gannets, which would have been very cheering. As it was, he was far from Ireland, or this place, with no thought of her. Mrs McCorn shuffled down the steps, one foot always forward like a small child, praying for the bottom.

Three hours later, in the safety of her hotel room, Mrs McCorn, although much happier, still found herself somewhat shaken. She packed her suitcase, so as to be ready for her departure in the morning, and it took her twice as long as usual. In her confusion she found she had put soft things at the bottom, and had to start all over again.

As it was her last night, Mrs McCorn felt it unnecessary to make quite the same effort she had made on previous evenings. She wore her plainest dress – very tight, now, across the stomach – and brushed half-heartedly at the mess the Skellig Islands had made of her hair. Somehow, she couldn't face drinks in the lounge – no energy, as yet, to recount the adventure of her day. She waited in her room until eight o'clock, then went straight into the dining-room.

She saw him at once. Commander Chariot was sitting at the window at a single table next to her own. Mrs McCorn's instant thought was to flee – to unpack her turquoise Lurex and change into that, and to have another go at her hair. But she was too late. He had seen her. He smiled, slightly.

Mrs McCorn followed the waiter to her table. She sat down and quickly ordered her dinner and half a bottle of wine. Then she allowed herself to look at the Commander, who was halfway through a plate of elaborate chops.

'Why, hello there, Mrs McCorn,' he said.

'Magda,' she said, with warmth and humour.

'Well I never, running into you here of all places.'

'It was your recommendation, you may remember.'

'Was it? Was it, now? Can't say I do remember. Anyhow, here for long, are you?'

Mrs McCorn gave herself time to think before answering. Perhaps it would be possible to make new arrangements after dinner, to extend her stay for a few days. But there was the question of money (she had spent every penny of her holiday budget) and getting another flight back – too many complications.

'I'm leaving tomorrow morning, actually,' she said.

'Well, well, what a ruddy shame.'

The Commander hustled a forkful of cauliflower into his mouth, shifting his eyes. His expression just might have been one of relief.

But this paranoid thought was quickly dispelled from Mrs

McCorn's mind by the next turn of events: the Commander suggested he might join her at her table, seeing as they would have only one evening together.

Scarcely able to believe her good fortune, Mrs McCorn signalled to the waiter. He moved the Commander's place to Mrs McCorn's table, picked up the bottle of wine, and lifted an eyebrow at Mrs McCorn. Her heart thumping, Mrs McCorn nodded. The waiter poured the Commander a glass of the wine: the Commander did not protest.

Outside, there was an orange sky over the bay, and a small hard gold sun. Mrs McCorn wondered if she should put to the Commander her funny idea about a *crab-apple* sun. But she thought better of it, and said instead:

'It's been quite a few years, hasn't it? And you haven't changed at all.'

'No. Well. I manage to keep myself up to scratch.'

Indeed, it was true he had not changed: no more grey hairs, no new wrinkles, the same handsome combination of angular bone and fine-drawn skin. Mrs McCorn found herself gazing at him in wonder and in disbelief. The only pity was the cruel timing. But she would not let herself think of the sadness of the morning. There was the whole night: time in which to play her cards with skill.

To keep a clear head, Mrs McCorn let the Commander drink all her wine, and ordered him another bottle. She delighted in his pleasure in the stuff: the way he sipped and swirled and sniffed with such expertise. They talked of their various trips, and the Commander acknowledged her cards from Norway and Sweden.

'I'm so glad they reached you. I thought that maybe – you know the foreign posts.'

'Oh, I *got* them all right. Should have written back, but I'm not much of a dab hand when it comes to letters myself.'

'I know just how you feel.' (This was a permissible lie. Mrs McCorn had no idea, as a great letter- and postcard-writer herself, how it must feel not to have the constant desire to keep in touch.)

By the end of dinner, the Commander had a bright pink spot on both cheeks (crab-apples, again, thought Mrs McCorn). He was friendly and seemingly happy, but not exactly lively. There were long pauses between each comment he made, and the comments themselves were not of the stuff that remains for ever in the romantic memory. Mrs McCorn, remembering his long mono-logues about fishing and the Navy, wondered if there was anything troubling him. Given the right moment, she felt she should make a gentle enquiry.

'It's really quite lively here, evenings,' she said. 'Shall we take our coffee in the lounge?'

The Commander followed. She led the way as far as the quiet room where the less lively guests read their papers round the fire, and the Commander indicated they should occupy the free sofa. But Mrs McCorn shook her head determinedly, and kept going till she reached two vacant chairs at the side of the dance floor. With a look of barely concealed pain on his face, as if the pianist's rendering of 'Stardust' hurt his ears, the Commander lowered himself into one of the chairs. Mrs McCorn, meantime, was smiling and waving to nearby friends in some triumph: they had all heard about her friendship with the Commander, and to be with him on this, her last night, was a proud occasion. So engrossed was she in acknowledging the waves and smiles – yet at the same time not wanting to encourage anyone to draw so near as to deflect the Commander's interest from herself – she was quite unaware that her own choice of seat was disagreeable to her companion. With the elation of a girl, she summoned the waiter.

'Let's be devils, shall we, Commander, and treat ourselves to Irish coffees?'

She knew, even as she made the suggestion, the treat would be put on her bill, and she did not care. What did strike her, with a brief iciness of heart, was her own word *devil*. She remembered the lugubrious island of evil gulls she had so recently visited. But the dreadful experience seemed wonderfully far away, now. She was back where she belonged, in a place of warmth and sentimental tunes and safety.

The Irish coffees came. Mrs McCorn sat back, revelling in the warm froth on her top lip as she sipped the sickly drink, one foot tapping the floor in time to the music. In truth, it would have been hard to have a conversation against the noise of the band, and the Commander, Mrs McCorn observed, was sunk in that pleasurable silence that is permitted between those of understanding. The broad-hipped dancers swayed about, sometimes giving their bodies a small flick, to show some vestige of youth still lived under the middle-aged clothes.

Mrs McCorn prayed the Commander would ask her to take the floor, to join them, to *show* them, but he did no such thing. And despite her vague sympathies for Women's Liberation, she felt it would not be quite the thing to make the proposal herself. She waved airily at one of the dancers, disguising her disappointment.

'I've made a lot of friends here,' she said. Commander Chariot nodded. They had a second Irish coffee. The Commander, making much of his gallantry, paid with a lot of small change out of his pocket. The pianist struck up, by wonderful chance, 'Hey, there! You with the Stars in Your Eyes'. Mrs McCorn could restrain herself no longer.

'Do you remember, Commander?' she asked. 'Our tune? On the cruise?'

The Commander looked at her blankly. 'Can't say I do. Music's all the same to me. Wouldn't mind if I never heard another note in my life.'

Her ploy having failed, Mrs McCorn ordered two further glasses of Irish coffee – the Commander made no attempt, this time, to pay – so that he should not be aware of the deflation she felt.

They spent the next hour drinking Irish coffee, unspeaking, except to agree to another order. By eleven o'clock, Mrs McCorn felt both reckless and sick. The Commander, she noticed, had a cluster of sweat on both temples, and was flushed. Time, she thought.

'Well, I must be turning in, Commander. Early start tomorrow, for the plane.'

Her words sounded thick as whipped cream. The Commander heaved himself up out of the deep chair and helped her to her feet.

'Jolly good idea,' he said.

Very slowly, Mrs McCorn made her way to the stairs. The pillars through which she threaded her way spun like acrobats' plates. When she tried to smile at various friends, her mouth slithered about in an uncontrollable way, and the feeling of nausea increased. But at last she achieved the foot of the stairs, and felt the mahogany banister solid beneath her liquid hand. She paused, turned carefully to the Commander, whose eyes were at half-mast, and whose mouth sagged.

'So it's *au revoir*, but not goodbye,' she slurred.

'*Au revoir* but not goodbye.' The Commander, too, held on to the banister, his hand only an inch away from Mrs McCorn's. The repetition of her own words gave her courage: in the floundering feather globe of her mind, she realised it was her last chance.

'Nightcap, Commander? Just a small one?'

A long pause. 'Why not?' answered the Commander eventually.

They negotiated the stairs, climbing each one as if it was a separate challenge, drifted like slurry along the moving ruby carpet to Mrs McCorn's room. There, the Commander dropped at once into the velvet armchair. Mrs McCorn hastily hid her peach Dacron nightie – nicely laid out by the maid – under the pillow, and telephoned for two more Irish coffees.

In her own room, she felt better. The sickness seemed to have passed, her head rocked rather than span. The coffees came. Once more, she and the Commander plunged their mouths into the comforting warm froth of cream, and sipped, without speaking.

Mrs McCorn lost all sense of time. Her legs felt as if they were cast in swan's-down, her heart beat wildly as it had in all her imaginings of this climactic scene, and she realised it was no longer possible to continue her life without the Commander.

The next thing she knew she was on the floor by his chair (one shoe had fallen off), her hands running up his trouser legs. A strange moaning came from her lips.

'Commander! Commander! You are my life, I am your slave, your obedient servant, your slave for ever!'

She was dimly aware of her crescendoing voice, and the Commander's bony fingers trying to unlatch her hands from his grey flannel thighs.

'Get off, Mrs McCorn! Get *up*, Mrs McCorn! Don't be so ruddy stupid.'

Through the humming in Mrs McCorn's ears, he sounded as if he meant to be stern, but the words lacked vigour.

'How can you say such cruel things to one who is your life, to one who has waited for you like Patience on a—'

'Get *up*, I say, Mrs McCorn. You're ruining the creases in my trousers.'

Mrs McCorn rose awkwardly as a zeppelin, poised above him for the merest second, then dropped on to his outspread knees, curling into a foetal position. Before he had time to protest, she had grabbed his jaw in one of her hands, squeezed his mouth into an open hole, and thrust her creamy lips on to his. For a blissful moment, she managed to taste *his* Irish coffee and feel the small points of his teeth. She heard him moan, and lashed his tongue more wildly. But then she felt vicious fingers in her ribs, and drew back, crying out with pain.

'Get off, you silly old baggage! What the ruddy hell do you think you're doing?'

'Magda! Call me Magda . . .'

'I'll call the manager. Rape!'

The word struck Mrs McCorn like a blade. She unfurled herself, holding the sore ribs. Stood.

'You don't understand, Commander.'

'I understand only too well, Mrs McCorn.'

'You've taken this all wrong.'

'You're blind drunk and disgusting with it.'

Somehow the words had little impact. They fell on Mrs McCorn's ears without wounding, but she felt it was incumbent upon her to protest.

'Commander! That's no way to speak when all I wanted—'

'I'm getting out of here.'

The Commander rose. His mouth was smeared with Mrs McCorn's Amber Fire lipstick, his sparse hair stood up in spikes. She felt sorry for him. He looked wounded, misunderstood. Mrs McCorn would have liked to have put a gentle hand on his head, smooth the hair, and say, There, there, it's all right now: it's all over. But she resisted.

The Commander moved to the door. He seemed both cowed and fed up.

'I'm sorry if I caused you any offence, Mrs McCorn,' he said quietly, in his normal voice, 'but a man has to protect himself from attack.'

'Quite.' Mrs McCorn nodded. She would have agreed to anything at that moment.

'And I realise you were overcome. Not yourself.'

'I'm sorry. Quite overcome. Not myself at all.'

'Well, I've survived worse things at sea.'

Gentleman to the last, thought Mrs McCorn.

'And now I must go to bed. You're not the only one with an early start. Tomorrow I'm off on a trip to the Skellig Islands.' He reached for the door knob.

Mrs McCorn had been aware of her spirits rising as the Commander made his apology. All was not lost. But with this fresh, final piece of news, they fell to a place so deep within her she had not previously been aware of its existence.

'The Skellig Islands?'

'Always wanted to go there. Well, goodnight.'

He left very quickly. When he had gone, Mrs McCorn fell back on to the bed. Too weak to analyse the failure of the evening, too disheartened even to chide herself, she cried for a while, and then fell asleep.

The maid who brought her breakfast found her next morning, still dressed, on top of the bed, one shoe still on, make-up awry. Somehow, Mrs McCorn roused herself and overcame this little embarrassment with considerable dignity, and even a joke about the effects of Irish coffee. Then she hastened to repair herself, and finish her packing.

Downstairs, she looked about for the Commander, but then she remembered the time of her own departure to the Skelligs yesterday and realised he would already have gone. When she was given the bill, she smiled at the huge sum the Irish coffees had amounted to, and with soft gentle fingers touched the headache that braided her forehead. Various friends from the hotel were there to see her off, and said how much she would be missed. Their declarations touched Mrs McCorn: at least she had made an impression in some quarters.

On the aeroplane over the Irish Sea, she found herself imagining the Commander retracing her own steps of yesterday, or a million years ago, or whenever the thoroughly nasty day had been. But she imagined *he* was enjoying it, and she admired him for that. He was a man of vision in some ways but, unused to much contact with women, could be sympathised with for not recognising true worth when he saw it. Her conclusions about the Commander thus neatly parcelled in her mind, Mrs McCorn searched in her bag for a boiled sweet. And as the coast of England, dear England, came into sight, she decided that on this year's Christmas card she would simply add, *Did you enjoy the Skelligs?* Thereafter would follow months in which she could look forward to an answer, and life in Cheltenham would continue to be lived in hope.

Not for Publication

Discipline as usual, today. Doubt if anything short of another war could make me change my routine now. Old men get stuck in their ways, haven't the heart to change them.

Grey sky, slight wind, leaves beginning to turn. I eagerly read the weather first thing every morning. A fine day makes me look forward to the afternoon walk, though I don't mind rain. I'd never retire to a hot climate. Seven-thirty: open the kitchen door for Jacob. He lumbers out into the orchard, squashing autumn crocuses with every step, the old bugger. Careless, but affectionate, is Jacob. Make myself a piece of toast – can't be bothered with a boiled egg these days – and a cup of tea. Put knife and plate into the sink, run the tap. Mrs Cluff says, 'You leave it, General, till I come.' But I don't like to. I like to do my bit.

Jacob returns, muddy paws. 'You brute, Jacob,' I say. He wags his tail. The most intelligent dogs have their soppy side. He follows me to the study. Goes straight to his place under the desk. The high point of Jacob's day is our walk on the Common after lunch. He knows this will be his reward for patience during my morning stint at the typewriter. He's learned the best way to get through the hours is to sleep. He sleeps.

I light the electric fire. Real fire in the evenings, when Mrs Cluff has done the grate. I lower myself into my creaky old chair (presented to me, at my request and much to their amazement, by my fellow officers when I retired. Well, I'd enjoyed sitting in it for so many years).

I glance out at the clouds behind the apple tree. Can just see a distant hill. It's not like my native Yorkshire, here. But not a bad bit of country. Tame.

I pick up *The Times*. I allow myself fifteen minutes to read it each morning, then begin writing at nine on the dot. 'Start when you *mean* to start,' my Commanding Officer used to say. I always try to take his advice. He was a sound man.

I'm having a bash at my memoirs. Military, mostly. I had a good war. Nothing personal, of course. Don't go along with all this exposure of private life in memoirs, myself. I was horrified only yesterday to see that some tinkering American professor had pried further than any previous biographer into Jane Austen's brief and innocent engagement to one Harris Bigg-Wither. (Imagine: *Pride and Prejudice* by Jane Bigg-Wither. Wouldn't have been the same at all.) Let her keep her secret to herself, I say. Stop nosing about. How will it further our knowledge and pleasure in her work to know that Miss Austen and Mr B-W held hands? Her secret should be allowed to rest peacefully with her in her grave.

Anyhow, I don't imagine anyone will want to read my story, let alone publish it. But I keep at it. Can't do nothing but garden in retirement. Have to keep exercising the old brain. Besides, one or two of the family might be interested once I'm dead. They never care to listen to me much in life.

I put on my specs. Telephone rings. Dammit. Very unusual. Not many people ring me these days and those who do are of the economical kind, won't lift a receiver before six o'clock.

'Hello? Gerald?'

Petronella – my sister. Petronella is a bossy, interfering, loud-voiced and large woman. She lives in Petworth and swanks about Sussex. She's married to a boring husband in commodities, and has four exceptionally dull and tiresome grown-up children married to suitably dull –

'Yes?'

'Seen *The Times*?'

'Not yet.'

'Despatches,' she snaps.

'Who?'

Not Laurence, I hope. My oldest friend, Laurence, in a Home near Folkestone. Been meaning to ring him . . .

'You look. Old friend of yours's husband.'

She gives a barking laugh, slams down the receiver. Petronella has always been of the mistaken belief that not to say goodbye lends a woman mystery. Silly cow.

Relief it's not old Laurence, though. I find the Deaths column. Eyes slip down. Bit slow, bit nervous.

Macdunnald, Vaughan Robert. Peacefully in his sleep after a long illness. Couple of days ago.

So, Mrs Vaughan Macdunnald, Mary Macdunnald, is a widow. That's what that means.

Mary, Mary, Mary Jay.

I put my hands flat on the desk, steady myself. *Brace up, General, greet the morning.* 'Don't hurry over the weighing up,' my Commanding Officer used to say – sound man, admirable fellow – 'then make the decision *snappy*.' His barking voice in my ears. I shut my eyes. Prepare to obey. *This, being something of*

a special day, dear Lord, forgive me for abandoning the military side
of my memoirs this morning . . .

The winter of 1947, you may remember, was cursed with some of
the worst snow of the century. I had recently moved in here, and
pretty primitive it was, too: no heating, hot water on the blink,
garden a jungle. I had bought it for its potential, but was uncertain
how to proceed with the transformation. What it needed was the
hand of some imaginative woman. As it was, it took me some
time to get the place shipshape with the help of a solitary builder.
That first winter was pretty grim. I had to sleep in my greatcoat,
chip ice off the windows every morning. I was grateful to have
only a few days' leave at a time.

Still, I did have a woman vaguely in mind. Veronica. We met at
a dinner dance given by Laurence – who's very rich – to cheer his
remaining friends after the war. It wasn't much of an occasion by
today's standards: food pretty drab, rationed clothes not up to
much. But we enjoyed ourselves. Veronica and I took the floor for
several quicksteps, and a fast waltz to end the evening. I was quite
a dancer in my day, could see she was impressed. I gave her a lift
home to a mansion block in Victoria. She talked about Byron.
She had quite a thing about Byron. 'Brains as well as a good
looker,' Laurence said.

Few weeks later, I took her to lunch at Brown's Hotel. More
Byron. She drank lemon barley which she said was a real treat.
Not a bad girl, not bad at all. On the big side, but friendly. Back
here in the cottage, I allowed myself to weave a few fantasies
about Veronica. She'd be the right sort to bring a house alive, I
thought. And good, child-bearing hips. I spent a few sleepless
nights – the cold, to be honest, more than the thought of
Veronica. After a week or so, I decided to make the next move.

Another evening at the Savoy? I suggested. Where we met,
after all, I said, thinking I'd have a stab at a show of romance. The
idea went down very well. We planned to meet the next Friday

evening. I would be in a black tie. She would be in a long blue dress.

That afternoon, I trudged through the snow to the village (not deep enough, then, to deter my gallant old Wolseley from getting to London) with Ralphie (Jacob's ancestor) at my side. I exchanged many saved-up coupons for a box of chocolates, and began to anticipate the evening with considerable pleasure.

I set off in plenty of time, punctuality being my byword. It had begun to snow again, lightly, and was bitterly cold. But the Wolseley started with its beautiful, reassuring purr. I drove cautiously down the lane, windscreen wipers doing their best against the dark flakes. A full moon, there was, I remember. In two hours I would be with Veronica in the warmth of the Savoy.

The snow fell more thickly. After three miles, the car whimpered to a halt. I tried everything, but the engine was completely dead. Snow piled up quickly on the bonnet. By a stroke of luck, I was fifty yards from my friends, Arthur and Janet Knight, both doctors. They lived in a farmhouse set a little back from the place in which I had come to a halt. Nothing else for it: I must call upon them for help.

Janet opened the door, light from the hall gushed on to the slippery step where I stood. She looked in amazement at my black tie and snow-covered greatcoat. Behind her, packing cases rose almost to the ceiling: she and Arthur were leaving for a spell in Canada the following week.

'Gerald! Whatever – ? Come on in.'

The door shut behind me. The warmth of their house lapped up at me like a welcoming animal. Arthur came hurrying out. I explained the problem. He responded with absolute conviction.

'Tell you what: give up. It's not the night to try to get a car going, and with the snow getting worse it'd be daft to try to get to London. Ring your date, tell her what's happened, and stay to dinner with us. There's plenty of rabbit stew and we need someone to entertain a friend of ours.'

The suggestion was practical, tempting. Before I could protest, my coat was taken from me and I was hustled into the sitting-room, a cosy, dingy room with a huge inglenook fireplace. Logs shifted beneath lively flames. Dense shadows, out of the fire's reach, confused my eyes for a moment. There was a distinct smell of apples – I observed a plate of lustreless Bramleys sitting on a bookshelf – and lavender. Bunches of the stuff, dried, were laid by the fire. Sitting near them, on a low stool, was the Knights' friend, Mary Jay.

She was quite small, I noticed at once, with a pale serious face, devoid of make-up, and huge brown eyes. She wore a dull brown dress of some woollen stuff, the colour of milk chocolate. It had a prim lace collar. Rather Lyons Corner House waitressy, I thought, as she stood up to shake hands.

Janet introduced me as Colonel Arlington. Mary smiled – a smile so slow, so contained, so enchanting that I felt the huge mass of my hand tremble as I briefly held hers. Then she sat down again, huddling her arms round her knees, as if my entrance had done nothing to interrupt her daydream.

In the forty years since that evening, I must have gone over every word, every look, every moment, a million times. With the assumption of old age (I hesitate to call it wisdom) I now understand that there are moments in our lives when some being within us craves something so amorphous it is not strictly definable, but the force of craving puts us into a state of readiness to receive. I believe that is how it must have been, for me, that night. After a life of almost chaste bachelorhood, I longed for something not yet experienced, the warmth of a fellow spirit, the notion of giving everything I had to a fellow creature. Veronica, I knew, was irrelevant to my search. To her, I made conventional overtures with a kind of vague, unanalysed sense of duty, but with no conviction.

In my state of readiness, perhaps, any woman who had been sitting by the Knights' fire that evening might have had the same impact upon me as did Mary. But I think not. It's impossible to imagine another woman igniting such devastating, instant effect. I felt ill, cold, terrified.

As a fighting soldier, I had lived so recently with daily fear, was accustomed to its manifestations: freezing blood, disobedient limbs, loosening bowels. I had learned how to switch on the automatic button in the brain that commands the body to go forth in strength, in faith, with calm. I had learned, as a leader of men, the necessity to inspire courage in others by disguising one's own fear in a guise of courage. Looking down at that small, still woman in her brown dress, I felt more afraid than on any battlefield. Here was someone who was about to change my life. (Ah, little then did I ever guess how.) I was giddy, weak, confused by the total unexpectedness of this break in my journey, by flames replacing snow, by warmth instead of cold. My heart was beating like a wild thing because of the presence of this stranger; had I reached the Savoy, it would have remained quite regular on the dance floor. I sat on a chair as far from Mary as I could manage. I hoped she would not be able to observe me well in the shadows.

Arthur went off to ring the garage, Janet to get me a drink. Mary Jay and I were left listening to the fire. I didn't feel there was any need to speak, but then I heard my own voice, all awry, blurting out some mindless comment.

'That dress you're wearing,' I said. 'It's the colour of a Mars Bar, isn't it?' Did my voice sound as peculiar to her as it did to me? 'Not my favourite colour,' I added, cursing myself as the words escaped.

What devil made me say such a thing, so rudely, to a woman I'd met just two minutes ago? Was it self-defence, resenting the shock she had caused me? Mary swivelled round to face me, fingering the stuff of the skirt, smiling slightly again.

'I know. It's pretty awful, isn't it? I was trying to find a real chestnut. But you know what it's like, still. No choice. Nothing.'

'I'm sorry.' I was wringing my hands. 'That was terribly rude of me. I don't know what- -'

She looked at me as if she really did not mind, perhaps hadn't even noticed.

'That's all right. I like people to say what they think, don't you?'

And those huge brown eyes, each sparkling with a minuscule candle of flame from the fire, looked straight into my soul.

Arthur returned. Mary and I both shifted our positions. Arthur noticed nothing untoward, which was strange: I could have sworn the recognition between Mary and me was tangible, visible to the naked eye. The garage would fetch the car in the morning, snow permitting. Hadn't I better ring . . . ? suggested Arthur.

Lumbering to the telephone in the hall, I felt as if each step was pushing against a heavy sea, so great was my reluctance to move. But the good soldier within me explained with military precision the situation to Veronica. She was very nice about it, quite understood. I said I would be in touch, knowing this was not true. What was the point of Veronica, now Mary . . . ? Janet put a large whisky and soda into my hand.

We ate bowls of rabbit stew round the fire, the kitchen being too cold. I asked no questions, but learned that Mary, whose home was in the Borders, was staying in The Black Swan, a small hotel near Henley. She was a painter, it seemed, but the purpose of her visit was not explained. She was here tonight to say farewell to the Knights before their departure for Canada. Janet was an old schoolfriend.

Our supper finished – an excellent sago pudding with tinned greengages and a small piece of Cheddar followed the rabbit – Arthur put Schubert's 'Trout' on the gramophone. Mary was still on her low stool, arms huddled round her knees again. The rest of us lay back in our armchairs, listening. I positioned myself so that she should not see me watching her. In that room as warm as fur, the musical water twinkled as never before, while the trout leapt, irrepressible, against calmer flames of the fire. My eyes never left the small, still shape of Mary, with her downcast lashes.

At eleven, this bewitching woman looked at her watch. She offered me a lift home, assured me that her Austin Seven would not let us down. It was on her way, she said. Had my head been clearer, I would have realised at once that my path lay in quite the opposite direction to Henley.

Mary wrapped a long scarf round her neck, put on a huge coat, woolly hat and gloves. Her farewells to her friends the Knights were prolonged. Mine were grateful, but brief. Still unsure of my voice, I was, and distracted by the glorious sensations searing through my body.

The Austin Seven was very small inside, but gallant. It snuffled through the deep snow, wonderfully slow. Mary concentrated on her driving. We did not speak. I concentrated on her profile – what there was left of it, between hat and scarf – the delicately tipped nose, the short curling upper lip pursed in concentration, and giving no hint of the smiles it contained. The sky was clear, but dark as those blackout nights when people crouched in shelters waiting for the siren to howl the All Clear. It had stopped snowing. There was an infinite arc of stars above us, and a powerful moon. Its light encased Mary's side view in a glittering frame. Every strand of escaped hair was visible, iridescent as cobweb threads. The fluffed outline of her childlike hat sparkled richly as silver fox fur.

At my gate, all too soon, I congratulated my driver. Congratulations! How steeped we are in convention: how it props us, clumsily, in heightened moments. So inappropriate, my congratulations in the midnight snow: would I had a poet's art of the right word. But again, she didn't seem to mind.

'Oh, it was nothing. I'm used to such conditions. Scotland . . .'

She smelt of sugared violets, the sweet iced cakes of childhood.

'I won't ask you in,' I said.

'No,' she said. 'I must be getting back.'

'It's perishing, when my fire's out.'

I felt I owed her some kind of explanation in case she was the sort of girl accustomed to being offered late-night champagne.

'I can imagine.' Her small smile snapped the last thread of my discretion.

'How long are you here for?' I asked.

'Another week, perhaps.'

'Would you like – well, lunch or something, one day?'

She hesitated. Then she said, Yes, that would be nice, and I should ring her at her hotel.

'Any special time?' My heart was racing, racing.

'Any time'll do. I'm not painting much. Just – thinking things over.'

'Very well, I'll be in touch.'

I took from my pocket the box of chocolates destined for Veronica, and gave them to her. She smiled again, said nothing. I thanked her for the lift, got out of the car. It trundled off down the snowy lane. The moon burnished its tiny roof. Its tyres left very narrow tracks in the snow. Neither of us waved.

In bed that night, frozen, shivering, wide awake, I began to think about the concept of romantic love. I had always been sceptical of its existence and was certainly innocent of its ways. Yet here I was, plainly seized by some extraordinary force, some unfamiliar form of madness, that made the rest of the night almost impossible to endure. I thought of the poets I loved – Shakespeare, Browning, Byron, Shelley – was this the sort of thing those chaps had been through? Was this the inspiration that had driven their genius? And to what measures would it drive me? My mind slithered, ineffectual as confused eels. Despite the cold, I was feverish, unable to lie still. Eventually, thank God, dawn paled the sky.

By mid-morning, I had established the nature of my brainstorm. It concerned love, and it was firing me with uncontainable restlessness. – The car, it seemed, was 'serious'. At least a week, they'd want it, with one man off, they said. I could not wait a week. I could not wait another moment.

Some instinct, though, forced me to endure two days. The weekend was the longest of my life. At last, on the Monday afternoon, in another snowstorm, I set off for The Black Swan with Ralphie. I had contemplated ringing Mary and asking her to come over in her car, but, after a thousand changes of mind, had decided that a surprise would be better. There were only two days left of my present leave. Already the weekend had been wasted, and Mary would be gone by the time I was back again.

Despite the deep snow, Ralphie and I made the seven miles to the hotel, across woods and fields, in less than an hour. A superhuman energy pressed me to keep up a wicked pace. By the time we arrived, I was sweating. Poor Ralphie was exhausted.

I saw Mary at once, through the glass door of the lounge. She was alone, reading a book by a small gas fire, a tiny glass of sherry on the table beside her.

'I've walked,' I said. 'The car won't be ready for a week. I couldn't—'

'Oh, Gerald,' she said. 'I thought you were never coming.' She looked abashed, as if she had not meant to say what she thought so quickly. 'But you're both frozen, soaked through!'

She patted Ralphie's head. At once the room, for all its emptiness, swirled with warmth and life, and I found myself sitting beside Mary in front of the pallid fire, shoes off, feet craning ungainly towards its pathetic heat, icy hands rasping together, speechless. As Mary seemed to be, too. At last, I said I was sorry I hadn't telephoned.

'I like surprises,' she said.

'Lunch?' I asked a while later. 'I'm ravenous.' This was a lie.

'Why not? Do you know, I'm the only guest here. God knows why they're open at this time of year. They say they have quite busy weekends, people coming to visit some home for disabled soldiers nearby. It'll be just us, and disgusting food.'

In the bleak, cold dining-room we ate the disgusting food and did not care: there was plenty of wine. An old woman with chilblained hands waited sullenly upon us, sniffing. Mary talked of her recent stay in Florence, and of her painting – 'not very good, but comforting' – and of her own labrador in Scotland, 'fatter than Ralphie'. Much of the time we ate in silence. There seemed no particular need for talk.

But come the castle pudding, with its smear of raspberry jam and skin-topped custard, and I could contain my curiosity no longer.

'Why are you here, exactly?' I asked.

Mary hesitated. I could see her working out an answer.

'Too complicated to explain, really,' she replied lightly. 'I'm just trying to work a few things out. I wanted to be somewhere a long way from home, by myself.'

'I see.' I would ask no more, naturally.

'I rather like being on my own. I really do,' she went on. 'In fact, if I never got married I'd be quite happy. My mother would call that a terrible failure, but I honestly wouldn't mind at all.'

'I don't suppose there's much chance of your remaining . . .'

The vicious thought of her being someone else's wife stopped me. Mary gave a small laugh whose echo was muted by the mud-brown carpet, the soggy grey walls, the thick curtains of stuff like woven bran. By now it was three-thirty. Chilblains had left long ago in a huff. Mary offered me another lift home. But I insisted on walking. There was still energy to be dissipated if I was to get a wink of sleep that night.

'Very well, then,' she said. 'I'll drive over to *you* for lunch tomorrow. How would that be?'

That was the only moment she was just the slightest bit flirtatious. *My darling, beloved Mary – what do you imagine? And stay for ever, please.*

'Early as you like,' I said.

At midday I began to imagine that she was snowbound, upside

down in a ditch, or had changed her mind. I suffered all the torments of a waiting lover, fretting over the smoky fire, the mud from Ralphie's paws on the sofa where she should sit, the draught from the windows. Provisions were a little odd, but by now I was confident she wouldn't mind that sort of thing. I had found one last bottle of port, given to me by my father on my twenty-first birthday, so pretty mature by now. Apart from that, there was a pound of sausages and a couple of stale rolls. The village shop had run out of pickles and cheese.

Mary arrived at one forty-five, by which time my equilibrium was in a wretched state. She had a shining cold face and wore green trousers: she gave no reason for being late.

'This,' she said, coming brilliantly into the room, a barren place, then, 'is *marvellous*.' She looked out of the window to the view I've lived with for forty years. 'Imagine when the apple tree is out.'

We grilled the sausages over the fire, burned and abandoned the rolls, and drank most of the port from my mother's old silver goblets. I put on the Beethoven violin concerto – scratchy old record, but it didn't matter. Nothing mattered. For the life of me, I can't remember what we talked about (the erosion of that conversation has been a mental torture ever since). But I do remember we laughed a lot, made tea when it was dark and the wind fretted at the bare windows, and planned a walk together the next day – my last.

Each day with Mary, somehow, was so extraordinarily different, as if the Lord was giving us a chance, at least, to see each other in a variety of weathers. The Tuesday was sunny: great strips of gold slashed across the wind-bitten snow, draining the blue from shadows. Robins shrieked from the apple tree. The hedges, snow-covered chariots, were parked on cobweb wheels of diamond cogs, spun by millionaire spiders. Unable to stay indoors, I set off to the village with Ralphie, thinking I would meet her on her way. I sang 'Rule Britannia' very loudly, not knowing the words of any love songs, and found children skating on the pond. I thought: this is my last chance. What can I do? How can I let her go?

An immediate plan came to my rescue. For the first time in my honourable career, I would make some excuse and take two more days' leave. Thus, before she left, we might have a little more time.

I heard the pooping of a small horn behind me. The Austin Seven was chugging towards me, Mary in her woollen hat, smiling. She was out of the car in a trice, running.

'I'm terribly early. Sorry! Hope you didn't – I mean, we mustn't waste the sun.'

We didn't waste the sun. We walked for miles. God knows where we went. I remember woods, the creak of snow in the hush of ash trees, the squawk of a frightened blackbird. I remember a lighted village church, women bustling about with clumps of evergreen, preparing for a wedding or a funeral, a smell of paraffin, the organist perfecting 'Abide with Me'. Wickedly cold, suddenly, when we came out again. The sun had gone. The sky was a starless navy.

Mary was tired by now. We had had a glass of mulled wine in a pub, but had eaten nothing. Time ignored the ordinary junctions of an ordinary day. We were surprised by the suddenness of the evening. In a lane a mile still from the car, Mary suddenly slipped, stumbled. I put out my hand to save her, pulled her to me. Instead of resisting, she clung to me, a childlike hug with the fingers of her woolly gloves spread out on my arms. She gave a small sob. I could feel it against my heart. Looking down, I saw tears pushing under the long lashes of her closed eyes. I kissed her forehead. She straightened up, dabbed at her eyes. In the failing light, a smear of tears glinted on her cheek. I could see a drop of crystal poised under one nostril. We began to walk again. She let me hold her hand.

And, back at the car at last, she permitted me to kiss her on the forehead once more. In retrospect, I am glad, so glad, I was spared from knowing at the time this was our last moment. For, then, I had plans. Tomorrow I would surprise her: turn up in the mended car, take her to London, lunch, the Tate, theatre, dinner, anything. I said nothing of this, however, and shut the door of the toy-like car. She waved, this time, with a smile that I think was rather sad, but I may have imagined that. Working over the same small fabric of memory so many times, the weave plays tricks. Anyway, it was quite dark by now, and tonight no moon replaced the sun.

The following day I put on a suit and my regimental tie, polished my shoes. The Wolseley, full of new life, deposited me at The Black Swan at eleven-thirty precisely.

I asked for Miss Jay at the reception desk, as the lounge was empty. But she had gone. Checked out. No forwarding address. Nothing.

No need to remind myself of the pattern of my despair that followed, the struggle to heal a broken heart. I cursed myself for the stupid risk surprises mean, drove wildly to the Knights' to make enquiries. They had left for Canada the day before. I skidded home to ring every Jay in the Borders' telephone book, but no one had heard of Mary. I wanted to end my life. I returned to being a soldier.

Six months later, almost to the day, I read in *The Times* the engagement was announced between Miss Mary Jay (address supplied, too late) to Mr Vaughan Robert Macdunnald of the Isle of Skye. (Oh God, had she waited six months for me to give some signal?) On one of Petronella's unwelcome visits, she mentioned that Mr Vaughan Macdunnald was a friend of her husband Henry, and the whole family would be going up to the wedding. Later, she tried to tell me about the nuptials. I told her that I had briefly met Mary Jay, but was not interested in hearing how her wedding day had passed. Petronella gave me one of her horribly knowing looks. I assumed, rightly, that I would have to avoid years of scraps of information pertaining to the Macdunnald household.

Three years after Mary's wedding, the Knights returned home. One evening I asked them, in a nonchalant manner, if they had ever heard of her again. They had not, though they had written to her at the time of her marriage. I went on, in casual fashion, to describe the nature of her departure.

'Well, it must have been very difficult for her, mustn't it?' said Janet. 'She'd come down here to try to persuade herself she couldn't go through with it, the marriage to Vaughan. But there was so much pressure on her. They had known each other since childhood, and he'd been trying to marry her for years, you know. Apparently he had a wonderful castle on the sea – everything you could want, if you loved Scotland, which Mary did. But he was blown up in '42 – helpless invalid for life. I think Mary believed that if she said no, that would be the end, for him.'

In the event, the end took forty years. Poor bugger. Poor Mary.

Mrs Cluff, I see, is coming up the garden path, basket over her arm, mind on the pork chop and baked apple she will cook for my lunch. She's a good soul, Mrs Cluff. And over those years, what for me? The odd fling, the casual affair, no thoughts of marriage: the saving discipline of army life, the pleasure of retirement here. I can't complain.

But, ah, what might have been? Should any old man ask himself that question? What might have been, with Mary Jay?

'Morning, General.' Doors bang. She's inclined to bang doors, Mrs Cluff.

'Morning, Mrs Cluff,' I shout back. We never come face to face until the dishes are on the table.

'Chill wind this morning.' Another bang.

And now she's free, my Mary Jay, and here am I still waiting. Still waiting, in the real sense? Has the hope never died? Is the love of my life still intact in my heart? What do you think, Jacob old boy? Would I be a fool to risk getting in touch again, now – or a fool not to? Is it too late? Are we too old?

The morning has flown in cogitation. Damn sight more inter-esting, as a matter of fact, all that sort of thing, than the military side. Dare say Petronella and Co would be fascinated. But they'll never know, because it's not for publication, of course. Nothing private for publication.

I've taken my time balancing up the pros and cons, though the summing-up needs another hour or so's reflection. Wind on the Common'll clear my mind. Then I'll make the decision, 'snappy', like my wise old CO said. By this evening, I promise myself. By 1800 hours, to be precise. Cheap dialling time. Quiet time to write a letter.

'Jacob,' I say, giving him a slight kick to wake him, 'Jacob, old man, it's an important day for you and me today. Come on, now. Stir yourself. It's almost time for lunch.'

Dressing Up

'Please, just one more chance,' cooed Prunella in her most persuasive voice. 'Just lunch and the afternoon.'

There was a long silence while her daughter Audrey, on the other end of the line, struggled to weigh up the pros and cons of her mother's request.

Prunella, although dreading this call, was fed up with watching time flood by with no sight of her grandchildren. It was over two months, now, since the unfortunate incident. Surely enough time for anyone to find forgiveness. But Audrey had never been rich in charity. Even as a small child she had shown signs of her father's hardness. She was vigorous in her condemnation, ungenerous in her understanding. Prunella had always been a dutiful mother, and hoped she always would be. But she couldn't like Audrey.

And how beastly she had been about the incident. A very minor mishap: no ill effects on the children. They had had *fun*, as they always did have when they came to their grandmother. More than they had at home, for the most part. It wasn't Prunella's fault Audrey had been held up in traffic, so arrived late to collect them on that particular day. Well, by six, half an hour later than her usual time for the first one, Prunella was exhausted, in need of something. She must have had two gins and tonics before Audrey arrived. Having started late, perhaps she had drunk them faster than usual. What with one thing and another, on the way down the path to Audrey's car she had stumbled, cut her knee, felt dizzy. There had been quite a palaver, Audrey pulling her up, grumbling away, telling the children to buzz off and find a plaster. 'You're irresponsible, Mother,' she had hissed when the children, all sympathy for their grandmother, had run off. 'How do you expect me to feel about leaving them with someone who *drinks*? Anything could happen. I shan't let them come again.'

Prunella hadn't felt like arguing. She had sat on a kitchen chair, one stocking an ignominious roll beneath her knee, watching Audrey savagely dab the bloody patch. The children hugged her goodbye, said they hoped they would see her soon. She had given them a box of chocolates, which afforded Audrey the opportunity for a familiar lecture on children's teeth before hurrying them away. Prunella hadn't seen them since then. Audrey was carrying out her threat. This was her punishment. Drink: and no grandchildren. Deprivation of the two people who gave her most pleasure on earth, these days. She was a callous monster, Audrey. How could she have given birth to one of so little compassion?

But this silly feud had gone on long enough, Prunella thought, at dawn the autumn day of the call she eventually forced herself to make. She must put an end to it. She must swallow pride and anger, apologise, make promises not to touch a drop before the children arrived or while they were there: promise anything. She must compromise herself in a disgraceful way. But any form of humiliation was worth it to see the grandchildren.

At eleven o'clock she drank two cups of coffee without their usual addition of brandy. This daily booster, she had found, gave her the necessary strength for the rest of the day. Unfortunately, Audrey's antennae were so acute she seemed able to tell if her mother had put so much as a dash of sherry in her trifle, just by her voice over the telephone. So this morning, wanting to take no risks, Prunella had denied herself fortification. Without it she was feeling very shaky. The receiver of the telephone danced at her ear. Sweat frosted the back of her neck. Her heart was leaping like a young lamb.

'One more chance, then,' said Audrey at last, in her tight little voice. 'You know the conditions.'

'I know the conditions. Of course I—'

'Just lunch and the afternoon. I'll drop them at twelve. And no chocolates either, please.'

'Poor mites! Very well, no chocolates. I've missed them so much. They must wonder why they haven't been for so long.'

'They haven't said anything.'

Prunella knew Audrey was lying. She was able to detect her daughter's lies on the telephone every bit as distinctly as Audrey could detect her own small indulgence of alcohol. But this morning she didn't care. The main thing was she had won the battle. The horrible waiting, the isolation, was over. She would see the children in just two days. Dear George, gallant beyond his years: Anna of the laughing eyes. Prunella poured herself a third cup of coffee, laced it with a fierce shot of brandy.

She was determined to take no risks. After breakfast on the day of the children's visit, she put the bottle of brandy in the dining-room cupboard – a cold, deserted room she scarcely visited – and locked it. She put the key in the pocket of her apron, hoping she would forget where it was. Back in the warmth of the kitchen she placed a tea cosy over the bottle of gin. The smile of its white label stretching across its elegant green shoulders was the temptation, evenings, afternoons, that she could not resist. So long as it was hidden, she would be quite safe.

The hours passed so fast in busy preparation of the children's food that Prunella did not stop for her usual cup of coffee, let alone brandy. At twelve, everything ready, the table laid, Ribena poured, she remembered this and smiled to herself. Sometimes, it was so easy. When you were happy, there was no need for a booster. Maybe she'd leave the brandy in the cupboard. Not touch it tomorrow, either. Make a real effort. Sling out the grinning gin. *Reform*, as Audrey would say. Though what would Audrey know about the near-impossibility of such a thing?

The bell rang on the dot of twelve-thirty. Audrey was always punctual, and superior with it. She gave a hurried smile, trying to disguise the twitching of her nostrils, the mean detection of drink on her mother's breath. Hoping to catch me out, the bitch, thought Prunella. But it didn't matter. With George and Anna wriggling under each arm, she felt bold, strong.

'Do I pass the breath test?'

'Don't be stupid, Mother. I'll be back at five.'

Once Audrey had gone the children burst from strait-jackets of polite demeanour – always worn in the shadow of their mother – and hugged their grandmother so hard she was almost knocked over. She managed to brush aside any answers to their questions about why they had not seen her for so long with the promise of small presents awaiting them in the kitchen. She produced shiny black pencils with their names engraved in gold, with notebooks to match – 'For your secret thoughts,' she said. The children laughed. They were always delighted by the quaintness of their grandmother's presents, so carefully chosen. At home, they were rich in computer games, Walkmans, miniature televisions – quick, easy, expensive presents which could be bought with no trouble. Spoiled in this respect, they still appreciated real worth: their grandmother's presents were of especial value.

Prunella's kitchen, where she spent most of her time, blazed with signals of her life. Old photographs, lists, theatre posters, half-finished pieces of tapestry were either stuck to the walls or piled on the floor or chairs. It was not uncommon to find grated carrot in a pair of satin evening shoes that had lodged by the stove for the past twenty years, or a rusty trinket in the fruit bowl. The children, accustomed to the white Formica sterility of their own kitchen at home, loved the room. It bulged with memories of happy afternoons since their earliest childhood, and was always full of the warm expectation of exciting things to come. Occasionally they would venture into the large, cold, unused rooms of the house, deserted since their grandfather had died. But they thought of them as sad, dead rooms, that made shivers run down their backs, and would quickly hurry back to the life of the kitchen.

As usual, they ate hungrily of their grandmother's food, made promises not to tell about the chocolate pudding. They listened enchanted as she told stories about her intriguing past, which had been a very glamorous time, and indeed she had been very famous. A dancer, a singer, a bit of both – and only twenty years ago some television company had come and persuaded her to talk about her past: they had seen the recording over and over again. She was a star, their grandmother, they could tell from the many photographs of a beautiful face that smiled from the mists of the old photographs on the walls. And even today she was a star, bright red hair – the children didn't believe it when their mother said it was a wig – long gypsy earrings, scarlet nails, silver eye-shadow. But for the wrinkles, she could be mistaken for a rock star, they thought. And underneath her apron she wore velvet dresses of crimson or purple or sapphire that flashed a patchwork of light, and she smelt of face powder from a bygone age.

'And what shall we do today?' she was saying. 'How best shall we pass the afternoon, little ones?'

'Dressing up,' they said.

'I thought so,' said Prunella. Of all the old-fashioned activities she thought up for them, dressing up was the favourite. 'I brought down some new things from the attic.'

In a trice they had leapt upon the huge cardboard box waiting under the window. (It had taken three whiskies, last night, to give Prunella the strength to drag it down from the attic.)

'How did you get this down all by yourself, Gran?'

'Easily!'

'You're brilliant, Gran,' said Anna.

Prunella, dumping dirty plates into the sink to be washed at some future time she had no wish to think about, beamed. She listened to the small cries of amazement and amusement as the children plucked pantomime clothes from the box. They would pull something on, then, more strongly attracted by something else, pull it off before it was in place.

The dishes cleared, Prunella sat at the table giving advice and encouragement. She panted a little, felt a little light-headed. Well, the children's visits were dizzy times, stirring up the stale old quietness till the kitchen became a place she could hardly recognise. Besides, she had worked so hard this morning, never a moment off her feet.

What she wanted was a drink.

The children were ready at last. George was a small laughing cavalier, ostrich feather swooping from his velvet cap right under his chin; Anna was a shepherdess with a laced bodice and yellow silk stockings.

'Wonderful!' Prunella clapped her hands. 'You look real professionals.' This, they knew, was her highest compliment: she had been the most professional professional in her time. 'Now for acting.'

'Not without you, Gran.'

'What, me? Dress up too?'

This moment of mock surprise was a small charade enjoyed on every visit. Prunella would feign reluctance, then find herself persuaded.

'Well,' she would say, as she did now, 'if that's what you want . . .' And they would shower her with myriad things to choose from till she, too, had become a character, a star from some world-famous theatrical show.

Prunella stood up. Knees shaky. She fended off the gust of scarves and jackets they threw at her.

'Just a moment, darlings. Gran just needs a . . . to keep her going. Put on some music, George, why not? Let's begin with our old 'Blackbird' to put us in the mood.' She opened the fridge, took out the bottle of white wine. She poured herself a tumbler.

George, child of the technological age, always had some trouble with the workings of the maplewood box his grandmother called the radiogram. But eventually he persuaded the old table to spin the 78 record – 'Bye Bye, Blackbird'. They had known all the words for years.

> 'When somebody says to me
> Sugar sweet, so is she
> Bye bye, blackbird . . .'

Within moments, Prunella found herself pumping the old power into the song. The once-famous voice trembled poignantly on every note, drowning the thinner voices of the children. She drank a second glass, picked up her skirts, pointed a velvet shoe with a diamanté buckle.

'Now, off we go. Follow the silly old bat, won't you? *Bye, bye, blackbird . . .*'

'You're not a silly old bat, Gran.'

The children knew the rules: copy every movement precisely. This afternoon Prunella was full of invention. They skipped around the table waving their arms as if carrying invisible boughs. They grabbed apples from the bowl and threw them high. They flicked their fingers under a running tap at the sink. They – and this was their favourite part – climbed up a chair on to the table, creaking the old pine top as they twirled between bowls of hyacinths – and then leapt down the other side. Those brief moments high on the table felt like being on a stage.

'Oh, happy chorus line, darlings,' Prunella sang. She downed a third quick glass. 'Up we go again, why not?'

This time, on the tabletop, she did a few steps of the can-can. Amazed by their grandmother's high kicks, the children gave up trying to copy her. They watched, entranced.

'Not the right music, of course, but I can still kick a leg, can't I? Let's see if I can't find a can-can record.'

Prunella, jumping ambitiously back down on to a chair, missed her footing. There was a crack, a thud and a dignified whimper, all muffled by the music as she flung one fat arm dramatically behind her.

'Gran? – Quick, George,' shouted Anna.

George slithered off the table, laughing. He bent over Prunella on the floor.

'Are you doing your dying scene, Gran?'

Anna prodded a vast velvet hip, its lights twinkling less brightly in the shadow of the table. She could see, so close to Prunella's eyelids, the smudges of silvery blue were thick and uneven. The lids looked like wrinkled blue worms lying side by side. When her eyes were open, you didn't notice this. Anna wished they would open now. The record slurred to the end. Now the only sound was the running tap.

'You can get up now, Gran,' she said.

'Think she's dead?' asked George.

'I suppose I'd better feel her heart.' Anna was top in biology at school. She ran a reluctant finger over the left velvet breast, feeling the warmth but no distinctive heartbeat.

'There's stuff coming out of her mouth,' observed George, 'and isn't she a funny colour? Maybe she's unconscious.'

'I'll ring for an ambulance.' Anna's coolness in a crisis had been rewarded by making her a prefect. All the same, the telephone jittered in her hand.

'Better not say she's dead,' said George, 'or they won't hurry.'

One of the ambulancemen removed the scarlet boa from Prunella's neck and quickly plunged down, locking his mouth on to hers.

'Kiss of life,' Anna explained to George.

'Wouldn't fancy that,' George giggled. The ambulanceman sat back on his heels, frowning. 'You've got lipstick all over you.'

'Pipe down, young chappie. What about you two?'

'Our mother will be here any minute,' said Anna.

'That's good, because we'd best get a move on.' He was helping the second man to attach a drip to Prunella's arm, still stiff in its last flourish.

It was a struggle to lift her on to the stretcher. One of her shoes fell off. The boa left scarlet feathers on the ambulancemen's uniforms. George deplored the sight of his grandmother's knee, suddenly revealed, that only moments ago had been so impressive in its kicks.

'Poor old Gran,' said Anna. She hated the sight of the shock of copper hair tipped sideways, proving her mother was right about a wig. She hoped George would not notice.

'If she's not dead, then it's her best ever dying Juliet.' Tears of admiration ran quietly down George's cheeks.

Audrey, hurrying punctually down the path, found her way impeded by the ambulancemen and stretcher. In the second she paused, she saw the multicoloured mound of her mother, clown-white face smudged with blue eyebrows, powdery blobs of salmon pink ironic on the old cheeks. She screamed.

From the front door the children watched her livid journey.

'Cool it, Mum. Gran had a fall.' Anna herself felt a strange calm.

Audrey swivelled round at the slamming of the ambulance doors.

'You *idiots*! Of all the stupid . . . Quick, we must follow her.' She ripped off George's hat and threw it nastily to the ground. 'What *happened*?' George retrieved his hat. He had no time to answer before Audrey ran into the kitchen, saw the empty bottle, the upturned chair. Again the children watched her from the door.

'Christ! I can't believe it. Never, ever again . . .' she shouted, exploding eyes glassy with tears.

Anna hitched up her skirt with pitiless hands.

'No use threatening us,' she said. 'Gran may be dead.'

'On the other hand,' said George, 'it may just be one of her best dying scenes.'

He knew about the sweetness of revenge from his history books, and the power it could engender. With a solemn look he replaced his feathered hat, tilting it in just the way his grandmother had assured him, light years ago, was appropriate for a laughing cavalier.

Laughter in the Willows

It was Isabel Loughland's second summer up at Oxford and in her own mind she was a failure. This feeling had come to her within weeks of arriving at New College, and settled more deeply every term. It was nothing to do with her studies. That part of her life, mercifully, was rewarding. She worked hard, taking advantage of hours unoccupied by romantic interest, and the results were encouraging. If she carried on like this, she had been advised, there was a chance she would get a good second-class degree – even a first.

This thought was no compensation for a loveless life. The few girlfriends Isabel had made had paired off with men very soon after they arrived. By now, initial partners had changed and changed again. Keeping up with the shuffle of love affairs was at first entertaining (how Isabel admired their ability to be so positive of their attraction to one, and then so quickly to another).

Now it was wearying. She no longer bothered. She had become used to being a lone figure in a coupled society, and reckoned a change in this situation was unlikely. Among the dozens of male undergraduates she had encountered, not a single one had caused her the ungrounding that she knew to be the prime indication of love.

Isabel felt no self-pity: merely, puzzlement. The men who had made advances to her – and even now, when the fear of committing sexual harassment makes for some hesitation, there was no shortage of them – had claimed her as pretty, almost beautiful. Certainly she was a good listener – her mother had taught her there was no aphrodisiac so potent as lending an attentive ear. She could make people laugh. She was the provider of imaginative gestures; she was modest and sympathetic.

The stumbling block, she knew, was the *unfashionable* air that blew off her, awesome as expensive scent. She did not dress like the others, in jeans and grubby layered things, and elephantine boots. She wore long, clean skirts of pure cotton or velvet, and pumps of pale kid. She brushed her hair and, in summer, wore straw hats stuck with real flowers to evensong. Her demeanour gave clues to her limitations. She had no desire to become close to a man after a single drink in The Blue Boar (although she was not averse to a pint of lager), and any suggestions of a kiss on immediate acquaintance were politely turned down. It was not that she was a prude – when the time came, she was convinced she would make love as keenly as her friends. But she was of the outdated belief that the only chance of a lasting relationship was friendship that developed into love and sex: the other way round did not augur well for permanency. While mere lust did not interest her, the height of her ideals caused her disillusion. Several times, her hopes were raised in the direction of a particular figure, only to be crushed by his expectations of instant physical gratification.

She should have been born in a different age, Isabel reflected, as she did so often. On this fine evening, sitting by herself in New

College gardens, she imagined the attraction of life at Jane Austen's pace: the *containing* of realisation. That's what she sought. That was the essence of the romance she believed in.

Isabel picked daisies from the perimeter of her rug. She tried to remember how to make a chain. Various couples walked by, caught up in the kind of rapture which, in her judgement, was too self-conscious to be anything more than temporary. She felt no envy: that was not what she wanted. But disappointment on finding no one of the stuff she imagined, in almost two years at Oxford, was sometimes acute. Now, for instance. It was a waste of such an evening, not to be sharing it. Returning to books was sometimes not enough.

The lilacs were beginning to unfurl. Blossom snowed down from a cherry tree. Shadows had stretched almost to the edge of the rug. (Isabel was ridiculed for her rug, with its mackintosh backing.) Others, nearby, sat on the grass. Time to go in, she thought. Back to her room. An evening of more study.

She looked up. A single man – a rare sight on a fine summer's evening in college grounds – was coming towards her. He was exceptionally thin, narrow. From a distance, his face was a blade. He wore pale baggy trousers of crushed linen, as if he'd just discovered *Brideshead*. Isabel smiled at the thought. She recognised him. Last week in chapel she had dropped her prayer book. He had picked it up, returned it to her. In the brief moment of the handing over, their eyes had met without interest.

It was evident, in the firmness of his step, that he was not about to pass by. He was intent on speaking.

Isabel shifted slightly, indicating reluctance to be encountered. She wanted to continue with her quiet evening, not have to make the effort to turn down an invitation.

The man was by her now. A concave figure, holding out his hand – an unusual gesture among students. Isabel shook it, surprised by such unaccustomed formality, but good manners instinctive within her.

'Jacques,' he said, 'de Noailles. We met in chapel last Sunday evening. I've been looking for you.'

Isabel suppressed a small sigh. She could not be unbent by flattery.

'Isabel Loughland,' she said reluctantly. 'This is my college.'

Jacques lowered himself, unasked, on to the grass beside the rug. It did not occur to Isabel to invite him to share it.

'I'm at Corpus.' Jacques de Noailles leaned back on his elbows, shut his eyes. In the instant that they were shut, Isabel observed a veil of pure evil cross his face. Or perhaps it was a strand of shade extending, now that it was almost eight, from the lilacs. There was something intriguing in the way his narrow chest dipped deeply towards his spine. She liked the cornflower blue of his clean shirt.

He opened his eyes, made no attempt to smile at her.

'Greats,' he said. 'How about you?'

'Mediaeval History.'

'That was an option for me. I would have liked that. But my father said, don't miss your chance of philosophies. He's French. You know what eager philosophers the French are.'

Isabel put down the book she had picked up in readiness to leave before Jacques had arrived.

'Yes,' she said.

'Strange: this is my third year and last Sunday was the first time I've seen you,' said Jacques.

'Not so very strange, so many . . . It's only my second year.'

'Ah.' They talked about their undergraduate lives for a while, and their vacations. Jacques said he divided his time between his mother in Scotland and his father in Provence. After coming down from Oxford, he said, he intended to take a course at the Sorbonne. Isabel told him she lived in Devon. Both her parents were botanists, often away in foreign mountains in search of extraordinary species. She and Jacques did not ask each other many questions. They took it in turns to offer small pieces of information, giving little away.

An hour passed. It had grown cool. Jacques raised himself on to his haunches, made ready to go.

'I was just wondering – is there anything in Oxford that you haven't done in your two years here? That you would like to do? It's difficult to come up with an original invitation. But I'm sorry. Silly question. It was only that I thought a girl like you must have done *everything*.'

Isabel felt herself blush. She let a long moment pass. Dare she tell him? Yes, she decided.

'As a matter of fact, there is one thing. It's so . . . childish. Such a cliché. It's what everyone does in their first summer, but somehow the chance never came. I want to go on a punt . . .'

Jacques did not laugh, as she had expected.

'Well, for that matter, I've never been on one either,' he said. 'It's never occurred to me. *Alors!* We shall go on a punt. I shall make arrangements.'

He stood, very quickly, rubbing his long thin thighs with his long thin hands. He pulled Isabel to her feet.

'Politically incorrect, I dare say.' They both laughed. 'You're taller than I expected.' He swooped down again, as if embarrassed by the intimacy of the spontaneous observation, and picked up the daisy chain. For a moment, Isabel thought he intended to take it: an unlikely romantic gesture. But he gave it back to her, dangling it lightly across her wrist. 'Now, I must go.'

Dusk had covered the grass, thickened the trees.

The next morning, Isabel found a message at the Lodge. *Be at Magdalen Bridge at three p.m. Bring your rug. Jacques.*

Impertinent, the rug bit, she thought. Though not impertinent enough to refuse the invitation.

She lay back in the punt, eyes half closed. All was just as she had imagined. Her rug was spread over cushions supplied by Jacques who tussled, tight-lipped, with the pole. Isabel pretended not to notice his lack of talent as a punter, and did not mind how long it took, the journey down the river. The heat of the sun and splash of water made her sleepy, too sleepy to speak.

At some moment, it might have been an hour after they set off, Jacques announced they had arrived. Isabel, rousing herself, saw they had tied up at the bank beside an enormous willow tree.

'I'd say that was pretty good for someone who's never done it before,' she said, sitting up.

'Thanks. But you were asleep most of the time.'

'Half asleep.'

They lifted out the rug, cushions and a small wicker hamper. This made Isabel laugh.

'Most undergraduate picnics travel in plastic bags,' she said.

'I don't like plastic bags.' Jacques' shirt was dark with sweat. 'If you're going to take a picnic at all, you might as well bother, no? What do you think of this place? Do you like it?'

Isabel looked across the river. The meadows were that bright green of early May with a pointillist covering of cow-parsley. Distant woods of new, transparent leaves made delicate fans against the sky.

'Good,' she said.

'And the willow? You like this old tree? It's famous. Lots of people come here. We're lucky to have it to ourselves.'

'You've been here before, then?'

'Oh yes, often. But never by punt. I've always walked.' He answered lightly. A sudden positioning of shadow on his face reminded Isabel of last night's brief illusion of cruelty. He was smiling. Remembering? Who had he come with? With what intent? Questions leapt in Isabel's mind, but they were empty. She wondered slightly at her lack of curiosity.

Jacques parted the thickly-leaved branches of the willow. Isabel followed him into the ribboned vault beneath it. Grass was scant here, worn away by previous visitors. There were other signs of the popularity of the hiding place, too. An empty crisp bag, a scrunched-up beer can.

'Bastards,' said Jacques. He picked up the rubbish, went back through the branches to bury it. Alone for a moment in this place of gently shifting leaf shadow, Isabel clutched herself with crossed arms. She felt a distant chill. The heat of the sun could not penetrate the walls of the greenery, though it made a million fire-flies among the leaves, points of lights that dazzled as they moved with the slight breeze. Isabel wondered if she should suggest they should eat outside.

Jacques returned.

'So hot. This is wonderful, no? The cool.'

They laid out the rug and cushions. The hamper was unpacked. Jacques had *bothered*: there was proper French bread, and *mille-feuilles* from the Maison Blanc; pâtés, tiny cheeses in oiled paper tied with twine. Black misted grapes, a bottle of white wine, red gingham napkins and china plates.

'Is all right? Enough?'

'It's fine. It's wonderful. You've gone to such trouble.'

They ate slowly, almost in silence. Isabel revelled in the deli-cious food, and the way Jacques handed her a piece of baguette with small yellow tomatoes balancing on a wedge of *pâté de cam-pagne*. But she still wished they were outside on the riverbank, despite the heat. The chill beneath the tree continued to strike: the bleak chill of milk bottles on a cold winter doorstep, the dank chill of turgid water – she could not quite place the exact kind of coldness, but it made goose pimples on her bare arms. Isabel pulled on her cardigan. Two glasses of wine had made her sleepy again. She longed to lie back on the cushions, but feared this would look like an untoward invitation. Then, eyes on Jacques' serious profile – he was eating a *millefeuille* with his fingers, forks being the only thing he had forgotten – she realised that no such thought would occur to him. She felt confident of that, though could not explain to herself why . . .

So she lay back, let her eyes trail among the long streamers of leaf that dangled from the branches above her. Focusing more sharply, she could see each one as an individual, with its just visible webbing of veins, its fragile whiplash of spine. There was grey in the various greens, through which the fireflies of sunlight splattered lemony freckles. A sudden gust of breeze made chaotic shadows dance on Jacques' blue shirt.

'Strobe shadows,' said Isabel, more to herself than to him.

Jacques turned to her, one side of his curious mouth, awash with *crème patissière*, lifted in agreement.

'Strobe shadows,' he said.

Isabel was grateful for his instant understanding. She fell asleep.

She was woken by laughter. It took her a moment to reorient herself. Willow tree: picnic: Jacques: that was it. Where was he? The picnic things had been cleared away, the wicker hamper closed and buckled. The neatness pleased her, but she was still cold. The shade under the tree was more intense.

Isabel sat up, looked at her watch. Five o'clock. She must have slept for at least an hour. A waste, really. But also agreeable. To be able to fall asleep in the presence of a little-known acquaintance who has taken such trouble with a picnic, she was thinking, when she heard the laughter again. A man's, a young woman's. Clashing, chiming. People outside. People seeking shade, perhaps. They would come in, blasting her solitude. There would be awkwardness, embarrassment. Please don't let us disturb you . . . No, no, not at all . . . do come in. Well, how lucky she and Jacques had been for a few hours, Isabel thought. To have had such a popular place to themselves was obviously a piece of good fortune.

She stood up, brushed an insect from her skirt. Head bowed, concentrating, she did not see Jacques return through the branches. When she looked up and saw him before her, she felt surprise. His face, reddened by the sun, was shredded by the straggling shadows of the willow leaves.

'I went for a walk along the tow-path,' he said.

'I'm sorry I slept so long.'

'I'm glad you did. But time to go now. The slow journey back.'
He gave a smile that flickered with moving shadow. 'Perhaps I'll
do better.'

'Others have arrived, anyway,' said Isabel.

'Didn't see anyone.'

'I heard laughter. Not a moment ago.'

'There was no one out there.'

'Maybe they were just walking by.'

'Well, never mind. We must go.'

Jacques bent to pick up the hamper. A distinct peal of laughter
came from behind Isabel. She jumped round. No one. Nothing.

'There,' she said.

'People playing silly games,' said Jacques. 'Can you manage the
rug and the cushions? We'll leave it to them. They can come in
now.'

'But the laughter was in here.'

'You're imagining things. People queue up for this place. It's no
longer a secret, unfortunately. They come in here to – well, have
their fun.'

He led the way through the branches. As Isabel followed him,
the long leaves tickled her face with a disagreeable touch. Out on
the bank again, she felt relief. A still-hot sun gushed over her:
gratifying, comforting warmth that made her shiver pleasantly.
The brown water of the river spread taut beneath the waiting
punt. A lark sang high above them.

On the way back Jacques said, 'There's a punting party in a few
weeks' time. A whole crowd of us. Would you like to come? It's
fancy dress, I'm afraid. Dressing up in Edwardian gear – some
silly idea. An awful bother, I think.'

'Nostalgia's so fashionable,' said Isabel. 'Yes, I'd love to.'

'You'll have to find something – some old dress, some fancy
hat, put your hair up.'

'I'll rather enjoy that.'

'We'll go together, then.'

By the time they tied up at Magdalen Bridge, the sky was a deep denim blue behind the tower. Crowds of punters were laughing, drinking, eating ice-creams.

Isabel found a second-hand shop near the station. She was trying to make her choice. It was dreadfully hot, stuffy. There was a smell of mothballs, old garments, dead starch. The walls were hung with dresses whose heyday was several decades ago, their gold embroidery and lace panels a little battered, but their spirits not extinguished. There was nothing suitable for the punting picnic, the kind of Edwardian tea-gown Isabel had in mind.

'Just got a new bundle in,' said the woman in charge, dumping a pile of twisted clothes on the counter. 'You can see if there's anything you like if you want to look through these.'

Isabel began to rummage through them. They were pale, faded colours, summery stuffs, torn and frayed, some of them, and very crumpled. Within moments, her eyes lighted on a piece of creamy muslin dotted with faint forget-me-nots: she pulled it from the pile. It was exactly what she was after, demure and pretty with small lace Vs that protruded from the long sleeves to cover the back of the hand. All it needed was a sash of palest blue moiré . . . Isabel felt reckless with excitement: the dress was more than she had intended to spend, but she did not care. A picture was beginning to form in her mind – a little hazy, but something to do with seduction, at last, in this dress. Something to do with *possibility*, and Jacques.

Back in her room, she shook out the dress and studied it more carefully: the hand-sewn hems of tiny stitches, the coarse hooks and eyes of the day, the enchanting fabric itself. She hung it over her chair, skirt spread out so that it touched the floor. Then she hurried off to Browns where, for the third time since their expedition on the punt, she was to have tea with Jacques. To date, there had been no invitations for anything later in the day. Things were progressing at just the pace so appreciated by Isabel. With each formal date – snippets of information accumulating – anticipation fizzed a little more: there was reason, Isabel began to think, for hope.

When she returned to her room at about six-thirty in the evening, her immediate impression was of the lack of air. It had been a very hot day, but she had left the window shut, being on the ground floor, for security: it was not unknown for undergraduates to rob each other these days.

On her way to the window Isabel's eyes fell on the dress – of which she had made no mention to Jacques. It was to be a surprise. It was not as she had left it. Slumped considerably to one side, so small a part of the bodice was now propped up against the back of the chair that the slightest movement would have caused it to fall completely.

This was strange. How could this have happened? There was no breath of air in the room. The door had been locked: no one had been in. Isabel's mind raced uneasily before quickly she found an explanation. Someone must have been running across the landing outside . . . the vibration of feet on old boards. All the same, her heart quickened. In the stifling room, the dress looked so desolate she felt a moment's chill. Goose pimples stood up on her bare arms, just as they had when she heard the laughter in the willows.

Scoffing at herself, Isabel picked up the dress with some distaste. She put it on a hanger. The muslin skirt, so soft and dry in the shop, felt slimy against her hands. Almost damp. Isabel hung it on the outside of the wardrobe. To check that she had been imagining the inexplicable dampness, she forced herself to screw up the frill on the hem with both hands. Obviously, her imagination had been playing tricks. The material was warm, dry, smelling faintly of musty flowers. Cowslips, Isabel thought. She opened the window, took out her books. She sat down at her desk, her back to the dress, wanting to put it from her mind.

But in the next few weeks before the punting party, it caused her some disturbance. She washed it, ironed it, skilfully mended a couple of small tears. All these jobs she found disagreeable: the silly thought came to her that by restoring it to its pristine condition she was somehow intruding. She bought a long blue moiré ribbon which she tied round the waist, a beautiful sash. Then, fearful of crushing it in the crowded wardrobe, she left the dress hanging outside. Each time she returned to her room she was greeted by its hanging presence – a presence more potent than an ordinary piece of clothing on a hanger. Always, she could swear, its position was fractionally changed – she made sure to straighten it before she left, and when she came back it had invariably shifted a little to one side or the other. This change was almost imperceptible, but Isabel's conviction that it *was* a change grew stronger every day. In her alarmed state, she began to imagine that in her absence the garment put up some kind of a struggle. Others, coming to her room, admired it, of course. Handsome symbol of another age, they said: imagine wearing something that prissy today.

Gradually, Isabel herself began to dread coming back to her room. The greeting from the still dress that moved when she was out became harder to ignore by concentrating on her work. She could not bring herself to try it on: she knew instinctively it would fit. And once the punting party was over, she began to think, she would resell the dress, throwing in the expensive sash as an added bonus.

Every few days, Jacques and Isabel met for the same teas – scones and cream and strawberry jam – in Browns, and Jacques unbent a little. One afternoon, he went so far as to suggest Isabel might like to visit his father's house in the Luberon in the vacation. Perhaps, Isabel replied. What she meant was, perhaps the time was coming for things to speed up a little.

'You would like,' he said.

'I expect I would.'

Their conversations were not marked by vitality. Rather, they shifted at a gentle pace, as does the talk of two people, bound by affection, who have known each other well for many years. Isabel found this comforting.

On the day before the punting party, they did not meet. Isabel spent many hours, in her disciplined way, getting ahead with work: she did not want the thought of an essay on Anna Comnena hanging over her as the gathering of punts drifted down the Cherwell . . . Tired by the evening, the essay accomplished, books neatly stacked, she went to bed soon after nine and slept at once.

She woke at three a.m. A thin spear of moonlight through the window had lighted on the waiting dress (re-ironed two days ago), bleaching its creamy colour to a milky whiteness, giving it a cloudy volume as if invisible thighs shifted beneath it. She distinctly saw it move.

Cold, Isabel sat up. Now, as her eyes grew accustomed to the fragile darkness, she could see the bodice and the long limp sleeves that seemed not as limp as the sleeves of an empty dress should be. It was the dress that had woken her, she was quite sure of that, with its sudden, living presence.

Terrified, Isabel switched on the light. At once she saw how foolish she had been: the dress was ordinary again, beautifully ironed, waiting, unmoving. The illusion of moments before must have been the tail-end of a nightmare. She smiled at herself, heart thumping: by now, she thought, she knew Jacques well enough to tell him of the strange experience, and of the odd feelings she had about the dress. Maybe there would be a chance tomorrow. Calmer, but not liking to put out the light, she picked up a book and read till dawn.

The following evening, when the time came to change, Isabel opened her door on to the landing. In some amorphous way, she wanted the reassurance of others nearby: the scurrying down the stairs, the heads looking in to check on progress. Now Isabel was seen by her friends to be 'in a relationship' too, they treated her with less polite kindness. This evening, finally in the dress, sash bow perfectly tied, muslin underskirt soft against her legs, she was grateful for their crude comments concerning virgin spinsters, and their coarse admiration of her finished appearance. She had piled up her hair in an Edwardian bun: on top of this she put her mother's wedding hat, a period concoction of silk roses clambering over creamy straw, with a tiny veil that half hid her eyes. A velvet ribbon she wore around her throat, to which she had pinned a small star. She was ready.

'You look much more the part than any of us,' said one of her friends. 'But then you've never been of this age.'

Isabel, arranging the Vs of lace over the backs of her hands, blushed. She felt intensely happy. All the misgivings about the dress, the absurd feelings of unease it had caused her, had vanished. She knew it suited her, that she looked well in it. And this was the sort of occasion she had been waiting for so hopelessly for five terms. *This* was the Oxford of her most extravagant imaginings.

It was seven p.m. when she joined a group of girls in long floating dresses to walk to Magdalen Bridge where Jacques, and other dates, would be waiting. Isabel's normal modesty was taxed: she could not help feeling she was the *belle dame* of the group. The others had strived, but somehow failed, in their attempts at Edwardian gear. They wore long shabby dresses with Doc Marten boots beneath. Some of them had piled up their hair, though nothing would disguise the contemporary haughtiness of their expressions, and their language would have been almost incomprehensible to those of the Edwardian era. But they were in high spirits, looking forward to a night of drink and music and love beneath the stars, when their fancy dresses would be ruined on the damp banks of the Cherwell.

At the meeting place there was a huge gathering of yet more girls in long dresses and men, transformed in appearance by striped blazers, cream trousers and boaters stuck with flowers. They bore no resemblance to the seedy, be-jeaned lot of normal day. There was much shrieking and incredulous laughter as food and bottles and ghetto blasters were handed into the punts.

'I thought of bringing my gramophone,' said Jacques, suddenly at Isabel's side, 'but I didn't think it would be appreciated.' His eyes moved politely up and down her dress. He made no comment, but gave her shoulder the briefest squeeze. All around them, others were already greeting each other with greedy kisses on the lips. Jacques had wisely not volunteered to be a punter. This meant he and Isabel could sit side by side, idle passengers, their attention free for the delights of the journey downriver.

By the time the convoy of punts set off, the sky was a deep blue-green, tipped with such refulgent clouds that Isabel imagined a giant peacock, standing on the horizon, had simply raised its fan-shaped tail to the heavens . . . As Magdalen Tower disappeared, and a tunnel of greenery loomed, she found herself sipping pink champagne, Jacques' arm about her. She could feel the boniness of his side. They had never been so close before. Nor had Isabel ever felt such irresponsible deliquescence: no matter what he asked her, tonight, she would agree. They had waited long enough.

Even as the party took place, Isabel was aware of that quality of luminescence that usually touches the memory of things past, rather than present reality. She clutched each moment to herself, wanting to preserve it in all its detail. She was not, after all, a girl so used to parties that circumstances had to be particularly vivid to cause the kind of impression that cannot fade. The wonder was increased by the constant presence of Jacques by her side. They shared her rug for the picnic on the bank by the willow, now a familiar place. A half-moon rose in the jade-black sky, its face smeared by unhurried clouds. Someone had brought jars containing candles, which were lighted in random spots, and a man with no apparent girlfriend (Isabel's heart went out to him in 'sublime compassion') sat playing a melancholy tune on his flute.

'This is very mad, very English,' Jacques said. He was folding dismal threads of ham into a piece of bread for Isabel. The food was not of the same standard as the previous picnic, but there was no shortage of pink champagne.

Once seated and eating, the chattering of the undergraduates lost its shrillness. It was as if, awed by the density of the warm night, intoxicated by the smells of ripe hay and damp long grass, they tempered their voices. Such innocence! Jacques replied, when Isabel whispered these thoughts to him. It was just that a good deal of drink and dope had already been consumed, he said. But it seemed to Isabel that the voices were quieter. It was always possible to hear the flute among them.

When the picnic was finished, more cigarettes and joints were lighted. One punt, bearing two couples, set off uncertainly into the darkness. Those left on the bank switched on a tape of rock music and began barefoot to dance. This enraged the others, who thought such crudeness broke the spell of the age they were trying to recreate, and sentimental tunes from the thirties were put on instead.

'Still wrong,' pointed out Jacques, 'but I suppose we can't dance to "The Last Rose of Summer".'

He helped Isabel to her feet, but not to dance.

'I'm not much good,' he said. 'No sense of rhythm. Let's see what's happening under our tree.'

They stepped from the moody darkness of the riverbank into the thicker gloom beneath its branches. On the ground were more jars of candles, the light not strong enough to turn the long leaves into ribbon shadows, as the fierce sun had managed on their last visit. Several couples were lying together, oblivious of each other, of everyone. Girls squirmed, long skirts thrown back over their knees. They lay on striped blazers, covered by thrusting flannel haunches: mouths locked.

'I told you,' said Jacques.

Isabel was glad of the darkness. She felt herself stiffen, blush. She was suddenly awkward. Jacques took her hand, led her back outside.

'What would you like to do? Dance with someone else?'

'Just watch,' said Isabel.

They took a bottle, the rug and cushions, and made themselves comfortable in one of the moored punts. They watched the dancing and embracing under gently changing patterns of moon and cloud. The music, thin recordings of sad love songs, fluttered down to them. They did not speak.

Isabel, on purpose, had not brought her watch. So she had no idea what precise moment of the night Jacques stirred, and concentrated on rubbing his ankle, which he had bruised some days before.

'I suppose I must admit the impossible has happened,' he said. '*Mon Dieu*: I would never have thought it. I think I have fallen in love. *Je te veux bien.*'

He turned to Isabel, unsmiling. Straightened her hat, lifted the veil. The lace pushed back, she now had an unobstructed view of his face, silvery green, with enquiring eyes.

At about four-thirty a.m. people began to go home. Punts set off alone at intervals, filled with loose-limbed revellers in stained and damaged clothes. When the last punt was about to leave, Jacques suggested he and Isabel should not take it, but walk back a little later. She agreed. She wanted the night to last, not for ever – people who expressed such views were thereby impeding the order of progress – but for a while yet.

So they were left behind. They stood on the bank, waving, the objects of much good-humoured speculation, till the punt rounded the bend, leaving only a few long, sleepy laughs and cries in its wash.

They stood in silence till the voices were finally no more, and then heard bright new laughter behind them. It was distinct, infectious. In the gunmetal light of the dawn sky, Isabel could see Jacques looked annoyed.

'So we're not the only ones, after all. Others are still here.'

He pushed his way through the branches of the willow tree. In a moment he was back.

'No one,' he said. 'I could have sworn I heard . . .'

'So did I.'

'Well, if there's no one, that's good. I wanted you alone.' He patted her shoulder. 'You're cold.'

'Not very.'

Jacques took off his blazer, put it round her.

'I feel,' he said, 'I don't know – restless. Stiff from all the sitting. Do you mind if I stretch my legs for a few yards? Back in ten minutes.'

'Of course.'

Isabel watched him walk away from her. He quickly disappeared into the mist that rose from the ground, a milk-grey mist that matched the paling of the sky.

The place, now everyone had gone, was lonely, the silence oppressive. Isabel longed for birdsong, the dawn chorus, the lowing of cows – anything to cloud the quiet into which the laughter might break again. She felt unsafe without Jacques at her side. Afraid. She wished she had her watch, so that she could time his return.

There it was again: the laughter.

This time it was nearer, but muffled. It was definitely coming from under the willow tree: people hiding, joking, trying to frighten her, was Isabel's immediate thought. Crossly, in her nervousness, she parted the branches and entered the hiding place. On the ground, the candles had burnt out in their jars. A blue suede sandal lay on its side, heel broken. But there was no one there.

Isabel heard herself utter a small cry, clap her hand to her mouth. She turned, ready to hurry outside, when a man appeared through the thickness of the branches.

'Jacques!' she screamed.

As she darted towards him, he backed away, indistinct in the poor light. But she clearly saw a flash of long white hand streaked with black mud, and a recognisable expression of something like evil. Then he was gone, vanished with no word. What terrible game was he playing? Isabel put a hand on the tree trunk to support herself. She was icy, shivering, confused. What had happened? What was this terrifying trick all about? Isabel looked round at the silent jangling shadows of the willow leaves, and knew she could not bear another moment in this horrible place. She must find Jacques, get him to explain . . .

She ran through the branches, hating their touch, and on to the tow-path. It was lighter now: that luminescent moment before real daylight. Isabel looked upriver. No sign of Jacques.

But, some twenty yards ahead, a girl. She was standing with her back to Isabel, looking in the same direction, upriver. Her presence brought relief. Obviously, she was a member of the party who had somehow missed a lift home.

Isabel called out to her. The girl did not move. In the silence between them, Isabel had the curious sensation that she was looking at herself, a mirror image, a reflection that she could not explain. The stranger on the path was the same height. She wore a long, bleached dress, though no detail was clear. Her hair was piled up in the same manner as Isabel's, though she wore no hat. Isabel put her hand to her head and found that her own hat, too, had gone. At the same moment, the reflection touched her hair. Isabel, remembering she had left the hat in the punt, shivered violently.

But, in her usual disciplined way, she called upon every source of common sense to come to her rescue. She was not a great believer in the supernatural: she had never seen a ghost. She did, however, acknowledge that strands of time can be confused, most particularly when some event of great significance has occurred. The complications of such theories were beyond her, and at this moment she gave them no thought. Curious, alarmed, she wondered what trick of the imagination, the light, her eyes, had caused this insubstantial vision of a girl who appeared to be a replica of herself. Perhaps, she thought, it was a mirage. Or even the unaccustomed quantity of pink champagne.

She called again.

This time the girl turned to her. For an infinitesimal moment she could see that she had no face – that is, no face delineated by its features. Instead, beneath the piled-up hair, was a simple disc, silvery transparent as the waning moon. In the second that Isabel was trying to readjust her focus, there was a loud crash, a hectic splash in the water. She swerved round to see that two swans had landed. They had set up their positions, cob following swan, in huge swirling necklaces of brown ripples. While the sudden noise had frightened her, the peaceful domesticity of the scene now reassured her. The swans were substantial, safe, not the stuff of illusion. She turned again to see what reaction they had caused in the girl. But she was no longer there.

Jacques was in her place, walking quickly towards Isabel. Happy, judging from his bouncing stride. Isabel ran to him. He waved. From a distance Isabel noticed his hand was streaked with mud. When she reached him, the hand was clean. There was no time for calculations.

Isabel flung herself into his arms. He held her.

'What's all this – hey? What's happened to the happy face of the girl I love?'

The face was buried in the concave chest, feeling the warm dampness of his cotton shirt. Jacques, confused, continued his teasing tone.

'I gave you ten minutes, precisely, to make up your mind. What were you thinking? Do you love me? Or is this heart to be unrequited?' He pushed Isabel away from him. 'Is it something serious? Tell me what's happened. Tell me as we walk back.'

Isabel could not be sure – she could not be sure of anything in this unnerving dawn – but she thought she detected a note of malice in Jacques' concern: the voice was hollow, somehow. Unsoft. Fighting such thoughts, fully aware of her confusion, she took his arm. Pressed together by the narrowness of the tow-path, they began the walk back to Oxford. Long grass each side of them was feathered with dew. Birds had begun to sing. In the security of near daylight, Isabel did her best to describe the hallucinations, knowing how ridiculous they sounded. Jacques made light of her experience – to comfort her, perhaps, she thought. He seemed untroubled, amused by her story: suggested someone could have spiked her drink. But he did agree that he, too, had heard unaccountable laughter.

By the time they arrived at Magdalen Bridge, the sun was up and buses passed to and fro.

'You must not give another thought to all the weird happenings,' Jacques said. 'I put them all down to unaccustomed drink, and much too much hard work. I'd say you're a little overwrought. You haven't had enough fun at Oxford so far. I mean to change all that. Now you must go back and get some sleep. When you wake, what I ask you to think about is . . . me.'

They parted with a chaste kiss. Isabel, never more grateful for the normality of daylight, hurried back to her room. Her immediate concern was to get rid of the dress. She tore it off, ripping fragile seams, stuffed it into a plastic bag and took it to a dustbin behind the kitchens. Too awake to go to bed, she then sat at her desk, her mind ablaze with a plan. It was only when details of this plan were finalised that she pondered on Jacques' declaration, tried to determine what it meant to her. But rational analysis was elusive, blotted out by image after image of a faceless girl and a terrifying man, both of them familiar.

That afternoon Isabel returned to the second-hand shop near the station. The owner well remembered the bundle of clothes from which Isabel had chosen the dress. They came from a friend, a Mrs Williams, whose husband was a retired lock-keeper. She gave Isabel the address.

Two days later, work finished early, Isabel found the Williamses' cottage. It was four miles west of Oxford, an unpretentious detached building on a small lane that ran between two cornfields. The only other habitation in sight was the lock-keeper's cottage, presumably where Mr Williams had lived before his retirement. Isabel was hot after the bicycle ride, sweating. She pushed stray wisps of hair under her straw hat, and walked up the cinder path between lavender, rosemary and white tulips.

A large man of about seventy answered the door: rolled-up sleeves, braces, a gardener's hands. He smiled.

'I wonder if you can help me,' Isabel began. She realised she had made no plans for an opening explanation. 'I recently bought a dress from a bundle of clothes you were selling in Oxford. I was interested to know if you could tell me something of its history.'

Mr Williams did not seem averse to the idea of the company of a stranger. He invited her in. 'The wife's just put the kettle on,' he said.

Isabel followed him into a small front room of large polished furniture. Everything was brown – wallpaper, bristling sofa, thick curtains, dull velvet cloth on the table, and the different tones of brown, all burnished by the sunlight, conveyed a low-watt life. How gloomy such a room would be in November, Isabel thought. It was stifling, airless. Windows all shut. She sat on a brown wooden chair at the table, where the only relief was a bowl of orange silk poppies. The wall in front of her was covered in sepia photographs of ancestors in brass frames.

'So what can I do for you?'

Mr Williams' braces were brown, his eyes were brown. Isabel repeated her interest in the dress. Mr Williams gave no indication he thought this an untoward request.

'Can't say I remember it, precisely, the one you describe. There was a whole big bundle – maybe the wife will know the one you mean. All I can tell you is they belonged to my grandmother, Ellen. She was a good woman but she was vain. Always buying herself pretty dresses. We got stacks of them up in the attic, selling them fast. It's quite fashionable, they say, all that sort of old stuff today. We get a good price.'

Mrs Williams came in with a tray of beige cups, tea and brown biscuits. Her husband let out a long sigh. Isabel's heart was beating uncomfortably fast. She felt faint from the lack of air.

'Can you remember a cream dress, Jean, in the last lot that went to Oxford?'

'With forget-me-nots,' added Isabel. 'Muslin. A frill at the hem.'

Mrs Williams poured tea. In the airlessness of the room, it seemed to Isabel, there was a certain reluctance in her action. Her mouth was grim.

'Can't say I can,' she said at last. 'She had so many dresses, much of a muchness.'

She passed a cup of tea to Isabel, then took one of the framed photographs from the wall. 'This is her,' she said. 'Ellen. And Jack.'

Isabel studied the photograph. It was so faded the figures were barely discernible, splattered by milky-white splotches. But she could make out the small, thin shape of a woman in a long, tight-waisted dress: impossible to tell if it was *the* dress. Her face was featureless, bleached out, a void beneath her piled-up hair. Beside her stood a tall, thin man, one side of his face too faded to see – in the other, a single eye was fierce, the corner of the mouth turned down. He wore a cricketing blazer, the stripes reduced to almost invisible sepia and cream.

'Can't see much, can you?' said Mrs Williams, a shade of triumph in her voice.

'Funny thing,' said her husband, turning to Isabel and snapping his braces one after the other, 'but you quite put me in mind of Ellen, the pictures I've seen of her. She was pretty all right. Trim.'

'Don't tell me you can tell what folk look like from old snaps, John,' said Mrs Williams. She left the room, taking her cup of tea. Her sharpness had no discernible effect on Mr Williams.

'To tell the truth,' he said at last, 'they were an odd couple, my grandparents. Can't help you much about the particular dress, young lady, but I can tell you they were a very odd couple. Tragic, really.'

Isabel listened to the muffled tick of the brown wooden clock.

'Why?' she asked, still light-headed from the lack of oxygen in the room.

'I shouldn't say this, but she came to a nasty end.' He glanced towards the door, checked there was no sound from his wife. 'The family doesn't like it talked about, but I'll tell you, seeing as how you bought one of Ellen's dresses. It was like this, so my father told me. Young Ellen was a pretty girl, lots of young men keen to court her, but she liked to keep herself to herself. Along came this Jack fellow, a farm labourer. He was tall, thin, but not half strong: could earn more than any of them in overtime during harvest week. Something a bit queer about him, though: wanted to get into the academic world, be a porter at a college, know what I mean? Ideas above his station. But he was the one who changed her mind about going out with a fellow regular, if you understand me.

'They used to do their courting, Jack and Ellen, down the riverbank, a mile or so from here. He was a strong punter, Jack. Used to take Ellen off in her party dresses, tie up by that big willow – you might know the one I mean – for a picnic and whatever – nothing wrong, I don't suppose, being those days. We've a photo of them somewhere, down there, taken by Jack's sister, my Great-Aunt Agnes. Those were the heydays, I suppose. Then it all went wrong once they were married. There are stories, but no one has the details.'

Mr Williams, even in his wife's absence, lowered his voice.

'Well, Ellen, she refuses Jack first time he proposes. She's quite adamant. She loves him but she doesn't want to be tied down in marriage. So Jack, he bides his time: asks her again. Again, no, says Ellen: she was an independent woman, my grandmother. "Well, I'm not going to give up," says Jack, and the third time he asks her she comes round. Says yes. So they marry and have the one son, my father. Jack stays on the land, no more talk of college work. He slacks off a bit, so the word goes, drinks a bit. Money gets tight. Ellen says she'll go out to work, get a job as a serving maid in one of the colleges. She does, too. Christ Church. That may have been the start of it, the trouble. We can't be sure, but there was a rumour. My father says he remembers as a boy over-hearing a row between his parents; something about a steward who'd taken a fancy to Ellen. Maybe she fancied him back. Anyhow, things definitely weren't good at home. Jack was drink-ing heavily.

'One day, about this time of year, they leave my father with the next-door neighbour, and go off for the day downriver on a punt. Maybe some kind of celebration – birthday or wedding anniver-sary. Maybe some sort of patch-up in the place they'd been so happy before they married. Next thing, Ellen's drowned, Jack's taken off for questioning. He swore it was an accident. They'd had a good day, he said, but admitted he'd had too much to drink. His story was they were bounding about in the punt and it had tipped up. Ellen fell over the side – funny story, that, when you think how heavy a punt is. Ellen gets trapped beneath it, can't swim, can she? And those long skirts. You can picture it, her strug-gle. Jack says he tries to save her, but then he's confused with drink, isn't he? Doesn't try bloody hard enough, is what the family think. He brings her body up, though, dumps it on the bank, gives her the kiss of life, and that's the last kiss he ever gives her. Big trial, all over the papers. People round here still remember the Williams case. Any rate, he gets off. Scot-free. Well, no witnesses, no evidence. Case over: my father gets adopted by a cousin, the lock-keeper here: that's how I came into the job. He and Jack never speak again, and I was never allowed to set eyes on Jack. By all accounts he was a nasty piece of work behind the sweet talk, and the funny thing is, he *did* end up in a college. I forget which one, some job in the kitchens.' Mr Williams paused. 'So I can't help you more than that. That's the story of my

grandmother Ellen. I bet your dress was pretty . . . she had an eye
for nice things, my gran. Sad ending, really. Moral is, as my wife
Jean says, you shouldn't say yes when you mean no, however
hard you're pressed.'

Isabel left soon after the story ended, apologising for the length
of her stay. His wife did not appear again, though Isabel could
hear sounds from the kitchen. Outside, butterflies lay spread-
eagled on the front path. Isabel guided her bicycle between them,
the sun heavy on her bare arms. She began the long ride back to
Oxford slowly, for the machine was old and cumbersome, and
the warmth of the afternoon sapped her strength.

Jacques' declaration of love spurred a slight change in his pattern
of invitations. No more teas at Browns were suggested but, the
evening after Isabel's visit to Mr Williams, he invited her there for
dinner. They ate gravadlax and ravioli and Jacques asked Isabel,
in his naturally formal way, if she would now go out with him.
Such were his feelings, he said, he could not imagine any week,
any day, without her. He loved her.

Isabel did not answer for a long time. Then she said, 'I think we
should just remain friends, nothing formal. For the time being,
anyway.'

Jacques' mouth tightened and a wayward shadow ran over his
face.

'I don't understand,' he said. 'I've been very careful to take
things at your pace. Not to alarm you, not to ask you too soon for
any kind of commitment.'

'I know you have, and I appreciate that. I'm afraid I can't
explain my reluctance . . . It's just a feeling, an instinct, that you
and I would be wrong.' She knew there was no possibility of
trying to explain to Jacques the signs, the reasons, that caused her
to hesitate to take up his offer. He would observe once again that
she was crazed from too much work, and suffered from a fevered
imagination.

Jacques laughed.

'While girls less conscientious than you are flayed by love affairs, two years hard study with no light relief has left you haunted by unreal things, visions, illusions fostered by an exhausted mind. The fact is, you're simply tired.'

Was that the truth of it?

He sounded arrogant in his conviction. He patted her hand.

'It's not that.' Isabel tried to be patient. 'Honestly. I'm sorry.'

Jacques laughed again, this time a shallow laugh.

'You may think you can get rid of me that easily,' he said. 'But I've waited a long time for the right girl. I'm not going to give up. What do you want – a proposal of marriage? I'd be happy with that. Would that convince you of my love? Will you marry me when you come down next year?'

Isabel, like someone drowning, watched the remembrances unfurl: their first meeting in New College gardens, their first picnic, so many pleasant teas at this very table, Jacques' admirable restraint that exactly matched her own. She pondered, too, on the realisation of her secret love for him, a love still undeclared. Was she a fool to resist, or should she take heed of the tragic Ellen and the strangely familiar Jack?

Jacques could not quite conceal his impatience. 'What is your answer?' he asked.

'The answer is no, Jacques,' she said at last. 'I can't marry you.'

Isabel was aware that the words, even as she said them, did not belong to her. Her refusal of his first proposal was merely an echo, a reflection in time.

Jacques smiled quickly, as if not to alarm her.

'I shall ask you again,' he said, as she knew he would.

To Rearrange a Room

Robert woke first. He glanced at Lisa. Tawny hair, slightly troubled look, even in sleep. He wondered if, when Sarah was back this time tomorrow, the image of Lisa would remain imprinted on the pillow, superimposed on reality.

He knew she had had a disturbed night. She had cried after he had made love to her, and promised it would be the last time he would see her weeping. Then she had turned away from him, restless. After a while, she had said 'Robert?', very quietly, and he had feigned sleep. He was exhausted by their interminable arguments – some calm, some whipped into the slashing words of anguished souls – while they tried to resolve the predicament that had suddenly (suddenly?) appeared six months ago. He did not want to spend their last night in further pointless discussion. There was nothing more to say. It was the end.

'Robert? In exactly five minutes I shall get up.' Lisa managed a

smile. Robert touched her cheek. He understood he had five minutes in which he could change his mind, explode their decision. If
he pulled her towards him, she could stay for ever.

'Right,' he said.

He tried for a neutral tone – should have been easy enough, a
single word. But it acted upon her like a gunshot. In a second, she
was leaping from the bed, cold air splicing the warm scattering of
sheets. In one long, continuous movement, she pulled on her jeans
and jersey, snapped her hair back into a band, produced her
severe, efficient morning face.

'Packing up won't take me long,' she said.

In the huge room that was both their kitchen and sitting-room,
Robert poured himself coffee, sat down at the table. Helping her
was beyond him.

'There's plenty of time,' he said. In fact, there was not. Sarah
had insisted on arriving at two.

'How much?' The depth of Lisa's desperation sang out in the
short question. Robert could not tell her she must be finished in an
hour, if he was to rearrange the room before Sarah's arrival. He
watched Lisa rip Indian shawls from the sofa. She had put them
there the first week she moved in, to hide Sarah's 'hideous' brown
corduroy cover. Robert had found them enchanting. When they
made love on the sofa, which they often did, they could hear the
tinkling of small silver bells sewn to the shawls' fringes.

Lisa flung them into an empty box, where they expired with a
few muted chimes. She gathered cushions, brightly coloured,
vaguely ethnic. Some were embroidered with squares of glass
mirror, angry eyes in the light of the February morning. Lisa
kept back one to hug to herself.

'Still smells of the sea,' she said.

They had stopped in an east coast seaside town. Waiting for a
shower to pass, they had sheltered in a gift shop, found it among
all the ugly things. When the sky cleared, and a white sun came
out, they took it to the beach. They spread their macs on wet

sand, laid their heads on the cushion and waited till the incoming tide reached their feet.

'Sea lingers,' said Robert. He could see tidemarks on the silk. His hand was shaking.

Lisa stretched up for the picture above the fireplace: sentimental watercolour of Edinburgh Castle. They had come across it in a shop behind Princes Street – Robert had slipped out of his conference on World Pollution to join Lisa for lunch. Later that afternoon, silent in front of Van Gogh's turbulent *Olive Trees* in the National Gallery of Scotland, she had cried out that he had never told her he loved her. Robert, startled, though they were alone in the gallery, told her to keep her voice down.

'*Why*?' she had cried, no quieter, not caring. 'Why've you never told me?'

Robert knew his helpless shrug appeared callous. It wasn't the place to explain.

'When you know it's the truth, what need?' he offered.

'That's not good enough.'

'I'm not a man of declarations, you know that. I try to act what I feel.'

'Women need declarations. At least, I do.'

'God, you do. I'm sorry I fail you there.' He gave her his handkerchief, kissed her wet cheek. It had been her first accusation. Their first row. After that, he often observed she tried to contain herself. But she could not stop asking the question.

Eventually, he did bring himself to say the words, in response to the hundredth time of asking. But it was too late. It was no good. Obliging with a response was not the same as a spontaneous declaration, Lisa screamed, just when he thought she would be pleased. He began to lose patience. From that moment, the fragile structure of their affair began to flounder.

She was swiping things from the shelves – ornaments, jars, postcards from mutual friends – throwing them into an empty box, careless of their fate as china and glass clashed against the cardboard. Then it was books, her books. Gaps left in the shelves, boxes full. The room stripped of all her things. Unrecognisable. Robert looked about, horrified.

'What about them?' He glanced at the curtains. Lisa had made them herself, cream linen. She had spent many evenings, at the beginning, sewing – saving money, she said, as her machine buzzed away. When she hung them, a veil of summer sunlight filtered through the folds. At night, the moon diffused itself through the loose weave of the material, making the room a shadow-cave.

'Can't take them. Much too big for my flat. Burn them, why not? *Keep* them, even?' She laughed nastily. 'Can you help me with the boxes?'

Why had he not asked her to be his wife? Why could he not have faced the whole palaver of divorce, Sarah's anger, Sarah's hurt? And spent the rest of his life with this wild, brave, sweet creature whose love for him had never been in any doubt?

''Course I'll help you with the boxes.'

'Then I'll be gone.'

They loaded her small car. She faced him. Snapped off the band from her hair so that it fell about like it did in the evenings. Thin legs parted, arms folded, defiant.

'I've left the snowdrops,' she said. 'She'll wonder about them, but that's not my problem. You could throw them away, too.'

Robert shrugged. He did not like to speak.

'Well: for three years – thanks.' Lisa shivered. 'At least I'm glad it's February. Most years, after February, things get better.' She gave a fractional smile. They kissed. She drove away.

Robert decided to do all that had to be done very fast. The short time to himself between the departure of his mistress and the return of his wife was inadequate for any internal adjustment. But Sarah had been insistent. (Years ago, he had loved her in her most adamant moods.) It was two o'clock or never, she said. Her lease on the rented flat was up, she had to be out. She had no intention of wandering the streets while her husband, apparently agreeable to her return, indulged in solitary reflection.

It was an awkward job, taking down Lisa's curtains. Robert stuffed them into plastic bags and hid them in the shed. Even more difficult was putting up the old ones. He shook them out, heaved them up the stepladder. Fat blue roses entwined with sour green leaves, clinging to orange trellis. How many evenings had Sarah sat in front of them, garish floral halo behind her, listing reasons why he was a useless husband?

They were in place at last. Terrible. Drawn back as far as they would go, their bunchiness further darkened the room. Robert found the lime and blue velvet cushions, so carefully matched in bad taste, which used to stand on the brown sofa. Sarah liked them to be on tiptoe, Robert remembered: on one point, so that they made diamond shapes against the back of the sofa. He tried. They fell over. He couldn't try again.

What else? The shelf above the fireplace looked naked. He reinstated his father-in-law's picture of a prim galleon on frilly sea. Remembered the candlesticks. Lisa had moved them to the table for *use*, she sensibly said. But had never cleaned them, so their pewter had turned to luminescent black. Robert dumped them at each end of the mantelpiece. He threw away the stumps of candles, finally burnt out last night. Searching for new ones, he came across the photograph. He looked at it. He and Sarah in Paris, late fifties. Their first illicit weekend. Taken by a student who had joined them for a drink in a café. They had bought the whole film from him, given him a few francs besides.

'God,' Lisa had scoffed when she found it one day, 'your *clothes*. You looked old *then*.' She had tossed the photograph away, no questions, not interested. You look even older now, she meant. Twenty years older than her – and don't forget it. At the time of the photograph, he and Sarah had felt very young. The solemn handbag was no indication of passionate spirits. His love for her had been on a different plane . . . still was.

He remembered that the day Lisa had sneered at the photograph was the day he began to wonder.

It was all done by twelve. Robert sat in the armchair pushed *back* from the fireplace, as Sarah liked it. Shorn of its crumpled shawls, scraped down to the skin of its beige brocade, it felt skinned naked, alien. He would have to ask her for a few changes . . . above all, the curtains.

His hands and feet were frozen. This time last year it had snowed. Lisa and he had walked through the Savernake Forest, snow-quiet, muffled breaking of twigs, arguing about the power of the past – its habit of intrusion. Oh God, what have I done?

Into the silence bit the quiet, menacing crunch of his wife's key. She had refused to give it back – said it would be symbolic of giving up hope. He had thought it impolite to change the locks. She could be trusted not to come round.

He stood, turned. Sarah's eyes were crinkled into a wonderful smile. Perhaps she had just been out shopping, never been away.

'Everything's the same,' she said, looking round.

He saw at once in her ageing body and lively face the woman he had always loved most, despite everything. He went towards her, hoping, dreading. His own smile, unexpectedly easy, responded to her innocence.

They kissed. In the tangle of guilt about her, about Lisa, only one thought occurred: you could spin a whole axis in a single morning. To rearrange a life, you simply had to rearrange a room.

Sarah, drawing back from him, had observed the Paris photograph on the mantelpiece.

'My worst nightmare,' she said, 'was that you might have changed things. But you haven't. Once we've had the curtains cleaned, you'll never know I've been away.'

'May it be that easy,' Robert said. Her busy eyes had now reached the table, and Lisa's bowl of snowdrops.

The Wife Trap

Seventeen years after their divorce, Peggy Jarrett received a Christmas card from her ex-husband George. She had recognised his writing on the envelope at once, and was puzzled. There had been no word of communication ever since their apathetic farewell in court, a sleety morning all that time ago. What was he up to now?

Nothing, it seemed. Peggy read the message several times.

Why don't you drop in for a cuppa if ever you're passing this way? Yours ever, George.

Whatever made him think she'd be his way? She had no reason to pass through Lincolnshire, some hundred miles north-east from where she lived. What a daft idea! Besides, in the unlikely event of her being in his direction, what would be the point of dropping in on a man with whom she had had seven years of nothing but boredom, irritation and disappointment? As a husband, George had been nowhere near up to scratch, in Peggy's mind, and she hadn't missed him once since their parting. Indeed, she'd scarcely given him a thought.

None the less, she searched the card for clues. She held it up to the opal wintry light that hung flatly across her small kitchen window, her lips puckered in critical contemplation.

It was a traditional scene: coach and four in front of an olde inn, swirling snowstorm blurring the artist's incompetent draughtsmanship. Rubbing her finger over the picture, Peggy could feel the raised paper that had been employed to depict the snow – a porridgy feel that made her shudder. A very low-grade card, she was bound to admit. But then George had never had her instinct for nice things. That had been one of the many life-dividers between them. His obliviousness to quality stuff – curtains, pictures, shoes, ties, anything you could mention – was one of the things that had driven her to despair. What's more, he had shown no inclination to *learn*. Things were just things, as he so often used to say, and as long as they functioned properly that was good enough for him. What do I care if a glass comes free from a garage or for twenty quid from bloody Harrods? he once asked. Funny how she remembered the question. He'd been standing in the kitchen clutching a tin of Quality Street to his stomach at the time. She could hear his sneery voice as if he were shouting at her this very moment. The Christmas card brought it all back to her, the remembrance of all the troubles she'd had with George; the fact that she had married beneath her, and regretted her mistake from day one of the honeymoon.

For a moment, Peggy wondered whether to throw out the card. But then she decided to put it with the rest, in a shoebox on whose lid she had written *Christmas 1995*. Might as well. She had quite a hoard of boxes now, proof that she was in so many friends' thoughts at the festive season. The presence of these cards was a peculiar comfort. Sometimes, even in the heat of July, she would take them out to re-count them, and reread the messages of goodwill and cheer. Not that even Jen, her best friend and neighbour, knew anything of this secret ritual. Jen was a great one for Understanding Most Things, as she often reassured Peggy: but instinct told Peggy that there were some things that should not be confided even to a best friend, for fear of misinterpretation.

When she had put the card in the box with the rest of her collection, Peggy almost forgot about it. Although, during the course of the next eight months, her mind did occasionally turn, curiously . . . Once, years ago, she had found a dormouse curled up under a floorboard in deep sleep. She had not disturbed it, but remembering its presence every so often caused a small wick of comfort to flutter in her stomach. George's card acted in the same way.

In August, Peggy's sister Lil suggested Peggy go up for a week to see the new house she and Jack had bought in Alnwick. Peggy didn't much fancy the idea, and knew from experience a week with Lil and Jack would be more like hard work than a holiday. She was driven to distraction by Jack's non-stop boasting about how he was a man for a bargain if ever there was one. In their last tacky little house there was not a single item that had not been a bargain, it was too plain to see. Peggy held no hopes that the knock-down terraced house in Alnwick would be any different. She hated Lil's scarcely disguised sympathy for her own single life – sympathy! That was the last thing she needed, considering her own superiority of judgement was of quite a different class to Lil's. And then the children. They were the sort of children who made Peggy feel glad she had none of her own. Still, despite everything against the idea, Peggy decided she would go, just for a few days.

The visit passed just as she imagined it would, and on the journey home Peggy was aware of an unaccountable weariness. The thought of home, and peace, was cheering, but not all that cheering. As she sat in a motorway café eating her lunch, she reflected on the year ahead of unchanging routine: part-time job at Oxfam, the bridge club, choir practice once a week and dear Jen's interminable visits and enquiries. Nothing to complain about, but nothing to lift her spirits, either. For want of something better to do, she studied the map, thinking that a different way home might relieve the tedium of the next few hours. It was then, by chance, she noticed the small town where George lived, and remembered his card. She measured the distance from her present position with her thumb: some thirty miles, she reckoned. A short visit – cup of tea, exchange of awkward pleasantries – would be under an hour out of her way.

Peggy took but a moment to make up her mind. However unexciting the reunion might be, at least she could make it into a good story for Jen, whose own life always seemed so much more exciting than Peggy's.

An hour and a half later she drew up at an undistinguished house in a suburban street: neat privet hedges and a newly painted wooden gate. She walked up the straight little path feeling nothing at all, and rang the bell. After no response to three rings, she took the liberty of finding her way round to the back of the house. She saw George at the end of a long, narrow garden. The familiarity of his stance – he had his back to her – caused a strange constriction in her chest. He stood there, same as ever, legs apart like a Colossus of suburbia, hosepipe in hands, playing its jet of pale water over a bed of brilliant flowers.

George had worked all his life for a horticultural firm which sold packets of seeds by the million. It had always been his habit to avail himself of free packets, and to furnish the garden so that it looked like pages from the firm's glossy mail order brochures. All too vulgar for Peggy's taste, of course: always had been. Though she had seen the point of free flowers, and in this one matter had conceded to George's determination never to pay for anything in the garden.

She stood quite still, knowing she would have a moment or two to take in his unchanging shape before he turned and saw her. He wore slouching trousers of indeterminate beige, and a polo shirt of a particularly nasty rust that she, Peggy, would never have agreed to. His hair was perhaps a little thinner, and the neat side wings, that curved same as always over his ears, were greying. Had she seen enough? Was this a mad idea? Should she turn and run?

Even as these questions fizzed through her mind, Peggy saw that it was too late. George had spun round and was looking straight at her. He frowned for no more than a second – possibly the strong evening sun was in his eyes. Then he smiled and moved towards her, the water from the hosepipe at his side making a sloppy track across the lawn. He stopped a yard from her – deeper runnels in his cheeks, grey eyebrows, teeth he still had not both-ered to have straightened – still smiling.

'Well, I'm blessed, Peg o' my life, I was just about to suss out the hydrangeas,' he said.

The years shot away from Peggy. His news had always been about gardening. Now, after a such a long absence, all he could think to greet her with was his own immediate plan concerning the hydrangeas.

'Were you passing?' he asked after a pause.

'More or less.'

'I knew you would. One day.'

Cocky bastard. All the same, Peggy smiled nicely. 'You've got quite a garden,' she said.

'Not a bad little patch. You should've seen it when I came here. Cup of tea?'

'I wouldn't mind.'

She followed him to the back door. He stopped to turn off the outside tap on the way, and kicked viciously at the green plastic snake of the hose. Once, he had kicked the cat, Pinky, so hard that he had caused a rupture. Peggy remembered Pinky as she looked about George's kitchen: a beautiful marmalade, lovely tempera-ment, everyone said. There wouldn't be any animals here, of course. George loathed animals. Pinky was one of the many things that had come between them.

The kitchen was a room that personified George's view of his surroundings: functional. The walls were a nasty green. There were plastic blinds at the window, a torn shade on the overhead light, a Formica table patterned with ribbons and roses of crude yellow and blue. The smell of stale smoke reminded Peggy of another division of opinion between them, as did the full ash-trays. She had eventually trained George not to smoke in the kitchen, but obviously that rule had lapsed with his freedom.

Peggy drew her angora cardigan tightly round her, and sat on an uncomfortable stool at the table. George, whistling under his breath, switched on the kettle and dumped two mugs on the table. One of them, a souvenir of the Queen's Silver Jubilee, she recognised as theirs. The other was new and ugly. But then in the sharing of things, Peggy remembered, George had been quite generous, allowing Peggy her pick and saying he would not need much stuff just for himself.

Eventually George sat at the other side of the table. A tin pot of tea and a bottle of milk stood between them. Peggy felt some old habit rumbling up through her veins: without asking, she poured the tea. George's first.

'Well, well,' he said. 'What brings you to this part of the world?'

'I've been staying with Jack and Lil. They've got a new place up in Alnwick.'

'Ah, Lil.' George had never shown much affection for his sister-in-law, though once, at a Christmas party, Peggy had found him giving her more than just a polite kiss under the mistletoe.

'You've got a nice place up here, I must say. Very quiet,' she said. Might as well be friendly.

'Quiet! Don't you believe it.' George banged his fist on the table, making the tin pot shudder. 'It's wicked. Break-ins, burglaries, rape, mugging, the lot. Terrible. I organised a local

Neighbourhood Watch, as a matter of fact. I'm what they call the chairman. I'd say things have improved a bit since we put the notices up, but not much. You can't be too careful. Had to spend a fortune on security, I can tell you.'

Peggy followed his glance towards expensive locks on the windows and huge bolts on the door. He'd always had a thing about security, she remembered. But the precautions he had taken here seemed to her a little out of proportion to the value of the contents of the house. No burglar in his right mind would want anything from this kitchen, surely.

'You lock yourself in all right, do you?' George asked.

'Oh, I take good care.'

'Sometimes I've thought, you know – funny thing, but there it is – I've thought, come along, George, send a card to Peg o' my life and tell her to be sure to check her locks. It's a violent world today. But of course I never did. You know me, not much of a writer. So then I sent the Christmas card and lo and behold here you are, so I can warn you in the flesh.'

He smiled. But there was a look in his eye that was new to Peggy. A sort of flinty, manic glare. Possibly it was her imagination. The sun had tinged everything with a glowering orange, making Peggy unsure of her original impression. Perhaps George had changed, in some way she could not put her finger on, which aroused both unease and something vaguely exciting.

They chattered on about the hydrangeas, and George's plans for a new greenhouse, and his addiction to snooker on the television. Two pots of tea were drunk, and then they turned to cans of shandy. These lived on the ledge above the sink and were warm from a long day in the sun: funny old George, still not much good at looking after himself. Never did remember to put drinks in the fridge.

Some time after eight (amazed, she was, how the time had flown) Peggy remembered the three-hour journey ahead, and said she had better be on her way. The three cans of shandy had made the roses on the table tremble as if through a heat haze. Still, she stood up quite firmly and announced her intention to leave.

'Oh, you don't have to go, surely,' said George. 'You can't drive till all the shandies have settled. It would be irresponsible to let you go. Sit yourself down and I'll get us a sandwich.'

Peggy let herself sink back on to the stool, whose seat had made grooves in her thighs. Suddenly exhilarated by a feeling that time did not matter, she made no protest. With incredulous eyes (in the old days George had never lifted a finger in the kitchen) she watched him open a tin of salmon, spread vegetarian margarine on sliced bread and cut up two home-grown tomatoes.

'Not exactly a feast,' said George, 'but there's plenty of raspberry ripple for afters, and I can probably lay my hands on a bit of Cheddar.'

By now Peggy was hungry as well as tired. She ate gratefully, and found herself accepting a glass of home-made elderberry wine. They talked more about the greenhouse, and about who had been promoted in the seed firm in the intervening years (George mentioned a lot of names new to Peggy) and no mention of her own life was made. After they had eaten, they went to the front room – forlornly brown – and sat side by side on the old G-plan sofa that Peggy, at the time of their parting, had said she would not miss at all. They watched the news, and the snooker, and by the time they turned it off a thin summery darkness had gathered outside the windows.

'Time to be turning in,' said George, as he had said every night of their marriage. 'Have to get up early. Why don't you stay the night, Peg o' my life? It's a bit late to start back now. I've got a perfectly good spare room: never been slept in, as a matter of fact.'

Peggy stifled a yawn. He was quite right, of course: it was no time of night to be setting off cross-country. She sat for a while in easy silence, not thinking about the answer she knew she would give, but wondering why the funny little irritating things about

George didn't seem to annoy her as much as they used to. She stood up, stretching in a way she would never consider in front of a stranger: George had never been one to complain of her habit of stretching before bed.

'I'll stay, thanks very much,' she said, arms above her head. 'But no hanky-panky, mind.'

In the dim light she could tell from his amazed expression that no such thought had crossed George's mind.

'Would I ever?' he asked. 'You can trust me. But it's nice seeing you again. Just the same as ever – well, in a way. Let's go and settle you in, sheets and whatnot.'

An hour later, her case unpacked, Peggy sat up in bed wondering at the curious turn of events. Her critical eye took in the ugly maple furniture, the hideous curtains, the central light – she missed a lamp by her bed – and she felt some pity for George. To have stumbled along in such discomfort and ugliness for so long . . . but then he had never been a great observer. Probably none of this affected him in the way it would affect her.

There was a knock on the door. Peggy's hand went to her chest. One of the two nightdresses she had packed to take to Alnwick had a low-cut front. She had chosen to wear this one tonight, for no particular reason.

'Yes?'

'Everything all right?'

'Fine.'

'I'll leave a light on, on the landing.' Pause. 'If I don't see you in the morning, good luck. Drop by again.'

'Thanks.'

Well, blow me down, if he didn't come knocking on my door, Jen. The cheek of it! I told him where to get off. But the fact of the matter is, George is still attracted to me. It was as plain as anything.

Peggy slid down in the bed. Before she could dwell on what could have been, what might have been, she fell asleep, hand still protecting her unassaulted breast.

She woke next morning soon after nine – a most unusual time for her, who was usually up and hoovering at seven-thirty. Hurrying out of bed, Peggy put her lateness down to the thickness of the curtains. No chink of sun slid into the strange room. She pulled them back, annoyed with herself, and looked at a landscape of 1930s suburban villas all staring blankly over their privet hedges. Then she dressed, folded her sheets – one blue, one pink – and packed her case.

Downstairs, there was no sign of George, and no note. He had plainly left in a hurry. Remains of his breakfast were on the kitchen table. The empty eggshell sat in a cup she had bought on the first anniversary of their marriage. They had been staying in Paignton at the time, and Peggy had been much drawn to this china donkey whose basket on his back served as an eggcup. It was painted with merry yellows and greens, imported from Spain. George, for all his immunity to pretty things, had been taken with it, too, from the start. Nowadays, of course, her taste more refined by the myriad glossy magazines she studied every month, Peggy could see herself rejecting such a donkey with some scorn. But she was touched that George should have kept it, and was still using it. Sentimental old thing, he had always been, in some ways.

Peggy made herself toast and tea, and resumed her uncomfortable position on the stool. In the morning sun the Formica roses of the table were even more dislikeable than they had been the evening before, when the shandy had thankfully softened their crude edges. And the old smell of smoke was sickening. But George would never give up smoking, never. He'd die of cancer one day, as she used so often to tell him, and serve him right. Peggy did not hurry over her breakfast: she took her time looking about, memorising every detail so that, tomorrow, she would have the pleasure of describing it all to Jen.

The awfulness of the kitchen, Jen, you can't imagine . . . curtains with a vegetable motif . . .

It was all printed very clearly on her mind.

But despite her uncharitable thoughts, it would not have occurred to Peggy to leave George's house in anything but a way that would show appreciation for his hospitality. She washed up – not only their breakfast things, but the dishes from last night that were piled in the unattractive sink. She wiped down the Formica surfaces, straightened things here and there, emptied the ashtrays. Then, finding the rubbish bin full, she decided her last act of kindness would be to empty it in the dustbin outside.

I felt I should leave a good impression, if nothing else, Jen . . .

But the back door was locked. This Peggy discovered once she had struggled to undo the giant bolts screwed at top and bottom of the door. There was no key in the lock. Patiently, she began to search for it – all the obvious places, the bread bin, under tins, top of the fridge. But no luck. No key.

Next she tried the small windows over the sink. Awkwardly leaning over the draining board, she struggled with locks that were completely unfamiliar to her. So then she went to the hall. There, the bolts on the stained wood door were drawn back – but it, too, was locked. Another search for the key: this took Peggy through all the nooks and crannies of the stuffy hall, even George's coat pockets that hung dully from a row of hooks. But again no luck. Peggy sat on the stairs to think.

I was screaming mad, Jen, I can tell you. The bastard had locked me in. Imagine! I was his prisoner.

She sat quite calmly for a while, intrigued by a sort of nefarious peace that seemed to have possessed her. Then, when the hall clock stirred her with its muffled strokes of ten, she went to the table on which the old-fashioned, undusted telephone stood upon an ancient directory. Obviously George's dislike of the telephone had not changed. She looked up the number of his firm in Lincoln, amazed by the weight of the old-fashioned receiver in her hand. She was put straight through to his office. His secretary, an efficient-sounding voice, said Mr Jarrett was out seeing retailers all day and would be going home from his last appointment.

No, there was no way he could be contacted. Unlike everyone else, he had always refused to have a mobile telephone. Here, the secretary allowed herself a slight giggle. Was there a message, in the unlikely event of Mr Jarrett ringing in? No, there certainly wasn't, said Peggy briskly – though she had a funny feeling her voice sounded curiously dreamy. And no, she would not be leaving her name.

The bastard, Jen. There I was, stuck. I thought, shall I ring the police?

Peggy returned to the kitchen. There, the overflowing plastic bin sat like an accusation on the threadbare linoleum of George's horrible kitchen floor. Something about it made her look round once more, and this time she saw all the things that could be done by way of improvement. A strange energy and desire to tackle them piped through her. She found an old mop, a balding broom, stiffened cloths, a packet of hardened soap powder, and set to work.

Well, I was dumbfounded. You can imagine. The cheek of it – trapped! Never occurred to me, all these years, poor old Romeo had been wanting me back . . . I just sat there, demented.

Peggy worked hard and efficiently, and it was lunch-time by the time she had everything to her satisfaction. As good as could be in the circumstances, considering the rotten fabric of the place. At least the air smelt more of pine-scented polish than of smoke . . . Pleased with herself, she found an aged piece of Cheddar in the fridge, some stale sponge fingers and a withered apple which, had she been less hungry, she would have thrown out. As she sat eating in the caged silence, she thought of all the thousands of meals George must have had here, alone, in all these years. Did he ever cook himself something good? What had he been thinking all those silent weekends and evenings on his own?

Revived by the food, Peggy then went upstairs. She crept, almost guiltily, into George's bedroom. What should have been the marital bedroom, she couldn't help thinking. The sight was much as she imagined it would be: unmade bed, familiar striped pyjamas and a single battered paperback detective novel on the floor, not a picture on the fog-grey walls. She went at once to the windows: they, too, were secured with the same kind of locks as downstairs. The sour, smoky air indicated they had probably not been opened for years. How could he bear summer nights in such an atmosphere?

It was horrible, his room, Jen. Bleak . . .

The least she could do was tidy it up a bit, have a go at the dust.

By the time she had finished the cleaning of George's bedroom, and the vile bathroom – curtains of cracked plastic, plugs of old hair in bath and basin – most of the afternoon had gone. Tired, Peggy decided to return to the spare room for a rest. She would have to set off the moment George came home. If he did come home. For a nasty moment she was stricken with the thought that he might have some wicked plan behind her imprisonment. He might intend to leave her to sweat it out for a while: punishment for the past.

She shivered in the dead air of the spare room. Windows locked there, too. Last night she had not liked to call George in to open them. Now – tea-time it must be – the afternoon sun hot outside, it was unbearable. Better go back downstairs: cup of tea, watch television, hope the hours would not drag too much till George . . . Peggy had no energy to tackle the sitting-room, riled though she was by its dismal state. She sat on the sofa with her cup of tea, switched on a children's programme, must have dozed off.

I was mad by the time he came back, Jen. I screamed at him, I can tell you . . .

She didn't know when it was, but he was standing over her. He carried a bulging plastic carrier from a supermarket, and he was smiling.

'You dropped off, then?'

'Must have.'

'Didn't expect I'd find you here.'

Peggy rallied, sleepiness quite gone. 'You locked me in, you old sod. What did you do that for?'

'I what?'

'Made me your prisoner.'

'Never. You must be daft.' He gave a small, guilty laugh.

'Every window and door in the place locked. I checked.'

'Locked, yes. That I don't deny. You know what I am about security. But I left the key. 'Course I left the key.'

'Where?'

'Come with me.'

Peggy followed him into the kitchen, suddenly uncertain. George dumped the bag on the table, went to the brush mat by the door. ''Course I locked the door from the outside – necessary precaution – but I left you this.' With some triumph he lifted up a corner of the mat and picked up the key that lay on the cement floor. He waggled it in her face. 'There, Peg o' my life. What did I tell you? Where, for all those years, did we always put the key at home? Under the kitchen doormat. Thought you wouldn't have forgotten that.'

Peggy sniffed. Foolishness engulfed her. 'Well, I did. I looked everywhere.'

'Silly old you, what? Still –' He looked round in some awe. 'I see you've been doing a bit more than just looking. Tidied up a bit, haven't you? It needed a woman's hand. I'm not much good at that sort of thing, you may remember. Here.' He put his hand in his jacket pocket and pulled out a couple of packets of seeds. 'You take these. A bushy new cornflower we're trying out. You've always liked cornflowers.'

Peggy examined the packets with their optimistic illustrations.

'I haven't much of a garden,' she said.

'Mine's quite sizeable, considering,' said George.

There was silence, then Peggy thanked him and said she'd like to take them.

He tried to calm me down with a packet of his blinking free seeds,

Jen: imagine. I said I don't want your seeds, George Jarrett, you can't buy me that cheaply . . .

'I'll be on my way,' she said.

'Better eat something first.' George pulled things from the bag. 'My shopping night, Wednesdays. Afraid you caught me when stocks were low, last night. We could make up for it tonight.'

Any fears Peggy had had earlier about George not taking care of himself now scattered. He had bought a selection of meats and chicken breasts and fruits and vegetables; an expensive rough pâté, French bread, and several bottles of good red wine. His tastes had changed. What was more, oddly, he seemed to have bought enough for two.

'Tell you what,' he went on, 'if you'd like to put something in the oven, I'll nip up to the greenhouse for half an hour, then I'll come back and join you in a nice glass of claret.'

. . . and then he had the cheek to ask me to cook the dinner! I said you cook your own blinking dinner. I said you haven't changed a mite, George: you and your chauvinistic ways that were the breaking of our marriage . . .

An hour later they were enjoying the pâté while the pre-made casserole warmed in the oven. George, against his better judgement, allowed Peggy to persuade him to leave the back door open so that sweet evening air pushed into the smoke and pine of the kitchen, dissipating the obnoxious smells. They drank the first bottle of wine and opened the second. By the time they were into the beautiful ripe Camembert, Peggy found herself weak with nostalgia.

'We did have some good times, George,' she allowed herself to say.

'Some, if you say so,' agreed George, and steered the conversation back to the possibility of a goldfish pond he had in mind for the bottom of the garden.

By the end of the second bottle of wine it was clear there was no possibility of Peggy driving home that night. Departure would have to be postponed once again. Still, there was no pressing reason to hurry home. So when George urged her to stay another night, she did not bother to resist. Once more he wished her a safe journey next day, and said what a nice surprise it had been, her dropping in, and he would leave the light on outside her room. Once more, despite the discomfort of the bed, Peggy fell asleep very quickly.

It was only next morning, going downstairs with my case again, Jen, I realised I'd forgotten to mention the matter of the key. I must admit fear gripped me. He'd had such a funny look in his eye the night before – nothing to do with the wine. And when I looked under the doormat, and there was no key, I knew it. I knew clearly what he was trying to do. He was trying in his horrible devious way to get me back . . . If you've ever had a man after you like that . . .

Quite calmly, Peggy boiled herself an egg for breakfast and made real coffee instead of tea. The kitchen smelt much better now: she sat looking at the lovely show of gladioli in the bed outside, hands round her mug, a comfortable summer warmth within and without. But she would not be caught out so foolishly again. When she had washed up she searched everywhere she could think of for the key to the back door. Unable to find it, she then checked the front door, and every window in the house: as yesterday, all locked. A prisoner again. She contemplated ringing George's office, but decided there would be no point: he was out on his rounds most days. And besides, she would do her best to escape this time, before he came back. This silly nonsense couldn't go on. Or could it?

The morning, Peggy thought, must at least be put to some good use. Back in the kitchen, she went through the groceries George had bought the day before and found ingredients for bread, a cake, veal stew, a gooseberry crumble. She set to work. The thought of the surprise George would have when he returned, reminding him of the good cook she had always been . . . A bee was trapped in the room. Peggy found herself sympathising with its pathetic buzzing.

'We're both prisoners, bee,' she said. 'But it's not too bad, is it?'

It was terrible, Jen, shut in, not a breath of air; dreading him with his frightening eyes coming back. What would he do tonight? Fill me with drink again? I wondered, should I ring the police? I was trembling all over by now, hardly able to think. The monster. Men who want a woman — they'll do anything.

Peggy was kneading dough with a firm hand, a slight smile on her lips. No questions as to why George had shut her in a second time came to perplex her. Rather, she found herself remembering some of the pleasures in their marriage. They had taken long walks, sometimes, in the Lake District, staying at farmhouses on the way. They both liked a bet on the horses, an occasional drink at the pub, quiet evenings in front of the television. It was hard to remember, in fact, quite what had gone so wrong. George had always been a terrible old chauvinist, never renowned for his open mind, but Peggy had become used to all that — couldn't remember the exact nature, come to think of it, of all the irritations and frustrations. Perhaps they had simply been too young, too wrapped up in their own preoccupations, no children to deflect them, to give them a mutual interest. Had they stuck it out . . . by now, they might have reached that state of coasting along in mutual tolerance that a good many people seemed to settle for. They would have had companionship, the comfort of security. Had they stuck it out . . .

I spent that afternoon, Jen, going back in my mind over all the awful things about George, thinking how well rid of him I was.

She spent the afternoon impatiently waiting for the delicious things to come out of the oven (the smell of baking bread finally overcame the last traces of smoke), an idea forming in her mind. It made her restless, her idea. Too restless to weigh it up very accurately. She laid the table for tea, chivvied about, willing the hours to hurry until the evening.

'I saw your car. What happened this time?' George began, soon as he was through the door.

'It was no joke, today, George. Locked in again.'

Peggy tried to sound angry. She knew she didn't succeed.

'Don't be silly.' He stomped over to the small alarm clock on the dresser. Picked it up. Produced the key.

'I thought you said under the mat?'

'Under the mat didn't work yesterday, did it? Thought I'd try our other place today. Remember: the key'll be under the mat or under the clock, we always said. Thought you couldn't be so . . . another day.'

'Well, I was. Stupid, I know.' George, she thought, gave her a funny look. 'There's tea in the pot.'

They both sat down at the table. George cut into the bulging loaf. The crust crackled and chipped under his eager knife.

'I say, jolly nice, this. Haven't had a bit of bread the like of this since . . .' He sniffed. 'Smells as if you've been cooking other things, too.'

'I made supper. Had to fill the hours somehow.'

'Sorry about the misunderstanding, Peg o' my life.'

'That's all right.'

There was a friendly pause. They both spread honey thickly on to the buoyant slices of bread. This is auspicious, Peggy thought. Now is my moment.

Greedy sod, got through my loaf in a flash. I could see he meant business . . .

'George,' she said, 'I could stay a few days if you like. Finish tidying the place up, put some things in the freezer for you. I mean, there's nothing pressing I have to be home for.'

'What about your little cat? I expect you've still got a cat, haven't you?'

'My neighbour Jen sees to her. I could ring Jen, tell her I was delayed for a few days.'

George sniffed again, put down his bread. His hand, his face, were suddenly, visibly, rigid. Peggy was awkward under his new look.

'Funny,' she said, 'I was thinking. You know, if we hadn't been so bloody silly we'd still be together today. None of that divorce business need have happened. We'd be quite happy, used to each other. We'd have security, company, for our old age. Not that I'm grumbling about things as they are, and you don't seem too badly off, could be a nice place here—'

'Vicious neighbourhood,' interrupted George.

'Vicious or not, we would probably have been better off together once we'd got over our ups and downs.'

In the silence that followed her little speech – not quite as she had rehearsed it to herself – George spotted the bee. Too exhausted to buzz, it now tumbled back and forth along the window ledge.

'That poor bee,' said George, at last. 'Must find the window key, let it out.'

'George, did you hear what I said?'

'I heard what you said, Peggy.'

'And what do you think?'

'I think, not on your life, Peg o' my heart. Not for anything. Too much damage caused, no one changed that much, probably. I'm used to it here, as I am. Happy, like.'

There was a silence. Peggy longed for the bee to resume its buzzing. But it had given up.

'Very well. It was just a suggestion.'

'You were always superior to me, see. I didn't like that.'

'Nothing's ever perfect.'

George looked round his newly cleaned kitchen.

'Thank you for tidying up, though. I'll try to keep it . . . You finish your tea. I must get down to the watering.'

George stood up, impatient to be off. Peggy had no appetite for the rest of her bread and honey.

'Keep in touch,' she said.

'Why not? Card at Christmas. That sort of thing. Drive carefully.' He pecked her on the cheek.

'I will.'

Peggy turned her head so that he should not see her face. Ten minutes later she was on her way, suitcase and bunch of hastily picked farewell marigolds on the seat beside her.

She was eager to be home now, could not wait to tell Jen. She arrived before midnight, so rang at once. Jen was a night bird, would be longing to hear from her. She had probably been worrying about why she had not returned on the promised day.

'Jen, it's me, Peggy. Just back. *What* a time, I can tell you. I've been with George. Yes, George, ex-husband George. Trapped! Almost raped! Begged me to stay, wanted me back, *locked me in* for two days till I managed to escape. *I was his prisoner*, Jen! Honestly!'

Peggy kept her friend up for a long time with her story.

Squirrels

Vera Brindle lived alone in a state of dishevelled solitude which the social workers who called upon her could not believe was desirable. They had begun their interfering ways some years ago now and their visits to her cottage were becoming more frequent. One or other of them – sometimes two together like policemen on the beat in a dangerous area – would knock on the door and, when there was no answer, press their faces to the downstairs windows, sheltering their eyes with both hands. Vera Brindle would watch the intruders from upstairs, hidden behind a curtain. On the rare occasions she gave in and opened the door, they would put to her the suggestion of a 'little chat over a cup of tea'. Vera, who disliked both tea and chats, would wave them into the kitchen and enjoy watching their incredulous faces as they looked around the room, making their assessments. She would make no move to put on the kettle. As for the 'chat' they were hoping for – that, too, they quickly discovered, was to be denied them.

Only last week a new young girl had been sent to try out her persuasive powers to make Vera Brindle 'see sense', as they put it. This particular representative of those who know best wore an anxious-about-deprived-people expression which, the old lady knew very well, would be switched off when she went home at five-thirty. She could just imagine the girl hurrying to the kind of party where the boasts of the caring professions meant instant admiration. The girl's narrow little face was contorted with the sort of professional sympathy that made Vera Brindle determine to be unhelpful.

'You must be Ms Vera Brindle,' said this unwelcome creature, when the door was opened a few inches. She was dressed in ugly clothes that signalled there was no frivolity in her do-gooding soul, and hideous, earnest shoes of yellowish leather.

'No, I'm Miss Brindle. I've been Miss Brindle all my life, so there's no supposing, my young girl, I'm going to change to some fashionable title now. And who may you be?'

'I'm Lee Barker. Social Services. But do call me Lee.'

'Certainly shan't do any such thing. I don't know you.' Vera Brindle edged the door open a little wider. She noted the intruder's bony nostrils rear up as various smells began their assault. 'I shall call you Miss Barker, unless you tell me you are a Mrs.' She sniffed. 'Which I very much doubt. Come in, Miss Barker.'

'I don't want us to get off on the wrong foot,' Lee Barker said, once they were in the kitchen. 'I wouldn't want that at all.' Her eyes carried on scouring every crevice of the kitchen. Perhaps she had been warned there was no use asking for a cup of tea, for they did not pause on the kettle. Vera Brindle, enjoying the young woman's unease, kept her silence. She listened to the scrabblings of the squirrels in the roof. Drat the squirrels, she thought. They were usually quiet at this time of day. If this cheeky young do-gooder heard them she'd start writing all sorts of exaggerated reports in her notebook, threaten to send along the pest control man.

'I have news for you, Vera,' Lee Barker said at last. 'There's a nice council flat come up, just a mile or so from Exeter. One of those sheltered housing arrangements. A lovely warden, should you need anything. All mod cons.'

Vera Brindle snorted, furious at the persistent attempt at intimacy, and enraged by the suggestion. But it was useless, she knew, trying to explain that mod cons held no allure. While she could scornfully understand they were part of contemporary utopia, they did not feature on her own list of essentials to a happy life.

'I'm not Vera to you,' she said.

'Sorry. *Miss* Brindle.' Lee Barker gave a patronising smile, which exposed a flash of brown teeth edging a long expanse of gum. Her breath smelt vile. 'Now, have you taken in what I'm saying?'

'I have and I'm not interested. I don't know why you bother yourselves, waste your time, keep coming here. Give the flat to someone who needs it. I'm all right. I'm not moving.'

Vera Brindle put a hand on the table to steady herself. She was not used to speaking at such length. So many words dizzied her. She felt exhausted, but knew she must gather her strength to tell this young woman to go.

'So you can be off now,' she said. The squirrels were scrabbling harder.

'Miss Brindle,' Lee Barker sneered, 'there's no use pussy-footing around any more. My colleagues and I have done our best to make you see sense. The time has come for plain speaking. This –' she looked up at the dark ceiling – 'your home, is generally considered unfit for human habitation. We fear for your own safety, Miss Brindle, if you choose to stay. Why, you're not even on the telephone. What if—?'

Miss Brindle licked her lips with the point of a small green tongue. They tasted of salt. Beneath the tight caul of their skin she could feel a prickling, a singing, in their blood. She knew that if she uttered another word her mouth would explode. Teeth, lips, tongue still attached to the messy glob of its roots, would blast off from her face and splatter across the room. So she said nothing, nodded towards the door.

Lee Barker, whose anger prowled up and down her face in mauve coils, responded to the utter negativeness of the stubborn old cow, as this Brindle witch was known in the office, by pushing her nose into a handkerchief. The offensive implications of this gesture Vera Brindle chose to ignore.

'Very well, I shall go for now. But be warned.' Lee Barker's eyes, even in the poor light, were bright with indignation.

'You'd better be warned, too.' Vera Brindle was determined to have the last word, though unsure of her exact meaning.

Lee Barker swung out, tossed her nasty little trousered hips from side to side as she hurried down the path, trailing her hand along the top of the dead lavender bushes. Vera Brindle waited until she was out of sight, then sat down at the kitchen table. She pulled towards her the white plastic weighing-machine that stood like a single symbol of modernity among the debris all around it. A little weighing, she thought, would calm her down. She reached for a slab of very old cake, broke off the hard end, placed it on the plastic dish. One and a half ounces, the clock said. Vera Brindle loved that moment, when the thin red hand raced so confidently to the exact weight. She added a few crumbs. The hand wavered. Miss Brindle smiled. The weighing-machine was the best toy she had ever had. It kept her occupied for much of the day. The interest of guessing what things might weigh, only to discover how right or wrong she was, almost obsessed her. The fluctuating of weight, as bits were added to the tray or taken away, gave her a strange thrill – the same kind of thrill as sudden icicles on a winter morning, or the drone of bees busy among the apple-blossom. Finished with the cake, Miss Brindle took a handful of nuts from the bag of squirrel food. Two ounces, she reckoned. Perhaps just over. She was happy again. Lee Barker and her threats had vanished from her mind.

Vera Brindle had lived in her cottage, a mile from a small village on Exmoor, all her life. Her father had been head gamekeeper on the Bancrofts' estate. Her mother, a housemaid in the big house, had died when Vera was twelve. All she had left was a very large and cumbersome old bicycle, which Vera still rode into the village once a week to collect her provisions. (She could get an astonishing amount into the copious wicker basket that rested, squeaking, on the front mudguard.) Not long after Mrs Brindle's death, her husband's employer had sold the estate and moved abroad. The sale did not include the cottage. With his usual generosity to those who worked for him, Lord Bancroft gave the cottage – only worth a few hundred pounds – to Sam Brindle, in recognition of many years of service. This noble gesture gave a new life to Miss Brindle's father, who for some time had been cast in the immovable gloom of a widower. Now a proud house-owner himself, he set about repairs and with a friend re-thatched the roof. This was the happiest time Miss Brindle could remember. Once she had left the village school, she stayed at home, with no urge to explore a wider world, looking after her father and the cottage. In those days, there was fresh paint, new carpet, uncracked windows and an up-to-date calendar on the wall each year.

But this idyllic period did not last for long. Her father, too rigorously stoking the boiler, suffered a heart attack and died two days before his daughter's twenty-first birthday. She broke up the iced cake she and her father were to have shared, and put it out for the birds. It was then she first began to take note of the squirrels, whose grabbing of the food was so much more sly than the birds'. It was then she took up a pencil and paper for the first time since she had left school, and began to make quick sketches. The results, she was in no doubt, were quite pleasing, if not perfect. She began to pin these drawings on the walls. She became aware of a faint sense of achievement.

Once her father was buried, Miss Brindle made some effort to take part in village life. There were those who feared for her loneliness, lack of company – her safety, even. She tried hard to convince them she enjoyed her solitary life and politely turned down most invitations. After a harvest supper, in her twenty-fifth year, a local farmer proposed marriage behind the barn. But Miss Brindle saw this was inspired by nothing more than quantities of beer and the hope of a more instant accomplishment than marriage itself. She took the precaution of not only turning him down, but of giving him so little hope that he thought it not worth the journey to her cottage when he sobered up.

For some years – her squirrel drawings acting as a qualification – Miss Brindle taught painting in the village school. She gave this up during the war to help out in the local hospital. Surrounded by so much death, she became alarmed by the shortness of life. Except for her weekly shopping expedition and an occasional bus journey to the dentist, she spent the best part of the next fifty years in the cottage or its small garden, feeding and drawing the squirrels, birdsong her only music when the old wireless finally broke down in 1951. Always a good needlewoman, she earned just enough money by taking in alterations and mending. To the amazement of those left in the almost deserted village, Vera Brindle seemed happy to lead this uneventful existence. She was never ill, never wanted for anything. A weird old bird, she became; a witchy threat to children. 'Vera Brindle will get you,' mothers would say. 'Vera Brindle lives with the squirrels and casts her spells.'

On the evening of Lee Barker's visit, such an agreeable plan came to Vera Brindle's mind that the social worker's unpleasant behaviour was almost forgotten. She would order a bigger weighing-machine. Fond though she was of the present one, Miss Brindle knew there was a limit to what it could accommodate.

And by now she was well acquainted with the weight of most things around her: a slice of cheese, a single slipper, a bag of nuts, two pencils and a rubber. It would be exciting to try out some larger objects, things that would not cause the red hand to dash right out of sight where it hid, alarmed by so much weight, in the bowels of the machine. It would be exciting to weigh the kettle – with and without water – her boots, her big wooden paintbox. With such plans in mind, Miss Brindle began to look forward to the postman's next visit, when he would bring the new mail order catalogue in which weighing-machines of all shapes and sizes were advertised. She would send off for one at once. Fill in the form with capital letters; by then she would surely have found her old biro. She would pay by postal order. Then wait impatiently for the parcel – new things to be weighed all lined up and waiting. Already she could see herself unpacking the machine, making a space for it on the table. The sweetness of anticipation began to seep through her. She had learned, in her solitude, that the occasional arranging of treats for yourself is the way to divide up time, cause a ripple in the otherwise smooth surface. She had discovered that anticipation of small pleasures, to those who live alone, is a necessity. A rhythm must be created in which there are times of exceptional happiness to counteract the occasions of amorphous melancholy.

So engrossed was Vera Brindle in the thought of her new machine, that at first she did not hear the thunder. She thought the rumbling was the squirrels again. They always danced more loudly at night.

But when, soon after nine, she went to draw the pitiful curtain across the kitchen window, she felt a stab of cold wind pressing through the space between long-dead putty and old glass. As she grabbed the material in her hand, lightning turned the small panes to the colour of watered milk, and she could see they were splattered with hard rain. Vera Brindle shivered, and longed for bed. On her way upstairs, she realised that more crashing above her was indeed thunder. Feeling the bones of the wooden stairs creak beneath her, she clung to the oak rail until the trumpeting outside had stopped. Storms held no fear for her. She had faith in the protection of the cottage, though in the hurricane of 1987 she remembered the cottage walls trembled as trees in the nearby woods fell to the ground with high-pitched, splintered screams.

Vera Brindle turned on the dim light by her bed. She saw that a piece of ceiling had fallen on to the floor. She kicked at the mound of crumbled plaster, automatically wondering what it might weigh. She decided not to sweep it up till morning and glanced up at the black hole it had left. The ceiling all around it was as cracked as an old cup. If the social workers had seen it, they would have gone potty. But it didn't worry Vera Brindle. She was used to it. For so many years, lying in bed, trying to sleep, her eyes would journey over the familiar pathways of lines, the patches that bulged, the baubles of paintwork that reminded her of withered balloons at the end of a children's Christmas party in the Church Hall . . . Long ago, it had occurred to her to have the room re-plastered. But then the thought of the invasion – builders, ladders, wireless, tea – was too awful to contemplate, and the moment passed. As time went by and the ceiling deteriorated, but never collapsed, Vera Brindle's faith in it continued. It would see her out, she thought. Once she was dead, if the whole place crashed to the ground, so long as the squirrels were not hurt, she did not care.

For a moment, unnerved by the whiteness of the plaster on her bruised and threadbare carpet, Miss Brindle considered moving to her parents' room. But no, that was inconceivable. No one had ever slept in there since they died. Their high brass bed was still tightly made up with clean cotton sheets. The piece of carbolic soap, still in the dish on the wash-stand, had been used by old Mrs Barley when she came to lay out Sam Brindle. His daughter could not bear to disturb the room. Besides, her own was quite safe. What on earth had come over her, such a thought?

Avoiding the spread of white dust, she took off her skirt but kept on the rest of her clothes against the cold night. The thunder seemed to be lumbering off elsewhere; just the odd rumble now. But the squirrels were disturbed. They charged back and forth, scrambled about in the darkness of the roof, a mysterious place which Vera Brindle could never quite imagine. Their scurrying footsteps brought to mind different things: most vigorously, the noise of waves on a grey shale beach she had once visited with her mother. That was the day Mrs Brindle had given up her own long wool scarf to her daughter, as they stood pondering the winter sea, saying 'You take it, child – your weak chest. Never do to catch a chill.' While all the time, as Miss Brindle later learned, it was her mother who had the weak chest, who was to die of pneumonia. So often, in the subterranean part of her soul, she had wondered . . . if only she had not taken the scarf, her mother might not have died. Just as clearly, the squirrels revived another sound: the kidney-shaped beans made of glass. They were kept in a jar on the high shelf above the kitchen range, only brought down as a treat on Sunday. Vera would be allowed to tip them out of the jar on to the scrubbed table. They would tumble out with a rush, fast as a small shoal of sparkling fish they came, crimson and sapphire and emerald, sparkling with lights. She would cup her hands around the mound they made, terrified lest one should escape and fall to the floor. Mrs Brindle would carefully choose a few of the beans to make flower patterns. Such imaginative leaves, she made with the green ones. 'How do you do it, Ma?' the child Vera would cry. Her own attempts at flowers were nothing like as good. 'Easy,' Mrs Brindle would say, and shuffle her bent white fingers through the pile of glass, pouncing on exactly the right one needed for her next petal. Vera, despairing at her own lack of talent in this favourite game, would simply run the beans through her fingers, loving the tinkle they made on her palm that was quite different from the scurrying noise they made as they jostled on to the table . . . That jar of glass beans, where was it now? Vera Brindle had never thrown it out. Perhaps it was still at the back of a cupboard somewhere. Might be worth looking for. She would like to weigh the beans, should she find them, on her new machine . . .

Some time much later in the night – no streak of moonlight or dawn paling the curtainless window – Vera Brindle was woken by a thump on her bed. She switched on the light. Edward, the shyest of all the squirrels, was poised, terrified, on the blankets over her feet, claws dug deep into the wool stuff. He stared ahead, not looking at her, jowls twitching almost too fast to see, tail raised high, ready to bolt.

Miss Brindle did not move, but looked up at the ceiling to see the hole was bigger; there was more powdered plaster on the carpet. Poor Edward, what a trauma, falling through the ceiling, she thought. On the other hand, she could not resist a feeling of great pleasure. For so long she had been trying to tame Edward, but he had always eluded her. His father Ernest, a huge animal with reddish eyebrows, spent more time in the kitchen than he did outdoors, while his wife, the lovely but greedy Rose, was a menace among the shelves. Edward's many brothers and sisters, cousins, uncles and aunts had all established that Vera Brindle's cottage was a perfect refuge, both as a place of hibernation and a source of food. They all had their names: the year each one was born was clear in Miss Brindle's memory. And, despite her failing sight, she could identify which junior members of the clan swung and squealed high in the trees. They were her family. She knew and loved them all. In return for her hospitality, they would keep her company just when she most needed it, perching on her chair, or shoulder, or sometimes on her head.

But Edward, strangely ungregarious, could never be won over. This was one of the great puzzles in Vera Brindle's life. Sometimes she mentioned it when she went to the Post Office to collect her pension, but the busy woman behind the counter, with her orange lipstick, didn't seem interested. And when she tried to tell Jack the poacher, who occasionally passed by, all he had to say was that she was a stupid old woman who should clear the vermin out of her house or the authorities would be after her. He was sensitive to the authorities, was Jack, skulking about after dark. But Vera Brindle held them in no respect. If she wanted to entertain squirrels in her house, she had every right to do so, and no one could force her to evict them.

Up until this extraordinary moment in the middle of the night, Vera Brindle had never managed to persuade Edward indoors, no matter how many saucers of bread and milk, or nuts, she tempted him with, or what olden-days songs she quietly sang – a device which always intrigued the female squirrels. The unexpectedness of his arrival caused her head to spin for a moment. What should she do to reassure him? Her instinct was to put out a hand, coo a few words, offer him a biscuit from her bedside table. But no, she thought, she must resist. Lie down with as little movement as possible, put out the light, pray to the good Lord young Edward would feel at ease at last.

In the dark, she felt a small movement over her feet. Sleepy, she imagined Edward might be sleepy, too. But in the morning he was gone. When Vera Brindle let his large gang of relations in for breakfast, he was not among them.

Later that day, she stood on a chair in her bedroom and filled the hole in her ceiling with a wadding of old rags and dishcloths. She decided not to secure it further with sticking plaster, in the small hope that Edward might fall on to her bed again. His rejection had caused a smarting in her heart that was hard to dismiss, despite the sunny day. The feeling was mixed with pity for his shocking experience, and her own pleasure at having at last come so close to him.

Vera Brindle ordered her new weighing-machine from the next catalogue and waited for its arrival with a force of impatience that made her restless. She found herself unable to concentrate on anything for very long. No sooner had she sat down in her chair to peel a potato than she darted up to look out of the window. An official-looking brown envelope was delivered one day. She took it to the door, spent a long time trying to light a match with trembling fingers, and at last set light to it. It was with considerable glee that she watched the unread threats devoured by a sudden curl of flame. They were followed by a wisp of black smoke that ventured out into the rain and was instantly extinguished. Pleased though she was by her act of conflagration, a fine wire of anxiety now threaded through the impatience; they would be after her again with their suggestions. Vera Brindle turned back so sharply into the kitchen that she alarmed the squirrels feeding from their breakfast bowl of nuts. They scampered away with unusual speed.

That October, there seemed to be interminable rain. The day the postman Alfred came with the parcel, it poured down so hard that the end of the garden was no more than a smudged outline. The guardian trees beyond were scarcely visible against the grey sky. Alfred's waterproof cape, as he hurried up the path, produced no more than a low-watt shine, a flash of dulled yellow. He stood at the door, holding out the parcel, dripping. Much though Vera Brindle dreaded anyone in her kitchen, she felt obliged to ask him in. The poor man was wet through.

Alfred stepped through the door. Vera Brindle quickly relieved him of the parcel, laid it in the space she had cleared days ago in readiness for its arrival. Once he had gone, this huge, wet, friendly man, she would unwrap it infinitely slowly, rolling up the string, folding the paper . . . Alfred's cape dripped on the floor. Raindrops glinted on his white moustache.

'Sorry,' he said.

'That's no matter. Would you fancy a cup of warm milk?'

Alfred, who had been hoping for the more conventional offer of tea, arranged his face into an appreciative smile of acceptance. He stood awkwardly by the sink, his cap just brushing the drooping ceiling. This was the first time in twenty-four years the Brindle witch had asked him in. He had delivered post to her in far worse weather than this. What, he wondered, did the invitation mean?

Would she offer him a nut as well as the milk? There seemed to be bowls of nuts everywhere . . . as if ready for a drinkless party. Something to tell the wife, this.

The postman began to look around. In the rain-dark room, nothing was very clear. But he could make out that the walls were completely covered with old scraps of paper, all browned to some degree with age, they were, and uniformly stuck to the wall with a black drawing pin at the left-hand corner, the rest of the paper left free. Altogether, they gave a shaggy impression, a feeling that the walls were ruffled up to keep out the cold, like a bird's breast. Very peculiar, very rum. But Alfred could see that the positioning of the scraps of paper was something of a work of art in itself. They were methodically placed, just overlapping, like a tiled roof. Very precise, very clever.

Vera Brindle handed Alfred a cup of tepid milk. He moved to peer closer at the strange wall-covering. Each one was a sketch, he could just see, sometimes a painting, of a squirrel – sometimes just part of a squirrel, a faded leg, a tail at many angles. The pictures were faded almost to extinction, only beady eyes, with minute highlights, remained distinct. For all that, Alfred – a man, he liked to think, of some artistic appreciation – could see the drawing was fine, sensitive. The Brindle witch was a talented old bird.

'These are beautiful,' he said. 'Bloody marvellous. You could make a fortune, selling squirrel pictures.'

Vera Brindle, who was anxious for Alfred to drink his milk quickly and go, shrugged. The time for appreciation of her art was long past. She was not interested in anything to do with fortunes.

'I don't do it any more,' she said. 'Paints all dried up.'

'Pity, that.'

They stood without talking while Alfred gulped the sour, tepid milk. Rain clattered more heavily against the windows.

'Mustn't keep you from your rounds,' said Vera Brindle at last.

'No.' Alfred brushed milk and rain from his moustache with the back of his hand. His huge presence in the kitchen had turned it into a strange, unrecognisable place that unnerved Miss Brindle. She wished he would hurry.

Alfred stepped out into the rain. He was glad to regain air that smelt of sodden grass and leaves. The stench in the kitchen – rotten food, mould, wet animals? he could not quite place it – had been almost overpowering. He turned to bid Vera Brindle goodbye. She was beside him, rain darkening her clothes.

'You go back in. You'll get a soaking.'

'I'll come to the end with you.'

'I shouldn't advise that, Miss Brindle. Look, you're soaked already.'

But she was walking up the path to the gate with determined stride.

'As for your roof –' The postman spoke more loudly. She was a yard ahead of him now, astonishingly fast on her slippered feet. He wanted her to hear. 'I was thinking, coming in, you should get that seen to. Looks dangerous to me.'

Vera Brindle reached the gate before turning to face him, face shining as rain squiggled down the furrowed skin, sparse white hair sticking up in small points. Her eyes moved scornfully to the roof of the cottage. There was, indeed, a grave dip in the thatch – she had not looked at it for some years. But quickly she realised Alfred was as foolish as the social workers; the roof had been expertly thatched by her own father not sixty years ago and had never caused a moment's trouble, apart from the odd starling caught up in the wire.

'Look at that moss –,' she snapped. 'That's been there for years. That protects the thatch, moss.'

'That moss,' began Alfred. But he could see the pointlessness of arguing in the rain.

'I'm not worried,' said Vera Brindle. She gave him a brief wave and was hurrying up the path before he had time to thank her for the milk.

So engrossed in her new weighing-machine was Vera Brindle

that she did not notice the persistence of the rain, or its heaviness. She delighted in the hours as she weighed all manner of new things – writing her guessed weight, followed by their actual weight, with her old biro. By evening, she became aware of a smell of damp that was perhaps stronger than usual, though it was always like that on a rainy day. It meant the squirrels would want to come in earlier. She opened the window for them – a pool of rainwater on the sill flopped on to the floor – long before it was dark.

On her way to bed that night, carrying the weighing-machine under her arm, Vera Brindle felt an almost tangible sense of well-being. It could rain every day till Christmas, for all she cared; she would spend her time weighing so many things on both machines. (It was important, she thought, not to desert the old one, just because of the newcomer. Mustn't hurt its feelings.)

In her room there was a pile of rags and dishcloths on the floor. They were mixed with more crumbled plaster. The hole in the ceiling was much bigger – funny she hadn't heard it fall. And at the end of the bed sat Edward, reddish elbows just twitching, watching her.

Vera Brindle managed to stand quite still, wondering what to do. She put her free hand into the pocket of her cardigan, found a couple of nuts, considered throwing these towards Edward. But she quickly abandoned that idea. Nothing must be done to alarm him. So she placed the nuts in the tray of the weighing-machine and put it gently on the floor. Still Edward did not move. His eye was bright as all squirrels' eyes; Vera Brindle suddenly remembered the tiny sable brush which she used for the white highlights in her paintings. After a while, she pulled back the blankets on her bed, slipped into it, not bothering even to remove her slippers. The most important thing in the world, having come this far, was not to scare away Edward now. In bed, awkwardly perched against the pillows, Vera Brindle studied his small body, tense as a trap, ready to pounce at the slightest sign of danger.

Rain beat in angry swarms against the small windows. It was cold.

For some time, Vera Brindle lay unmoving, waiting. Then Edward suddenly jumped off the bed, with lashing tail, to the top of the pile of rags and leapt into the plastic tray of the weighing-machine. The noise of his nails, scratching the plastic, unnerved him. But in a moment he was calm enough to attend to the nuts. He clasped one of them in his paws, his jaws working with frantic speed. Vera Brindle, still very cold but dizzy with excitement, strained to see what the machine clock registered. But without her glasses it was impossible. She made a silent guess.

Then she allowed herself a contented sigh. The extraordinary sight, not a yard from her, was beyond her most unlikely dreams. The weighing of a squirrel . . . her ultimate, most secret desire. No one would ever believe her claim that the squirrel had taken it upon himself to jump on to the machine. But that was of no importance, as there was no one to tell. The shock of it all wearied her more than she could have supposed. Her clothes were still damp from the rain. She shivered. Up in the roof above her, Edward's relations began their nightly dance, their feet tapping almost in time with the rain. Very peculiar, she thought, as she fell asleep.

Vera Brindle dreamed of dozens of squirrels lining up to be weighed and of Edward, quite tame now, visiting her every day. She dreamed of sun on her mother's opal ring and the noise of waves breaking on the grey shale. Their crashing became so loud they briefly woke her. For a moment she saw that moonlight on the windows, shredded by rain, lit a room in turmoil: chunks of rock – was it? – on the floor. Black spaces in the ceiling. She heard more crashing, thudding, the high screams of terrified squirrels. Then she saw them raining down on her, flashes of tooth, eye, frantic tail. How kind they were, coming to comfort her. Behind them, she could see a huge slab of ceiling, shifting, unhurried as a cloud. She shut her eyes and struggled to breathe beneath a sudden new weight. Never in all her years of weighing, she thought, would she have imagined her family of squirrels to be so heavy.

Some days later, Alfred the postman returned to Vera Brindle's cottage with another brown envelope. It still rained, and he saw that the thatched roof had fallen in, breaking up the livid green covering of moss.

The kitchen door was locked, the windows shut. Alfred called loudly, but there was no reply. He peered through the kitchen window and could see that among the chaos of things on the table a squirrel lay on its side. He could not tell if it was alive or dead. An iciness went through him, nothing to do with the weather. He hurried away, reported what he had seen.

The rain had at last begun to ease a little when Lee Barker and her colleague, both in turbid anoraks, drove to the cottage. They had brought with them a small metal ladder on the roof-rack. They carried it between them down the muddy path, elated by their feeling of smugness. This would teach the old girl not to listen to those who knew best.

'Stupid daft witch,' said Lee Barker, in her off-duty voice. 'This'll make her see sense at last. The sooner she's sitting round the telly in an old people's home, the better for all of us. We can't keep putting up with all this aggravation.'

'Quite,' said her colleague.

Like Alfred, they received no response from knocking on the downstairs windows. With a gesture of some triumph, therefore, Lee Barker stuck her ladder into what had once been a flower-bed beneath Vera Brindle's window. Clumsily she climbed, her huge trainers hesitant on the metal rungs of the ladder.

'Got the mobile on you, Di? Expect we'll need an ambulance.'

'Operation Witch Evacuation, right.' Di, awkward on the spongy grass, tapped her mobile telephone and laughed. She watched her friend push away lumps of rotten thatch that hung over the casement window and look in, pressing her face to the small panes.

Lee Barker screwed up her professional eyes and saw that there was life in the bedroom. There were squirrels everywhere. They ran up and down over huge lumps of plaster on the bed, where Vera Brindle lay facing the window. She stared back with dull but open eyes. Sitting on the old woman's hand was a squirrel with reddish elbows, a small tuft of her white hair between its paws.

Angels Bending Near the Earth

'I do believe,' said Ivy Bell to her friend Florence Kidd, 'I spy reindeer tracks on my icing sugar.' She poked at her piece of Christmas cake with a fork. 'There must have been a little sledge carrying Father Christmas through a copse of those tiny fir trees – on top of the cake, I mean.'

Florence adjusted her glasses. She could observe no sign of reindeer tracks on her friend's icing. But then Ivy had always suffered from an imagination.

'I doubt that,' she said. 'Tea-rooms like this would be bound to exercise a certain economy in the matter of cake decoration.' Then a silence between them was filled with a moody version of 'It Came upon a Midnight Clear', piped through grilles in the ruby flock walls.

Ivy Bell and Florence Kidd were very old friends – they'd been friends for longer than either cared to remember, as they told anyone who enquired about the exact length of their acquaintance. They had been at school together, worked together as landgirls during the war, been bridesmaids at each other's weddings. There had been a spell when, as married women bringing up children, geography had forced them a hundred miles apart. But they always kept in touch. And when, curiously, they were both widowed in the same year, it was an obvious decision to move to the same place. They chose a seaside town on the south coast, never too crowded in summer and wonderfully empty in winter. They bought bungalows at opposite ends of the esplanade. This was on purpose, for they agreed that the strength of their affection was due to keeping a certain distance. They knew much about each other's lives, relations, pleasures and troubles. But they were careful never to encroach on each other's privacy.

Florence and Ivy were both women of energy and drive. Each one was involved in various clubs and activities in the small town, and proud of their busy lives – not for them lethargic retirement. The coming of Christmas, with so much to do preparing for visits from the family, meant it was difficult to find a moment actually to meet to exchange news of their plans.

'I'm at my wits' end, Ivy dear,' Florence had explained, 'right up till Christmas Eve itself. There are the church flowers to be seen to – I'm in charge of the rota system this year, as you've no doubt heard. Then I've the Writers' Circle here one night, the vicar for mince pies another—'

'Yes, yes,' Ivy had interrupted, not to be outdone. 'I'm rushed off my feet too, as you can imagine. The Choral Society's rehearsing every evening right up to the concert – to which I hope you're coming by the way—'

'—Nothing I'd rather, if I'm free—'

'Well, I very much hope you are, Florence, or I shall be disappointed. Then I've promised to help with the Christmas party up at the hospital –'

Florence was beginning to feel that in the competing list of pre-Christmas activities there was a chance she would be out-shone this year. To deflect any further boasts on Ivy's part, she cut in with a spontaneous suggestion.

'Then why don't we treat ourselves to a wild tea at Marshalls?' she said.

In her demure youth Florence had been good at instilling ordinary events with a touch of excitement simply by granting them inappropriate adjectives. Ivy could scarcely imagine anything less wild than tea at Marshalls. But she noted the gleam in her friend's eye, and found herself accepting with a pleasure out of all proportion to the proposal.

Thus it was that the two friends met in the hosiery department at four o'clock on Christmas Eve, and wandered through the other departments of their local grand store observing the general transformation by tinsel. They enjoyed the fact that, unlike the crowds of last-minute shoppers, they had no desire to buy anything whatsoever, having completed their Christmas shopping in October. They enjoyed scoffing at the tacky gold stars poised above the sock counter, and the nylon trees with their pathetic sprinkling of fake snow. They reminded each other of a time when Christmas was less vulgar, when they were young, and they sighed a little in sad remembrance.

In the top-floor restaurant, where they were to take their tea, the management had run out of decorating ideas: gold paper-chains were merely slung in careless loops across the ceiling. It was a gloomy room whose numerous small tables showed a spirit of optimism, for only two were occupied. But Florence and Ivy were pleased to see a comely waitress approach them. She wore a small tiara made of pleated muslin on her head, threaded with black velvet ribbon, and conveyed neither her surprise nor scorn when the two old ladies withdrew their gloves and placed them neatly by their plates. Plainly this was a meeting place for a generation who appreciated the niceties of a well-laid table and sparkling white cloth, and the waitress was used to such decorum.

'I wouldn't mind a small glass of sherry, myself, Ivy. How about you?'

Ivy nodded. But there the waitress was unable to oblige. She was sorry, but Marshalls store held no licence for the consumption of alcohol. So they settled for China tea, and Christmas cake with the icing that had alerted Florence to reindeers. A mist of carols rolled endlessly through the room, almost indistinguishable in their blandness. Neither Ivy nor Florence appreciated this cheap contribution to the festive season. But they knew that background music was the general requirement these days, and those who abhorred it were the odd minority.

'Busy, busy, busy I've been,' said Ivy, pouring tea. 'I'll be glad when it's all over.'

'Well, exactly,' agreed Florence. 'Always the same, every year. Always tell myself I'm going to have a quiet Christmas, and never seem to manage it. Absolutely rushed off my feet . . .'

The competitive spirit between them was rising again, enjoyably. Florence dabbed at her mouth with a paper napkin decorated with holly and bells.

Even now, with her head poised at certain angles, Ivy was reminded how pretty her friend had been. In the old days Florence was quite blasé about the amount of invitations she received. Nowadays, of course, the only ones that really counted were those from the children.

'Jack and Dawn want me the day after Boxing day,' Florence went on, 'so I'm splashing out and hiring a car to Epsom. I'll have to take the children off their hands, but it should be fun.'

Ivy took her time before striking back.

'John and Magda have threatened to come over and take me out to dinner, possibly tonight,' she said. In fact nothing very definite had been planned. And though Ivy had no wish to lie, she could not instantly think of a way of conveying the truth that would not incur her friend's pity.

'Then you're rushing?' said Florence, looking at her watch.

'I'm in no rush, no,' admitted Ivy, with a slight frown. 'They haven't confirmed the plan yet.'

Florence allowed a moment's silence to precede her next piece of information.

'I'm supposed to be helping with the mulled wine after the early carol service,' she said. 'And I have to say that from now till the New Year there seem to be parties, gatherings, endless entertainments. For such a small place it's very lively, don't you find?'

Ivy paused.

'It is, isn't it?' she agreed. 'Did I tell you that Grace and Fred suggested I went to Scarborough next week? But no, I said, I'm much too busy. And frankly, grandchildren for a week are exhausting.'

'Of course they are,' Florence agreed. 'Exhausting. But the *pleasure* of them at Christmas. I love seeing them round the tree. Families gathering at Christmas is what it's all about, rather than all this overemphasis on decoration.' She waved a disapproving hand towards a silver-foil fringe that drooped from the window-sill.

'But we must remember how lucky we are,' mused Ivy, ' both of us, to have such large families, to be so involved. – To be a child-less widow would not be nice at all.'

'I'm glad to say my children are very good to me,' Florence reflected with a little twist of her mouth, 'though I do understand that with their busy lives—'

'And is everything ready for the influx?' Ivy, reluctant to have to reflect on the generosity of her own children, wanted only to hear more of Florence's plans.

'Weeks ago. And you?'

'Absolutely. Though I have to admit I succumbed to ready-made stuffing this year – saved a lot of bother.'

Florence raised her eyebrows. Ivy had always been such a good cook, taking so much trouble, making little beribboned pots of this and that for her grandchildren. Perhaps she had just run out of steam.

'Any coming to stay, are they?' Florence asked.

Ivy swallowed.

'Not actually to *stay*, no,' she admitted.

The curtainless windows were slabs of black sky now, faintly ruffled with neon lights from the street below. Florence and Ivy were the only customers left. The waitress was putting transparent covers over untouched cakes. There was an edge of impatience in her movements.

'When did you say they were arriving, though?' Florence indicated her desire for the bill with an imperious wave.

'I don't believe I did say,' Ivy answered sharply. 'And your lot: when are they descending on you?'

Florence scanned the bill very intently, moving her lips as she mentally checked the total.

'What with one thing and another,' she said, 'it seems that Jack and Dawn and the twins can only manage a fleeting visit on their way to some New Year party.'

Ivy picked up her gloves.

'One has to understand,' she said, 'what very frantic lives they all lead. It's a wonder we see them at all. Grace and Fred are unable to get here before next week either – some last-minute hitch, they said.' She paused for a long time. Then she took what she knew was a risk. 'In which case, Florence, it would seem that neither of us is very much occupied on Christmas Day.'

Florence, with a sniff so delicate it was scarcely more than the twitch of a nostril, looked up from counting out change.

'That would seem to be the case.'

Ivy cleared her throat.

'We could always rectify that, could we not, with some small celebration in your house or mine?'

Florence pulled herself very upright in her chair.

'I have to admit I made an incautious amount of mince pies, presuming that the family—'

'Fatal to presume,' snapped Ivy. 'But most fortunate we discovered – well, what we discovered. You could call it a case . . .' She petered out, unable to put a name to the idea that struggled in her mind. It was something to do with relief at Florence's confession of a Christmas as bleak as her own – and yet, in the crispness of their exchanges, they had managed both to preserve their dignity and avoid any notion of self-pity.

In the ruby gloom of the tea-room 'It Came upon a Midnight Clear' had rolled dismally round again. Suddenly remembering the unsung words, Ivy was fired with an explanation. 'You could call it a case of angels bending near the earth,' she added.

'What do you mean by that, precisely?'

'Don't put me on the spot, Florence.' Ivy smiled. She had not envisaged gaiety would permeate the careful pretences of this meeting. But now her head was filled with gold she could not describe. 'It's Christmas Eve,' she said. 'No call for an explanation.'

They rose from the table. The overhead light was snapped out, the music switched off. Florence and Ivy, in semi-darkness reaching for each other's kid-gloved hands, made their way through the tables with the jauntiness of those suddenly secure in the knowledge that the most perilous day of the year would not, after all, be spent alone. As they passed the table on which the Christmas cake was displayed, Ivy was just able to see that it bore no reindeer or sledge carrying Father Christmas. But on account of it being the season of goodwill, she decided not to score this point over her friend, and made no mention of the fact to Florence.

Mistral

I don't know why, and there is nothing I can do about it, but I have this way of irritating people. It's a sad affliction but, as I am unable to change matters, every day is a minefield. I know that at any moment I am liable to do or say something that causes Mr Arthur or Mr Gerald such annoyance they can barely trust themselves to speak.

My name is Annie Hawker. I am housekeeper to Mr Arthur and Mr Gerald, and have held that position for eleven years. Both gentlemen are in their mid-sixties. Mr Arthur was once briefly married to a certain Lucretia. The very thought of this lady brings out the worst in him, though her name is rarely mentioned. There are two grown-up children: Deirdre and Brian. Both of them are over thirty, unmarried, and still searching their way in life. Their telephone calls to their father don't inspire much sympathy. I hear him snarling down the telephone several times a week, though I have reason to believe he is a generous father, and sends cheques to England with some frequency. When Deirdre and Brian come for a visit – some would call it a prolonged free holiday, as I'm bound to observe to Mr Arthur – tension in the house rises. Mr Arthur gets no pleasure from their company, and the feeling is all too plainly mutual. Well, I have to say it: they aren't very reward-ing offspring: lumpen, dull minds, lazy, spoiled, purposeless.

Their visits put Mr Gerald into a bad temper, too. He stomps off most mornings, walks the hills or visits friends all day, and then is barely civil to them over dinner. Jealous, I suppose. Mr Gerald was never married, and the children remind him of Mr Arthur's past. Or it may be that he simply finds their ungrateful presence in the house annoying. Which it is. Secretly, all three of us look for-ward to their departure.

I took the job two years after my husband Simon died in an industrial accident. Arm torn off in a machine in the mill, and he wasn't even a manual worker, but an inspector. Trouble was, he was always poking his nose – in this case, his arm – too far into things, being a conscientious inspector. I knew in my bones some disaster would happen one day. So I wasn't surprised by the amputation, or the complications that followed. Or indeed his death within the week. Nor did I waste much time grieving his departure. Our marriage had never been of a high calibre: we had just chuntered along for ten years, childless, him travelling round the North inspecting, me working for the Inland Revenue.

I had always had a secret inclination to write. But I knew there was no hope there, for all that I was good at essays at school. Everyone wants to write and thinks they can. But there was no evidence to make me believe I'd be any good, or stand a chance of publication. So I abandoned that dream in order to avoid disap-pointment, and funnily enough quite enjoyed my time at the Inland Revenue.

Anyhow, two years after Simon's death the thought came to

me: now's your chance, Annie, I thought. Make a dash for it before you're too old. Go for a complete change. Try a new life.

I started looking at advertisements for jobs abroad, and as luck would have it came upon Mr Arthur and Mr Gerald's within days. The description of the place appealed to me – hilltop cluster of houses in the Luberon region of France. Beautiful scenery, peace, swimming pool, sun: the stuff of most people's dreams.

They were interviewing applicants for the job in London. I went down the night before, stayed with my sister in Barnet so as not to be in a fuss on the morning. I dressed carefully in a nice navy suit and pink blouse. It occurred to me a younger type of person would probably be applying for the job, of the jeans and T-shirt school, the kind who care more about being in the sun than what they give in return. I wanted to make a good impression, assure them of my reliability, willingness to work hard, and above all my unfailing sense of humour.

Well, it worked. They were a little stiff, the two gentlemen, sitting side by side on a plumped-up sofa. Very tanned, they were, with almost identical thin grey hair. In a word, we liked each other from the start. 'Do call me Annie,' I said, when the interview was concluded. 'None of this Mrs Hawker stuff, now, if you please.' They smiled a little instead of agreeing to this, and made no reciprocal proposal. I realised at once that they were the sort of gentlemen who, at their age, liked to retain a little of the old-school formality, and hoped I had not blundered in my friendly suggestion. Evidently I had not, for they offered me the job, two days later.

Just a week later I fell in love with Le Beau Banc at first sight. They had bought the place, a deserted hillside hamlet, some twenty years before, built a road (still pretty rocky) and renovated the whole place with great skill and imagination. Today, the small houses are a monument to local craftsmen: beautifully converted with mellow tiled floors and lime-washed walls, their old shutters scrubbed and oiled, their old beams stripped and sealed. One of these – quite the nicest, I think, with its little ter-race overlooking a vast valley that is always blue with either lavender or mist, is entirely mine. A very far cry from our house in Sheffield, I can tell you. I put up my few things – my picture of Morecambe Bay and my mother's shell mirror and so on – and it felt like home from the start. I can't imagine living anywhere else.

Mr Gerald, being a keen and skilled gardener, planted the whole place, too. There are peach and olive trees, English roses and mimosa. Every path is lined with lavender, and a huge fig tree shades their terrace. Butterflies flutter all day and the crickets sing every evening, ruffling the silence. Oh, it's paradise, as I tell my sister. I know how lucky I am.

The original idea, Mr Arthur told me, was to make the place a kind of commune or colony for artists and writers. The plan was that each would have their individual house in which they worked in peace, and meet for dinner in the evening. But long before my arrival this plan failed. It seemed many a young so-called artist, plus boy or girlfriend, checked in for a long free holiday full of delights of a certain kind, but in which little artistically was accomplished. So they decided only to put friends and relations in the guest houses: they themselves live in the large main house, which is my responsibility.

To be honest, in all these years I have never quite discovered what Mr Arthur and Mr Gerald actually do. Obviously they are gentlemen of some means, and have no need of regular employ-ment. But Mr Gerald seems always to be on one of the many telephones in his study, often to auction houses in London and New York, as far as I can gather. Very thick expensive art maga-zines arrive for him every week, and sometimes foreign gentlemen come for lunch. On those occasions Mr Gerald suggests I cook something French rather than the Yorkshire favourites we have on our own. The guests bring with them such funny-looking old ceramic pots which they handle with great care, and talk about in low voices.

Mr Arthur, in his study, is on the telephone a great deal of the time, too, and I understand he has interests in South Africa. But it doesn't bother me that I don't know the exact nature of their professions. All that concerns me is what I have to do to be satisfactory in my job: and that I know precisely.

My employers are gentlemen of routine. They thrive on the domestic timetables they have devised for themselves, and I do my best to see they are not interrupted. It's not hard to take care of them in the manner which they enjoy, because they are easy to please as long as everything is spick and span and meals are on time. They pay me a very fair wage and give me plenty of money for housekeeping, so I am able to call in a plumber or electrician, if need be, and pay him, without having to bother one of the gentlemen.

My day starts early. I'm in the kitchen by seven, all nice and orderly as I've left it the night before. I step outside, enjoying the early morning before the sun has become too hot, and pick a ripe peach or fig for the bowl. I lay the table, blue and terracotta cups and plates from a local pottery, put croissants in the oven and the coffee in the jug. Mr Arthur and Mr Gerald appear regular as clockwork at eight o'clock, each in his blue-and-white kimono.

'Morning, Mr Gerald Mr Arthur,' I say. 'Had a good night, have we?'

I have to admit they don't answer me any more because, I believe, although they appreciate my question is the height of good manners, they don't want to bother me with the troubles of their nights. (Mr Arthur suffers from asthma, Mr Gerald has problems with his digestion.) But I always like to be polite and show an interest. It used to worry me when they gave up answering, but I don't mind any more. I'm used to their ways and they're used to mine.

To be quite honest, the position of housekeeper is an amorphous one, not easy. The problem of address, for a start. I appreciated they wanted to maintain their little barrier, to denote

my position as employee rather than friend. So when they insisted
on calling me Mrs Hawker I did not object, and soon got used to
it. They did make one big concession: I should not call them sir,
they said, this being a newly democratic world, and as they both
had complicated double-barrelled names Mr Arthur and Mr
Gerald was the compromise we settled on. That was how they had
been addressed by the staff at home as children, they explained,
and thought it a charming custom. I agreed.

   To begin with, I found it hard to know what was expected of
me. What exactly was my place? I never asked the question specif-
ically and they never made it clear to me. Normally, for instance,
I would lunch with them at the kitchen table, or on the terrace, but
the invitation was never extended should there be a visitor, no
matter how often that person came. For some reason they always
liked to dine on their own, so once their food is cooked and on the
table I have to hang around waiting to clear away. I mean, I've
never got on with watching French television – after all these
years I haven't managed to grasp the French language at all,
though I'm pretty good at making myself understood in the shops.
So the evenings are a little bleak, though I enjoy my knitting, or
my latest Catherine Cookson. Then again, it's a little confusing
when people come for a drink. 'Fetch the bottle of Chablis out of
the fridge, if you will, Mrs Hawker,' says Mr Arthur, and in a
moment I'm placing it on the table by the sofa, on a tray with six
crystal glasses and a pottery bowl of fresh olives. 'And have one
yourself, Mrs Hawker,' he often says, when the guests have all
been given their glasses. At that point, what am I supposed to do?
Early on, I made the mistake of lingering, supposing that having
accepted a glass of wine I was required to join in the conversation.
I remember the occasion so well: the local architect was there to
discuss renovations to the old barn, along with his wife, not an
English-speaker, and her brother. Nobody knew each other very
well in those days, so I saw fit to fill the rather awkward silence
with some comment upon the pleasantness of the weather. As

nobody leapt in to follow up my lead, I took it upon myself to compare the climate of Provence with that of Morecambe where, I explained, I had spent so many of my childhood holidays. Possibly I let my tongue run away with me a little, in striving to be helpful, for I remember describing my fondness for whelks. I went on to recall the time I fell off the pier and was rescued by the famous comedian who was starring in the summer show that year. The very thought of all this made me laugh, of course, and it took me some time to realise I was the only one laughing. The three French guests looked completely bemused, and Mr Gerald and Mr Arthur, behind tight little smiles, seemed to be gritting their teeth. Then Mr Gerald came up to me and in a low, urgent voice suggested it was time I began preparing the dinner. I left the room with all the dignity I could muster, as Mr Arthur began to speak to the guests in French, no doubt explaining my extraordinary behaviour.

I have to say, nothing was said. They did not reprove me. And after that, when wine was being served, one of them would bring a glass to me in the kitchen. Well, I got the message: I did not take offence – I'm not one to take offence, it's so time-consuming. I had learned my humiliating lesson and thereafter strove to be the essence of tact. I also realised at that time that there was no question of Mr Gerald and Mr Arthur *ever* being intimates: while they were rarely anything but friendly, they would never be friends. It was necessary to them to keep their distance. They liked the protection of formality and it was not my place to try to persuade them to behave in any other way. 'Despite the small grumbles, Annie,' my sister once wrote from Barnet, 'you sound very happy. Mr Gerald and Mr Arthur's formal ways of speaking and so on seem to have had their influence on you, too, if you don't mind my saying so. Do you realise you write in a very grand way now? You use lots of new grand words and complicated sentences these days. It's hardly ever you break into your old way of writing.' I had not realised that, though Mr Arthur and Mr Gerald's way of describing the simplest things had always intrigued me. They were elegant in their use of language. Had this really had some influence on my own writing? It was quite a thought. 'It must mean you admire them,' my sister added.

This, my eleventh summer here, has been unusually hot. Mr Gerald and Mr Arthur have never quite accustomed themselves to the heat, and they react badly. They both become short-tempered, petulant, though they do their best to disguise this state. They change their minds a good deal, and give me conflicting orders, all of which is very taxing as the sweat pours down my face in the kitchen. But I try to keep my calm, and reassure them cooler weather must be on its way. Of course, neither of them is getting any younger. In the unkind light of the midday sun I notice that their hair, identical pure white now, is also similar in its thinness. They puff it over their shining pink temples in an effort to make it look thicker than it really is. Mr Arthur goes a funny colour, sometimes, after lunch, and extends his afternoon siesta by at least an hour. Mr Gerald has become fanatical about his pills – vitamins of every kind – and only takes very short walks these days, always with his stick. Time hasn't been particularly kind to me, either: I've inherited my mother's arthritis in the knee, which keeps me awake many hours of the night. And my childhood migraines come back from time to time. But I keep these things to myself. If Mr Arthur and Mr Gerald thought there was any danger of my cracking up, heaven knows what they would do. I may inadvertently irritate them, but I am their prop, their life-blood, their absolute necessity.

Two days ago the mistral began. I've learned to dread the mistral. It's the only thing that makes me seriously contemplate returning to Morecambe for my retirement. All the stories about its weird and unsettling effects are true. As soon as the wind begins to tug at the trees and beat hotly against my window at night, I feel my blood rise. Anxieties turn my skin to gooseflesh. I try to be reasonable, work out what they are about, but they remain nameless. I find it hard to be myself. Mr Arthur and Mr Gerald are affected, too. Their appetites go, and they snap at one another and spend more time on their telephones. 'We must all brace ourselves, Mr Arthur Mr Gerald,' I say. 'It affects us all the same,' I say, and they slam their doors.

The wind started up with its familiar tugging and snapping, blowing my skirts into warm billows above my knees when I went to hang out the washing. It sneaks through any door left open for a moment, ruffling papers and blowing things to the floor. For a few hours I took a positive attitude: the relief, I thought, of a light breeze to stir the heavy heat we had had for so many weeks. But in truth the mistral is not so much light as malevolent. Its aim is to taunt, to goad, to drive you mad. Well, it's not going to beat me, I told myself, as I slammed shut the kitchen window and scooped up the pile of flour I had arranged on the table for my dough. 'One of God's little tricks sent to try us,' I said to Mr Arthur and Mr Gerald at breakfast. Their temples shone with sweat. They answered with silence.

At lunch I could see that both gentlemen were agitated. I put the pot of chicken casserole on the table, then took up a plate to help Mr Arthur first, as I always did.

'I couldn't eat anything hot on a day like this,' he said, and wiped at his forehead with a silk handkerchief.

'But we always start casseroles in late September, Mr Arthur,' I reminded him.

'I tell you, I can't eat a bloody casserole in this heat. I'll have bread and cheese and fruit.'

He looked quite flushed and Mr Gerald, I noticed, was pulling at his earlobe, a habit he has whenever he is out of sorts.

'Don't you worry yourself, now, Mr Arthur,' I said, cool as anything, determined not to be offended by his rejection of my casserole. 'It won't take me a moment to run you up a nice tomato—'

'Did you hear what I said, Mrs Hawker, woman? I'll have

cheese and fruit so you can stuff your infuriating concern . . .' He trailed off, picked up a length of bread.

Of all the offensive elements in his response, it was the word 'woman' that got me most, cut me to the quick. *Woman!* Indicating chattel, inferior, nuisance. *Woman!* Never had I been so insulted in all my years here. But I quickly took a hold on myself. No point in shouting back. It was, after all, the mistral that acted like some devil within him.

'And you, Mr Gerald?' I asked, plunging the ladle into the casserole. 'You'll have some, will you?'

'Just a little, Mrs Hawker. Thank you.'

It was a silent lunch. Mr Arthur left before the coffee, his fine poplin shirt darkened with patches of sweat. Mr Gerald anxiously watched him go.

'It's this heat,' he said, by way of conciliation.

'It gets us all down, Mr Gerald.'

'Quite.'

Once I had poured his coffee he stood up and said he would take it to his room. I suppose he no more wanted to be alone with me than I wanted to be alone with him. In this kind of atmosphere it was safer for all of us to be on our own.

'Mr Arthur will be hungry by tonight, at least,' he said with a very faint smile, which I took to be an apology for his friend's behaviour.

'We'll have cold collations,' I reassured him. 'Don't you worry.'

'Thank you, Mrs Hawker. That would be advisable.'

Once he had gone I continued to sit at the kitchen table, stirring my coffee. I could hear footsteps on stone floors, several doors banging. I could hear shouting, though the words were not clear. Then all was quiet. Just the buzzing of several flies and the snip, snip, snip of the wind against the warm stone of the outside walls.

I don't know how long I sat there listening to the frayed rhythms of the wind. But eventually, true to habit, I stirred myself to clear the table and wash up. Then I went out into the garden. There, the fig and peach trees were tossing restlessly about, their great heads of silvery leaves trying to dodge the nagging and the teasing of the wind. Their usually calm shade was broken into a thousand moving pieces. Butterflies, driven from their resting places, were tossed in the air like tiny sailing boats on an invisible rough sea, and bees clung tightly to the lavender, silent in their concentration. I walked to the edge of the grounds to where the huge oak tree guarded the precipice. Its branches moved slightly, and its leaves snarled, but it acted with none of the frenzy of the fruit trees. It had learned to resist, I thought. I looked down into the great bowl of a valley where fields of lavender and corn dipped and swayed, confusing the bee-eaters. And overhead clouds scurried like lemmings in a dark blue sky. My skirts whipped about my legs. My hair lashed my face. There was not a moment's stillness. I felt so sad, so profoundly, inexplicably sad. The idea came to me that all I had to do was take a couple of further steps to be consumed for ever by the blue of the valley.

When eventually I returned to the kitchen I found, to my horror, that Mr Arthur and Mr Gerald were seated at the table, thunderous expressions threatening their watches.

'Ah, Mrs Hawker,' said Mr Arthur, all polite sarcasm, 'and what has happened to our tea?'

'It's nearly twenty past four,' said Mr Gerald. 'Very unlike you, Mrs Hawker, to have no tea prepared by now.'

There was a moment's quiet, just the wind still tugging away at the windows. Then I let them have it.

'Fucking hell, *gentlemen*,' I screamed. 'For once, just for once in eleven years I'm ten minutes late with your tea. What a disaster. What a bloody disaster! For you two lazy spoilt selfish slobs, that's a *major* disaster, because you're such hopeless bastards you can't so much as switch on a kettle, fill a pot, fetch the butter from the fridge – do you know which the fridge *is*, Mr Arthur Mr Gerald?'

Perfectly synchronised, their flabby old mouths fell open. But their eyes could not meet, nor could they look at me.

'Aren't you ashamed,' I raved on, 'at your absolute uselessness, your total inadequacy? You employ me to wait on you hand and foot, do your bidding at every turn: you rely on me completely, useless prats for all your money—'

'Mrs Hawker,' said Mr Arthur.

'Mrs Hawker,' added Mr Gerald.

'Calm yourself.'

'Calm yourself.'

'Calm!'

In fact, I did feel calmer, now. I knew my words would come more tightly, with more menace. 'Who could be calm at the thought of a future waiting on two spoiled old sods? Who could be calm thinking that old age would still be darning your socks, getting your porridge just right while my own life just ebbs away? 'Course, if you live to bury me, I've no doubt you'll commission a nice marble headstone engraved with the tribute *A good and faithful servant . . .*'

'You've gone too far, Mrs Hawker,' said Mr Arthur, dabbing at the string of sweat on his nose.

'Much too far,' said Mr Gerald, running a finger round his damp collar.

'You're not yourself. The mistral, it affects us all.'

'Not yourself, indeed.'

'Not myself?' I gave a nasty laugh that made them both jump in their seats. 'As a matter of fact, Mr Arthur Mr Gerald, that's just what I am being at this moment – *myself*. For the first time in all these years, *myself*. The bit you've never shown the slightest desire to know about, to see. Well, I've only just begun. Sorry to shock you, but there's much, much more I'd like to say . . .'

I saw a look pass between them, then, and Mr Arthur gave an almost invisible sigh. The words I had ready to shoot at them were exploding in my head in such blinding lights that I could not quite read them – something to do with bitterness at the waste of my life, nothing but the satisfaction of two spoilt old men to show for it: the regret at so meagre an achievement, and the sadness – could they not understand the sadness?

They seemed to be waiting for me to go on. But anger had left me inarticulate. Words, insults, evaporated. So I began to moan, a noise similar to the wind. As I picked up the huge pottery bowl Mr Arthur and Mr Gerald looked scared. I thrust the fruit at them, moaning louder. A brilliant aim: figs caught Mr Arthur on the chest, making smeary pink marks on his clean shirt, and bursting obscenely over his fingers when he put up a hand to shield his face. An over-ripe peach slobbered down Mr Gerald's temple. I laughed again. I picked random crockery from the dresser and began to throw it on to the stone floor. The shotgun explosions of cups and saucers and the large dinner plates were pure music: pottery breaks into noisy crumbs. Glass, next. Half a dozen wine glasses landed in the stainless steel sink. They smashed with a high-pitched scream, drowning the noise of the wind. Then a jar of olives – they rolled about the messed-up floor like jet marbles, smearing it with olive oil. The home-made jams: two large jars, Mr Gerald's favourites, burst on to the floor, sticky plums sploshing among the olives and china. And finally the inspiration of a bag of flour. As I picked up a kitchen knife to slash the bag for speed, Mr Arthur and Mr Gerald turned a matching deathly white. In a moment they were whiter still as I held it high and let it scatter down like a snowstorm. I loved its silent descent into random piles that covered everything.

'This is . . .' Mr Arthur stood up, a floury spectre. Flour fell mistily from him.

'. . . too much, Mrs Hawker.' Mr Gerald, still troubled by peach in his eye, stood up too.

Something told me they were right. Besides, the energy was ebbing, just as the words had done earlier on.

'If I've caused you just a moment's thought, Mr Arthur Mr Gerald,' I said, 'then this has been worth it.'

Head very high, I left the room.

That was all some four hours ago. Since then, back in my room, I've been writing like a lunatic. All this stuff. Giving vent to, as they say. Letting it all out. As I pause for a moment I look out of the window and notice the trees are still. A bee-eater on the telegraph wires, eyes speared on to the lavender bush below, does not sway. The wind has died. Only the scratching of my pen in the silence.

Then the buzzer goes, frightening. I pick up the telephone.

'Mrs Hawker? It's almost eight o'clock.'

'So it is, Mr Arthur,' I say.

'Dinner-time,' he says.

'I'll be along, Mr Arthur.'

I stand, stretch. It's one of those dusky blue evenings I love so much. The crickets will start up again now the wind has gone. Funny how much I've enjoyed the writing. The hours just flew. Perhaps I shall try it again. Perhaps that's how I shall spend my time off in my old age, writing stories at last. I brush a streak of flour from my sleeve. I am very calm.

In the kitchen Mr Gerald is laying the table – three places. Very unusual, for I only dine with them at Christmas and on my birthday. He wears one of my aprons. Candles are lighted. A bottle of good wine is open. Over at the oven Mr Arthur is prodding expertly at the chicken casserole and tossing a salad. There's no sign that anything untoward (a favourite word of Mr Gerald's) has ever taken place. China and glass from the cupboard have replaced the missing things on the dresser. There's a bowl of olives – one of them must have been down to the village to buy more – and the flour jar is filled. What an afternoon they must have had! I try not to smile. I say nothing.

'Sit down, Annie,' says Mr Arthur, back to me.

'It's our turn to wait on you, Annie,' says Mr Gerald, without looking at me.

I do as they ask, and we have the dinner of a lifetime.

Now, it's past midnight. Even as I finish this story I find it hard to believe it all happened. The merging of fact and fiction in memory, however soon after the event, is intriguing. How much of what I have described was exactly like that? I have tried to be accurate, but if someone were to ask Mr Arthur and Mr Gerald to describe the events of today, some years from now, I've no doubt they would tell quite a different story. What I do know is that everyone is entitled to such terrible days now and then, and that, in the end, is what Mr Arthur and Mr Gerald understood, and that's why I love them and will work for them for the rest of my days.

Besides, they called me Annie. Of course – and I must stop now, I'm feeling suddenly tired – I know that was only for tonight. Mrs Hawker is how they like me to be, and why not? So Mrs Hawker I'll be again in the morning. But at least I have been Annie for a night.

I set my alarm.

The Wife and a Half

I know what it's like to fly, thought Kelly. I know what it's like to rise on a gust of wind, then soar between balanced wings.

She stood at her kitchen window watching the magpie who lurched – a little ungainly for so handsome a bird – from the ground to the apple tree. He was becoming less skilled at taking off, only heaved himself on to the lower branches once or twice a day now. A few years ago he would swoosh upwards easily as a firework, black and white feathers fanning through the leaves.

Kelly looked at her watch, guilty. These days she often caught herself staring at nothing very much, thinking thoughts of no importance. All duties were done: dusting, tidying, tea for Jacqueline ready. The precious hour of free time, familiar to all mothers who are bound by the school run, was almost up. Kelly knew she should have taken advantage of this free time. Read her book, or turned on some music. Instead, she just stood, studying a magpie, despising herself.

An old man shuffled past the gate – a construction of nicely turned, rather prissy wrought iron, Kelly had always thought – though Richard, an expert on ironmongery, had brought it home soon after they were married, declaring it a very fine gate indeed. It afforded a narrow view of the world beyond the thick privet hedges. Some of the passers-by had become familiar to Kelly. She would guess at their lives, wonder if she and some of the women with children had anything in common. – The old man moved so slowly he seemed to be soldered to the pattern of iron. He wore a belted grey mackintosh of soft-looking stuff. She imagined he was expecting rain, despite the blue sky. Perhaps he was wise enough always to anticipate surprises.

Last night, at the civic dinner she had been obliged to attend with Richard, he had called her a wife and a half.

'Kelly, here,' he had said, hand on her hip, 'is not in the run of normal wives. Definitely not. She's a . . . wife and a half.' A group of his colleagues had laughed at his joke. Admiringly.

What he didn't know, and never would know, thought Kelly, is about that extra half. She did not know herself, really. She could not be specific. She had little to complain about – their marriage was solid and friendly – but there was some void in the marital pattern. Something that she had imagined, when she was younger, would be there – was not there. What was it? A shared secret world to do with mysteries and art and stars and poetry? Even as such words came to her, Kelly laughed inwardly to herself. By now she was two minutes late for her daughter. She'd have to hurry to be at the school gates in time. – No: Richard was not the man for secret worlds. Never had been, never would be. His imagination concerned only the practical. 'Poetry,' he once said, 'is not for the likes of businessmen, unless you mean the poetry of stocks and shares.'

Last night at the civic dinner Kelly had sat next to one of his junior colleagues, Alan Burns. 'A ladies' man,' Richard had explained, before introducing them.

Kelly and Alan never turned to the guests on their other sides. All through the melon medley and beef Wellington they raced through opinions of Byron, Wordsworth, Keats and Shelley. By the time they were served a solidified little lemon mousse a-glitter with glacé cherries, Kelly had drunk enough red wine to commit her first ever act of infidelity.

'Richard says businessmen have no time for poetry,' she said.

'Nonsense.' Alan gave the faintest sneer. His handsome mouth was briefly disagreeable.

Any further thoughts he may have had on the matter were curtailed by the loyal toast. Then came the moment when a formal occasion begins to crumble: with an air of relief wives begin to seek out their husbands to drive them home safely. Alan whispered: 'I hope we can meet again some time. I've loved talking to you.' In that brief second his mouth had dislodged her hair. She could feel her long earring swinging for several moments after he had moved away. She stood holding the back of her gilt chair, steadying herself against the tide of departing diners. The chemical colours of silks and satins seared her eyes, pricking them with unaccountable tears.

'Saw you two getting along all right,' Richard observed on the way home. 'You want to watch out. Something of a lad, Alan.'

Today had not felt quite normal. That is, she had done all that was required of her, and had her moments of idle reflection – the magpie, the old man. But it was as if the solid things of every day were ruffled by an invisible breeze. Nothing was completely still. The civic dinner, Alan's words, lapped to and fro, disturbing. By the time she reached the school gates – no, thank goodness, Jacqueline wasn't there yet – Kelly knew that the one person she did not want to avoid, should he care to approach her, was Alan Burns.

Later, cutting toast fingers for her daughter's tea, a plan lighted in the whirligig of her mind – a plan so wicked and exciting and completely out of character, that the evening chores – helping with algebra homework, chopping carrots – were enlivened by a dust of such bright gold that Kelly wondered at its invisibility.

She spent a wakeful night composing two innocuous lines, and next morning, high on lack of sleep, wrote them carefully on a postcard – a picture of Lord Byron. '*There wasn't time to say how much I loved talking to you, too.*' (She hesitated over the *how much* but finally decided to leave it.) '*Hope we can carry on some time, Kelly H.*'

The nefarious act of actually posting the card caused her an uneasy morning. She snapped through the household chores with unaccustomed speed, half-dreading the reply, but impatient for it. She knew that even in this age of female liberation it was probably unwise for a woman to make the first move – despite a positive signal that it would not be rejected. But since the civic dinner an agitation had come upon her that she found hard to contain.

What these feelings conveyed, exactly, Kelly could not explain to herself. Something to do with *time* with a sympathetic man, perhaps: the innocent excitement of a walk by the lake, a spontaneous picnic, a glass of wine on a . . . well, a terrace or something. Nothing to do with an affair, sex, blatant infidelity. Kelly entertained no such crude intentions. Innocent friendship was all she sought. Beyond that, she was loath to imagine.

No answer came from Alan Burns. Each morning, rising before Richard so that she should be first to reach the post, Kelly would study her husband's sleeping face and wonder what he would do if he knew of his wife's betrayal. His innocence touched her, just as her own sense of guilt affected her. Every day that brought no response from Alan was, in a way, a relief. At the same time, her longing for a single sentence – what was his writing like? – consumed her.

Richard himself, never an acute observer, noticed something was amiss.

'You're jumpy,' he said one morning at breakfast, before return-ing to his paper. 'Anything up?'

Then Jacqueline accused her of not concentrating when Kelly handed her the wrong pair of shoes.

'Your head's in the clouds, Mum,' she said.

Six weeks after Kelly had sent her card, a reply came by second post. A lunch-time delivery was unusual, the envelope with unfa-miliar handwriting doubly unexpected. Kelly, hands trembling, sat down at the kitchen table – the horribly expensive maplewood table Richard had recently bought as a surprise. Alan, too, had chosen a card, but no picture. '*Dear Kelly*', she read, '*thank you for your card but I trust you will understand it would not be appropriate for us to meet again. Yours, Alan Burns.*'

In disbelief Kelly read this several times. Then suddenly she understood. Plainly Alan's wife had observed her husband's enjoyment at the dinner, and had threatened him. So Alan had been forced to write this pompous little card. Unreasonable anger replaced Kelly's understanding.

She gave herself no time to reflect. She rang Richard's firm: asked for Alan's office. It was a personal friend, she told his secre-tary – she preferred not to give her name. There was a long pause. When the secretary at last returned to say Mr Burns was in a meet-ing, Kelly was convinced there was a note of triumph in her voice.

In the next few days Kelly rang several times. Alan was always out or at a meeting. She never left a message for him to return her call.

How much time passed? Kelly scarcely knew. Obsession lengthens hours, hardens days. Alan's silence spurred Kelly's desire to see him into a longing that had begun to alarm her. The agony of not knowing what was going on in his mind increased daily. – But then came another opportunity to see him: a dinner for some departing director of the firm. Kelly spent extravagantly on a new dress.

'Have I seen that before?' Richard asked, as she came downstairs. It was as near as he would ever get to a compliment, and made Kelly smile. But she did not mind lack of appreciation from Richard tonight, because in half an hour the man for whom she had made the effort would be looking upon her.

She saw him at once, half turned from her in a group of serious-looking businessmen. No sign of his wife.

It was impossible, in the crowd, to reach him before dinner. By cruel chance he was on another table, but within sight. Kelly tried to catch his eye as she listened dully to her companions talk across her about our brave new computer world. Kelly could not believe Alan was unaware of her presence. But he did not respond.

After long, lustreless speeches, Kelly saw Alan rise. With others who had had enough of tributes to their old director, he hurried towards the door. Kelly, careless of Richard's surprise, also got up. Followed them out. But she was too late.

In the lobby she saw him spinning, fainter, fainter, through the glass of the revolving door. Gone.

Richard's hand was on her arm.

'See young Alan's scarpering,' he said. 'Silly, that, if you're as keen for promotion as he is.'

So that was it. For the ambitious, to dally with the chairman's wife would be foolish indeed.

Kelly drove carefully home, unable to speak. Later, she could not sleep. Next morning, in the silent house, she telephoned again. Should she manage to speak to Alan, this time, she would say she understood.

'Oh, the personal friend again,' said the secretary whom Kelly had come to dislike intensely. But she connected her at once. Alan began to speak before Kelly was able to utter a word of her understanding little speech.

'Look here, Kelly, please leave me alone. No more calls. It was nice talking to you that night, but meant nothing more than that. Sorry, but you misread. As I wrote to you, it would be inappropriate to meet. To be brutal, there's no point in our ever meeting.

My life's rushing in a different direction. But I wish you well. I must go now. Goodbye.'

Kelly did not attend to her duties for the rest of the day. She sat on the untidy sofa half smiling at her own foolishness, able to see the comforts that rejection can bring. She realised the cruelty of Alan's words was fired only by feelings he dreaded – becoming as involved with her as she would like to have become with him. She admired his strength. He was right, of course. To resist temptation shows great force of character. To recognise possibility, and spurn it before it gets out of hand, is the behaviour of the morally admirable. Kelly understood that, too.

At least she was left with the private treasure of what might have been, unspoiled by what it might have become. She would always have that to look back upon. Richard would still have the whole of her, of course. It was just the other half beyond the whole – so unwittingly praised by him – that he would never know. That would remain her private life, relishing things her husband had no time for – small, inconsequential things. A harmless kind of infidelity, that, surely.

When Richard returned at the end of that long day, he went to the window and stood looking out into the garden – very unusual for one who normally poured a large gin and tonic and opened his briefcase as soon as he was home. Kelly was puzzled by her husband's reflective mood. Could it be that he suspected anything? she wondered. That was impossible, surely. Was the oddly gentle look in his eye a figment of her imagination? Or did it indicate she had miscalculated his blindness to her recent, unnerved state?

'Our old magpie,' Richard was saying, 'is aiming hopelessly for the top of the tree. Silly old thing: trying to outreach his grasp, or whatever. Didn't one of your poets say something like that?'

Kelly could see he was making an effort. Why, she didn't know, but she was grateful. Now that an event that never happened was over, she was intent on beginning a new era of married life, armed by new resolution.

'Trouble with that old magpie,' she said, joining her husband at the window, 'is that he doesn't know his limits. He should stop trying to fly above his station.'

Richard patted her arm. He could not pretend to be further interested in his wife's theories concerning the magpie's failure to reach the top of the apple tree: so he made for his drink, his brief-case, his normal evening, and Kelly was glad.

Another Kind of Cinderella

'Now come along, gentlemen, *if* you please,' urged Lewis Crone, waving his baton. 'What we want is a little more *up*lift in the last bar, don't we? Up, up and *away*.'

'Stuff it, Lew,' murmured Reginald Breen, second violinist, under his breath.

He dabbed at the sweat on his forehead with a large white handkerchief. It was bloody hot down here in the pit, even in winter. And he was damned if he'd give the last bar a lift. It wasn't exactly Beethoven the Winterstown Concert Orchestra was struggling to bring some life to, after all. Just wallpaper music to fill the gap where the Fairy blooming Godmother turned the mice into ponies. They hadn't half had some trouble with the ponies this year, what's more – doing their business just at the wrong moment, and so on. Reginald sniffed.

'So once again, gentlemen,' the mighty Lewis, conductor with airs above his station, was saying. 'We'll take it once again, *if* you please.'

What's the point, Reginald wondered, being this particular for this kind of show? Not a soul in the audience would notice whether or not there was a wretched uplift in the last bar. Half of them would be under twelve. The other half, pensioners' outings, were plugged into hearing aids. For them a pantomime was no different from a silent film. He tucked his instrument under his chin, and turned with an exaggerated look of scorn to his friend, Tom, first violin.

'Better give it the works,' whispered Tom, 'or he'll keep us into the dinner hour.'

'Righty-ho. Last time. Up, up and *away*.' Reginald had perfected his mimicry over the years.

He and Tom lifted their bows in unison. Tom caught the conductor's agitated eye. The orchestra crashed once more into the last few lines of forgettable music. Their sudden energy came from indignation. Lewis Crone had kept them at it since ten this morning. They were now hungry, bored and fed up with his absurd attention to detail. Trouble was, Lewis had once seen André Previn rehearsing an orchestra on television. Since then he had applied his own version of Previn's methods to the WCO, causing much suffering and discontent. In the old days they'd played through the score a couple of times at the beginning of the season – *Jack and the Beanstalk*, *Aladdin*, *Mother Goose*, whatever – and that was it. Now, all this pernickety fussing was driving them to near rebellion. Most of the players – weary, professional men – had considered resigning, but none actually did so. There were not many openings for their class of musician on the south coast. Tom was the most vociferous in his complaints. Reginald encouraged him in his discontent, for Tom's resignation would be to Reginald's own benefit. Once Tom had gone he, Reginald, would surely become first violin. He had waited some thirty years for this position. Over and over again others, outrageously, had been placed above him –

incompetent musicians, mostly, from outside the orchestra. And once, worst of all, a very junior 'talented' violinist from the WCO itself. He hadn't lasted long: no stamina. Many times Reginald had suffered the humiliation of being passed over, and had kept his silence and his hope. He could not afford to resign.

The morning's rehearsal over, Tom and Reginald made their way along the front. They exchanged few words: music was their only common interest. Proper music. Tom carried his violin case under his arm. Home, this afternoon, Tom would be practising the Mozart concerto. Reginald would be attending to his mother.

The sea breeze on their faces was good after the stuffiness of the orchestra pit. Reginald always enjoyed the short walk home. It refreshed him, gave him strength for the tasks ahead.

'Still haven't got the coach finished, I hear,' said Tom.

'Coach and beanstalk, it's the same every year, always late.' Reginald smiled at the thought of the familiar incompetence.

'At least we'll see Valerie in her spangles tomorrow.' Tom was something of a woman's man, keenly sensitive to the potential of leading ladies.

'She's as good a Cinderella as I can remember, I'll say that.' Reginald himself had been quite taken with her – what he could see from the pit – during the past month of rehearsals.

As the men parted, Tom paused for a last look out to sea. There was a small fishing boat on the horizon.

'Give anything to be out there,' he muttered, more to himself than to his friend. 'Always fancied playing on the deck of a boat, up and down in time with the waves.' He gave a small, helpless laugh. Reginald smiled in reply. He, too, had known fantasies that would never materialise.

He slowed his pace, once Tom had gone. He was always reluctant to return home and face *that* kind of music: but face it he must, as he told himself every day. If he didn't hurry and buy his mother her paper there would be more to answer for.

*

'Is that you, Reginald?'

The familiar peevish tone bit into his ears as soon as he was through the door. Who the hell do you think it is? he wanted to shout back. Who else would let themselves in at twelve fifty-five precisely, as he did five days a week?

'It's me, mother, all right,' he called, and clenched his fists, taking a grip on himself before going in to the front room.

Mrs Breen sat in an armchair in the bow window. Her vastly swollen legs hung from widely parted knees, slippered feet not quite touching the floor. A mustard crochet cardigan – made in the days when she still bothered to sew the crochet squares together – covered a bosom so cumbersome she was unable to see her own hands in its shade. But the fingers (the worst kind of sausages, Reginald thought, among other savage thoughts) worked skilfully on their own, crocheting away, square after square, hour after hour. The furious, pale eyes, scowling on their ledge of fat purple cheek, were attending to some cooking pro-gramme on the television. Mrs Breen had not moved since Reginald had left her that morning. She was not able to move on her own. Her illness meant she was almost completely immobile, though Reginald had reason to think that on secret occasions, when she wanted something badly enough, she was able to reach it. Chocolates in the tin on the bookshelf, for instance. Their unac-countable disappearance, observed by Reginald on many occasions when his mother was in bed, could only mean one thing. But the time had not yet come to challenge her.

Her mauvish bulk backlit by the netted light from the window, Mrs Breen made no effort to drag her eyes from the television.

'I fancy the Ambrosia today, Reginald,' she said, 'with that tin of plums you got last Friday.'

Incapable of shopping herself, her recall of exactly what her son had bought, when, was extraordinary. She would plan the life of half a pound of cheddar down to the last slice, insistent that only an ounce should be used for the sauce for the macaroni, and the merest scrapings for the Tuesday cheese supper with biscuits and tomatoes. Should Reginald miscalculate, and the cheese be finished before its allotted time, Mrs Breen would be moved to one of her famous rages, when every blood vessel in her body enlarged, darkened and threatened to burst through her glowering skin.

'Anything else?'

'Tin of curried spaghetti still there, is it?'

'It is.'

Reginald's heart pounded in relief. Last night he had had half a mind to eat it, but had resisted on the ground that he had had no energy to ask his mother's permission.

'Then I'll have that.'

Reginald went to the kitchen to set about opening tins and preparing the tray. The room faced north. Any light that managed to challenge the old curtain at the window was diffused by the coarse-grained and very dirty net. A smell of disinfectant clashed with the smells of years of frugal meals. Opening the window was forbidden, so the air was never cleared. The kitchen gave Reginald a headache every day. He dreaded it. But there was no escape. How many years, now? Eight? Almost nine. And how many more . . . ?

When he had placed his mother's tray of lunch beside her, he returned to the kitchen. But he could not face either washing up last night's supper dishes and the breakfast, or making himself a sandwich. Instead, he went out into the strip of ill-kept grass that was the back garden. When his father had been alive, herbaceous borders ran down both sides – borders that kept the old man's every spare moment fully occupied. From the thin earth, he had managed to persuade a magnificent show of hollyhocks, tulips, dahlias (his speciality) – the lot. But Reginald could never be bothered with gardening. Everything had gone to seed, died off years ago. Now the lawn was bordered with weeds. But the apple tree, the single tree in the Breen family possession, still blossomed.

And the blackbird still lived there. Reginald listened to its song now – vibrant, optimistic notes that gave him the courage to go on, sometimes. He lit a cigarette. Into his mind came a picture of Valerie, who in tomorrow's dress rehearsal would be in all her finery at the ball. He looked forward to that. He found himself pecking quite fast at the cigarette, then grinding its stub under his heel with a force that surprised him. Valerie was the sort of girl, had things been different, Reginald might well have approached. He had no great ambitions concerning her, of course, even in his imagination. With the difference in their ages, marriage was naturally out of the question. No: all he wanted, or told himself he wanted, was a friend. Her funny crooked smile and short bouncy hair inspired him with exciting ideas of friendship. Perhaps one day he would summon the courage to speak to her, see how things went.

'Reg! It's time.'

Reginald allowed himself a moment's more reflection, then returned to his mother. It was time for the dreaded visit to the bathroom, the ungainly negotiating of the dim passage, the old woman's entire weight on his arm, her invective spewing in his ear. Then, the long afternoon. He would have liked to go to his room, have another go at the Tchaikovsky. But his mother could hear, she said, however quietly he played. It hurt her ears, all that screeching, she said – she had always wanted Reginald to go into insurance, like his father. The violin was forbidden in the house.

Instead of music, it would be shopping at the Co-op, hoovering the stairs, two hours of bad-tempered Scrabble, another tray for high tea, television and the terrible ritual of putting Mrs Breen to bed. By the time Reginald went to his own room he was exhausted. Like a disobedient child, he would play his radio under the bedclothes for a while, very loud. This was the part of the day he most looked forward to. Much though he enjoyed his nightly blast of illicit music, it put him to sleep almost at once.

*

On the noticeboard at the stage door it was announced that the transformation scene was the first to be rehearsed. Reginald felt a slight prickling of anticipation as he undid his violin case, took out the instrument and wiped its bow. The awkward notes of his fellow musicians, tuning up, usually filled him with gloom and unease as he faced the long morning of indifferent music ahead. Today the squawks of striving notes could not touch him. He tried out a few notes himself, tightened a couple of strings. He scarcely noticed Lewis Crone blundering up on to the podium, cocky, grinning, one hand fingering a yellow tie.

'Making a statement, what?' whispered Tom, who was using a duster to polish his violin – a very superior instrument which could not have been better cared for had it been a Stradivarius.

'Won't get anywhere,' replied Reginald. He had no idea why he made this comment, or if there was any truth in his speculation.

The stage lights were switched on, bringing life to the Ugly Sisters' grim kitchen.

'Idiot,' yelled a voice from off-stage. 'That's the ballroom effing light.'

The peach light was dimmed, replaced by the kind of light usually glowing in the front room at Reginald's house. No wonder Cinderella, shortly to be sitting by the giant fireplace, needed a Fairy Godmother. Reginald could have done with one most days himself.

Bev Birley, in fishnet tights and a short satin tunic, came striding on to the stage. Bev was Prince Charming. Last year she had been Jack, the year before Aladdin. Beginning to show her years, too, thought Reginald, noting the definite thickness of her hips. He had never liked Bev – not that he had ever had occasion to talk to her. But she was stuck-up, haughty, tongue like a whiplash to junior members of the cast, though all agreeable smiles to visiting stars. Between seasons, Reginald saw her sometimes in the town, walking a terrier. Once, he recognised her picture in the window of an optician. She was wearing flyaway blue-tinted glasses and her hair had been stuck down with grease. She still did not look very nice. Presumably, not being in national demand, she had to do any job she could to keep herself going between seasons.

'Anyone wanting me this morning?' Bev shouted into the darkness of the auditorium, legs spread wide, hands on hips, her annual stance in every proposal scene. There was a slight titter in the orchestra pit. Tom nodded towards Reginald. Bev scowled.

'No one wanting you till two, darling,' the director called from the back of the stalls. 'See you then.'

Bev stomped off.

'Stuck-up bit; know what I'd like to do to her,' whispered Tom.

Reginald had no time to imagine what this might be because Cinderella came on to the stage just then, wrapped in a large cloak. She wore a great deal of scarlet lipstick which made her crooked smile look very grown up. As Bev passed her, she whispered something that made them both smile, and ruffled her hair.

'Cheek,' said Tom.

'Taking liberties, sucking up, usual thing,' agreed Reginald.

'Quiet now.' Paddy Ever, the director – or Ever Anxious, as he was known – had moved forward to take command. He leaned over the pit and shouted up at the stage.

'Why are we wearing a cloak, darling, in the kitchen?'

Cinderella, Reginald could see, looked confused.

'Wardrobe said it was a cloak for this scene. Suppose I'm cold in this bloody great kitchen, no central heating.'

The musicians smiled among themselves. At the beginning of the day they were ready to respond to any kind of joke, no matter how feeble.

Paddy scratched his head. 'I mean, *would* Cinderella suddenly be in a cloak? Why would she be in a cloak, now, but only in a dress in the last scene? Is it viable, is all I'm asking. Is it *rational?*'

Paddy's worries were known to hold up proceedings, sometimes for ages. The musicians flicked their music, rested their instruments. They could be in for a long spell of problem-thrashing before Lewis requested their first chord.

'Don't be daft, Pad: cloak on, amazing quick change in the dark. Stands to reason.'

Paddy's face briefly relaxed. Reginald did not envy him his job. 'Balldress under . . . point taken, darling. But why the sudden lipstick?'

They could hear Cinderella sigh. 'Can't put lipstick on in the dark, can I?'

'Righty-ho, lipstick on. Let's go.'

The Winterstown pantomime was all a very different kettle of fish to the Palladium, Reginald thought, as he did every year.

The rehearsal began. Cinderella and the Fairy Godmother, a dear old thing who had been in panto for years and whose under-arms, these days, swung as the wand waved, played the scene too far downstage for Reginald to see anything. He could only just hear Valerie's sweet voice and strange emphasis. 'Oh, god-*mother* . . .' He liked such original rendering.

It wasn't till after the mid-morning coffee break that the musicians were required to play the few high notes whose purpose, as Lewis so often explained, was to convey excitement. There was drama with the ponies, as usual: two nasty little Shetlands, hired at great expense from an animal psychiatrist, but who had minds of their own just the same. They refused to stand still, and laid back their ears warning what would happen should they be pressed to act against their will. One of them nipped young Andrew, the coachman. A part-time actor mostly out of work, Andrew proudly admitted he started off at the bottom year after year, but remained convinced that one day his moment would come. Trouble was, as he once confided to Reg, he was so nervous of the ponies, despite their small size, that it was all he could do to keep holding their reins, let alone think himself deeply into the part of the coachman. A lamp fell off the coach as soon as Andrew returned from being bandaged, and then the door wouldn't open. 'Bloody useless wand,' snapped the old godmother, longing for her lunchtime Guinness as the carpenter hammered away at the door.

It was a morning full of laughs – the kind of morning that made up for so much of the aching boredom of the job. And at last Cinderella appeared alone in the spotlight, cloakless, dazzling in a dress of sequins splattered on to net. Reginald still could not see her properly: he would have to wait for her upstage number, 'I'm Going to the Ball', for that. As it was, the wolf-whistles and laughs from the stagehands – an old tradition at any leading lady's first dress rehearsal – made him uncomfortable. For all its good humour, Reginald did not like the idea of Valerie in all her finery being laughed at.

At the lunch break, Reginald hurried out alone from the pit. He had to break the news to his mother – whose dinner was, thank God, provided by Meals on Wheels today – that there was to be an unscheduled rehearsal this afternoon, due to delays this morning caused by the coach and ponies. Her outrage was predictable. He would have to listen to ten minutes of abuse and insult – 'If you were Sir Thomas blinking Beecham I might understand' – before providing her with a calming glass of brandy and making his escape. Dreading the scene ahead, he barged clumsily round the corner that led to the stage door and bumped into Valerie herself. She was still in her ball dress. The sequins, in the poor winter light, looked asleep.

'Excuse me, I'm so sorry . . .'

'Reg, isn't it?' Cinderella gave him a wonderful smile. Her grasp of every name in the company endeared her to all.

'I have to let my mother know . . .'

'Like the dress? Isn't it gross?' She laughed. 'See you later.'

Reginald spun home, weightless. His mother's fury, the cold sausage for his lunch, the smell of the kitchen, the jibes at his general uselessness, meant nothing to him. Impervious to everything but the extraordinary thumping of his heart, inspired by Cinderella's smile, he was in and out of the house with astonishing speed. As he hurried back up the garden path, almost enjoying his mother's wailing in his ears, Reginald knew he was in love with

Cinderella, and was to spend the afternoon playing for her alone while she danced above him at the ball.

In the next two weeks of rehearsal, Reginald did not run into Valerie backstage again. But in his new state of love he was quite happy to be patient, to hear her sweet voice above him, hear the tapping of her feet, and to catch the occasional glimpse of her when she was upstage. Her prancing little body and enchanting smile were particularly appealing in her ragged dress, though he saw her best at the ball: the choreographer had naturally arranged for the prince to waltz with his Cinderella as far upstage as possible. Reginald, putting his soul into every note of the banal waltz, followed her steps as Bev swung her about. They gazed into each other's eyes, the woman and the girl, acting the kind of happiness which was so convincing it caused Reginald a jealous stab. Fact was, they were much better actors than he had ever given them credit for. The audience would believe this was Prince Charming – not Bev the part-time optician's model – in love with Cinderella, not Valerie who, Reginald knew, sometimes sang in a pub to make ends meet.

He longed for an event that he knew would never happen: waltzing *himself* with Cinderella in some posh hotel ballroom with chandeliers, far from Winterstown. Then on the balcony of their suite, the moonlight and roses bit: he would play a little tune – one of his own compositions, maybe, while she sipped champagne. Next, he would kiss her. So hard she could no longer smile. After that . . . but there his fantasies stalled. He could only imagine a paling dawn sky.

None of that would ever happen. It was some consolation, watching her, to know that at least *this* was all make-believe. What Reginald could not have borne would have been Val (she had become Val in his mind) dancing, in real life, with another man. He closed his eyes as he pulled the final note from his violin. He longed.

*

At the first performance of *Cinderella*, as always, there was a full house. The audience, mostly pensioners and schoolchildren, loved it. Val, taking many bows, had never looked so appealing. She and Prince Charming held hands and smiled copiously at each other. Reginald would have liked to have gone round to her dressing-room and joined the crowd of admirers he presumed would be there, tell her she was wonderful. As it was, he had to hurry. His mother would be furious at his lateness caused by the prolonged applause.

Once again, he ran into Valerie, surprisingly, in the passage that led to the dressing-rooms. She was still in her ball dress, an old cardigan slung around her shoulders.

'Good first house, wasn't it?'

Reginald nodded. The compliments rose, then withered in his throat.

'Bev and I are just off for a hamburger. See you.'

She was gone.

On his way home, Reginald decided what to do – for now, he believed, he should waste no more time, act fast. He would send her flowers. Huge great bunch in cellophane, small card in the envelope saying *From a secret admirer*. The thought of this plan went some way to dispelling his fury with himself for not speaking to her. She must think him a useless old man. But time would change all that. Plans beginning to crowd his head, he opened the front door.

'Is that you, Reg?' His mother's shriek was more than usually annoyed.

Protected from her by his inner strategies, Reginald went calmly to deal with her cocoa, the wearying process of putting her to bed and all the arrows of her fury.

Reginald dreamed that night of himself and Cinderella at a princely ball, but he never sent the flowers. He managed to leave early enough, next morning, to get to the florist before rehearsals for a concert. But he was so confused by the scents and colours and prices, he left without buying. He'd had in mind pure white lilies, or old-fashioned cream roses mixed with cornflowers – the kind of thing his father had been so proud of in his border. The florist seemed to have only crude red or rust flowers on stiff stems, leaves unbending as swords. Nothing worthy of Cinderella.

Then, just as he was coming out of the shop – the assistant's eyes contemptuous on his back – he observed Val and Bev walking down the other side of the High Street. Both wore jeans and anoraks. For a moment it was quite hard to recognise them. They paused, kissed each other on the cheek, and Bev disappeared into Boots. Valerie, turning to continue on her way, saw Reginald. She waved, smiled her glorious smile, arming him for the day against all adversities.

There were plenty of those. At the rehearsal for a concert in the Winterstown Hall, Lewis was at his most waspish and petulant, quibbling with Tom's tone and Reg's high C, and sneering so hard at poor old Jim Reed on the drums it was a wonder the man did not resign on the spot. But as his bow soared through the *Enigma Variations*, transporting him to the English countryside in May, walking in meadowlands with Cinderella, it came to Reginald that the only way to make any progress with her was to *do* something. Like ask her out for a drink.

At the lunch break that day the other members of the orchestra left for an hour in the pub. Reginald could not be persuaded to join them. He wanted to be on his own: Meals on Wheels was dealing with his mother. There was no reason to move.

He sat, violin across his knees, in the forest of empty chairs on the stage. The music played on in his ears, not disturbing the real silence. Down in the vast hall, chairs were stacked against the walls ready to be regimented for the next concert. A thin rain pattered against high windows. The light on the bare walls was dull as old stone, and it was cold. But Reginald spent an undisturbed lunch hour, oblivious of everything around him, walking with Valerie in Herefordshire (a place he had always longed to visit). He was, for once, at peace.

After the performance that night he hurried to the stage door, and then out into the alleyway at the back of the theatre. It was still raining, a cold hard rain that damply spotted his mackintosh. He stood, eyes on the square light of the glass door, violin case under one arm, heart pumping audibly. Members of the cast and orchestra came out in groups, and singly. Once a show was under way, nobody planned much of a social life after performances. They were all keen to get home.

Almost last, Valerie emerged. She wore a scarf wound high round her neck, but no hat. In the rain, and the light from within, the frizzy mop of her hair glittered like a swarm of fireflies. Behind her, Bev was talking to the porter at the stage door. She wore her imitation leopardskin coat and seemed to be cross about something. Val saw Reg.

'What's up, darling?' she asked.

Reg moved his free hand on to the solid, familiar curves of his violin case.

'I was wondering,' he said, 'if you'd care for a quick drink on your way home?'

He deliberately said quick because there was not much time. He had taken the precaution of making up some story to his mother about having to see the manager, but her credulity would not stretch far. Half an hour's grace, at the most.

Val laughed. It was not the friendly laugh. But perhaps sound was distorted here, out in the rain.

'Why not?' she said. 'Bev and I and some of the others are going down to the Drake. Want to join us?'

Reg paused for a second. Val's idea did not fit in with his plan at all. The last thing he wanted was to be with her in a crowd, perhaps unable to exchange a word. He wanted her to himself, just a small table, somewhere, between them. He wanted her full attention while he told her some of the things that had been piling within for as long as he could remember, and had never been spoken. His violin had been the sole recipient of his feelings, the music his only consolation. But man cannot live by music alone, as Tom, who had many an eager woman on his arm, so often said.

'I don't think I will, thanks. My mother . . .'

'Very well. Another time.' Val was not interested. But then something of the approaching Christmas spirit, Reginald supposed it was, entered her funny little head. She decided to be kind. 'But tell you what: tomorrow after the matinée? Bev's going to the dentist so we can't go over to her mum as per usual. We could have a coffee.'

'A coffee?'

A kaleidoscope of difficulties swooped through Reg's brain. More excuses to his mother would have to be thought up, and where would be a suitable place to go?

'Very well,' he said.

'Meet you here after the show then. Bev!'

Bev hurried out, glanced at Reg. Val was all smiles.

'Blimey, what a night.' Bev snapped up an umbrella, put her arm round Val, drawing her beneath it. 'Cheers, Reg,' Bev said, and Reginald watched Val slip her arm into the crook of the nylon leopardskin one.

They moved away, in step, huddled snugly under the umbrella, confident of its shelter, like those people in the advertisement for a life insurance company. Reginald waited till they were out of sight. Then, hugging his violin case, he turned into the full blast of the rain, in the direction of home.

Reginald and Val sat at a small table in the window of the Wimpy Bar – nearest eating place to the theatre. Reginald had suggested they go to the tearooms further down the High Street, altogether a more comfortable place, but Val had insisted she fancied chips in the Wimpy.

Two cups of thin coffee sat between them. Val covered her chips with spurts of ketchup from a plastic tomato. Reginald kept one hand on his violin case, propped up beside him. His head was empty from lack of sleep. He was drained, exhausted, by his imaginings. He didn't know where to begin. Ten minutes of their half-hour had passed, and all he had done was to make a disparaging remark about Lewis Crone. Val had disagreed. She said far as she was concerned he was a good sport.

'It must be boring down in the pit,' she said eventually, 'not seeing anything.'

'You can see enough. I get a good view of you dancing in the ball scene.'

'That!' Val laughed, more friendly than last night. 'See Bev treading on my toes? She's a horrible dancer.'

She laid one hand flat on the Formica tabletop, examined her nails with great interest as she slightly lifted each finger in turn. Reginald wanted to cover her hand with his.

'You're a lovely dancer, though,' he said.

Val gave him a teasing look. 'Reg! Haven't you got a wife, a woman? Someone? You always look so down in the dumps.'

'There's my mother to be looked after.' Reg suppressed a sigh and tapped his violin case. 'There's my music. I'm all right. Just not one of life's jokers.'

'No.'

The speech Reg had rehearsed most of the night, inspired by Bach under the bedclothes, welled. It was now or never, he thought.

'But I'd like to get to know you – nothing . . . out of line. Cup of tea sometimes. Talk. You know. I haven't much of a life socially. What with my mother. Drink with Tom, Saturdays. End of a concert drink with the boys. Not occasions to talk . . .'

Reg petered out, aware he had lost the thread of his message. The rubbish he was talking sounded close to self-pity. He didn't want Val's pity: last thing he wanted. And she had stopped picking at her chips. She pushed her empty cup away, stiff-handed. Gave a tight little smile, as if she decided she must get through this little scene as graciously as possible, but it was boring.

'Poor old Reg. Well, it's fine by me if we have another coffee some time. Though I'm leaving Winterstown, March. Doing three months in Manchester, an Agatha Christie.'

Reginald's heart contracted. He would have to think about that later: the bleakness of the spring.

'Anyway,' she smiled, nicely this time, 'you must be fifteen years older than me, Reg.'

'Probably.'

It was dark outside now. The pair of them made awkward shapes reflected in the plate-glass window. Madness seized Reg so fast he was unable to control it, to reason with himself.

'But I'm over the moon about you, see. Nothing bothersome, mind. Just, watching you dancing away, Cinderella in her ball gown, I fancied your pretty smile was for me. Daft, I know.' He saw her look of alarm, tried to slow himself. 'All I want is to talk to you, don't I? To tell you things, give you a good time, spend my savings on you. I've a fair bit put on one side – nothing to spend my wages on all these years. What do you think, Val? Would you let me, sometimes?'

Val gave a small laugh, perturbed. 'I don't want anything like that, nice though you are.'

'No. Well. I didn't rate my chances high.'

'It's not that I'd mind a chat from time to time. But Bev wouldn't like it. There'd be trouble. I've had enough trouble.'

'Trouble with Bev?'

'Bev's my friend.'

'I know Bev's your friend. But she can't order your life about. A woman.'

Val sighed. 'Have to be going,' she said. 'Meeting her at six.'

'Meeting Bev? What's she got, this Bev?'

In his confusion, Reg could not be sure of anything. But for a moment – so short he might have imagined it – he thought Val looked scared.

'A nasty temper if things don't go her way.'

'You shouldn't put up with her. I mean, do you *like* her?' Later, Reg reflected, his boldness may have been impertinent.

Val shrugged. 'Thanks for the coffee 'n' chips.' She stood up, swirling the scarf round her neck.

'Cinderella,' said Reg. 'Cinderella.'

She bent briefly towards him. He could smell her breath: ketchup, chips, coffee. She patted his shoulder.

'Chin up, Reg.'

'I want you to know' – her hand fled from his shoulder – 'that every performance it's you I'm playing for, Val, down there, all that rubbishy music. One day I could play you Brahms, on a beach somewhere, tide coming in, never go back to the orchestra. They'll never make me first violin is what I'm afraid of, not even when Tom goes. You could, you could come with—'

Val turned from his jibbering, impatient. Reg could tell from her eyes she thought he was a silly old fool, letting go.

'What you must remember is this, Reg.' Her voice was harsh as flint now, cutting the quick of him. 'You're a nice guy, but I'm another kind of Cinderella.'

She was gone. Striding through the purplish light, the ketchup tables, the bleak landscape of Formica and burgers. Reginald remained standing, clutching his violin case, peering through the window. In the late-night shopping crowds he thought he glimpsed a leopardskin coat, but of Val he could see nothing.

That night he kept his eyes on the music, did not look up to see Cinderella in her ball dress dancing with Bev the prince. Reg had always known she was not for him, any more than was the position of first violin. But who was she for? What did she mean, another kind of Cinderella?

After the performance he hurried off to avoid an accidental meeting. It was a night full of ironic stars. Just twenty-four hours ago, in the rain, she had given him some hope. He didn't know why he bothered with hope, anymore.

'Is that you, Reg?' Furious voice. Usual thing.

Reg made his way slowly across the small, stuffy hall and into the front room. He opened the door, surveyed the familiar picture of the monstrous old woman who was his mother: the mother who had messed up his entire life. Plumped up with indignation, she sat upright in her chair, accusation flaring across her purple cheeks, obscene legs swinging. If it hadn't been for his binding duty to her, things would have been different. If he had been a worse son he would have had a better chance.

'What kept you then? Dancing with Cinderella?'

She gave a sneering laugh, thumping one swollen hand into the soft mess of crochet on her knee. Reginald swung his violin case above his head, and moved towards her in silence before they both screamed.

Men Friends

Conrad Fortescue, on his way into the church, trod on a beetle. In the silence of the Norman porch he heard the tiny crackle as it crushed beneath his foot. Looking down, he saw the smashed shell, each fragment shiny as his own highly polished black shoes, linked by a web of blood. Damn, he thought: how Louisa would have hated this – Louisa who would rescue dying flies from summer window-panes. Conrad felt his throat clench. He coughed. Up until this moment he had been all right, in control. Death of the beetle shattered his calm.

He made his way into the church. He was early. Walking up the path banked with expensive wreaths of flowers at the foot of the yews, he had been pleased to think he was probably the first. He wanted time to himself to think about Louisa. But he was not the first. Half a dozen others were already seated, curious vulture eyes upon him, people behaving as if the gathering was for a party rather than a funeral. Conrad took a service sheet from an usher, chose a seat by a pillar from which he would not quite be able to see the coffin. *Louisa Chumleigh*, he read: *1st Sept 1956–2nd April 1992*. Not a long life. The organ began to play a Bach prelude. Conrad closed his eyes.

They first met seven years ago, one of those smudged summer afternoons when the tremor of heat makes everything illusory. He stood on a thyme-planted terrace, leaning over the balustrade to admire the descending shelves of impeccably mowed lawns. Friends had brought him to the house for tea, drinks – he couldn't remember which. He had stood transfixed as he watched Louisa, in the shimmer of heat below him, take the arm of an old man with a stick. She supported him as he stepped from the lawn on to the path. Her solicitousness – she had no idea she was being watched, she later told him – was mirage-clear even from so great a distance. She kept hold of the old man's arm – Jacob, it was, her husband. They walked towards Conrad, joined him on the terrace. As Jacob pointed his stick towards the arboretum, spoke lovingly of trees, Conrad regarded his wife. It was a case of instant enchantment. Something unknown to him before.

They had had five years. Five years of adultery, though Louisa would never use such a word. She had made it easy for him – writing, ringing, taking the initiative to get in touch, so that he was spared taking the risk of contacting her. She never involved him in her deceits. She even managed to make him feel, sometimes, that the woman in his arms was free. But that was the one thing she was not, nor ever would be until Jacob died. Until that time, her husband came first. If she did not ring Conrad for a week – and the agony of silent days never lessened – he knew it would be because Jacob had made some demand that she would not dream of refusing, although when she did ring she gave no explanation for her silence. And Conrad knew better than to ask.

Once, they had managed three whole days together: Jacob was on business in America. Louisa took the opportunity to visit relations in Paris. Conrad followed her on the next flight. Louisa saw little of her relations. On a warm spring afternoon in the Bois, Conrad declared his intention to wait for her: to wait until Jacob, thirty-six years her senior, died. He saw at once his mistake. Louisa, who had been laughing only moments before, retracted from him, though she kept hold of his hand. Conrad, apologising for his clumsiness, felt a lowering of the afternoon. 'Who knows what will happen – then?' Louisa said. 'It's something I can never think about, Jacob's dying.'

Soon she was laughing again. Back in England nothing seemed to have changed. Conrad accustomed himself to the imperfections of loving another man's wife, and privately determined to wait, however many years it might be.

Then, two years ago, there had been such a long silence that Conrad had been forced at last to write. What had happened? Louisa rang at once, her weak voice apologetic. Some wretched bug, she explained. She hadn't wanted to worry him. She had been forced to stay in bed for two weeks.

The bug needed treatment – radiotherapy. Conrad visited her occasionally when Jacob was away. He observed her thinning, beautiful skin gleaming with an incandescent menace. Noticeably more frail each visit, she lay back against a bank of linen pillows in the huge marital bedroom whose windows looked on to the garden. Conrad would look down on the lawns, misted with rain, and see the brilliance of that first summer day. A nurse filtered in and out, filling water jugs, straightening covers. Conrad brought pansies, in which Louisa silently buried her face, and elderberry jelly. She spread it thinly on toast, but could only eat a mouthful to please him. They held hands, talked about the past. But mostly sat in silence watching the rain on vast window-panes. Sometimes, Louisa felt like being up for a while. Once they walked down to the lake and back, which exhausted her.

Conrad learned of her death in *The Times*. None of their mutual friends knew of their affair so, not surprisingly, offered no condolences. He had written at once to Jacob, who replied by return, a stiff polite letter in an infirm hand, inviting Conrad to the funeral and lunch afterwards at the house.

Now Louisa was dead, Conrad would never marry. She was the only woman in whom he had found all the qualities he had never known he needed until he found them in her. He doubted he would ever love anyone else.

The church was filling up: men in black ties, women in dark hats. A large man with extraordinarily wide shoulders sat in front of Conrad, uncomfortable on the narrow bench of the pew, shifting about. Conrad recognised Johnnie Lutchins, a childhood friend. Louisa had sometimes talked about their times together in Cornwall.

Cornwall, Scotland, the south-west of Ireland – Johnnie and Louisa had spent many holidays together. Johnnie's widowed mother had been the best friend of Louisa's mother. She and her son spent much of their time with Louisa's family. Johnnie remembered his first sight of Louisa, a skinny angel in filthy dungarees. *Feeble*, he remembered thinking, at ten: but within the day he had discovered she was tough and daring as any boy. They climbed trees, sailed in brisk seas – the rougher the better, Louisa used to say. They teased an old donkey, put pretend spiders in the cook's tea – always laughing, always daring the other into greater mischief. At fifteen, Johnnie kissed Louisa in the greenhouse among unripe tomatoes. Then he couldn't stop kissing her. When he went up to Oxford three years later, she would visit him several times a term. He was the envy of all his friends, and showed off the beautiful creature at every opportunity. After he had graduated, and found a decent job in antiquarian books, he finally declared his love and proposed. But he had been beaten to it by Jacob – Jacob, a man older than Louisa's own father. When Johnnie had recovered from the shock, he had tried to dissuade her from such madness. Then he had turned to teasing. 'I can only conclude you're marrying the old boy for his money and his house,' he had laughed, bitterly. Louisa denied this. Neither Johnnie nor anyone could stop her from becoming Jacob's wife.

Still, as Johnnie soon found to his delight, the marital state made little difference to their friendship. Jacob, who had known Johnnie since he was a boy – indeed, he was Johnnie's godfather – issued constant invitations to the house. Johnnie was urged to look after Louisa, keep her amused, when Jacob was away on business. Which meant that with a half-clear conscience they could go out together in London. Opportunity was on their side: Johnnie considered himself the luckiest man in the world. He knew Louisa loved him, even if not in quite the same way as he loved her. It was only a matter of waiting . . . sometimes she had frustrated him by her silences, but he knew they meant she was being dutiful to Jacob, and he had no right to be either impatient or greedy. When she had become ill he had spent hours, days, by her bedside, laughing at the many flowers and cards sent to her by 'admirers' whom, she claimed, she hardly knew. Johnnie believed her.

He saw her on the day before she died – asleep, but holding Jacob's hand. The old man sat with fresh tears replacing dried tears on his cheeks, making no effort to brush them away. But when he rang Johnnie next morning with the news, his voice was firm as usual. He was a dignified old boy. He would have been horrified by Johnnie's uncontrolled weeping.

To deflect his thoughts, Johnnie glanced round the church. Hundreds of pansies were woven into ivy round the pillars, and along ledges where they mixed with the reflections of stained-glass windows, and twined into edifices on the altar. Candles burned as if it were Christmas Eve. The pews were full. People were hunting for seats in the side aisles. Many of them resigned themselves to standing. One of those, Johnnie realised, was Bernard Wylie. Johnnie had met him and Louisa one day in Bond Street, very briefly. He had only just caught the name. Later, he remembered to ask Louisa about him. She said Wylie was a solicitor – something to do with her late father's affairs. They had both laughed about the slickness of his coat, with its too-wide velvet collar. Today, Johnnie recognised the coat before the face.

Bernard Wylie wore his favourite coat accompanied by expensive black leather gloves, and a black satin tie lightened with the tiniest white spots which he had judged would not be offensive. He stood clutching his service sheet to steady his hands, staring straight ahead, feeling the uncertainty of his knees. And he wondered for the millionth time what it was about Louisa that had so bewitched him that his life, since meeting her, had fallen apart.

She had come into his office one November afternoon – some trivial matter to do with her father's estate – wearing a hat of grey fur sparkling with rain. Completely confused by the legal niceties of the matter, she had suddenly said, 'Oh, I give up, Mr Wylie,' and had laughed her enchanting laugh. 'In that case,' he had said, 'let's go and have tea while I explain it all to you very slowly.'

So slowly that their tea at the Ritz drifted into champagne, and then dinner. He had driven her back to her flat, come in for a drink, stayed the night. There had been dozens of nights since – nights and lunches, little notes and presents from her, calls from all parts of the world when she was travelling with Jacob. Then, a year or so before she fell ill, there was the final note. 'I'm awfully sorry, darling B, but we can't go on. I realise now it was all *infatuation* on my part . . . and know it was not real love for you either, but great fun, and thank you.'

For the rest of his life, Bernard would regret not having made his declaration – Christ, he had loved her from the moment she walked into his office. But he had abided by Byron's principle of never telling your love, merely conveying it. Had his conveying been invisible? Too late he wrote to her, pages of the long-contained passion now set free. But she did not reply. The last time he saw her was at a party, laughing in the distance with some unknown man. She had not seen him. Bernard had left at once.

And now instead of Louisa he had a second-best wife at his side who would never know the loving man he once was . . . She nudged him, this loyal, unexciting wife, her sense of occasion offended by the sight of a young man standing not far from them in a dark jacket, grey trousers and no tie. In the unknown youth's eye, Bernard thought he saw reflected the same despair that lodged in his own heart: but it may have been his imagination.

The young man, Felix Brown, had cried for many nights. Cold, exhausted, drained, he feared he might faint during the long service, but there were no seats left. He it was who late last night, and at dawn this morning, had transported pansies from the greenhouse to the church, and arranged them on his own. Only three years ago, Lady Endlesham – as he still thought of her, as he would always think of her – had come into that very greenhouse and admired them. Said they were her favourite flowers. They had talked of planting and pruning, and made plans for the south bed. Felix had done his best to conceal the mesmeric effect the shape of her breasts beneath a pink cotton shirt had had upon him. He had told her how happy he was to be working in the garden. He could scarcely believe he had been promoted to being in charge only two years after leaving horticultural college, he said. Lady Endlesham had smiled, and said they must make more plans. Then he gave her a pot of pansies for her desk.

Some weeks later she came into the tool-shed, admired his clean and gleaming tools that hung in order of height on the walls. The warmth of that evening was almost tangible. In the stuffy air that smelt of dry earth Felix was embarrassed by the pungent smell of his own sweat. He could also smell Lady Endlesham's scent, a mixture of fragile flowers. In the shadows it seemed to him she hesitated, planning perhaps to mention some gardening matter. Then she put out her arms, and said, he thought – though he could never be quite sure of the exact words – *Come here, you handsome thing*. Handsome? Gathered to him, Felix could hear the racing heart of his employer's wife. They ran like children through the orchard to a hidden place Felix knew. Lord

Endlesham was away, she assured him, but not in a rejoicing way. She sounded almost lonely. Felix was twenty-one at the time.

Since then they'd made love in every corner of the garden, and, in winter, in the hayloft. Felix would marvel how one moment his mistress (as he liked to think of her) was laughing in his arms covered in grass or hay, and the next he would see her in the distance walking beside her aged husband, immaculate, admiring the flower-beds whose geography she and Felix had discussed between a thousand kisses.

When she was ill, no longer able to come downstairs, he sent up a new bowl of flowers to her room each day. The last time he saw her she was standing at her bedroom window – looking for him, perhaps. He was raking the terrace. He glanced up, saw her wave. Then she disappeared. She disappeared, and with a crescendo in the organ music Felix knew at last she was gone. Never coming back to their garden. He took out his handkerchief, blew his nose, realising he was the only man in the church to resort to such weakness at this stage. Through tear-blurred eyes he watched the shuffling procession of coffin-bearers hesitate up the aisle, and caught the eye of his employer, Sir Jacob, seventy-two at Christmas. He was a good man to work for. Felix respected the old codger, but wondered if he could bear to continue the job now the inspiration of the garden no longer existed.

Sir Jacob, seeing young Felix, the first face to come clearly into focus, gave the briefest nod to acknowledge that his floral work in the church was appreciated. Louisa would have been amazed. She loved decorating the church. She and Felix, before the illness, had done a grand job always at Christmas and Harvest Festival. She had been wonderful with the boy. In her usual generous way she had inspired him, encouraged him, suggested his promotion – typical of her, always seeing the best in people, bringing out their qualities.

Sir Jacob trod very slowly, in time to the gentle music. In front of him on the coffin lay a single gardenia. He had chosen it with

Felix – the best in the greenhouse. Inside, placed in the stiff hands, was the equally stiff card with its private message of love which would not fade until long after the body had perished.

Beside Sir Jacob walked Louisa's mother, a bent old lady with a still-beautiful profile that had been inherited by her daughter. It occurred to Sir Jacob, as he put a finger on the knife-edge of his collar that cut into his neck, that they might look more like man and wife than he and Louisa ever did . . . Louisa could have been his granddaughter. Walking down this same aisle, their wedding day – but he hadn't cared then, or ever, what people thought. All that mattered to him was their mutual, perfect love for each other. Which turned out to be proven. While Sir Jacob recoiled at the thought of his own smugness, he couldn't help reflecting that never once in their sixteen years of marriage had Louisa ever let him down, disappointed him, betrayed him. He knew he came first in her life, just as she did in his. He had trusted her absolutely. The only worry they had ever had was about her life after his death. She often said that no one ever could replace him.

The coffin-bearers reached the altar, placed it on its plinth. Sir Jacob and his mother-in-law took their places in the front pew. A shaft of sun, at that moment, pierced the roseate glass of the window above the altar. Sir Jacob remembered Louisa remarking on the strength of its colour – 'a small pink pool on the altar steps, darling – did you notice?' In truth he had never noticed, in all the Sundays he had been coming to this church, until Louisa had pointed it out to him. She had drawn so much to his attention that gave pleasure. She had opened his eyes to the extraordinary qualities of the ordinary, and made him the happiest of men.

The vicar clasped his hands. In the moment's silence before the first prayer, Sir Jacob looked round at the congregation – so many people who would always remember his wife. It occurred to him there was a large proportion of men. Men of all ages, he saw, all with that sternness of eye that strong men employ to conceal grief. He knew some of them: others were unfamiliar. Darling

Louisa: untouchable to all but me, he used to say. And she, kneeling on the library floor beside him, would laugh her thrilling laugh in agreement. How proud of her he was! There was nothing like having a wife who was desired by all, but faithful only to the man she loved, her husband.

May the vanity of such thoughts be forgiven, Sir Jacob found himself praying. Then he joined in the general words of thanks for Louisa's life. He could not close his eyes: in his disbelief they never left the coffin. Like so many of Louisa's men friends in the church for her funeral that day, Sir Jacob could only picture her alive.